THE LANDKIST SA

VALLEY OF EMBERS

STEVEN KELLIHER

VALLEY OF EMBERS

Printed in the United States of America

ISBN-13:978-1535244350
ISBN-10:1535244356

For David, for showing me that reading is pretty great. Also dragons. Those are great too.

For Mom and Dad, for believing I could do anything.

For Krysten, for being my light in the dark.

CHAPTER ONE

A GOOD SCAR

Kole woke to the steady beat of drums. The booming percussions were amplified by the timber walls of his home, acquiring a wavering quality as they crept in through thatch and shingle.

He went first to his leather armor, which soaked in oil water. He looped an Ash bow over his back, strapped on his water skin and drew his blades. The Everwood knives were black with old char.

When he opened the door, the steady bass of drums cleared, their sharp retorts ringing and now intermingled with the baying of the wall hounds. Kole picked out the steady baritone of the First Keeper as he issued orders in a staccato rhythm at odds with the chaos of the night, the rain adding its own crescendo to the familiar proceedings.

A small slope of packed earth separated Kole's quarters from the front gate. As he moved off, boots finding purchase difficult in the muck, he heard panic issuing from the merchant sector. He knew there was no such sound further south, where the children would be ushered into the Long Hall.

Everyone, it seemed, was heading south, toward the Shore of Last Lake. They sought the armor provided by moving away from something.

The walls rose before him, the timbers bathed in the red-orange glow of flame. Kole took the steps to the gate two at a time. He scanned the curving arch, picking out the intermittent stone braziers that glowed along its length. The rest of the defenders were scrambling up their steps and getting into position, the Keepers settling next to their braziers. Kole closed his eyes and felt the heat tickle his blood as his own brazier thrummed.

He surveyed the earth before the walls. Brown water pooled in shallow depressions, slick canvases that acted as natural complements to the drums that were only now quieting their complaints, something the hounds were less inclined to do.

He eyed the tree line. On a hot morning, he could bury a stone in the nearest clearing with a strong throw. Tonight was cool bordering on cold. Kole quickened his heart and set his blood to boil, feeling the heat coursing through his veins, the hafts of the blades across his back glowing a dull red in anticipation.

The moon was no ally tonight. The Dark Months might be tailing off, but it was small comfort. One could almost feel the World Apart brushing by, whispering its promises and issuing its soft challenges. Kole did not listen.

"You look worried."

Kole looked to his left. Across the breach before the gate, Linn regarded him coolly, a faint smirk tugging the corner of her mouth.

"Finished tucking your sister in?"

"You know her," Linn said, turning her attention to the trees. "She always has to make sure everyone's in their place, from the elders right down to the fauns."

"Somebody has to," Kole said.

"I suppose."

Kole nodded, but both kept their eyes locked on the shadows beneath the trees.

"See anything?"

"Everything," Linn said as she scanned. "Which is to say, nothing."

Two scamps were along in short order—boys not yet used to shaving the stubble that sprouted haphazardly along their chins. They carried a black cauldron stocked with flaming pitch between two poles, depositing it next to Linn. Beside it they placed a bundle of arrows whose ends had been wrapped in birch and sealed with wax.

Linn nodded her thanks without turning and the boys hopped off the archer's platform, picking their way eagerly among the moss-covered stones that trickled toward the lakeshore.

Kole did not begrudge them their flight.

Something was off. His father had yet to return from his weeks-long ranging, and Kole was beginning to wonder if Tu'Ren's fears were well placed. Kole trusted his gut, but he trusted Linn's eyesight more. He watched her—she was still as stone—as often as he watched the shadows between the trunks of the trees.

The shouted orders of the First Keeper faded away, Tu'Ren's voice going out in a wisp. Everyone was in position, and Kole rested a palm on his brazier, the heat flowing into him with a welcome shock that set his skin to steam in the drizzle. The other Embers along the wall were calm as mantises, with the archers and spear-wielders in between watchful and ready.

Kole caught a flash of movement to his left—Linn's bow shifting in her hands fast as thought. She had a steely look, and Kole dropped his own bow from his shoulders and snatched a shaft from the pitch on his platform, lighting the end with a burst from his palm. He drew the string half-taught, feeling each feather slide along the grooves of his fingers.

He took it for a trick of the light at first. Here was a shadow that grew shallow before deepening once more, and there a flicker of jet black between a copse of trees.

"There."

Kole looked as Linn rolled her shoulders back and drew.

At first, it looked like a great pack of worms, or a giant's hand made only of rotted fingers, fat and questing. The tentacles reached out fast as centipedes, hissed in the ruddy torchlight and withdrew for a breath, drenching the trees in an inky stillness.

Usually it was a 'They' come bursting out of the forest—a roiling mass of spiked tails and barbed tongues lashing in the wavering light, leaping and slithering toward the walls. This time was different.

Now it was a singular thing—a mass of purple darkness, like a coil of snakes that move as one body. Its great arms ended in jagged claws, which raked earth, grass and stone with its passing. Roots cracked under its mass and the demon poured itself out from the trees, the horror lit by flickering torchlight.

Linn squinted against the torches at her periphery and let fly. Her aim was true and the shaft pierced the beast's head, which shifted chaotically on impact, the mass of squealing serpents attacking the flaming arrow like an infection.

The beast roared throatily, and the wall hounds renewed their baying, iron will covering their nerves.

Tu'Ren took up the call, and Linn had already sunk two more burning shafts into the creature when Kole found his range. Other shafts arced up from the yard behind the gate, the wind of their passing teasing the hair on the nape of Kole's neck. All along the wall, volleys flew, finding their mark and doing little to stop the demon's momentum.

It was like a titan of nightmare, a god of the forest—a Night Lord from the World Apart, whose like had only been seen once before in the life of the Valley. That was a creature against which only Creyath Mit'Ahn, Ember of Hearth, had stood his ground, and Kole was not he.

Great forelegs curled into apelike fists, pounded the sloshing earth as bowed hind legs propelled it with lurching strides. And it headed right for the gate on which Kole and Linn stood.

"We need to steer it away," Linn said, voice steady as she loosed another shaft. Her lips formed a tight line.

Kole dropped his bow and drew the Everwood blades from the sheath strapped across his back.

"Taei!" Kole yelled, and the other Ember turned to regard him from his own brazier further down the line. "We need Tu'Ren!"

"I think he's occupied elsewhere," Taei said. He was a matter-of-fact sort of fellow, and Kole was just now noticing the facts.

The din of pitched battle echoed on all sides as the Dark Kind they had expected issued forth like a frothing river. It started first on the right flank, where First Keeper Tu'Ren was stationed alongside Jenk. The hounds were already up and over the walls there, their quick strides leading the swarm on circular routes between wall and wood as the archers picked their marks.

On the left, Larren gave his own commands in his measured way, his spear tip glowing amber as he drained the fire from his brazier with the opposite palm. A pack of Dark Kind was already scrambling up the walls there, and the warriors around him dropped bows in favor of blades.

All around, men and women fought for every inch, throwing back the creatures with steel, flaming shaft and—in the case of a select few—Everwood blades burning bright as dawn, spraying their glowing arcs across the night.

Kole had never seen this many at once.

He sent his own sabers into a spin, feeling the familiar warmth coursing through his veins as he concentrated on the brazier that crackled beside him. Light flared and his blades ignited in a shower of sparks that had Linn cursing beside him as her latest shaft veered off the mark.

"Kole," she said, drawing out his name in an uneasy warning as Dark Kind found their holds in the timbers of the gate and started their climb. The great black beast roared and beat its chest, the worms that were its skin charred and flaking around the burning arrows flecking its hide.

The beast came on again, and it was very close now.

"Kole!"

He left a smoking black stump where the first clawed arm reached up and over the carved timbers and whirled to face another.

There was a crash, and he was flying. And then he was falling.

His lungs expelled what air they held as he landed with a shock that sent pain lancing up his spine. Splinters—some the size of him—rained down around him as the gate exploded. Kole only realized he had lost one blade when a warrior scorched his gloved hand retrieving it from the debris. The man tossed it at Kole's knees and nodded before being launched through the air by a black fist the size of a wagon.

Kole considered all of this through a haze, dimly aware of his surroundings, until he felt a burning slash across his cheek as a passing arrow cut him almost to the bone.

"Up!" Linn screamed from her perch, which leaned precariously over the wreckage of the gate. She already had a second arrow nocked, her eyes wide with uncommon fear.

The rush of pain renewed Kole's heat, and he gripped his blades tighter, flaring them to life as he rose … and came face-to-face with the demon.

The writhing mass of undulating darkness crouched before him on bowed legs. It was half as tall as the gate it had brought down, and its eyes were the color of blood, deep and dark and staring—no, they were considering him. The eyes traced the contours of Kole's face and then moved down, widening ever so slightly as it took in the glow of his living blades.

Kole's broken brazier had spilled its guts into the shattered remnants of the gate. The beginnings of a bonfire started in the mud-caked pile, lighting the battle like daylight.

Linn had gone back to shooting as the Dark Kind made for the gap. Wall hounds and warriors alike clashed with the creatures, and Kole saw Jenk's flaming sword and Kaya's blazing staff flashing in the breach.

The Night Lord loomed over Kole, red eyes shifting like a hawk. And then its head tilted sickly, sharply, as if it heard something he could not. It might have been comical if it weren't so horrifying.

For half a breath, he thought the demon might leave them alone. And then the look shifted, the recognition washed away in an instant as it roared and raised a great black fist.

Kole took his chance.

As the beast rose up to smash back down, Kole dove for its belly, plunging his blades in as he twisted and landed in the mud. Red-black blood that smelled of fresh rot poured out in steaming gouts, hissing around Kole's burning blades as he withdrew and came up in a scramble.

A maddening roar was accompanied by a concussive blast to the chest and Kole was flying for the second time, only now he came up in a roll and weaponless.

Kole looked up to see the beast being harried on three sides by weapons of fire. Kaya slammed her staff into its hind leg with gusto, and Jenk slashed it on the opposite when it turned for her. Larren faced it down head-on, his spear glowing almost white hot, flames sprouting from its tip as it used the air itself for tinder.

The beast made Larren the object of its rage—a poor choice, as his spear made a hole in its neck, burning its life away in a single clash.

The creature fell to join its writhing fellows in the muck, twisting and squelching. It landed on its side with the force of a falling tree. As the rain washed away its corruption, turning the writhing snakes into pools of ink, Kole saw the red eyes fade and turn a pale blue.

He stood on shaking legs and stepped forward, joining the other Embers in a circle around the great, ape-like body as the battle raged around them. Above, Taei moved to intercept a Dark Kind that had Linn cornered on her perch. He cut it down in a sizzling spray.

"This one's come a long way," Larren said before moving toward the breach, Kaya following after.

Jenk looked down at the giant, brows drawn. He glanced at Kole, offering him a strange and unsettling look before reigniting his sword and rejoining the fray.

Despite the chaos, Kole lingered a moment longer, and then he, too, moved off to recover his blades, the gash on his cheek having already scabbed over.

The First Keeper's orders echoed in the night, the hounds howled and the Ember blades flared and flashed. All was back to the way it was, but even as he fought into the pre-dawn hours, Kole could not shake the feeling that something else had been looking at him through the red.

CHAPTER TWO

SAGES AND EMBER KINGS

As it turned out, Kole was feeling the effects of his row with the Night Lord keener than he had first thought. Ember blood had a way of masking minor concerns of the body until the fire ran its course. When it did, Kole collapsed.

Being carried on a litter back through the town he had helped to defend was not Kole's idea of heroic. But then, nothing about the Dark Months was, not like the stories from the desert he and the other children had been told before bed each night.

His thoughts drifted as the sorry caravan wended its way down the lichen-choked steps, the wood homes on the outskirts giving way to older, sturdier stone in the basin. The structures here were squat and weathered, pressed into the side of the slope like the mussels clinging to the mud on the beach.

Kole strained and tilted his chin, attempting to raise his head, but a callused hand pressed it back down. First Keeper Tu'Ren walked beside him, his stern countenance augmented by a white mustache and beard.

"Lake'll still be there when you're at the bottom, son," he said.

Kole struggled to speak through a cracked tongue and raw throat, so the other Ember leaned awkwardly as he walked.

"What losses?" Kole managed to whisper.

Tu'Ren shook his head, staring off into the distance. "Not what they could have been. More than they should have been."

He looked down at Kole, his expression morphing.

"A fine thing you did."

"Holspahr struck the fatal blow," Kole said.

"True enough. Still, a fine thing. If you don't know where to aim—

"Aim for the gut," Kole finished weakly, and the First Keeper smirked.

Closer to the bottom, the path split, and Kole's bearers turned him right and gave him a view of the lake. Even through the fading morning mist, it shined brightly, fishing boats bobbing, oddly content on their moorings.

"Never seen one like that," Kole said, finding more of his voice with each word. An image of the great ape—pale, blue eyes staring at nothing after it had fallen—came up unbidden.

"Wasn't a Night Lord," Tu'Ren said. He nodded at Kole's surprised look. "I know what it must've looked like to one as young as you. Hell, I know what I thought when I saw it bearing down on Holspahr. It was something, alright, and there's only one place a thing like that came from."

"The Deep Lands," Kole said.

"Aye. Nothing's come out of there near as long as I can remember. Then again, the Dark Months get worse each time, more of them finding their way into the Valley. Things must be getting bad out there."

Their exchange stopped abruptly as they reached the Long Hall, the last pattering rain slowing to a steady mist that carried on the breeze, soothing and cool. Kole was set down in the reeds beside the road and Tu'Ren squatted beside him with a groan.

"Kole!"

"Ah," Tu'Ren sighed. "There she is. Linn ran off to find her straight away, seeing the state you were in." He winked. "How you managed to ensnare those two lovelies is beyond me, but now you've got a nice scar to show them, eh?" He touched Kole under the cheek, his skin pulling with a pinch at the deep scab.

"It's going to scar like leather," Kole said, leaving out that it was Linn who gave it to him. He probably owed her his thanks for that.

"All Embers do," Tu'Ren said, rising with a few more creaks and cracks than the reeds he stood on. "The fire in our blood cares for closing wounds, not stitching them proper."

A flash of blue and green and Iyana Ve'Ran was kneeling beside him, the First Keeper moving off with a bowed gait that stood at odds with his reassuring demeanor.

"She was corralling a group of children and elders toward the shore-line," Linn called over as she crossed the road. "They had boats waiting."

"You had so little faith in your fearless protectors?" Kole asked, fighting through the fog to lock eyes with Iyana.

"The attacks get worse each time," she said, squeezing his arm tightly as she closed her eyes and began to concentrate. "Perhaps a little fear would do our protectors well."

People were forming a crowd outside of the Long Hall. The rest of the fighters must have been up at the wall, manning it in case of another attack, though the light was nearly upon them.

"Fair enough," he said, smirking at Linn as Iyana bent to her work.

The filtered moonlight merged with the cold rays of the distant sun, casting a silver-blue hue on Iyana's light hair as Kole studied her. Her ears bore the unmistakable slant of a child of the Valley Faey, though she had been born among the Emberfolk. Young as she appeared—childlike, almost—she was only a Valley bloom Kole's junior.

Unlike Kole and his Embers, the Faey had a healer's touch. Like all Emberfolk, Iyana traced her bloodline back to the snaking sands in the deserts of the north, but the land chooses its own, and the Valley had made her only the second from among their people to bestow its gifts. She was one caught between worlds, Kole knew, and though her touch was smooth and caressing as river stones, he marveled at her solidity.

"Ow," Kole said, wincing as the sting spread through his veins. He struggled to keep from burning her hand as his blood threatened to rise.

"Your blood was thick," she said, heedless of his complaints. "Something in that beast got into you. But it looks like you burned most of it out on your own."

"Who said Embers can't be healers too?" Kole asked, and he was rewarded with a stare even more withering than those Linn could muster.

Iyana pulled a small mixing bowl from some secret compartment in her pack; the stone was greened from frequent use. She withdrew a patch of pungent herbs and set to crushing.

"This will help you get back to yourself quicker."

"Lovely," Linn said sarcastically as she watched the crowd passing by, nodding at the elders who thanked her with heads bowed.

Kole followed her line of sight and saw Tu'Ren locked in an argument with another group. Seer Rusul and her crones watched from the shadows with their beady eyes before moving off toward Eastlake.

The Long Hall was raised above the water on wooden pegs. The door opened, spilling an orange glow onto the dusky road, and the press surged inside. Tu'Ren was still locked in verbal combat as he entered.

Kole put some of the paste Iyana gave him under his tongue and she laughed at the face he made.

"I have a feeling that whatever energy you just gave me is going to be sucked out in there."

"You're going in?" Linn asked.

"I am."

"Why?"

"Decisions are going to be made soon, and we'd better make ourselves a part of them."

Iyana sighed and rose.

"Go, then," she said haughtily. "I've other wounded to tend to."

"Don't burn yourself out," Linn said, gripping her sister's shoulder affectionately. Iyana smiled at her and tossed a different look back at Kole.

"That's his job," and she walked off.

Linn and Kole were among the last filing into the overstuffed meeting place. Smoke choked the rafters and its trailing vapors mixed with the orange glow of the fire pit, lending the whole affair a hazy, dream-like appeal. The scents weren't at all unpleasant: burnt lake grass, holly and sage—the last shaken by a pair of elders who made their aching way around the chamber.

"I imagine that's supposed to cool tempers," Linn said sardonically.

"I imagine."

The Emberfolk liked to pretend hierarchy was only enforced among the Keepers, but outsiders would immediately be able to mark the relative import of the assembled by their proximity to the coals burning in the center of the room.

Kole spotted his father Karin off to the left, his dark complexion making it difficult to read his expression in the smoke. Their eyes met, and Karin's tired mask fell away in a warm and caring smile.

"Your father was the one who found you," Linn said. "You had chased the Dark Kind into the trees. I lost track of you."

"What was he doing in the woods?"

"I imagine he was on his way back from Hearth. He couldn't well march in while the Dark Kind were at the gates."

"How does he avoid them out there?" Kole wondered aloud.

"He is First Runner of Last Lake," Linn said, as if that explained it all.

It was a strange image, Karin Reyna alone in the woods and surrounded by creatures of night and shadow.

Kole shook himself back into the present. Perhaps Iyana had given him stronger stuff than she had let on.

An old man sat directly before the coals cross-legged. Doh'Rah Kadeh, father of Tu'Ren and the second oldest of the Emberfolk in the Valley, commanded respect. Kole knew that had not always been the case, particularly among the Emberfolk of Hearth, whom Doh'Rah had split off from decades before.

Ninyeva sat across from him. The Faey Mother was the only soul older than Doh'Rah among the Emberfolk, and the iridescent green in her eyes only glowed brighter with each passing year. Her standing had been well-earned.

"What have we done with the beast?" Doh'Rah asked. He was often the one to break the silence.

"It's being dragged to Eastlake as we speak," Larren Holspahr said in the same manner in which he said everything: grim. "The Seers wanted a look at it before we burned it away."

"Wholly unnecessary," Doh'Rah said, and there were murmurs of agreement in the hall. "The beast is no problem we haven't faced before."

"If that ain't a problem, I'd love to hear your idea of one."

Heads tilted and twisted to see Bali Swell, the fisherman. He stood by the door, arms crossed.

"That thing took out two of our finest lads and carved up a good handful more."

"And we carved him up right back," Tu'Ren broke in.

There were several experienced blades in the room, but none commanded quite the respect as the First Keeper. Tu'Ren had led more defenses against the Dark Kind than any other. Ever since the Breaking of the Valley, when the mountain passes had sealed them in and the horrors started leaking in from other lands, he had been their rock, their flame in the darkness. Breaches like the one that had happened tonight were rare; Kole knew that Tu'Ren took it personally.

Bali nodded in deference, but cleared his throat to say more. There were a few groans at that, but Kole saw that he had the attention of most in the room.

"I heard some calling this one a Night Lord," he said, and there were a few audible gasps. "Lucky we have Embers like yourself, First Keeper, but how many are there? A dozen, between us and our cousins in Hearth? And when was the last one born? Ten years ago? More?"

There were nine. And Kaya Ferrahl was the last to be born in the Valley, twenty years ago. Kole watched the younger Ember as she leaned against the far wall, not far from Jenk, who was born a year after Kole and before Kaya. He watched the proceedings with far more interest than she.

"Night Lord!" Doh'Rah veritably spat the term. "What, pray tell, is so lordly about a giant ape riddled with sickness? The Dark Kind have ever been a scourge on all lands. That creature was as much victim as foe."

"That was no average Dark Kind," Bali said, knuckles going white as he squeezed his forearms. His son Nathen grabbed him on the shoulder, but he shook him off. "I say he's come back for us, come to finish what he started with our king back in the desert."

There were no gasps there, just a palpable silence. Kole felt it like a shadow on the heart. The Dark Kind were a fact of life in all lands, as far as they knew. When the World Apart drifted close enough to touch during the Dark Months, they made their way in through whatever seams they could find. It was not the Dark Kind the Emberfolk had fled when their king led them out of the desert a century and more ago; it was one who spoke to them, commanded them. He was one of the Six—the one all Emberfolk grew up fearing, and the one Kole most wanted to meet.

Ninyeva unclasped her hands, and even in that small movement she commanded the room.

"Bali is not wrong," she said, which caused quite the stir. "The beast was not so unlike a Night Lord, but a sign of our enemy returned this is not. The Night Lords fell in battle against the White Crest, our protector."

Her green eyes searched the room, settling on Larren.

"Capable as our few remaining Embers are, this beast was a pale shadow of the ones that tangled with him in the passes. The White Crest fell that day, but he took those titans with him."

"That doesn't mean he took his brother with him," Rhees, a blond craftsman a few years older than Kole, put in. "Him that took our king from us."

There were half-hearted cheers at that.

"The Eastern Dark has never been one of the strongest of the Sages," Ninyeva said. "Quite the opposite. If his servants couldn't do it for him, I don't expect he stood much of a chance against our Sage."

A woman spit and made for the door.

"Sages and Wizards and Ember Kings," she muttered. "Keep your ghosts. I have children to feed."

"All due respect, Faey Mother," Bali said. "But our protector is gone along with our king. If it weren't for our Embers—like Kole Reyna there—I fear we'd be following in their footsteps."

There were cheers at Kole's name, and his father beamed beneath his bangs, but Kole felt himself blush.

"For all we know, he fell in battle with the White Crest along with his Night Lords," Ninyeva said. Kole was happy to have the attention shift away from him.

Bali looked as if he wanted to speak, but even he could sense when his wick had run. He held his peace.

"Kole Reyna," Ninyeva said, and all eyes again turned toward him, including those piercing greens of the Faey Mother. "I wonder what you think of this. It was you who came face-to-face with the beast, was it not?"

Kole stared at her for a spell until Linn elbowed him in the back. He coughed.

"Larren saw it plenty up close as well," he said, and the Second Keeper merely watched him, expression unmoving.

"Larren's spear knew the beast longer than he did, and we're glad of that," Ninyeva said. "But I wonder what you saw. Do you think you came face-to-face with a Night Lord?"

"I can't speak to that," Kole said hesitantly.

"But you want to speak to something," Ninyeva said, green eyes boring in.

Kole cleared his throat, and the whole of the hall seemed to swell in anticipation.

"It was looking at me," he said after a spell, the words sounding even more foolish spoken aloud than they had in his head.

There was a silence that stretched before Kole broke it.

"I mean to say, whatever it was, it felt like it was really seeing me."

"And?" Ninyeva prodded. Her eyes were a command unto themselves.

"I felt that someone else was looking at me. Something greater. Something worse."

Grumbles in the crowd around Bali.

If the room held the mood of a burial rite before, it now exploded into something verging on panic. Accusations were levied and put down, and Kole's words were thrown in his face only for those around him to lob them back with twice the venom. Through it all, the greens of the Faey Mother never left him. She raised a hand, and either that or the sudden flash from Tu'Ren's palms got everyone settled back in.

"You never say much, Kole Reyna," Ninyeva said as the scent of ozone curled throughout the hall. "But you say more than many know. Give us your true feelings. Do you think it was him? Do you think it was the Eastern Dark who glimpsed you and whom you glimpsed behind those eyes?"

"You asked for my thoughts and you have them," Kole said. Karin had shifted toward him in the crowd, silent as the rest were loud. His father's presence was as reassuring as Ninyeva's gaze was unsettling.

"I have a part of them," Ninyeva said, her tone unyielding. "As a child, you doubted the existence of the White Crest, just as you doubted his dark adversary."

Kole felt his blood go hot. Karin must have as well, as he laid a hand on his son's arm.

"I have never seen either of them," Kole said through a jaw made suddenly stone tight.

"I have never seen the eye of a storm on the lake, as Bali has," Ninyeva said. The sailor's demeanor softened at the mention. "I have never seen the far reaches of the Untamed Hills, though I trust they exist."

She looked as if she was about to go on, but Kole interjected.

"It's true that I doubted them as a child," he said. "Who could blame me? I have never seen any of the Sages, but I have known them closer than most, closer than any should. I see the havoc their magic sows every night in my dreams. You know this."

Ninyeva said nothing.

"I know all here hold the White Crest's memory up as a shining example of the great exception among the Sages, but I have never felt it. I've heard the tales spun since I was a babe: how he opened the Valley to the Emberfolk and then closed it up behind them, how he battled the Eastern Dark and his Night Lords in the passes in a clash that formed the Deep Lands and shattered the River F'Rust."

Kole paused. His skin had gone hot, and he was feeling light-headed, Iyana's paste doing its work in the wrong way now.

"I have heard you, Faey Mother, tell the tale of how you saw him as a child—our protector—dressed all in white, whose robes billowed around him and cast rainbows in the sun."

"And you doubt me?" Ninyeva stated as much as asked.

"I don't doubt what you saw," Kole said. "But I doubt if it wasn't exactly what he wanted you to see. Just as I doubt if the White Crest was ever on our side in the first place. Just as I doubt if his dark adversary, whom we have not heard from since our king fled the desert like a whipped dog, would challenge one as powerful as he."

Faces went slack—some of them so white one could be forgiven for doubting their links to the desert.

"You believe it was him you sensed?" Ninyeva asked. "Our Sage, and not the Eastern Dark? You believe the White Crest still lives?"

"Our Sage was never my Sage," Kole said. "I do not know what presence I felt except to say I've felt it before. I felt it when my mother died alone in the rain, clawing the earth and asking for help where none came."

Silence.

"Do you think she was asking the White Crest to come save her from the Eastern Dark?" Kole asked, venom entering his tone. "A storybook villain from the sands none save you have seen. Or do you think she was asking him why he had betrayed us?"

Kole stared a challenge around the room. He flushed when he noted Linn avoiding his gaze, and the shame redoubled when he saw his father's haggard look return; it was the look of one lost in the painful haze of memory, and it was Kole's doing.

"I know the Sages exist," Kole said, looking back at Ninyeva. "Unlike all of you, however, I don't distinguish between them. They took their powers from the World, after all. We Landkist were gifted our own. I used to wonder why that was, but I think I know now. Just as I know why our jailor painted himself as our savior, right before he slew our Ember king."

The hall exploded again, and no matter what fiery displays Tu'Ren affected, it was a long time before it quieted. This time, it was Doh'Rah who managed to restore peace.

"What is it, then?" he asked Kole, his tone weary. "What is it you think you know?"

Kole cleared his throat.

"The Embers are the strongest Landkist in the Valley," he said. "You elders claim we're the strongest in the World."

Doh'Rah did not argue.

"The Sages have been at war for centuries," Kole continued. "How convenient, then, for all of the Embers to be cloistered away in one of their nests, in a Valley for safekeeping. Until the time we're needed to answer his call. How convenient that our Ember king was lost to the Eastern Dark when the White Crest returned from that battle to roost and lick his wounds."

"You would put the ambitions of the Eastern Dark onto our protector," Doh'Rah said. "And you would belittle the sacrifice the King of Ember made in striking out against him. The White Crest returned here on his orders, to protect the Valley and its people."

"Haven't the Sages been looking for an advantage in their private war forever?" Kole asked, exasperated. "Hasn't each of them, in his or her own way, drawn the peoples of the World and their Landkist into their conflict?"

"For a time, perhaps," Doh'Rah answered. "But the White Crest abandoned that pettiness."

"Or so he would have you think. He convinced our king of it as well."

"Why, then, would he send the Dark Kind to slay us, Embers included, if he meant to use us in his war?"

"An Ember of the Lake has never fallen against them," Kole said, and the words sounded horrid even to his ears. "Neither has an Ember of Hearth. Not since they first entered the Valley when I was a boy." Images of all the soldiers—and everyone in between— who had been killed flashed before his eyes.

"The Dark Kind serve no master in this World," Doh'Rah said. "No master save the Eastern Dark, who has ever been our enemy."

"Perhaps they have been let in," Kole said, but he knew he had lost them. Whatever interest he had piqued had soured. If he was honest with himself, he could not entirely blame them. In matters concerning the Sages, he had never been able to remain clear-headed. His thoughts were guided by rage, his words by revenge. In truth, it was revenge as aimless as the wind itself.

Was he wrong? Was he truly projecting his anger, his loss, onto a figure that had sheltered them against his own kind?

More of the gathered had begun filing out into the night, and Kole suspected that whatever good will he had garnered in the assault went with them.

"You are not the first Landkist to think to challenge the Sages, Kole Reyna," Ninyeva said in a room grown quiet enough to hear the waves of the lake lapping beneath the boards. "Nor are you the first to question the loyalty of the one who swore to our king to shelter us against the rest. The Dark Months have never been as perilous as they are now. Whatever answers are to be found at the peaks, I expect they will still be there to be found when the World Apart is no longer so close. For now, we cannot risk one of the few Embers we have."

Kole blinked, taken aback. He had expected her to rebuff his claims, to shout him down in defense of her Sage's memory. He had expected her to turn her ire onto the scourge that had hunted them in the deserts of the north and quite possibly had returned to hunt them now.

By the look on her face, Linn had expected the same.

"You would give me leave to try for the peaks?" Kole asked, hating the quiver in his voice but unable to suppress it. Was it excitement, or fear?

"I would give you leave to set your mind at ease, Kole," Ninyeva said, "and in so doing, to do the same for your people. Questions are a powerful thing. In the past, it was easy to forget what it must be like growing up in the Valley but being of the desert." Tu'Ren nodded gravely, staring into the dying coals. "And worse, how difficult it must be for your generation to grow up with no sign of the White Crest, with nothing but war and warriors for company. It is by necessity we live this way, but we cannot continue like this forever."

Ninyeva scanned the gathered crowd, her eyes finding each set among those who remained.

"If the White Crest lives, he must be found," she said. "If the Eastern Dark has returned, he must be found. Whatever path we take, I suspect, as I have long suspected, it is not to be found in the Valley. But these are pathways closed to us in the Dark Months. For now, we will endure, and we will hope another of those beasts does not come to our door with the eyes of a Sage, no matter which one."

Linn and Kole walked together for a spell in the soft light of dawn, while Karin stayed behind to give his reports. They did not speak, and Kole felt his scab burning angrily, though the rest of him had cooled. He was troubled by dark dreams that night. As always, they carried a core of hot flame and the echoes of a mother's cry.

CHAPTER THREE

STARLIT HUNT

Restless was not a sharp enough word to describe Kole's sleep that morning, so he settled on broken. The shards of dreaming were still nesting in his mind. He tried to shake them as he walked.

The clouds had moved off and the moon shone bright and blue. No Dark Kind would harry them now. Attacks were more frequent than they had been in any of the previous seasons Kole could remember, but they never occurred consecutively. Karin had done his job thorough. There were no Dark Kind moving in the South Valley as far north as Hearth, and those that had fled the wrath of Last Lake had done so in numbers too few to scatter hares.

Still, Tu'Ren was taking no chances, Kole saw as he approached the yawning and splintered gap where the gate had been. Men and women toiled into the night rebuilding a barrier out of the wreckage. Every brazier was lit, each Keeper on guard but for Kole. They thought they were doing him a favor. Perhaps they were. Or perhaps Linn Ve'Ran had had something to say about it.

She froze when she saw his brown eyes reflect amber in the torchlight, and the smile she forced did little to ease the unspoken tension from the night before.

"You're awake," she said, straightening from the beam she had been leaning against.

"Can't sleep."

She shifted uncomfortably, but the smile soon dissolved and she blew out a sigh.

"Iyana forced my hand," she said, nodding up toward the nearest platform, where Jenk stood beside his crackling brazier, his eyes focused on the trees ahead as he pretended not to eavesdrop.

"Embers heal fast," Kole said. "I'm more than fit to keep watch."

"Good," Linn said, tossing him a pack. "Then you're more than fit to hunt."

Hunting in the Valley was rarely a solitary effort. In the Dark Months, it never was. Kole was about to reprimand Linn for striking out on her own when someone approached at a trot from the road behind.

"Nathen," Kole said, nodding appreciatively at the fisherman's son. "How are you?"

"Hungry," Nathen said, all good humor. He was a genuine lad from a hard working family, and younger than Linn and Kole by close to a decade—young enough not to know a Valley without the Dark Kind. As it happened, he was also the best hunter on the Lake. It was a fact not lost on his father's friends, who never let Bali hear the end of it.

"If Nathen Swell is hungry," Kole said, "then it truly is past time to bring in some fresh game. Not that we don't appreciate your father's fish, but there's something about sinew to get you through dark times."

"And Dark Months," Nathen said with a smile before taking the lead as they passed under the scaffolding.

"You three going out now?"

It was Kaya, leaning on her Everwood staff and craning over from what was usually Linn's perch. It was a slight intended and received.

"We need some fresh air," Linn said without breaking stride.

"Plenty of that all around," Kaya called after her.

"Especially around you, Ferrahl, since you've no brazier stealing it away," Linn shot back. A string of curses followed and Linn left a trail of bubbling laugher in their wake as they ducked beneath the canopy.

Though there were six Embers at Last Lake, there were only five braziers. Kaya was a powerful Landkist and formidable enough with her flames, but she was want to suck up more heat than she could easily channel, and the results had been near-catastrophic in the past. Kole held no ill will toward her, but facts were facts.

Nathen was always quiet on a hunt, a skill the others possessed but felt no need to adopt as they marked a path west toward the nearest of the Untamed Hills. Linn and Kole had never been known to share words over tea. They thought best beneath the trees and spoke freely in the clearings.

"You may as well ask," Kole said, earning a confused look from Nathen up ahead before Linn answered.

"You really think it's the White Crest doing this to us?" she asked, her tone making her own thoughts on the subject abundantly clear.

"I don't know what I think," Kole said, as if he hadn't done a good enough job proving that in the Long Hall. "But he is one of them, isn't he? One of the Sages."

"Was, you mean."

Nathen put a bit of distance between him and the pair, partly to avoid the distraction and partly—Kole suspected –to avoid getting involved. The stars lit the branches overhead like a thousand tiny mirrors, but the light faded as the woods grew dense, the path choked with roots and loose stones. The animals of the Valley were silent in their nests and burrows.

"He is gone, Kole," Linn said in that hard way of hers. It was the way she said things when she wanted him to prove her wrong.

"We don't know that."

"We know that the Night Lords attacked him in the Valley passes thirty years ago," she said. "We know the battle lasted three days—

"And three nights," Kole put in. "And their clash brought down the peaks and broke the River F'Rust, and the Rivermen who lived in the canyon were trapped in the Valley—those that survived, at least. Their bones litter the Deep Lands now, and the Steps still echo with the faint clashes of our Valley Sage and the Night Lords sent against him. I know the tale."

"It wasn't so long ago to be called a tale, Kole. It happened in the lives of our parents. The White Crest fell and the Dark Kind entered the Valley. We've been fighting them ever since."

Kole said no more, and Linn grabbed him by the shoulder and turned him around roughly. They were in a small clearing beset by filtered star-light. Though she was angry, she looked oddly beautiful.

"Did you really sense something looking through that beast?" she asked, a hint of fear in her voice. "Kole. Did you see something?"

Kole sighed.

"Something saw me, Linn," he said. He knew Nathen had stopped moving along the path up ahead, that he was listening with those hunter's ears. "That was not your average Dark Kind. It had a master."

"The Dark Kind are a force of nature. Not in our world," she said, noting his expression. "In theirs. Only one has the power to control them. If what you say is true, then Bali is right. The whispers are true, and the Eastern Dark has found us. He's come back. The White Crest didn't manage to kill him in the passes after all."

Kole did not look convinced, and that seemed to snap something in Linn. She grabbed him by the straps of his pack and nearly shook him.

"What makes you say otherwise, Kole? Why are you constantly chasing the ghost of a Sage you've never seen? A Sage that died before we came into the world."

Kole looked away, dropping his voice so even Nathen could not hear.

"I saw him the night she died," he said, and Linn's grip slackened. "I sensed him. He was there, Linn." Kole's brown eyes took on their amber glow as they met hers. "He could have helped her. I know it."

But he didn't.

"There were shadows with the same red eyes as that beast. They were in the peaks above the Deep Lands. Not Dark Kind, but something stronger." Kole's eyes widened as he remembered waking up in a cold sweat for the last time, before the fire had found him. Before he was Landkist. "If he was there, why didn't he help her? Why did he let them …?"

Linn shook her head and released him.

"We've all lost, Kole," she said, her eyes all sympathy. "But not all of the Sages are the same. There has ever been one the Emberfolk have counted an enemy. With the White Crest gone—gone, Kole—we can't rely on anything but the strength of our people to repel him."

"Ninyeva knows something," Kole said. "She led me like a lamb to the slaughter. If she knew he was back, she should have said so."

"You got exactly what you wanted," Linn said, moving ahead of him. "You can make for the peaks when the Dark Months end, see what there is to see."

"She knows what's happening, or has a guess," Kole said, following after.

"Ninyeva always has a guess."

Sure enough, Nathen was lounging idly on a leaning trunk, chewing some root or another. He stood when they approached, flashed that quick smile and continued on the path without a backward glance.

"You're right about one thing, Linn," Kole said, unconcerned about Nathen's presence. Linn stayed quiet, picking her footfalls carefully as the branches grew thicker overhead. "The Dark Kind are getting bolder, the Valley more deadly by the year. We can't keep waiting at the edge of the World. Either our enemy's out there or he's not. It's time we took control of our destiny rather than waiting for the ghost of a dead king to point us in the wrong direction. He already did it once."

"You don't know that. For all we know, the wider world is completely overrun by the Dark Kind, the Sages dead and gone—all of them."

"They're not gone," Kole said bitterly. "Powers like that linger."

"We need powers like yours to linger here," Linn said. It was clear she was running out of patience, and Nathen's nerves seemed about to fray as they reached the darkest parts of the woods that bordered the Untamed Hills. The Dark Kind were the least of their concerns out here.

"Good as my bow arm might be, Reyna," Linn said, "it'll never be able to stop what came through that gate. You and yours are the last Embers born in a generation. Even Ferrahl is someone we can't afford to lose. Whatever you do, make sure you're doing it for the right reasons."

The conversation stopped there. And the hunt began.

Despite the early tension, Kole felt lighter after having it out. He could not say he sensed the same from Linn, but the White Crest had been a revered figure in her household as well as in many others among the Emberfolk—a deity of sorts to replace their lost king. He was a Sage who had turned against his own kind, had sheltered the Emberfolk against the Eastern Dark and had even struck out with the King of Ember to bring him down.

He had failed on that last count. As far as Kole was concerned, he had failed on all counts. Kole had no way of knowing whether or not the White Crest was dead. He had no way of knowing what had been looking at him through those reds. But it had the stink of magic. If one of them openly flirted with the Dark Kind, why wouldn't the rest?

The Emberfolk had put the White Crest on a pedestal polished by memory and fear. Kole had no use for idols. His had burned bright, and her flame had died away, leaving only ashes. He would find the truth, and whichever Sage was at the end of it would rue the day.

Kole tried to leave the choking thoughts behind as they crossed another brook and approached the final tree line before the first glade. Starlight bounced off of the moon and painted the grassy hilltops silver in an approximation of the capped peaks in autumn.

The Untamed Hills were a place even the Dark Kind avoided. The creatures there grew tall and fierce, and unlike the rest of the Valley game, the prey there did not hide.

Linn unloosed her bow from around her shoulders as Nathen readied his own, a shorter and thinner band in keeping with the weapons of the Faey. Linn's eyes were intent on the first rise, where the hint of outlines shifted in the half-light.

Kole fished through the pack Linn had given him and withdrew a sling. He picked out several tightly rolled balls of sticky pitch and lined them up on the ground before him, shifting beneath the branches to get a better view.

Linn nocked an arrow and drew, Nathen doing likewise. She nodded so slightly it could have been mistaken for a twitch, but Kole knew better. With a burst from his fingers, he lit a ball and launched it sky high with a guttering whistle, then did the same with two more in rapid succession.

The flares punctuated the cool semi-darkness and the tiny comets streaked into the stars, Linn and Nathen following their arcing path as they trended downward. Linn let fly half a breath after each ball struck the turf and announced its presence with a flash that blinded the horned animals gathered there. Their flight tore up clods in the earth as they scattered, but Linn's arrows caught two clean before they turned, bringing them down in a heap. The third was either lucky or damned, depending on how many legs it would need to live out the week, and Nathen cursed his aim.

"It changed directions quickly," Kole said, patting his arm. "The herd will look after it."

Nathen forced a tight smile.

As Linn and Kole stood watch atop the rise, Nathen worked at the bodies of the fallen beasts, removing the shafts with expert precision and saying the words that needed saying. It took some time for them to drag the carcasses back to the trail, where they rested and refilled their skins in the brook. Sitting with his bare toes steaming in the water, Kole watched the last wind-blown embers turn to ash in the breeze, snuffing the orange lights from the field.

After a spell, Kole stood, his feet drying before he had taken two steps, and helped Nathen strip the most elastic branches from the boughs overhanging the water. Linn tied the best knots, so they let her secure the poles to the litter before loading their bounty and setting off. Their progress was slow, but they reached the unfinished gates before the moon had finished its slow arc across the night sky.

Nathen insisted on seeing both animals to the stores and bid Linn and Kole a good day. As he disappeared into the center of town—still bustling despite the recent attacks—Kole could not help but laugh.

"What is it?"

"Why that boy isn't a soldier is beyond me," Kole said. "Are we sure he isn't Rockbled? He's even stronger than he looks, and he looks plenty strong."

"People have said that about my eyes since I took up the bow," Linn said. "But alas, not all of us can be Landkist. Besides," she shouldered her pack, "we're all soldiers when we need to be. Some would rather leave it at that, especially when you've got a heart like his."

Kole nodded and handed his own pack over.

"My turn at watch," he said, earning a reproachful glare from Linn.

"First light is almost upon us," she said, indicating the lake, which sparkled in the pre-dawn light. "Besides, I may not be as doting as my little sister, but you haven't really slept in days, and, Ember or not, your mind needs rest as much as your body. If you get any warmer, you're going to ignite, and I don't want to be there when it happens."

"That bad?"

"I can smell the ozone coming off of you from here," she said, wrinkling her nose. "It always happens when you're stressed."

"Plenty of reasons to be stressed," Kole said.

Linn said nothing. She turned and marked a path toward her lakeside abode. Kole walked her back. Iyana was gone when they arrived, likely more exhausted than any of them as she cared for the wounded.

Kole sat and watched the gray ash in the hearth swirl in the dying beam of moonlight coming in through the slatted window while Linn washed and changed. He liked being this close to the water, a trait that clashed with his base nature. He thought about the gentle waves as they lapped against the lichen-covered pegs beneath the house. He thought about their moonlit hunt and how the horned runner had cried as it disappeared beyond the rise, and if it really did have a herd to look after it.

His last hazy thoughts before drifting off were of Linn's face in the moonlight.

When she returned, she brushed his dark hair back from his eyes and kissed his forehead before heading out, taking the path north for the wall.

Kole never slept without dreaming. But tonight's dream was not in the rain-choked passes, as all the others were. Tonight's was a dream of beginnings.

CHAPTER FOUR

DREAMS AND PORTENTS

Karin had told Kole of dreams and their power.

There were dreamers in far-off lands, over mountains and spanning snow-covered fields that held their visions of sleep in higher esteem than the trials of day-to-day living. There were dreamers now passed on that had lived in shimmering jewels in the deepest deserts where now there were only red wastes. To them, a day was merely a dream's portent. And there were others beside, in the crenellated walls of rain-soaked keeps that felt any vision of the mind was wrought with illusion and deceit, its only outcome desire or despair.

The Emberfolk held their dreams private, and Kole was no different.

Now, he dreamed of the first time his blood had caught fire. He was eleven, and though he acted much the same then as he did now, he carried himself with the wobbling uncertainty of a child freshly bereft of his mother. For his people, it was a rare thing grown commonplace, and about to grow more so.

He remembered searing pain, as if he was boiling from the inside out.

Now he saw Ninyeva come to take him, Linn chasing after them while Iyana cried in the back garden. He saw his father wipe the tears from her eyes and sing songs of growing. Kole sat down beside her and listened, trying his best to ignore the wails of his younger self as he was carried away, his father flinching all the while.

"Just as the seed blossoms into the shoot," Karin was saying as he ran Iyana's pale fingers along the green stem, "so a child grows into a little girl." He pushed her nose like a button, drawing a giggle through the curtain of tears. "And just as all young women flower, so too do the Embers that give our people their name, and their pride."

And their power.

Iyana had that uncertain look children get when they're being led. Karin saw it, so he led her on a walk along the cobbled garden path. She skipped over the sprouting moss between the stones and Kole followed after.

"This is a proud moment for Last Lake, for all the Emberfolk," Karin said, inflecting his voice with a sense of awe and wonder, though Kole could see he already bore the deep creases he would come to know so well. "Once his body accepts the change, Kole will be the first Ember to awake in half a decade, since Taei Kane did before him. And he won't be the last."

Just third to last.

"The Dark Months are coming, and we need our Embers to help protect us."

"But the monsters don't come here," Iyana said, looking suddenly afraid. "The White Crest protects us."

"We do not know where the White Crest has been these last few years," he said, smiling to reassure her. "But the Emberfolk are strong. We can look after ourselves."

They said more, but Kole lost track of the exchange. He felt himself being pulled along, his attention turning and aiming him toward the shore. He stepped tentatively out onto the water and walked across its surface, standing beneath the creaking timbers of the Long Hall.

He walked further out and looked up into the sky. Clouds circled overhead, darkening the water, which grew violent around him. Kole felt his heart quicken. He spun, looking past the houses and up the hill, past the wall and over the trees. A darkness deeper than black polluted the clouds there. It rushed and scattered like smoke in the wind. It was a wall of night, a portal into the World Apart.

Anger swelled, mixing with the fear. The surf churned and boiled beneath his feet, steam rising in a torrent as his muscles bunched. The drums rolled and the braziers lit the gloom with a sick glow.

Kole leapt, leaving a jet of steaming water in his wake, his passing creating a crater on the surface that crashed down like an avalanche. He sailed up and over the Long Hall, past the market, and slammed down before the gate, breaking the earth there and sending up shockwaves that announced his presence to the dark.

This was how powerful the Embers of old must have felt.

The darkness receded like an inhalation as Kole rose. And then it came for him, spilling from the trees, an army of lashing talons and red eyes intent upon his blood. Kole had no blades, so he summoned great living weapons of flame—spear and axe. He set to hacking.

Kole laughed a devil's laugh as the Dark Kind fell before him, and all around him the forest that ringed his home burned.

There was a piercing cry. At first, Kole thought it the strangled, inhuman wailing of the Dark Kind, but it soon resolved into a woman's scream. Kole tried to regain control, to reel the flames in, but they would not be contained.

He sat bolt upright and fought to orient himself in the momentary panic that comes from unfamiliar surroundings. There was a fire in the grate now, and motes of ash with cinders for tails floated by him. It took him far longer than it should have to notice Iyana's presence.

For a sickening moment, Kole thought hers must have been the voice he heard screaming in his flames, but she was unharmed. She sat in a latticework chair with a steaming cup of lemon-scented water clasped neatly in her small hands. Her eyes glowed like green versions of the cinder motes as she studied him.

And what a sight he must have made, bunched up and steaming as his skin turned sweat to vapor.

"Hello, Iyana," Kole said meekly, fighting to suppress the panic that still welled within him. He was used to settling after his dreams, but the settling was taking time.

"You've had quite a time the last few days, Reyna."

"I imagine you have as well."

She set her cup down. He marveled at how much older she seemed and how much younger she looked.

"Feeling better since last we met?"

"Physically."

Iyana moved to fill him a cup. The stone was warm and reassuring in his hands and the smell reminded him of the markets of Hearth, all citrus and clove.

"Maybe you should take some time away from the wall."

"We're nearing the end of the Dark Months," Kole said, indicating the pink light of dawn, which filtered in through the slatted window. "The days will grow longer and the World Apart will recede."

"Until the next cycle," Iyana said, adding, "During which time we will undoubtedly require your services again."

Kole sighed.

"I'm worried, Iyana," he said.

She set her cup down and put a hand on his knee, flinching slightly at the heat.

"I'm not sure it's going to end this time."

"What's not going to end?"

"The Dark Months, the Dark Kind," he swept his hand out in a meaningless gesture that was meant to span the whole of everything. "All of it."

Iyana stared at him, all concern, but Kole was having trouble meeting those green eyes lately. She took his hands in her own, ignoring the pain it must have caused her.

"You are Landkist, Kole Reyna," she said. "Ember-born and chosen of the flame."

"And I'm among the last," he said bitterly.

"We don't know that for sure."

"The desert has forsaken us," he said. "We are not its children any longer."

Iyana shrank back a bit and Kole squeezed his temples.

"I'm sorry," he started, but she broke in.

"Our new land has gifts all its own," she said, fighting to keep a civil tone.

"They aren't gifts meant for war," Kole said, shaking his head.

"No," Iyana clipped. "They're gifts meant for mending. A lot of that goes on in wars, in case you hadn't noticed."

There was nothing to say to that, so Kole said nothing. But something in his look must have worried her, because her temper—often hotter than his own—cooled quickly.

"What is it, Kole?" she asked. "What do you know?"

"Nothing."

"Was it the Night Lord?"

"Tu'Ren says it wasn't a Night Lord—not a true one, at any rate."

Iyana just looked at him.

"It's just a feeling, Iyana," he said, standing and stretching. "And dreams."

"Your dreams are as vivid as Ninyeva's sometimes," Iyana sounded concerned.

"Don't let it worry you."

"It worries you."

Kole was silent.

"Some hold Jenk Ganmeer up as the future hero of our people," Iyana said. "There are whispers that he will lead us out of the Valley and back into the deserts to reclaim our lands."

Kole looked at her, his expression unreadable.

"But those who count know that it's you, Kole. Why do you think Ninyeva is allowing you to go where no other has since—

"Since my mother," Kole finished, and Iyana fell silent.

Kole thought to tell her he was sorry, or that he knew she was. Instead, he said nothing.

"Thank you for the drink."

He left, feeling those green eyes on his back long after he'd rounded the bend.

<hr />

Linn had not gone north after all. Instead, she took a circuitous route through Eastlake. Her watch did not begin for a few hours and she would not be missed as sorely as one of the Keepers.

Sunrise in the Dark Months was always slow in coming. It painted the stones in the road pink and orange, like coals left on the edge of a fire. The sun would barely rise above the lake, its path more horizontal than vertical as it skirted the edge of the horizon before disappearing a few hours hence, leaving them stranded in darkness once again.

She turned west, taking a path through the squat homes that ran parallel to the shore. From her vantage, she could see the salt water calm as mirrored glass all the way to the jagged spine of obsidian that broke its surface in the center. Though Last Lake was in the south of the Valley, she felt that she could hit one of the Sage's peaks in the north with a well-placed shaft on a clear day. Looking south, over the obsidian spires, she could make out only the faintest outlines of the ridges that separated the lake from the mother ocean that ringed it, the salt tunnels breathing like dragons beneath the surface of water and rock.

Westlake sat on a hill, which was sheltered by a shelf of gray stone that might have been the child of some ancient peak now fallen down. The weak sun rarely marked the roads clearly up here, so lanterns lit her way.

Linn always focused on her surroundings when her mind was troubled. She saw everything except for what she did not want to see. Sometimes she wished she knew her mind as well as she knew the details of each branch in the woods before the wall. She wondered if Kole knew it better. She did not have to wonder if Iyana did.

Though she was not sentimental, Linn's mind wandered this morning. She remembered her moonlit hunt with Kole. She remembered their first faux hunts as children, and then a little older, when they had changed from pretend to real and ended with killing. They had discovered more after that first hunt, lying in the moss by the river after washing. But it seemed those days were behind them.

They were memories so pure as to be agonizing, and her fondness for them scared her so much that she had hidden them away. She wondered if they both had, and if it was best that way. Still, they cared for each other deeper than knowing.

It was a sad thing that killing had first brought her and Kole together, and it was killing that bound them together now. It was killing out of necessity, but she envied those in the Valley that found ways to avoid it. She passed them on the streets and they thanked her for it with their looks and glances—thanked her for taking the bloody burden. A part of her hated them for it, but it was a small part. It was the part of her that railed silently against the world, and the part she had buried beneath the same hill as her parents.

The truth was that she and Kole knew each other better in those moments than in all the quiet ones in between, the cold efficiency of her work painting a stark contrast to the firestorm that consumed him when his blades were lit. There was a trust at the center of it—a trust she was betraying now.

But she had to protect him. She had to protect Iyana. She would protect them all, Landkist or not.

Linn thought of the difference between secrets and lies as she came to a green door and rapped.

CHAPTER FIVE

BURDEN OF LEADERSHIP

While the homes near the wall were newer, built primarily of wood and thatch, the structures further down the slope took on a more permanent shape. The cobbled streets were overgrown with moss and weeds, wending their way through the market and around the wells before giving way to the gravel where the fishermen kept their cabins.

Although many of these hovels were ramshackle in appearance, they were the oldest at the Lake, having been put up before there was even a true settlement along its banks. Back then, there had been no need for walls; in fact, it was the very decision by the Merchant Council of Hearth to build their own gaudy white barriers that prompted the Emberfolk to fracture, with a great number coming south to the salt and spurs. The strategic advantages provided by the land around Last Lake were more of a happy accident than any genius in engineering. The settlement was protected on three sides by water and rock, and on the fourth by a thick timber wall manned by some of the stoutest warriors in the Valley.

Ninyeva considered how all she now saw before her would have been swept away long ago if not for those warriors—if not for Tu'Ren and his Embers, Landkist much more useful than she.

She rapped gnarled knuckles on the mahogany rail of her leaning tower, looking out over the docks below, the Long Hall a stone's throw away. These had been her chambers for as long as she had made the Lake her home, which was near as long as any save for Doh'Rah, the man that had convinced her to come in the first place.

What if she had stayed out among the Faey? What more could she have learned from the other Landkist blessed as she was blessed?

But her people had needed her, she supposed. Or thought they needed her, which was as near a thing. Ninyeva was the oldest of the Emberfolk in the Valley and the first to be Landkist by it. To the young and leaderless, this made her wise. For a long time, she felt wise, when the killing and dying had been done on human terms—meaningless conflicts between the three tribes of the Valley. Quelling those conflicts took doing. For Ninyeva, it was all a matter of listening and getting the right ears to listen back.

The Dark Kind had no ears for mercy and no hearts for forgiveness. There was no wisdom could stop a thing like them. They were as inevitable as the Dark Months themselves. The Valley had made her people soft. Try as she might, she could not remember the sting of the sand in her eyes or the sun on her back.

Of course, it was the young and leaderless that guarded them now. They were made of stronger stuff than any that had entered the Valley in the legendary caravan of which Ninyeva was a part. But it was not enough to stop the inevitable.

There was a chill in the room, and if there was one in the Valley who dealt with chills even worse than she, it was Doh'Rah. Ninyeva sighed and turned away from the railing, moving to the threaded carpet in the center. She lifted the blackened grate and slid another stack of scented oak into the sloped pit beneath it, fanning the eager flames back to life. Her thoughts continued to tumble around as she waited—thoughts and their cousin doubts.

Doh'Rah would have news from Hearth and the Scattered Villages. He might even have word from the Rivermen at the Fork. He was well known and respected, if not entirely liked. Ninyeva held the hearts of the Emberfolk of the Lake, but he held their minds.

In the distant past, Ninyeva might have been anxious at his approach. In the not-so-distant past, she would be excited to match wits. Now, she felt neither frayed nerves nor the swell of anticipation. The Dark Kind had come for them every year for the last generation, and they had lost many of their best and most of their brightest. Together, they shared the burden of leadership, whatever good it did their people.

Ninyeva was sitting cross-legged before the flames when he entered. They nodded a greeting, and he took the cup she proffered out of habit, setting it down without sipping. Doh'Rah looked past her, marking the path of the half-sun as it moved across the surface of the lake.

"Still calculating, exhausted as you are," Ninyeva said sternly.

"No harm in knowing the time."

"Now, then," she said. "What news?"

Doh'Rah spoke, and while he said nothing altogether concerning or untoward, his tone was forlorn. It was a tone he might have affected once only in the company of his late wife, now reserved for her alone. Not even Tu'Ren saw his father like this.

"Villagers from the Western Wood have been pouring into Hearth— scores each day. If Karin's reports of the refugees are accurate, we should count ourselves lucky to have lost so few."

Ninyeva flinched, her green eyes flickering.

"The day we count any loss as lucky will be a dark one indeed."

Doh'Rah grunted his agreement.

"Our cousins in Hearth experienced no losses in the attack?"

"They never do," he said, an edge of bitterness in his voice that made him blush when he caught it.

"Rah," she said, locking him in place with that unyielding stare. "There's something else."

He took a drink and coughed a bit, unable to take his eyes from hers. He broke the trance with a shiver.

"I hate it when you do that."

"Sorry," Ninyeva said, blinking. She meant it. It was so easy for her to feel his emotions; they were like a thread she wanted to pull at to unravel the thoughts beneath.

"No matter," he feigned indifference. "Just the odd talk of dark men in the woods— demons and the like." He waved his hand dismissively. "If I've learned anything in my considerable time in this Valley, it's that the only folk more tall in their tales than the Rivermen are our own."

Ninyeva smirked, but his words had her feeling paler than she must look.

"What did they say of these dark men?"

"Nothing of note."

"Rah."

He grumbled, but she caught him in those greens again, and he blubbered what words were swirling just behind his tongue.

"They are blacker than night," he said. "Unclothed and with eyes shining blood-red with a ruby glint."

"Sentinels."

"No!" he nearly shouted before coming back to himself. He wiped the sweat from his brow and took another drink. "The White Crest slew him. Why would he wait this long? What could he want?"

"The same thing he's always wanted," Ninyeva said, hazy with memories of the tales her father told her of the Eastern Dark as a child. "It must be, Doh'Rah. The Dark Kind have ever been a scourge on the World, coming in through their rifts, but these attacks are coming too regular and too direct. A Night Lord died within our walls."

"It was no Night—

"An approximation of one, then. And now the Sentinels? They are being guided now as they were then."

"And you mean to send one of the last Embers we have out into the passes to see?"

Ninyeva paused.

"I don't know," she said. "But I know that we will not endure if we stay here. When the Dark Months end, we need to see the state of the World. It's been generations."

Doh'Rah was silent. He settled back, imploring her to speak.

"When we first came to this Valley," she said, "we were a pragmatic people. Our home was in the deep deserts. Sand and wind were no strangers to us, and we were warmed in the bosom of the buried mountains."

Ninyeva was never sure how Doh'Rah would respond to stories from the past. He had been born in the Valley, his memories of the desert false things implanted by those who had come from there. He seemed at once both eager and afraid to dwell on what had come before, uncertain or unwilling to consider what had been taken or what had been lost. The buried cities that should have been his home warred with the Valley he knew and loved.

"To my grandsires," she continued, "the fire flowing within their veins was as natural and as common as the snakes carving their crooked paths across the dunes. It was not a matter of if, but when your flames would emerge, since those were the early Ember days. We lost much when we left the deserts. My father used to say that we never knew how full the desert was until we left it."

She smiled fondly.

"Lately, I keep hearing those words in my dreams. They follow me into waking. Doh'Rah," she looked intent. "The Ember blood was never our birthright. It was never a part of us. It was a gift of the sun and fire, of the beating heart beneath the sands and the black rock that held it all up. The Embers of the Valley are weak. Only the oldest among them—your son, Larren, Garos Balsheer and Creyath Mit'Ahn of Hearth—hold a candle to the old flames. The young show flashes, but nothing more than burning ash on the wind, soon to be snuffed out entirely."

Her eyes widened.

"I am Landkist by the Valley. I am blessed by pine, oak, ash and yew. But I am no Ember, nor is Iyana. The Landkist of the Faey and the Rivermen cannot stop the coming tide. Our Embers are burning out. When that happens, our children die. All of them. And he wins."

"He wants their power," Doh'Rah said, speaking slowly. "That is what he has always coveted, according to the stories."

"Then he will take them and pervert them," she said. "He is ready to make his war on the other Sages, if he hasn't already."

"He already did more than a generation ago, against our own."

"That was a retaliation for the attack the White Crest and the King of Ember launched against him."

"That was a hundred years ago. Why did he wait so long to confront the White Crest? And why did he wait so long to send his Night Lords and his Sentinels—supposing that is what they are?"

Ninyeva sighed, shaking her head.

"The World Apart cannot be controlled," she said. "Only guided, aimed."

Doh'Rah was silent for a time. He looked tired, and she was sorry for it.

"Do you really think our Sage could be alive?" he asked with the naïve hope of a child.

"Kole Reyna is scarred by a poisonous mix of dreams and memories from that night."

"The night Sarise made for the passes," Doh'Rah said. "He said you saw it as well. What did he mean by that?"

Ninyeva looked away. It was a rare enough thing, and one he caught.

"I don't know," she said in a whisper. "But I saw the White Crest, Rah. I saw him as a girl, standing with the King of Ember, his great silver wings shining on the cliffs. I felt his eyes on me, and later came to learn that everyone who passed under him that day had felt them, intent and unflinching. He was to be our protector, our guardian, and a rock to break what waves might come from the wars without his lands. These lands."

"These lands," he repeated, seizing on them like a vice. "These are the lands we must look to, the lands we have always known and the lands that have sheltered us."

"They will be our burial grounds."

"They already are!" Doh'Rah shouted. "But so are the lands beyond, more so. They are rent apart, broken in the Sages' private war. That is why we left. That is why you left."

They both fell silent.

Doh'Rah pressed a palm to his face and attempted to drag the anger away, leaving fatigue in its place. He looked like defeat. She was not sure which version of him she preferred.

"The truth," he said quietly, lifting his cup a final time. He drained it in a swig and placed it back by the grate, rising to his feet and smoothing the folds from his red-brown robes. "The truth, Faey Mother, is that we have no idea what lies beyond the mountains. Maybe you did, once. Whatever horrors may come, they pale in comparison to what we'll find out there."

He took her hand and gently helped her to rise, kissing it lightly, all his bluster having blown out with the breeze from the balcony. He turned for the door and Ninyeva emptied her own cup and moved back to the rail. The day was cool, and the night was coming fast, the sun nothing but an amber jewel on a sapphire horizon. She heard the door open behind her as Doh'Rah readied himself to leave.

"Who are we to bid them stay?" she asked, more to herself than him.

"Even Reyna does not truly want to leave, Ninyeva," he said. "He wants to save us all. The trouble is, he's one man—an Ember, yes—but one man regardless. We can't send him out to die."

"Then I suppose I'd better see what I can find," she said, turning with a smirk that eased some of the tension.

"You're a little old for a trek through the Deep Lands, over the Steps and into the peaks," Doh'Rah said with a laugh.

"I learned much in my time with the Faeykin," Ninyeva said. "There are many paths in this world. Not all of them require walking."

He closed the door, and the odd look on his face before he left did little to bolster her confidence. The Between was a road perhaps more dangerous than those in the north of the Valley itself. And she had never travelled far. But night was coming, and all the terrors with it.

If not her, then whom?

CHAPTER SIX

DOWN AMONG THE ROOTS

Kole had spent a day and the following night's watch ruminating on the difference between dreams and visions. Karin used to tell him that the two were like cousins: any mixture could not be trusted. He knew what haunted his son every night because the same thing haunted him.

The Faeykin, Landkist of the Valley, had visions. They saw them as paths to walk and waters to swim. Ninyeva knew their ways. She knew how to navigate them, but Kole did not go to the Faey Mother. He wondered if Iyana had been taught how to wend her way between worlds, but he did not think so. Now more than ever, the healing abilities of the Faeykin were in higher demand than sleepwalkers.

The lake still boiled and frothed in his mind's eye, the trees whipping violently under the black gales. He still heard his own primal screams rending the forest. There was anger there with a touch of fear just below the surface. It was at once repulsing and intoxicating.

There had been something else, and the more he meditated on it, the more certain he became: something had been watching him from the trees.

At first, he had dismissed the feeling as a byproduct brought on by the fog of sleep, but the closer he drew to the woods, the more he felt it, like a nagging tickle on the nape of his neck.

He thought of going to Linn or Nathen for help, taking them with him into the woods. But they would have convinced him not to go, and besides, he would not deprive Last Lake of any more of its defenders than necessary. No, Kole would not risk them. But that did not mean he had to go alone.

Kole crossed the road well before the torches that lined the path to the half-built gate. Progress was quick, the timber supports already laced with rope and doubled with angular frames of stout oak. This was not the first time the builders of Last Lake had been forced into quick action, and it would not be the last.

The kennels were sprawling and unguarded, the hounds trusted more implicitly by the people here than their own children.. There were no gates or latches to keep these soldiers in; they were free to come and go as they pleased. Though they could not take up residence with humans, attachments formed, especially among the fighters of both species.

Kole reached into his belt to produce an old standby. He snapped the end off a carrot with a wet crack, and heard the telltale sounds of claws in the gravel almost immediately.

Shifa greeted the carrot first, crunching hungrily before finding the courtesy to reward Kole with a lick. She walked a circle around him, sniffing as she went, both to reacquaint herself and—he suspected—to ensure he was not further burdened with orange vegetables.

"That's my girl," he whispered, scratching behind a white-tipped ear. The other hounds looked on from their places beneath the thatch-covered slats, unimpressed.

Together, they moved around the back of the wood barracks, skirting the edge of the wall to the west, Shifa following Kole's lead and mimicking him as he avoided the pools of orange light that marked the braziers' glow. He chose the section of wall nearest Kaya to scale.

Shifa was a wall hound of the Lake, fleet of foot and cunning as a sharpened blade. The hounds here had to be, since it was their prodding and feigned retreats that helped to corral the attacking Dark Kind during assaults. The Emberfolk of Last Lake did not have the great white walls of Hearth to hide behind, so they worked with what tools nature gave them.

Kole sat the hound down in a darkened bend in the wall. He motioned with two fingers and she was up and over with a bound and scratch so faint one could be forgiven for thinking it a squirrel. He waited a short spell and then followed her over, finding her sitting and waiting, ears perked and matching tail wagging. They took off into the woods, and if there was a small part of him that felt foolish for following his flights of fancy, there was a keener part intent on discovering the source of that constant prickle, which was now a steady burn at his temples.

His veins felt hot, and Shifa's hackles raised as she crossed in front of him on the trail, scenting the ozone he released. The Woodsmen of the Scattered Villages often said there were two choices when it came to trust in the deeper forests at night: the moon and the path. The moon was unreliable, dipping behind clouds and canopy alike; the path could be tricky, snaking this way and that, mingling with the Faey roads or washed out in the rains. Kole supposed it mattered little which he trusted now.

There were no Dark Kind laying in wait for them. If there had been, Shifa surely would have sensed them. Still, she had caught something. Kole could tell by the pace she set. He marked her progress by following the bobbing tufts of her ears through the dark.

Hunter and hound slowed their pace before halting altogether at the borders separating the Greenwoods from the Black. The branches were thicker here, the fur-covered vines forming dense curtains that reached to the forest floor. There, they intermingled with the roots and worms in the soft earth.

Shifa looked up at Kole, tongue lolling as she waited for him to make a move.

Kole slowed his breathing to a crawl, closing his eyes as he listened, intent on the woods. He heard nothing, a common thing in the Dark Months, but this was a thick and watchful silence. He felt Shifa go rigid beside him. She issued a low growl, a final confirmation. He moved forward, parting a fur-laden curtain with one drawn Everwood blade, which he left unlit.

In the deep forest, the roots grew thicker than beams, forming a sort of latticework—a second canopy above the tunnels and the soft, moving things below. If you had to traverse the great roots, you were better off going high than low. Kole picked his way carefully from root to root. He remembered coming here with Linn as a boy, when they used to imagine sliding down the tails of drakes.

The feeling of being watched intensified to a point of near-mania, and Shifa reacted accordingly, issuing her growls to the forest floor and the twisting branches above. Kole redoubled his heat, and his skin prickled, the sweat turning to a misty veil that enwrapped him like a forest ghost.

A misjudged hop and then a rotted root betrayed him, announcing his blunder with a resounding crack that echoed off the encircling wall of trunks. Kole slid into a role, cursing as he crashed down into the leaf-laden sludge between roots thick as serpents. He managed to come up with his blades drawn, flexing his core and releasing a spark that set them alight.

Shifa issued a startled bark and navigated the root system down to him. At the bottom, she darted in front of him, tail stiff, forming a shield between Kole and the deeper darkness of the tunnels beneath the trees. The ground was uneven, and the roots made arches and snares. It was a poor terrain in which to fight, if it came to that.

The sensation of motion ahead caused him to drop his blades away from his eyes, the better to see. It was a mistake, as the blackness formed itself into the hurtling shape of a man that came on with unnatural speed. Shifa leapt, her jaws snapping a piece of the blackness as it shot past, and then it hit him full in the chest.

Kole landed in a rolling heap and tasted blood as he came up slashing. Hands that were impossibly strong grabbed hold of his wrists and launched him back with a kick, ripping the burning blades from his grasp as he flew back. The creature screamed and flung the blades aside as Kole tumbled down a steep embankment of rock-hard roots that took the wind from him. He looked up. Standing on the crest of the gnarled rise was a black form silhouetted in the guttering light of his discarded blades. It leered down at him with eyes that shone like bloody rubies.

A small form hit the demon in the back, but it twisted and slashed with its black fingers, Shifa yelping as she was thrown aside. Kole rose on shaking legs and heard more than saw the form land next to him with a crunch among the dried refuse of the canopy. He turned and extended his hip, lancing a kick that missed. He was driven back and the demon pummeled him, his head spinning as it ricocheted off something hard as bone.

"Shifa!" Kole screamed it with all the strength he could muster. His blood pumped hot liquid fire and he lashed out weaponless, but the demon was strong and unyielding. It parried his blows and sent him tumbling into the deeper darkness. Kole rolled to his knees as the red-eyed form approached, the darkness seeming to swell around it.

And then the light exploded, Shifa shooting over the lip of the ledge above, one of Kole's Everwood blades clenched burning in her maw. The black hands made a grab for her, but she was too swift, and Kole snatched the blade from her jaws as she tore off into the brush toward the sound of rushing water.

Kole flared the blade back to life and stabbed upward, driving the black form back. With his feet under him, he sliced the air in sharp angles, forcing it to dodge, its red eyes burning with hate. His head swam, the fire in his blood unable to fully undo the effects of the demon's attacks. It circled like a wolf, darting in and out, always staying just out of range of the slashing blade and its fiery trails.

In the space between beats it came on again, and Kole tore a black hand from its body in a crescent of yellow. Still it came on, scoring deep gash in his forearm and making his hand go lax, fingers numbing instantly as the blood ran. They danced, cutting and slashing among the ancient roots, until finally Kole's legs failed him, his arm going slack, blade tearing free from his grasp as he fell to his knees.

Those red eyes seemed to lock him in place, its mouth opened in a toothless screech, and the details of the forest around melded into a swirl of agony. Kole cursed his stupidity and felt a voice in his head whose words he could not distinguish. It urged him to stillness and he struggled against it, fearing he would die alone in the dark.

Just like his mother.

The surge came from a place beyond himself, a well deeper than thought and older than memory. The light of its burning was impossibly bright and the demon's screech turned from triumph to searing pain. It tore at him with its black claws, pulling at his burning hands, which were now clasped around its throat. It twisted and wrenched like a trapped animal and Kole poured his fire into it.

He collapsed when it was done, the flames extinguished in an instant. He looked around with blurred vision and found himself at the center of a charred circle, the roots all burned away.

Kole retrieved his smoking blades and staggered through the brush in the direction Shifa had gone, holding his bloodied arm to his chest. He found her breathing shallow on the edge of a muddy stream the color of rust. He lifted her and she whimpered softly, the echoes of the demon's dying careening in his skull as he walked on unsteady legs.

The rest passed in a haze of pain, and the feeling of pursuit never dissipated, though the demon had burned like birch, its face curling in the flames. His blood felt slow and stagnant, the darkness around him close and stifling, and his mind wandered, delirious. He moved with a singular focus as he fell to ruins on the path back to Last Lake.

He reached the gate without knowing. Torches waved and boots splashed in the mud, carving the night with light and sound as they approached in a fervor. Kole tried to speak, but his voice failed along with all sense. He collapsed in a space between wake and sleep, and lingered there awhile.

A long while.

CHAPTER SEVEN

GREEN DOOR

T he smell of hot mint and sage assailed Linn's nostrils when she opened the door, and the voices she had heard from outside muted upon entering. She wafted the steam out of her face and took stock of the gathering in the guts of the modest bathhouse.

There was an elderly man dressed all in green: this was Towles, the proprietor; he was nicknamed 'Trusted' for reasons Linn hoped were well founded. Linn's sudden appearance caused him no untoward alarm as he bent back to his work, pulling a lever that announced a jet of steaming water—and another flush of mint—the pipes rattling their protests as they emptied the mixture onto a large grate covered my smooth, black river rocks.

The latest cloud parted to reveal the handsome face and close-cropped hair of Jenk Ganmeer, who sat on an oak bench slick with residue. He smiled lightly at her, features warping strangely in the shimmering heat.

"Ve'Ran," he said. "Fashionably late."

The other men and women, who sat in their various places between and around the benches and steaming grates, regarded her with a discomfiting assortment of expressions. But these were the faces of soldiers she knew well.

"It's a gift," Linn said, setting her bow down in a pile with the rest of the weapons—a considerable set—before making her way toward the front of the small room. As her nerves built to a steady, screaming crescendo, an image of Kole's black, unseeing eyes set into a face drained of all color flashed. She could not shake it, just as she could not shake the sounds of her sister's silent sobbing as she had worked over him in the tower.

"We've been dragging our feet long enough," she said, forcing a layer of calm into her voice that she did not feel. "It's time we made good on our talk and left."

There was a pregnant silence of which Jenk was at the center. The Ember stood and moved to her side, rewarding her with a curious expression as he turned to address the rest.

"These aren't the type of people you can push, Linn."

Linn ignored him and studied the gathered soldiers. It was unlikely Larren Holspahr held any great opinion of her either way. He kept his own council, but her keen eyes had saved plenty throughout the Dark Months, and that was something he would not forget. In fact, it was likely all that had brought him here to her summons when he could have been resting for the following night and whatever terrors it might hold. Larren's spear dealt the final blow to the beast that had smashed the gate, but she could tell the experience had rattled him. That was good.

To the right of Holspahr sat Nathen Swell, her hunting companion whose jovial manner painted a stark contrast to the Second Keeper. Further along the bench, which bowed under his considerable heft, was Baas Taldis, who was one of the Emberfolk in name only, his father well known as the son of the River Patriarch of the Fork. Taldis had largely been raised among the Emberfolk of the Lake after his father had settled with one of their own. Though he was undoubtedly the strongest man on the Lake, Baas left the guard duties to the Embers and their ilk. He preferred fashioning weapons to wielding them. As for why he was here, Linn had it on good authority that he found her particularly fetching. She had no qualms about using that to her advantage.

Standing off to the side was a duo that likely made up the most deadly pair in the Valley—the twins Taei and Fihn Kane. They were a strange lot, and though only Taei was Landkist, Fihn could more than hold her own with a blade. Where Taei was calm, cool and collected, his sister was quick to anger and long to forgiveness. Linn had no idea where they would fall in this.

As for the final member of the gathering, Kaya Ferrahl had likely only come because Jenk had. The youngest Ember in the Valley held no love for Linn or Kole, and the feeling was mutual. Given the covert nature of this meeting, taking place out of earshot of the First Keeper, Linn was not entirely comfortable with her presence. But beggars could not be choosers, and for all her faults, Ferrahl wielded the flame. That was reason enough to have her along.

Kaya mostly ignored the front of the room, focusing instead on the gouts of steam that issued up from the grates. When she did glance at Linn, she did so with hateful eyes. Truth be told, Linn did not know where they had fallen off with one another, though she suspected it had something to do with the fact that Linn took a more active role in safeguarding the Lake than an Ember. Sometimes, however, Linn had to admit to herself that she knew exactly how Jenk looked at her, and how Kaya looked at him.

"We've been meeting like this for weeks," Jenk said, blushing as Larren raised his brows. "We cannot keep doing so without making a decision. That said, you do seem a bit unhinged at the moment, Ve'Ran."

Linn bristled.

"I'd say the whole of Last Lake should be feeling the same," she said, trying to keep her voice level.

Jenk pulled up a stool and moved aside. He sat, nodding at Linn to continue. She had trouble deciding if he was condescending or not, and then decided that it did not matter either way.

"What's this about?" Larren asked gruffly.

"I'd hazard a guess it has to do with Reyna," Kaya sneered. "What state is he in? What on earth was he doing out in the woods during the Dark Months? He's not half the Runner his father is."

Linn winced. She tried her best to ignore Kaya, but she cursed herself for not approaching Larren and explaining her plan separately. Her demeanor must have been more off-putting to him than she had expected.

"The Dark Months should have ended a week ago," Linn said.

"They're tailing off," Nathen said. "The sun floats higher in the lake each day and hangs longer before sinking."

"Yes, Nathen. But the attack that took down our gate was the worst we've ever seen, and now one of our Embers, our Keepers," she looked challengingly at Kaya, "has been attacked in the woods by something far worse than the Dark Kind. You've all heard the whispers, try as Ninyeva and Doh'Rah might to dispel them. You've heard the word they've been tossing around."

"Sentinels," Baas said. He did not elaborate.

"Tall tales from the desert days," Larren scoffed, but he looked unsettled.

"What is a Sentinel?" Nathen asked.

Jenk cleared his throat.

"If the stories are to be believed, then the Sentinels are the sentient Captains of the Dark Kind in the World Apart," he said, staring at Linn all the while. "Where the Dark Kind are an unthinking mass of tooth, claw and tail, the Sentinels are cunning and deadly. Some say they even control the Night Lords themselves."

Nathen's eyes widened, no doubt thinking of their moonlit stroll.

"Why have they not come before?" he asked. "I thought the Dark Kind came through in waves—through rifts."

"Not the Sentinels," Linn said, seizing on the covered fear in the room. "They're too powerful to make it through, too easy for the World to mark and destroy upon entering. They need to be let in."

"Now you believe the Sages have turned their eyes on us, just because Kole says so?" Jenk asked. He looked far from convinced. "He doesn't know what he saw when the Night Lord caught him in its gaze. And he's not one known for being objective when it comes to the Sages."

"The attacks are getting worse every year!" Linn shouted. "And now we have Night Lords and Sentinels in the Valley. The World Apart skirts no closer now than it's ever been before. This is direct. It's just like the stories."

There was a silence.

"I hear Reyna was more than injured when they brought him back."

The speaker was Fihn. Her voice was high with a sharp edge.

"They say his eyes are black pits, staring out at nothing."

Linn was about to speak, but Larren cut her off.

"I heard his screams echoing from the tower on my way over." He looked around the chamber. "That boy is stout. He is Ember. It is troubling, Ve'Ran." He looked at her hard. "But solutions lie in preparation, not rash action. What is it you want us to do? Why is it you called us here, out of sight and out of mind of Doh'Rah, Ninyeva and the First Keeper? You saw what happened to Reyna for chasing demons in the woods. Why would we do the same?"

Linn swallowed. She had to tread carefully here.

"Kole said he sensed the White Crest."

Everyone in the room shifted at that.

"He couldn't decide which of his hated Sages he saw," Larren said, and Kaya snorted her agreement, earning a withering glare from the Second Keeper that put her back in her place.

"Kole is an Ember," Jenk said, speaking slowly. "We have powers, yes, but none of them stray into anything like the sight of the Landkist native to this land—of the Faeykin. If Ninyeva had said so—

"She may as well have," Linn said, her words short and clipped. Steam from the grates clung to her brow, sticking her dark bangs and giving her the uncomfortable feeling that she looked very much like a little girl fresh from a bath. "Ninyeva did not dispute anything Kole said, not even when the White Crest was brought up."

"The White Crest is dead," Baas said, his tone flat. His people held no love for the Sage or his legacy. After all, it was his battle with the agents of the Eastern Dark that brought down the passes over the heads of his grandsires. It was not so long ago. The White Crest had not been seen or heard from since.

"Kole says he is alive," Linn said, her voice growing desperate. "I know what it must sound like, especially to those of you who don't know him like I do. But Kole," she paused. "He has this sense about him. He's had it ever since—

"Ever since his mother fell in the Steps," Larren cut in. "Sarise A'zu was as strong an Ember as there's ever been in the Valley. I have no shame in admitting that. Her loss was keenly felt, by that boy most of all. But the sense you're talking about is obsession. Sarise was killed by the Dark Kind. They've always been thicker in the north of the Valley, especially around the Deep Lands. She was a fool for having gone. Had the White Crest been present, he'd have protected her."

"He is alive," Linn said, though her voice was now soft as a whisper. "He has to be alive. Ninyeva knows it."

Larren looked about to speak, to cut her words down again, but something in her expression gave him pause. He swallowed and looked away.

"The old bird gave him leave to find out what he saw at the close of the Dark Months," Fihn said.

"Does it seem to you he'll be able to make that deadline?" Linn countered.

"Doesn't matter much to me. Not sure why it matters to you."

"Because she wants him to be alive," Jenk said, understanding dawning as he studied Linn's face. "And she fears what Kole will do if he finds him."

"Where has he been all this time, then?" Kaya asked "Hiding?"

"It would make sense," Nathen said with a light shrug. "If he was gravely wounded. We don't know how long Sages take to heal."

Larren scoffed, something entirely unlike him. But he did not speak, just stood there with his back to the wall, shaking his head slowly.

"He's been gone our entire lives," Taei said, and all eyes turned to him. He glanced at Larren. "Most of our lives." It was rare enough for the Third Keeper to speak. Rarer even than Baas Taldis, but it was the Riverman who answered.

"Here's hoping it stays that way," he said and Larren straightened.

Trusted Towles sidled awkwardly between Linn and the others carrying another bucket of scented water. This one smelled strongly of lavender and sour orange, a pungent combination clearly meant to signal that he had had enough of harboring this particular meeting. The baths were no doubt heated overhead and he had customers to tend to.

"Who says the Dark Kind will stop with the coming of longer days?" Linn asked.

"All of our prior experience, since the first attacks occurred not long after I was born," Jenk said. "These creatures are perverted wretches from the World Apart, leaking in from the broken kingdoms in other lands. They have grown in number, yes, but they have not grown so bold as to attack us in daylight."

"The Dark Kind used to be a force of nature, and a random one at that," Linn said. "Now they attack like clock work, as if their scourge is a season unto itself. Before last night, they have never been bold enough to take down an Ember on our borders."

"An Ember who went out alone," Kaya said.

Still, Linn could tell all in the room save Baas were unsettled, the Embers most of all.

"What of the Faey?" Baas asked.

"What of them?" Jenk asked.

The hulking Riverman turned to him, the bench creaking under his weight.

"They meddle in the ways of magic, no? Perhaps they have turned the Dark Kind on us, seeking to purge us from the Valley."

"We settled our issues with the Valleyfolk before you were born," Larren said. "Besides, only the Eastern Dark can control the Dark Kind." He looked at Linn, and she was surprised to see that he was waiting for her to speak.

"If the White Crest is alive," she said, "we will need him to stop what's coming."

"What's already here, according to some," Larren said.

"We have a week to decide," Linn said. "Maybe less. We need the days to get a bit longer, but if the Eastern Dark is intent upon us, I doubt it will make a difference."

"We would be depriving the Lake of many of its stoutest defenders," Larren said. "On a fool's errand, to brave the Deep Lands and the Steps, and to see if a Sage that has not been seen in a generation will save us once more."

"Look at it this way," Linn said. "If our old enemy has returned, where do you think he's holed up?"

"He could be anywhere," Baas said.

"Maybe."

"We should wait until Doh'Rah, Ninyeva and Tu'Ren make their decision," Jenk said.

"They are not our leaders," Linn said, and the unintended venom with which she said it caught the room off guard.

She swallowed.

"They will drag their feet, as they ever have, while we wait for the days to shorten once again. And then we will be asked to hold out another year, to hold out before we make an attempt on the peaks, before we see the state of the World. No. It is time we took our destiny into our own hands."

"But not with Kole along," Jenk said flatly. Linn had no response to that.

Baas clapped once, loudly, and rose, the bench sighing in relief. He slapped Nathen Swell on the back and nearly drove the wind from him before heading toward the door, leaving the others stunned. As he walked past Linn, she grabbed him by the shoulder and stopped him.

"You will not come?" she asked, eyes shining.

Baas blushed.

"I will come," he said, turning to look at the others. "Was that not obvious?"

He smiled warmly at Linn before shouldering a stone-crusted shield that must have weighed as much as him and heading out onto the road, the pink light of the half-day filtering in behind him.

Nathen nodded to Linn and Jenk, boyish features hardening as he tried to match the mood of the room.

"I don't imagine you'd get too far in the woods without me," he said, patting Linn on the shoulder with a wink as he followed the Riverman.

Kaya looked unsteady and nervous. She kept switching her gaze from Jenk to Linn and back, unsure what to do and unwilling to commit. With a huff, she shouldered past Linn, the twins following in her wake. While

Fihn looked miserable as ever, Taei looked reluctant, even apologetic, as he showed them his back.

Larren straightened and moved to the front of the room, Jenk following his progress. The Second Keeper stopped between them and looked at both, his expression stern as ever, but Linn sensed a touch of unease that made her distinctly uncomfortable.

"What we plan to do is no small thing," he said.

Linn and Jenk looked at one another before turning back to the Ember.

"Nor does it leave Last Lake in an enviable position," he continued. "Still, I have had the same thoughts these last few years. No matter what lies in the passes—be it an ailing power we once counted as friend or the agents of one who has long been the scourge of our people, we have a duty to find out." He looked at Linn. "The burden is not yours to bear alone."

Jenk's sense of relief was as obvious as the sigh he expelled. Linn's was masked, but no less profound. Her knees felt weak. Larren Holspahr was as close to a legend as you could get in the Valley, an Ember of rare power and perhaps the most skilled combatant she had ever seen. Even as she felt the one weight lift off of her shoulders, however, she felt another press down, and had to admit that there had been a part of her hoping Holspahr would be the one to talk some sense into her.

Whatever might come, their path was now set.

"I will leave correspondence with a trusted guard," Larren said, oblivious to Linn's swirling psyche. "Tu'Ren and the other defenders will know precisely where we have gone and when we plan to return. That should give them some basis by which to formulate a proper defense."

The Ember started for the door, grabbing his spear, which nearly scraped the ceiling. "Let us hope that the attacks diminish with the coming of longer days." He turned back once more with the door half-cocked. "And let us pray that they are not fool enough to follow us."

The green door closed with a scrape, and they heard the clink of the butt of Larren's spear on the cobbles as he retreated into the morning light.

"I think I'll be praying that we're lucky enough to return," Jenk said, getting to his feet, much to the delight of Towles, who busied himself pretending to clean the place where he had just been.

Jenk extended his hand, and Linn took it, their eyes meeting through the mist.

"You've pushed us onto the right path, Ve'Ran. The only one there was, I expect."

Linn tried to feel proud of what she had accomplished, convincing even half of the assembled warriors to join her. But Kole's inhuman screams still echoed in her mind, the Ember crying out from his tower with nothing but a worried father and the salt of her sister's tears for company.

"Next moon, then," she said, her usual calm returning like a familiar cloak as she made for the door, grabbing her bow on the way. She flicked a piece to Towles, who fumbled before catching it. "Can't say I loved that last mix you put in."

She left Towles blushing and Jenk smirking as she braved the cool blast of Valley air and steeled herself for the walk to the tower.

CHAPTER EIGHT

STEADY BREATHING

The fishermen were already calling it 'The Tower of Screams.' Their jests covered the dark nugget of fear the hardened men of the shore kept hidden, but Iyana knew better.

She had spent the better part of a week caring for Kole. In fact, she had hardly left his side, a fact not lost on her sister. Even Karin, himself distraught and tortured, cautioned her not to burn herself out. She reminded him that, though Landkist, she was no Ember. Her own fires came from the Valley: these were fires of healing, flames that repaired rather than destroyed, and those were not easily blown out. Not so long as she cared.

Karin Reyna had only left to gather what linens and poultices Iyana needed to work. In truth, she had sent him out as often out of worry for his mental well being as necessity. He was, after all, First Runner. Remaining in a stifled tower with the prone form of his only son had not done him well. Iyana knew him to be a calm-if-introspective man, but the lines of worry on his face had never shocked her so as they did when the golden rays of the first dawn had struck his face.

As she touched her bare hands to Kole's brow—sticky and cold—Iyana pictured him as she had first known him, when the Ember had been an older brother to her. Though he and Linn had been hardened like all in the Valley, they had experienced some semblance of a childhood before the Dark Kind came. Iyana could not say the same. Though her people counted her gifts a blessing in such times, she often wondered if they were not more curse.

It had taken time before the Embers had managed to shield them from the worst of the night. Iyana's parents had not made it, and she often wondered if she could have made a difference had she discovered her abilities at an earlier age. But then, Ninyeva could not save them, and she had been trained by the Faey themselves. What could Iyana have done?

She felt the pain leaking into her own veins as Kole fought through whatever nightmares assailed him. She gritted her teeth, willing the pain to dissolve and trying to find him in that bitter darkness. Thus far, she had not come close.

There was something else going on, here. Iyana knew it both because of what she felt when she touched him, and by the fact that Ninyeva had been scarce since examining the Ember when he was first found collapsed in the rain beyond the ruined gate. Something about Kole's state had disturbed her enough to retreat to her own leaning tower. In the days since, she had only left her chambers to walk in the fresh air. According to those that saw her, her pace was furious, her demeanor increasingly erratic.

Kole had encountered something out in the woods, something more sinister than the usual Dark Kind. Whatever war he waged now, Iyana feared he would have to see it through himself.

Karin was dozing off in his seat in the corner. That was good.

When the other healers had told Iyana to rest, she had told them to leave. When Karin told her later, she had listened, taking what rest she could as father watched over son. The screams had stopped shortly after. Perhaps Karin had managed to reach him somehow. Perhaps Kole had given up. It was impossible to know, the relative silence that had at first been welcome was now disturbing in its own way.

And then there was the matter of Linn. Her sister had come every night for the first three, and then nothing. There had been another attack, and Linn had helped to throw the Dark Kind back. The next day, she was gone, along with Larren Holspahr, Jenk Ganmeer and a handful of others. Tu'Ren had visited Iyana before Linn's flight, but she had not seen him since.

Iyana tried to concentrate on Kole. Whatever troubles her hero sister would find in the northern forests, it was nothing compared to the storm Iyana would unleash when she returned. She kept special care not to allow 'if' into her mind. There were enough of those close by.

"His color has returned some."

Karin's voice was soft and reassuring, impossible to startle. Iyana welcomed the reprieve.

"I think the worst has passed," she said, turning a smile. She took care not to include the 'hope' that had been tickling the edge of her tongue.

Karin smiled back. He was not convinced, and they both knew it.

The bond between parent and child had grown into something less warm and more poignant after the Dark Kind had come. Death was a constant companion for the Emberfolk. As such, the community took on the roles formerly reserved for family. Still, there was something to be said for blood. Iyana did not remember her own, but watching the ghosts of emotion pass over Karin's face as he watched his son, she knew that link was something more.

"Thank you," Karin said, his eyes watering as Kole's never could. He said it without looking at her, but the pang of its sincerity struck her like a blow and threatened to shatter the thin veneer that was her resolve—threatened, and then made good on its promise. A single tear began a waterfall, and Karin embraced her as she poured the shared pain of herself and Kole into him.

Karin was made of something stouter than iron. He did not wince, though she felt his heart near to breaking.

CHAPTER NINE

HIGH AND LOW

Doh'Rah and Tu'Ren argued as only father and son could, and Ninyeva observed with a detachment unbecoming of the Faey Mother.

The first rays of dawn were creeping over the treetops to the north, painting them golden-red like the lit ends of matches. The sun climbed higher each day, but what was usually a time for rejoice was now something else.

In truth, Ninyeva was too spent to involve herself in their quarrel. She had traveled the disorienting roads of the Between twice in the last week, and both journeys had ended with resounding headaches in the place of answers. She knew she should share their concern; a part of her did. After all, Larren Holspahr had apparently gone rogue, taking a handful of Last Lake's finest north with him.

Of course, Ninyeva knew which of the powerful company had likely engineered the plan, but she kept that to herself. The Dark Months were nearly up, which made the roads to the north safer for traveling. Still, the northern peaks were uninhabited for a reason. The Deep Lands still held residual magic from the White Crest's fatal clash with the Eastern Dark and his Night Lords, and while Kole Reyna's condition was improving by the day, his run-in with the Sentinel in the woods had been cause for serious concern.

Word had spread about the young Ember's condition, and about what had caused it. But only Ninyeva—and by extension the two other men in the Long Hall with her—understood the implications. The Sentinels were no mere foot soldiers from the World Apart, mindless beasts made more of shadow than sinew. These were Captains, cunning and with purpose, and capable of infecting anything with their corruption, even Landkist.

Even Embers.

If Sentinels were in the Valley, they had no doubt been sent. The Eastern Dark had turned his eyes back on them. None of the elders truly believed he had perished in the fight with the White Crest. But his seeming absence had stretched over such a period as to catch Ninyeva in the illusion of permanence as well. Her thoughts kept turning back to Kole Reyna and to his contentious words in the Long Hall the week before.

Reyna was young, but he was a Keeper of the Lake and more powerful than any Ember she had seen at his age, including Tu'Ren Kadeh. Kole had glimpsed something in the red eyes of the Night Lord, and though all signs pointed to the Eastern Dark as culprit, he was as convinced of the White Crest's presence as he was doubtful of his allegiance.

Could it be so? Could their guardian truly have survived his ordeal? And if so, where had he been?

The memory of Sarise A'zu spinning in her tornado of fire, shadows with red eyes in the passes all around her, was never far from Ninyeva's thoughts these last days. A vision of death that only one of the Faeykin should have the eyes to see had somehow imprinted on her Ember son.

Kole experienced that night in his dreams, and while Ninyeva had done what she could to shield him from their burning reality, he had come through those nightmares changed. He now bore a singular focus. He was bent on the Sages.

The questions swirled, and Reyna seemed to be at the center of it all. Even Holspahr's mission reeked of Linn Ve'Ran's desire to interfere on Kole's behalf.

"I swear, that boy reminds me more of his mother by the day."

Doh'Rah was not a quiet walker; his cane betrayed him at every opportunity, and still she had not registered his approach.

"I see less of myself in him with each argument."

Of course. He was talking about Tu'Ren.

Ninyeva turned from the railing at the back of the Long Hall and saw that the First Keeper had left, the door still swinging from his abrupt departure. It was unlike him to leave without addressing her. Perhaps he had.

"The rest of us see more than enough of you in his veins," Ninyeva said, turning back to the lake.

Doh'Rah snorted.

"Your thoughts?" he asked, trying in vein to hide his concern.

"The sun rises higher each day. Holspahr and the others will be as safe now as ever."

Until they reach the Deep Lands.

"When they reach Hearth," he said, "they will be turned back by my contacts there."

"They will not go to Hearth," Ninyeva said with a small laugh.

Doh'Rah frowned.

"You have been to see Reyna," he said as much as asked.

"He will wake within the week."

"Do you truly think this to be the work of a Sentinel?"

"I do."

Doh'Rah sighed, and each time he did, it seemed that a bit of him went out with it. Ninyeva was older, but looking at her friend, she sometimes found it hard to believe.

"What do you think they mean to do?"

"Something, I would guess," Ninyeva said, and when he looked at her with that confused expression, "something more than nothing."

"Defending one's people hardly qualifies as 'nothing,'" he said, but then he looked out onto the shifting water, the light filtering down from the angled roof of the hall to strike its surface. "Still, I suppose we have grown shorter of sight, more concerned with surviving than living these last years."

Ninyeva said nothing.

"As a boy," Doh'Rah said, drawing her attention, "I clung to the image of the White Crest as our fearless and benevolent protector." He laughed sardonically. "Later, when the denizens of the Valley—I don't excuse our own people from that—turned to killing one another and he stood by, I thought him merely a barrier to the Sages without."

He looked at her, and now he did look like the man he had been, the youth who had split off from Hearth and led his people south.

"Now I wonder. Was he ever truly on our side? Did the King of Ember bring us to a paradise, or a prison?"

Ninyeva placed a comforting hand on his shoulder and affected a gentle smile.

"I imagine he did the best he could," she said. "Just as we have."

Doh'Rah smiled, and together they looked out on the lake that was their home. As the soft afternoon light touched the furthest waves, Ninyeva thought they looked like the shifting dunes of the deserts she had left.

"The young among us deserve to mark their own path, now," Ninyeva said after a time. Doh'Rah regarded her. "They were born in a Valley deprived of peace. They deserve better, and they deserve to find it for themselves. I only hope the Eastern Dark has lost some of his potency, if he has returned."

"Even a Sage such as he must take care when courting the World Apart," Doh'Rah said with a frown.

"We do not know how the conflict goes with the others of his kind," Ninyeva said. "He could be growing desperate. Why else would he send his Sentinels now?"

"Why indeed?"

They parted in the soft gravel of the fishing village, sharing nothing else but the bowed heads that come from long understanding and slow regret. Ninyeva navigated the bustling streets and pathways back toward her leaning tower. The gravel roads close to the shore were choked with people, most of them fishermen. The sun provided the means and incentive to strike out for game in deeper waters, and the men took advantage.

As she walked, she replayed her previous attempts to travel the winds of the Between. Where had she gone wrong? For a time, she even considered consulting with Rusul and the Seers of Eastlake, but decided against it. They would likely spend more time judging than assisting, no matter the stakes.

No, she would do this herself. Holspahr and the others needed to know what awaited them in the Deep Lands and beyond. She would worry about how to contact them after she solved the first issue. Perhaps Reyna would get his wish early. The Dark Months were ending, but Ninyeva felt it in her bones that the danger had only just begun.

She still remembered the winged figure standing on the cliffs as their sorry caravan had trundled through the villages of the Rivermen, their gray eyes suspicious. And she remembered the figure in red that had stood beside him, their Ember King, whom they would never see again.

How could any despair when they had such figures—such gods— watching over them?

Ninyeva and hers were refugees, but their children and grandchildren had not chosen to abandon the northern deserts. Their blood was of the sand, but their hearts were in the Valley. Until the Valley betrayed them.

She took a wide berth around the market, unwilling to be clogged in the various choke ways sprouting from the wheel. When she reached the chipped paint of her front door, the sun was high in the sky, but she knew it would not stay there for long.

Once inside, Ninyeva removed her green robe and made her aching way up the stairs, closing the shutters and sliding the thin pine frames shut to block out the light, an irony not lost on her. She lit the candles, dusted the pit beneath the grate and built a fire fit for her purposes. She went to the jars in her cubbies and each contained lifelong friends: there was the blue of sage root, wet and pungent. She took a handful of that and lined a stone bowl with it. Next, she grasped the dry, caked mass of yellow sand nettle, which she broke up and added to the mix. The green grass of the Faey gardens joined it, along with the charred fungi from the Blackwoods, its bright red flesh emerging as the blackened shell cracked and dissolved upon mashing.

The paste churned and as it did the colors turned, affecting a striking hue of orange and purple. The kettle whistled and she added the boiling water with a hiss and bubble that sent up a curling mist thick as cream. Ninyeva allowed herself to drop into the back of her mind and leaned forward, breathing long and deep.

Somehow, she always forgot about the pain. It hit her like a swarm, the smoke buzzing with an electricity as it moved through her lungs, its product leeching into her blood. The first few seconds marked an eternity of agony, but Ninyeva stepped away from it and watched it pass, as it always did.

All sights, sounds and smells of her clothes, her room and the salt lake below faded. These were not a part of the Between, but rather the World. The Between was not a place, but it could be something similar.

She told it what to be and it complied, though it would rebel with increasing angst. She bade it bring her up, and she felt the rushing of wind and moist clouds thick with the promise of storm. She flew over the deep green canopy of the northern woods and raced along the rivers that fed the green fields of Hearth.

As she shot north, she felt the pain of the earth and tried not to look, still catching the glaring scars that marked the Deep Lands in her periphery. Gray stone rushed up to meet her, and she climbed the Steps two at a time without touching down. These were great plateaus dotted with fields of green with purple flowers. They were lands bursting with life and absent movement, for none in the Valley dared brave them for fear of the darkness lurking in the shadows of the higher passes and the memory of the fallen Sage that had made them his home.

Cresting the top now, and the sight stole her breath and nearly threatened to send her careening back. The golden pools and sharp black ridges stood out stark and beautiful, but the lands beyond were indistinct as a brushed painting not yet dry.

At first it felt like a spider crawling. She twitched and turned, feathered wings wheeling, sharp eyes searching. She felt eyes boring into her, cold with hate. The mind intent on hers betrayed itself, and its intensity sent her spinning. So fractured it was—so mad. There was a power there, but it was scattered and frayed, and it emanated from the red-tipped citadel that had been their guardian's abode.

She fled, and as the lands below passed in a blur, she saw the shadows grow long beneath the trees and felt the red eyes glaring up at her as they heard their master's call. Larger things stirred in the trenches of the Deep Lands and she did not look at these. And there was a beating, like the hearts of giants that followed her south, warping the air around her and setting it to thrum.

Before she woke, she saw the sky change, the white clouds growing sick with dark, the threat of storm making good its violent promises as blue light broke the horizon. Hearth stood out starkly, red-tipped roofs cloistered within the pearly white walls. The city looked alone, surrounded on all sides by an encroaching darkness, its braziers cold and unlit.

As she fled, she stole a glance behind, toward the peaks that now stood tall and leering as dark sentries framing a blood-red sun. They vibrated with the beating drums in their guts, with the hidden power trapped therein.

A power she had just awoken.

CHAPTER TEN

STORM CLOUDS

Talmir was a practical man, but his thoughts were want to wander. Now, he thought of the many folk living in the Valley, and the many things between folk, from the great beasts of the Untamed Hills down to the shrews in their burrows. The Dark Months had ever been a fact of life for folk of Valley and the lands beyond, but it was not until the World Apart sent its children through that they became something to be feared. Later, something to be endured.

The whys were debated in the stone huts of the Fork just as they were in the taverns of the Emberfolk. Even the Faey blamed the increasing intrusions on the War of Sages, the residual magic from their clashes spilling over into their relatively peaceful corner and upsetting the balance between worlds.

Many died in the wilds those first few years. If not for the Runners of the Lake, it was possible that the Emberfolk of the Scattered Villages beyond Hearth and Last Lake would have starved in darkness. After that, the people focused less on the whys. The Valley conflicts had ended a generation before, but the fighters among the Emberfolk, Rivermen and Faey found need of their blades again.

Though they survived, some argued that life in the Valley had been no more than a life of waiting on the edge of nightmare, the dawn nothing but a reprieve from the terrors that dogged them. If the Dark Months were a time of war then the dawn was a time of preparation.

Morbid as the thought was, it made life a hell of a lot simpler for Talmir. He was Captain of the Rock, and he surveyed the green fields before the walls of Hearth.

Talmir had always been one for preparation. He left no stone unturned, a fact that had resulted in his slow, inevitable ascension through the ranks of the largest Emberfolk settlement remaining in the World. What's more, Talmir was not Landkist, though he commanded some of the strongest Embers in the Valley.

The traditionalists still whispered when his back was turned, but he paid them no heed. Talmir's charge was to keep the people of Hearth safe, whisperers included, and that he did, ensuring that every Ember, soldier, hunter, villager and stray cat within a day's travel was prepared for the next attack. Under his watch, the great white walls of Hearth had never been breached. He planned to keep it that way, and though the sky was a little more dour now than it was the day before—the threat of storm clouds curling in the distance in an odd change for this time of year, they had made it through another spell relatively unscathed.

Of course, the same could not be said for his cousins on the Lake, but he had no doubt that First Keeper Tu'Ren had regained control in short order. Much like their own First Keeper, he was not a man to be trifled with.

Talmir watched the pale sun shine its light on the serpentine river that snaked its way through the rock-strewn fields. It passed beneath Hearth's portcullis, where dark clouds turned it steel gray.

The Dark Months were ending.

Why, then, was he so uneasy?

Thunder rolled in from the north as if in answer, and the scent of ozone carried on the wind. Talmir was not a superstitious man. He would not have believed there was a White Crest if he had not felt the tremors of the great battle in the passes as a youth, the same battle that pushed the Rivermen south and sparked the early conflicts. His father had played a prominent role in those clashes. It was strange, that Talmir broke bread with the Rockbled along the same Fork that had been stained red not so very long ago.

Talmir shook the dark thoughts away and walked the battlements. He looked down over the city that was his charge. If Last Lake was the nourishing mouth of the Emberfolk, Hearth was the heart—or the guts, depending on whom you asked. The buildings here were squat and stacked one atop the other as they climbed the crooked, cobbled streets toward the Red Bowl, the great market at the center. The very wall on which he stood was the only thing in sight that had been built with an eye for engineering. It was not lost on him that the Rivermen and their Landkist were mostly responsible for that.

If Last Lake provided the fish, Hearth provided the hooks.

A piercing screech assailed him as he was about to descend to the streets below, and Talmir spun to the west. He half expected to see a swarm of Dark Kind pouring from the trees in a last desperate bid for the walls. Instead, he was greeted by a sight jarring in its normalcy: a small, mule-drawn cart laden with rain-wrapped bundles leaned weirdly, one wheel stuck fast in a rut along the stream.

An old man bent to work over the delay. Talmir could see him cursing as a young woman shouted at him over the reins. The gray mule screamed again, eager to be off, and the Captain shouted orders.

The grinding gears of the portcullis began their slow rattle, but Talmir's attention was drawn by something else. A figure emerged from the tree line behind the old man. The figure moved with the predatory grace of a cat, and Talmir thought he glimpsed a flash of ruby red in place of eyes, causing him to rub the sleep from his own.

His vision cleared, but the scene before him grew no less perilous.

"Riders!" he screamed, knowing it was too late.

The old man had barely risen before he was cut down, his head parting neatly from his shoulders. The woman shrieked as the dark figure turned on her, the mule startled at the sudden commotion.

Talmir silently urged her to run as soldiers raced about him, horns blaring, gears continuing their raucous grinding as the gate rose slow as agony. But she did not run.

The Captain snatched a silver horn from the nearest courier and blew out a note that cracked the sky apart like fresh thunder. Hearing this, the mule bucked and rushed forward, snapping the reins and sending the woman crashing to the mud. She regained her feet and ran like something hunted. The black figure gave chase, splitting the distance between them with ungainly leaps that erased all lingering doubts as to its inhumanity.

Finally, the welcome thunder of hooves followed the slam of the gate reaching its zenith, Creyath and his riders pouring forth and carving the fields like a scythe. Even from this distance, Talmir could see the shimmering haze leaking from the Ember's armor as he bent over his covered steed.

The dark figure launched itself skyward in a final pounce, and a flaming shaft took it in the chest and sent it rolling in the turf as the horses circled. Creyath signaled for a rider to retrieve the woman, and he swung her onto the saddle and spun toward the gate. As for the Ember, he dismounted and walked toward the black figure. It was difficult to make Creyath Mit'Ahn appear pale, but this creature surely did.

The dark thing writhed under the Ember's boot, but he held it fast, lighting another shaft with the fire in his blood and launching it down to split the earth beyond the monster's skull with a sharp retort. The

Ember signaled to Talmir that the deed was done and remounted. He echoed the Captain's fears as he glanced worriedly toward the western trees before turning back for the city.

Even as the last of the riders cleared the looming teeth of the raised portcullis, the shadows beneath the distant branches lengthened and took on a life of their own.

Talmir heard the men and women under his command issue a collective gasp. He could not say he blamed them. The inky shadows resolved into the figures of men as they arrayed themselves in the space between wood and field. One of their company bore the same striking red eyes as the one Creyath had felled. It raised its hand and seemed to glare a challenge over the great expanse before slicing the air.

The black tide surged forward. Arrows were nocked and braziers lit.

Before the panic set its hooks too deep, Talmir exhaled. He had his Embers. He had his soldiers. He had his walls. Creyath joined the Captain, the Ember's skin warming the space around them.

"The woman?" Talmir asked without turning.

"Unharmed but for a few scrapes in the mud."

"Good." He paused. "We'll have to find her a new cart."

CHAPTER ELEVEN

LIVE

Linn woke with a startled yelp, her heart throbbing so hard it hurt. She was sweating, and now she was embarrassed as she took in the five pairs of eyes regarding her over the white smoke of a small cookfire.

"Dream?" Baas Taldis asked.

"Morning," she answered without warmth. She stood and stretched immodestly, the Riverman's eyes roving all the while. Linn was not entirely sure how she felt about him. Baas had always been a quiet sort at the Lake, but the open road seemed to agree with him—or disagree— depending on your perspective.

Aside from the familiar sights and now-familiar smells of her traveling companions, the ache in her joins returned to Linn her sense of time and place. It was day four of their magnificent, heroic, utterly ridiculous quest. By their looks, she guessed at least half of her companions felt the same. If there was a bright spot, it did not follow any of the three Embers in their company, but rather the fisherman's son.

Nathen Swell's boyish enthusiasm clashed oddly with his impressive forest lore. The same attitude that threatened to drive Larren Holspahr to quiet violence resonated with Linn, Baas and Jenk Ganmeer. Even Kaya Ferrahl shot her glances at him when she was sure none were looking. In truth, Nathen was likely the only member of the group they could all agree on liking, or at least not openly disliking.

"I, too have had dreams these last nights," Baas intoned gravely, as if Linn had not summarily ignored him a moment earlier. "I thought the sun would burn them all away, but it has strengthened their resolve in an attempt to weaken my own."

"Sun's losing today," Kaya said, indicating the gray skies.

"What sorts of dreams?" Jenk asked, sounding genuinely curious. He displayed a keen and unwavering interest in each of them. Linn had yet to decide if it was the politician in him or the heroic leader. Perhaps he was just a curious sort and she had never taken the time to notice before.

"No matter," Baas answered after a time. He scanned the trees suspiciously. "Some spell of the Faey, I think."

Larren scoffed at that as he worked over a piece of dried venison. It was no secret that Baas was Rockbled. The Landkist of the Fork were not as overt in their power as the Embers, but they were impressive in their own right. Incredibly strong, tireless and blessed with natural resiliencies to weapons of the earth—most weapons—they might not be as offensively potent as the Landkist of the Emberfolk, but they were exceedingly difficult to kill.

Of course, Linn had never seen those powers in action. Her mother had, but there had rarely been cause for Ember to fight against or alongside Rockbled in the decades since the early conflicts, no matter how many demons the World Apart sent into the Valley.

Their makeshift camp fell into a silence that each of them worked to cover with the checking of gear, the washing of teeth and the pulling of strap and buckle. There was a grim mood about. In place of the shining sun that should have been greeting their backs through the filtering branches, they had woken to a pall hanging about the sky, which was punctuated by the echo of distant thunder.

Linn was thankful that the twins had decided not to accompany them. Taei was fine enough, and certainly useful in a pinch, but she could do without Fihn, whose mood as often as not resembled the gray skies above. It was all about small victories in the Valley, and Linn would take them where she could find them.

While Linn had assumed the Second Keeper would be the de facto leader of the group, it was Jenk Ganmeer taking the center of the clearing to address them now.

"We've had our discussions, and now we've had the night to sleep on them," he said. "Hearth is barely a league to the east. We'd be able to see the walls from here if it weren't for the trees. We could re-stock our supplies, get some more fitful rest and maybe even recruit some woodsmen who know the lay of the land up north. On the other hand, if Doh'Rah's contacts make us, we'll be quartered and sent back south before we can have a cup of milled wine in the first tavern."

Linn cleared her throat.

"It's no real question to me," she said. "We continue on, or we can be bundled up like children caught stealing from the baker and sent back to the Faey Mother." She shouldered her pack, and the others did likewise, Jenk last.

If the forests to the south were dense cloisters, those further north were sparse by comparison, the trees growing taller as the canopy thinned to pine. Nettles littered the forest floor and cushioned their footfalls. Sap leaked from the rough bark in patient rivers, giving the woods a sour and pleasant odor. It was amazing how varied the lands of the Valley were, like a world unto itself. For Linn and the other members of her party, it always had been.

Linn did not fear an attack by the Dark Kind, even in the gloom the gray skies cast. With each passing day, the World Apart drifted further, making their intrusions less likely by the hour. Still, the Deep Lands were bathed in constant shadow and magic still seeped up from the ground there. If they could find a way around those chasms, it would be well worth it.

Lost in thought, Linn nearly smashed her nose into a sheer wall of blue—Baas's shirt; the hulk had stopped dead in his tracks.

"What—

He hushed her with an upraised hand, neck rigid as he stared intently ahead.

Linn craned her neck in an attempt to see beyond the Riverman—a considerable effort—and noted Larren crouched beneath the lip of a small rise. Jenk and Kaya flanked him, weapons in hand. Nathen touched her on the shoulder and motioned toward the branches above. He held a finger over his lips and then touched his ears with a shrug.

The forest was silent. Even a week ago, that would not have seemed strange, but the birds had been calling from dawn to dusk since the Dark Months had begun to fade. It was a wonder how quickly one could get used to the change, and how quickly its absence could be forgotten.

Linn unloosed her bow from around her back and followed Nathen east, curling around the road from the opposite direction as Baas and the three Embers bunched up in a copse to the west.

There was a sound like the screech of a drake, and Linn nocked arrow to string, leaning against a trunk. She spared a glance to her right, where Nathen stood taught as the arrow he pulled, sinuous arms locked and straining with practiced ease. His eyes, normally a welcoming blue, now bore the unmistakable glint of ice. If not for the slight rise and fall of his chest, you might think him a still image. Seeing him thus, it was no wonder many hunters had attributed Bali Swell's most legendary kills in the Untamed Hills to his son, despite his miss on their recent hunt.

When the ass first rounded the corner, Linn's mind had cast it in the image of some demented beast out of nightmare, shadowed as it was by low-hanging branches over the road. She heard Baas's laugh and the scene resolved itself into a farce as the brown cart trundled toward them, an old man and his daughter hunched over the reins.

The archers moved to rejoin their Landkist vanguard, which had already taken the road, Jenk conversing easily with the pair of early-season travelers.

"There's no wind," Nathen said, grabbing Linn by the elbow and pulling her back. He looked unsettled as he indicated the swirling clouds overhead.

Linn shivered but pulled her arm away.

"It's a high wind," she said, but the hunter did not look convinced.

As they approached, Jenk was speaking amiably with the old man while the young woman watched nervously from her place on the bench.

"It's early yet to be traveling the roads through the woods," Larren cut in, eyeing the old man reproachfully.

"My daddy always told me there isn't no better place to be but first," the old man said with a toothy grin. "Dawn's here." He swept out his hands and then pulled his cloak tighter about him as he noted the overcast sky. "Well, nothing you can do about the odd storm, eh?" He laughed.

"From which village do you hail?" Baas asked.

"Mirax," the girl said, blushing when the Riverman looked her way.

"And they let you out to travel the roads this early?" Larren asked, and now it was the old man's turn to blush.

"What are you looking at?" Kaya snapped at the girl, who nearly fainted.

"Leave her, Ferrahl," Jenk said. "She has every right to be nervous. It isn't every day you come across four Landkist armed for war."

"Landkist?" the girl's mood did a full turn. "I thought it felt warmer around you." She blushed again, looking at them each in turn. "You are Embers of Hearth?"

"Three Embers," Jenk said with a bow, indicating Larren and Kaya with nods. "And—"

"And only three," Baas said, his tone broaching no argument. Jenk merely shrugged and shared a conspiratorial wink with the girl, who giggled.

"Speaking of," the old man said, "what business have you in the western woods?"

"We're not going west," Baas said before wilting under a sharp, cutting glance from Jenk. It was a look like steel, and it disappeared as quickly as it had come.

"We are heading west soon," Jenk said, adding, "but not right now. Before we check on Mirax, we need to see how the folk of the Fork have done through these Dark Months."

"Isn't that what the Runners are for?" the girl asked.

"It never hurts to be thorough," Jenk said. "After all, this was a difficult period."

"But we're glad to see you and yours have made it through all right," Linn put in, smiling warmly. She was eager to be on the move. Luckily, Kaya had none of the others' decorum.

"We need to be going," the Ember clipped, and the old man nodded sagely.

"I'm afraid my compatriot is right," Jenk said, shaking the old man's hand. He went to do the same with the girl, but she sat stock-still, rigid with fear.

Jenk, Linn and the others followed her gaze up to the pine canopy, where the great boughs creaked oddly.

"Girl!" The old man shouted, and not for the first time, but she was focused on a particularly dense bunch of swaying green.

"A forest cat?" Baas asked, bringing his great shield to bear.

Linn ignored him and nocked the arrow she had only just put back in its quiver, Nathen doing the same. She peered into the shifting shadows and was dimly aware of the others fanning out on the road beside her. There was a darker patch that seemed too dense for the canopy, and when a dark cloud overhead brightened with heat lightning, she saw the thing crouched there.

"There!" Baas yelled, breaking her concentration as he pointed in the opposite direction. An arrow whizzed by her cheek as Nathen let fly and an unnatural shriek pierced the sudden dusk. Linn took aim and fired, but another flash from the sky above made it difficult to track her mark, and she heard the shaft bury itself in the bark.

At first, Linn thought she had missed, but the shaft had been well placed and well launched. The dark form fell with a lifeless thud next to the mule, which exploded into panicked motion. Kaya screamed as the cart rolled over her foot, the bones snapping like birds' wings. She fell, dropping her staff before she had it lit.

The forest came alive with shadows. These were not the Dark Kind, Linn recognized with mounting dread. They moved in the lurching shapes of men, silent but for the crunching of twig and the rustling of brush as they poured from the woods. Linn loosed another arrow that dropped another shadow and spun. She saw the cart careening around the far bend, the hood of the old man thrown back as he struggled to regain control of the panicked mule.

Her decision was made in the next beat, as Linn ducked under the slashing claw of the nearest shadow and got her legs churning, taking off after the runaway cart. She heard Larren shouting orders and felt the atmosphere explode with sudden heat that shocked the back of her neck. She looked over her shoulder as she ran and witnessed the uneven line of nightmare soldiers crash into the formidable wall of fire formed by

Larren's spinning spear and Jenk's slashing sword, the Everwood blades lighting the trees with their own sun.

Baas Taldis launched the shadows back one by one as they attempted to get around the Embers, and those that got between his stone shield and one of the flaming blades died writhing in scorched agony. Larren backed up to defend Kaya, who was struggling to rise. He spitted a shadow as it leapt for the prone Ember and sent a jet from the tip that immolated the featureless face of the next.

Linn tore past Nathen, who loosed shaft after shaft, picking off the shadows that managed to dodge the smashing shield or burning blades. He nodded to Linn as she ran, sweat standing out on his brow as another blast of heat set the air to shimmer like water, the work of Holspahr's latest torrent.

An avalanche of needles and black earth announced her presence as Linn leapt and slid down the far bank of the bend. She landed at the bottom and came up sprinting, bow clutched tightly as she carved a diagonal path toward the bouncing cart. A few of the shadow men gave chase, but she was too fast for them. When one impeded on her path, she rewarded it with an arrow to the neck and it fell gurgling, flailing hands catching on her ankles as she cleared it in a bound.

She broke through the last curtain of brush, the branches tearing her face and arms, and affected a controlled fall onto the rocky road below the bank. As she rose and shook the dizziness away, she focused on the charging mule as it made directly for her, mouth frothing, each step more haggard than the last.

Linn pulled back the feathered shaft and eyed the gray beast, sighting it between the eyes. She exhaled and then heard the impact more than felt it. The black form slammed into her from the side and bowled her into the ditch as the wild-staring mule trundled past with its bouncing cart.

She felt her bow snap beneath her and the air was forced from her lungs, but she went to work with her knife as soon as she was pinned, taking the shadow's fingers and a good portion of its opposite hand. The mangled limbs gripped her around the jaw and she saw that this one had eyes that shone red. It glared hatefully, its fellows rushing past her after the cart and toward the fields before Hearth.

Live.

She bucked, but the demon was too strong. A skinny thing, but its weight was like a mountain on her chest. Those red eyes bored into her, and she felt more than heard a voice in her head, urging her to stillness. But Linn Ve'Ran was not one to be cowed, so she fought with what her mother and father had given her, launching a barrage of tooth and claw that had the creature reeling.

A struggle that felt as though it spanned weeks likely lasted a minute, and the demon forced her back down. It was then that a clear note broke the sky, drawing the red eyes away, the horn's blare carrying from the fields beyond the trees. Linn felt her questing fingers brush something metal, and she seized it, breaking her skin on the blade of her knife and spearing the shadow through jaw and skull. The light went out from the demon's eyes before she had even pushed it over. She retched, adding her own bloody mix to the mud.

Linn knew her victory was short-lived, but as the dark forms streaked past her in the woods beside the road, none spared her a backward glance. The horn rang out again, driving them on, and Linn stumbled back onto the broken path she had carved between the branches.

The woods stilled around her as she made her way back toward the road, fearing what she would find when she arrived. Though the sight that greeted her upon rounding the bend was macabre, she saw none of her friends mixed among the corpses. Many of the shadow men had lost their faces under the press of Baas's shield, and Nathen must have spent all of his shafts clearing the borders of the road. In the center, scorches in the shapes of men scarred the road, and the heat of the Embers' expulsions still lingered, the air crackling with ozone.

As she walked among the bodies, Linn noted that the shadows had faded, draining away like ink to reveal the garish faces of men and women beneath. They were not Emberfolk, nor Faey, and they had not the bulk or sinew of the Rivermen. These were foreigners, pale as light and sick with dark. She thought of the red-eyed attacker she had impaled—a Sentinel, she knew—and shuddered when she realized there had been nothing beneath its blackness but thicker shadows.

"Ve'Ran—

She spun toward the harsh whisper, knife whipping, and nearly collapsed when she saw Jenk standing beneath the boughs, light hair crusted with red. He grabbed her by the wrist and led her stumbling through the rolling nettles.

"The others," Linn managed through a cracked tongue and pounding headache.

"Alive," he said, though it sounded strained.

"Jenk."

He glanced at her as he supported her, his skin burning like the blade that still glowed at his hip.

"What happened?"

"We were lucky," he said, and then, to her continued staring, "I don't know what they are. But there was a Sentinel."

"I fought one," Linn said, stopping and standing still.

Jenk looked stunned.

"How did you survive?"

"Luck." And she knew it to be the truth.

"Larren was distracted." He looked at the ground. "He killed it, but it did something to him, left him screaming in the dirt."

"It seems we picked the wrong time to leave the Lake," Linn said, but Jenk shook his head.

"Maybe it was the perfect time, Ve'Ran. The Dark Months are ending. The World Apart is too far for chance to send a force like that through. Someone sent those shadows for us, and they came from the north."

They came to a trench between boulders, the trees silent around them as Baas stood vigil. Kaya clenched a piece of leather between her teeth as Nathen worked over her foot. A spear rested in the crevice, and below it, Larren Holspahr breathed shallow and slow.

She supposed it could have been worse.

CHAPTER TWELVE

THE WAKING FIRE

K ole Reyna was strong, but all the strength in the world counted for less than nothing here, in the swirling, burning darkness. At first, he felt the pain. It was constant and unbearable—a pain that threatened to consume him. But slowly, surly, it ebbed away, and the other had made its presence known.

It was not so much a voice as a series of impressions that filled his head, but he knew them to be the work of the Sentinel. It showed him things: there were men falling in the rain, cut down by shadows. As they fell, some rose again, red-eyed Captains bidding them to find homes for their blades in the hearts of their former brothers.

He saw Hearth surrounded, bugles blowing their death knells. There was a mass like ants climbing the walls, piling one atop the other in a leaning tower that bent sickly in the driving wind and rain. A solitary figure climbed to the top, dodging the spears of the defenders or burning them away. The figure stepped over the crenellated walls easily and the Embers of Hearth fell to one of their own.

It was his own face Kole saw laughing amidst the flames.

It was then that he remembered himself. He pushed back and the other was revealed in his mind's eye, the same black contours, shining red eyes and gaping maw. Kole remembered fighting it beneath the roots of the Blackwoods. He remembered the way its eyes had glowed and its maw had stretched in a silent scream of agony as it had writhed and died in his flames. At that remembrance, it raged, spit, hissed and died all over again, expelled like a cleansing flood.

For a time after, the space between waking and sleep was a gulf of endless depth. When he did wake, he brought only half of his senses, but they were enough to recognize his father and Iyana watching over him.

Kole fell into dreaming, and one was as vivid as a story from the past replayed.

He saw himself as a boy. It was a cold, overcast day, and he was stripped to the waist. He heard the calling of lake gulls and felt his mother's eyes on his back. Ahead, just above the dark line where the slow waves lapped at the shore, Tu'Ren stood next to a great brazier, his face stern as stone. There were rows of Emberfolk, his people, lining the road to either side of him. Their faces became a blur at the borders of his attention. Behind the brazier, Ninyeva, Doh'Rah and the other elders watched him stoically, but he could feel their hope burning hot, their fear cold kernels of ice.

In the years that followed, Jenk Ganmeer and later Kaya Ferrahl would make the same walk, but Kole was the first. They did not know he would be the first of the last. He wondered if they still would have sung their songs if they had. It was the last good dream on the edge of nightmare, for the Dark Kind had yet to encroach on their peaceful Valley.

"Your hand, Reyna."

Kole looked up into the face of the First Keeper. He was not frightened of him like the other children were, so he examined him calmly, catching the glowing brazier beside him. He was afraid of that.

The stone thrummed with life. Motes of red flame floated out of the narrow slit, stinging his face as they passed. Kole raised his palm and studied it, committing the lines to memory, and then he offered it to the flames without further hesitation. There was a collective gasp, and even the lake seemed to inhale, dragging the next swell further in anticipation.

He could feel the heat, and even the pain, but in place of a desire to be free, his body sought to drink it in, and the flames responded eagerly. When Kole removed his hand, he brought the flame with it, curling and uncurling his fingers and making the fire dance.

Before he woke, Kole saw the boy he had been walk along the pathways he had known all his life, only he did so carrying a small fire that was the heart of his people, their past and future dancing in his palm. The only face he remembered was his mother's.

Karin Reyna began the chant that followed him into waking.

"Landkist," he said.

"Ember," they answered.

And on it went.

Kole woke and found that he was alone. He enjoyed his first true feeling of clarity in what felt like a month and listened to the sound of the rain as it pattered on the open sill. The muffled talk of the guards flitted up from outside. There must have been a break in the clouds, as a soft beam of sunlight streamed in, and he parted the covers to soak it up with his bare feet, sighing as the energy flowed into him.

Slowly, achingly, he stood, and it was then that Iyana announced her presence with the sound of shattering porcelain. He turned and saw her standing on the hardwood in the doorway, her silver hair bound back in a tail. She ran to him, and they embraced. Iyana's shoulders did not shake, but she left damp imprints in his shirt nonetheless.

"Kole," she said through tight lips, bright green eyes boring into him as they separated. Those eyes went along with the gifts of the Faeykin, and they could simultaneously entrance, placate and unnerve. It would stand to reason that Kole would be used to their effect by now. He was not.

"What news?" he asked, fighting to keep his voice level. Half-remembered nightmares and the leering face of the Sentinel reared up in is mind.

She hesitated.

"You are back with us," she said, sighing. "That is good."

"If that's the best we have going, I'm not sure I'll like the rest."

She eyed him steadily, lips pursed.

"You're not the only one who's felt a need to take a stroll through the woods these last days," she said, accusation barely masked.

Kole's heart nearly stopped.

"Where is Linn?"

"Everyone's got it in their minds to save our world," she said, perhaps a little more biting than she intended. "My sister is the latest. She's gone north to find one Sage or slay another. And she happened to take most of our best warriors with her."

Kole swayed unsteadily, and Iyana's empathetic side took over.

"I think you might like some air," she said, guiding him by the hand with a grip that was soft and firm.

"Yes," he said, thoughts reeling.

They stopped at the kennels first to check on Shifa. The hound had improved much more quickly than Kole had, nothing but a hairless patch at one corner of her mouth betrayed her involvement with his flight and ensuing fight. From there, they turned south, moving along Eastlake toward the shore, the threat of storm rumbling in the distance as the rain misted down.

As they walked, Iyana filled him in on all he had missed. The Dark Kind had attacked a final time while he writhed in his tower, but they had been thrown back without much effort. Not long after, word had come from Hearth's Runners that the northern city was encircled by an army the likes of which the Valley had never before seen. Karin had been dispatched to get a closer look; Tu'Ren was unwilling to send martial aid without knowing the lay of the lands around Last Lake first. Linn's departure likely played no small part in that decision.

They stopped at the docks and Kole sat on the edge, dipping his bare feet in the water with a pleasant hiss. He knew Iyana's infinite patience had stretched farther than it had any right to. He had to speak with Ninyeva, Doh'Rah and Tu'Ren before long. But for now, they enjoyed the salt breeze and watched the sun dip behind the black ridges as the dark clouds overhead claimed the sky.

"Did she say anything?" Kole asked. "Before she left."

"No," Iyana said. "Though I should have seen it coming. Linn has been quiet lately—more than usual, I mean."

Kole opened his mouth to speak, but closed it, the words half-formed. Iyana took up the thread anyway, unaware or unconcerned that Kole had not consciously expressed them.

"I know better than to tell you not to blame yourself," she said. "You know my sister. You know her better than I do, and you know her better than you know me."

Kole looked at Iyana. There was no accusation in her tone, just a firmness of belief—a statement of things that were.

"What is she trying to do, Kole?"

He swallowed.

"I think she took my words in the Long Hall to heart," he said, looking back down at the water, which fizzed around his ankles. "Linn has always believed in the power of the White Crest. More than that, she's believed in his goodness. She thinks he's alive, and—

"She thinks he's alive because you told her so. Because you told all of us what you knew to be true."

Kole merely looked at her, trying not to flinch under that green stare.

"Well?" she asked. "Do you know it to be true?"

"I know what I've seen. I know what I feel."

"And what of the Eastern Dark?" she asked, challenging. "What of our true enemy?"

"A Sage, just like all the rest," Kole said, voice level. "If he has truly returned, we need to fight him on our own. The White Crest, if he lives, will be no help to us."

"And you think we can defeat him when another Sage cannot?"

"I do not pretend to know what one Sage or another is capable of," Kole said. "But I know what the Landkist can do, especially those in this Valley."

"The Embers, you mean," Iyana said. "You."

"Your powers are for mending, Iyana. Mine are for something much different."

"Guarding—

"Burning."

There was no arguing with his tone, so Iyana did not. They both looked out on the water for a spell.

"I'll find her, Iyana," Kole said after a time.

"I don't think it makes much difference either way. She has three Embers with her—Larren Holspahr among them—and Baas Taldis. She's in good company."

Kole did not look convinced. He did not feel convinced. That black face leered up out of memory, and he pushed it back down.

Dusk fell on a whim and the wind picked up, driving the rain until it had soaked them through. Kole stood and pulled Iyana up next to him, the rain steaming off of him in lazy currents. They walked back toward the shore in silence, watching the fisherman tacking their tarps and stowing their gear. None would venture out onto the water with the skies turning.

There were many Emberfolk at Last Lake, but the folk were a family, tight-knit and protective of their own. As Kole and Iyana walked streets both dirt and cobble, passersby greeted them warmly.

"Seeing is an entirely separate thing from hearing," Iyana said after one of the elders nearly swooned upon spotting Kole. "They knew you were on the road to recovery, but apparently the words of the Lake's healers, even a Faeykin like me, are worth little."

She smirked as she said it, and Kole regarded her with a serious expression. He stopped dead and turned her toward him.

"Thank you," he said, eyes shining. Iyana smiled, and then the smile dropped, turning to something wrenching and afraid. She nodded and continued on, Kole following after as they traveled the winding roads of Eastlake.

"You know," he said some time later, "I used to fear the rain, after the fire awoke."

Iyana looked curious. She touched Kole's arm, which was bare, the droplets sizzling as they made contact.

"I sometimes wonder if the rain for us feels like burning to you," he said.

"I don't think you'd be out in it, if that were the case," Iyana laughed.

"No," Kole said, smiling absently. "But I do forget what it feels like to burn."

Again, the image of the Sentinel's face was called up, and again he watched it burn away in a torrent of hellfire he had summoned.

They crested the rise, and the crooked, ramshackle tower of the Faey Mother loomed. The blue roof tiles were faded from a mixture of salt and wind, the green paint on the shingles peeling. Some thought it a gaudy, misshapen thing, but to Kole, it oozed warmth and called back to images of what Sages and Wizards were supposed to be.

"We are both Landkist, Iyana," Kole said as they neared the porch. "But you were blessed by the Valley, the moss along the streams. You're a mender, not a killer. You see things in others they cannot."

"Kole," she started, but he stopped before the first step and turned to her.

"My blood is a hot river," he said. "It could run through rock and stone, because it comes from the deep deserts. I have always found it difficult to control—more difficult than the others."

"Kaya always had trouble," Iyana offered.

"There's something in me that's not in her," Kole said. He thought that Iyana wanted to say, 'I know,' but she didn't.

"What is it, Kole?" she asked, concerned. "What happened out there, in the woods?"

"I followed a dream. It carried the face of a demon, and one that looked an awful lot like the Sentinels from the deserts Ninyeva spoke about."

"And you killed it."

"I burned it until there was nothing left," Kole said. He felt the thrill all over again, which was quickly supplanted by the shame at having felt it. "It was a power unlike anything I've ever felt. It was freeing, and it was frightening."

They stood under the awning, and Kole held his hand out, palm up under the sloshing gutter. At first, there was the mild hiss that always resulted from a meeting between water and an Ember's skin, and then his muscles bunched and he coaxed out a kernel of the thrill he had felt before. The sound morphed from a soft hiss to a steady rattle, like summer insects. Then, as the steam curled thick as a gauntlet, it was a sound like a pit of vipers.

"Something in me woke out there in the trees. I don't think it's going back to sleep."

He did not look at the face Iyana made. He did not want to.

The first thing Kole noted upon entering Ninyeva's tower was the monstrous Everwood blade that leaned against the doorframe. It was almost as tall as Iyana, and only one man could wield it.

"Looks like the Faey Mother already has company," Iyana said. It was difficult to tell where observation ended and mindreading began with her.

"Dark times," was all Kole said in reply. His skin had dried completely by the time he had pushed the pine door shut.

"Ironic," Iyana said, "that such times should hit as we're entering the Bright Days."

A shadow passed over Kole's face and Iyana touched the red scar on his cheek where Linn's arrow had slashed him.

"I think you're trying a bit too hard to grow into that scar, Kole Reyna," she said, somewhere between scolding and sincere.

Kole tried to smile, but they both looked up as the floorboards creaked overhead, a gruff and muffled voice filtering down from the dusty rafters. They moved through the entryway and came to the foot of the stairs. There, a matronly voice cut over the first.

"Shall we?" Iyana asked tentatively.

"All Valley roads lead to Ninyeva," Kole said with a sigh and a shrug. "Damn whatever the merchants in Hearth say."

Iyana shivered beside him.

"What's the matter?" he asked, laying a warm hand on her shoulder.

"What you just said, about roads and Ninyeva—I caught an impression from it."

"And I'm guessing it wasn't an overly positive one."

She hesitated.

"I only hope you know what you're doing," she said, green eyes flashing like emeralds.

Kole smiled even as his stomach churned. He started up the stairs and she followed after. The voices had already quieted as the creaking stairwell announced their presence, but Kole still rapped on the oak at the top.

"Come in, Reyna," Ninyeva said curtly, as if annoyed he had bothered knocking.

The scent of burning sage and citrus assailed their nostrils upon entering. Ninyeva raised her brows at the face he made, stood and moved to open the screen to the balcony, admitting a bit of the wind and rain in, something that had the already dour-looking First Keeper frowning. Tu'Ren floundered as he remembered himself, standing to clap Kole on the shoulder and to share an embrace with Iyana.

"Good to see you on your feet, boy," Tu'Ren said, the red in his cheeks turning rosy in good humor. "We can agree on that, if nothing else." His laugh was forced as he looked at Ninyeva.

The Faey Mother was as tired as Kole had ever seen her, her usual warmth dulled.

"You've done good work, Iyana Ve'Ran," she said, stepping forward to look Kole up and down appraisingly. Over the years and by close association, Kole had become somewhat used to the alien quality of Iyana's eyes, but he could not say the same for her teacher. She was, after all, the oldest of the Emberfolk of the Valley, and the first to be Landkist by it. It stood to reason those eyes held more nuance, and perhaps more potent gifts than any of them knew.

The old woman flashed him a knowing smile and he returned a weaker one.

"Feeling sprite and spry after your jaunt through the woods?" she asked, the joke stinging in more ways than one.

Kole did not answer.

"Good," she said, taking her seat by the fire. She glanced at Tu'Ren—there was much in the look—and then turned those emeralds on Kole, waiting.

Kole shifted uncomfortably.

"I'm ready to do what needs to be done," he said.

"And what, pray tell, needs to be done?"

"Well," Kole started, "I think we can all agree that, whatever it is needs doing, it needs doing in the north. That's where it's all come from. We're just waiting to be buried down here."

Tu'Ren crossed his arms and issued an unintelligible grunt, but made no move to speak. Ninyeva only smiled a smile of victory.

"That settles that, then," she said. "Our esteemed First Keeper here feels that we should shut ourselves off from the north and wait out the storm."

Tu'Ren bristled, but did not rise to the jab.

"This is no storm," Kole said. "Not one of the World's making, anyway."

All eyes turned to him. He did not elaborate, and they did not ask him to.

"Excuse my short manners, Reyna," Ninyeva said, sounding genuine. "I'm sure Iyana filled you in on the basics?"

He nodded.

"My dreams did the rest, though I hope the truth is not half as dark."

"Look out the window, Kole," Ninyeva said. "What do you think? If you told me the Dark Months were in full swing, I'd believe you if I didn't know it to be a lie. As for your dreams," she paused, smirking a bit despite the mood, "I think there may be a bit of the Valley in that Ember blood as well."

Tu'Ren cleared his throat and Ninyeva rolled her eyes.

"Then you know Larren Holspahr, Jenk Ganmeer, Kaya Ferrahl and some others you're distinctly familiar with have gone north," he said. "Do you know their intended purpose?"

"I'm guessing they intend to save us all," Kole said. "How they plan to do that, I don't know. But I could guess it has to do with finding one Sage or killing another."

Ninyeva looked about to speak, but Tu'Ren broke in, his tone matching the sky outside.

"You count this a good thing?" he asked with mounting anger. "An aimless quest by some of our best and brightest when their people need them here most of all." He was speaking to Ninyeva, but now his attention shifted to Kole. "You may be the most naturally-gifted Ember we have, Reyna, and look what happened to you when you tangled with one of the Eastern Dark's Sentinels. How many more do you suppose are out there?"

"Enough to overwhelm us if we let them continue to build their army," Kole said evenly. He looked to Ninyeva. "That is what they do, no? If these are the same Sentinels you spoke of from the desert days, then they can turn our own against us."

Ninyeva nodded, but Tu'Ren was not done.

"How did they not turn you?"

Kole looked to Iyana, who shuffled forward uncertainly. The First Keeper's mood seemed to calm a bit then, his face coloring now in shame more than anger.

Ninyeva poured herself a cup and bade the younger Landkist sit. They did.

The Faey Mother's green eyes seemed to glow as she took Kole's measure, and he felt suddenly like a moth caught in her lantern's web. The part of him that felt his tricks of light to be marks of true power felt foolish when Ninyeva brought her own power to bear. She held him in thrall, and Iyana swayed from hip to hip, eyes opening and closing as the energy in the room changed.

"You have had dreams, Reyna," Ninyeva said. Tu'Ren shifted away from her as quietly as he could. "I have as well, and I have traveled their roads and found their ends." She looked at Tu'Ren and then back at Kole.

"Hearth is besieged," she said, and Kole's heart caught in his chest. He had seen it. "Tu'Ren has sent your father to learn the details, but there's the truth." She paused. "Be that as it may, your path is to the north, the far north. It was intuition that saw me agree to your desire to make for the peaks, to learn what there was to learn. Perhaps Linn Ve'Ran and the others have forced our hand in a positive light. I felt misgivings about sending you alone with nothing but your own heart to guide you."

"I had plenty of reasons," Kole said, though speaking felt like swimming through molasses. He was unable to tear his eyes away from hers, and images from her mind flowed into his. He saw the dark clouds issuing like smoke above the peaks, and in a dark cloister of spurs, he saw the hint of a red-tipped structure that suggested a dark keep.

"Your reasons are not good enough," she said flatly. "But now, with your friends out on the roads you were set to travel, that might change for the better."

Now Kole saw images of an entirely different bent, Linn always at the center, and he did not know if these were of his own making or not. Iyana seemed to share them, either feeding off of him or the Faey Mother. She shuddered at their potency.

"The enemy you will face out there," she continued. "The enemy you did face, and that your friends will face soon enough, is not the same as that we have battled since you were a boy."

"I know—

"No," Ninyeva interrupted. "You know a small piece. You came upon a single Sentinel. There are more, and they have brought with them their Corrupted. Even last night, I saw things stirring in the Untamed Hills—great beasts being turned in the image of the Night Lords."

"I don't understand," Iyana said. "If The Eastern Dark has come for us, why does he not send the whole of the World Apart? Why do it piecemeal?"

"The World Apart is a place of chaos," Ninyeva said. "I do not even think a Sage is confident mining its stores. He sent true Night Lords, powerful generals, against his brother and our protector before you were born. I think the experience nearly killed him. Most of us thought it had. The Sentinels are a virus, incredibly dangerous but not so powerful on their own to draw the notice of the other Sages. The war he makes on us now is one meant to be made in private."

"It felt powerful enough," Kole said, shivering despite his warmth.

"Yes," Ninyeva said. "Now you know what to expect. The Corrupted will not be nearly as potent as their masters, but you need to avoid conflict where you can. You need to make for the peaks and find the source. It lies beneath a red roof, the one I have shown you."

"How?" Kole asked. "How do you know this?"

"I have seen it," Ninyeva said, and even she looked to waver for a moment, her eyes glazing over. She cleared them and refocused. "I do not pretend to have all the answers, Kole. I only know that we will not endure this flood unless we stop the source, and the source is nowhere near here."

"I want to know how Reyna has been having these dreams," Tu'Ren broke in.

Ninyeva's attention splintered and something in the room went with it. Iyana seemed to come back to herself. She stopped her swaying and blinked sharply.

"What you felt when the great ape looked into your eyes and you into his," Ninyeva said, looking to Kole. "Did you feel the same when the Sentinel locked you in its gaze?"

Kole nodded.

Ninyeva turned her eyes back to Tu'Ren.

"We know that our King of Ember, together with the White Crest, attempted to bring down our enemy in the east," she said. "We know that he failed, but knowing how powerful he was—a Landkist capable of striking a bargain with one Sage and challenging another—I can guess he made an impression."

Kole swallowed, feeling suddenly quite sick.

"You think he has designs on Kole in particular?" Iyana asked. "What of Tu'Ren, or Larren, or the Embers of Hearth?"

"I do not know," she said, and she looked to be telling the truth of it. It was a truth that bothered her greatly. Her eyes hardened. "You have long felt that the Valley was more prison than refuge, Kole. I do not know if that is the case, but given what I've seen lately, and what comes against us now, I cannot entirely dismiss the possibility that we've been right where he wanted the whole time. I think it's time we showed him why we are not to be trifled with."

"And what of the White Crest?" Tu'Ren asked.

"I don't know," Ninyeva said. "I awoke something in the Between. In some way, I think it may have been the catalyst for the darkness that assails us now, though it was always coming. But these are not weapons of his, no matter where you think his allegiance rests or rested."

She looked to Kole as she finished and looked as if she wanted to say more. After a struggle, she did.

"I won't send anyone else on a fool's quest to find a guardian long since dead," she said, swallowing after the words had been said.

And there it was, Kole's world come crashing down, and the apparent source sitting right before him. His mother had not struck out for the peaks those years ago of her own accord. Ninyeva had played some part, however great or small.

Kole felt his blood go hot, but he worked to cool it. He reminded himself what he remembered of his mother, and more so what others had told him since. She had been headstrong to a fault, making Linn Ve'Ran look like a conformist by comparison. Any choice she made, she made herself. Still, it was a bitter pill to swallow, but one that had no doubt taken courage for Ninyeva to admit.

"I made a choice, Kole," she said. "A choice based on things I believed and on things I wanted to believe. Only take care that, whatever you find in the north, you do not make the same mistakes. It won't always be you who pays for it."

Ninyeva swept her gaze to encompass all in the room.

"You are all children of the Valley," she said, eyes misting over. "Even you, Kadeh." Tu'Ren nodded with a blush. "Landkist or not, the fire within our people has never burned brighter. I see now the folly of the King of Ember: it was fear that drove us out of the deserts, and it is fear that has kept us here."

She looked to Kole and Iyana.

"You are children raised in a war against the dark," she said. "I am sorry for that, but it has prepared you to be the stewards of your own destiny, and that of your people."

After a time, Kole looked up.

"Perhaps if our noble heroes have charged themselves with saving the Valley in my stead, I'll have to resign myself to saving them."

CHAPTER THIRTEEN

ANT HILL

Hearth was built on the lone hill that rested on the great plains of the Valley. White stones jutted up from the dark soil to form a patchwork with the green grass and silver-blue streams that snaked through it. The biggest stone of all rose up in a sheer cliff and formed most of the northern section of the city's walls, the rest having been built out from it.

The Rivermen had taken to calling it 'Ant Hill' soon after the first conflicts. For a long time, the Emberfolk had assumed the name derived from the settlement's physical structure: the streets rose onto a great crest before dipping back down into the Red Bowl at the center, which formed the Valley's main market. All in all, it was an easy comparison to make. But that was not the reason for the name.

Instead, they had named Hearth so after its inhabitants: though smaller and seemingly weaker than the great warriors along the Fork, the Emberfolk were akin to a swarm when agitated. The Rivermen had learned that lesson hard.

Talmir Caru used to despise the name and all it represented. Now, having risen in Hearth's ranks from courier all the way to Captain and commander, he thought it fit. He thought of Hearth as a nest, one to be defended and one that should not be kicked lightly.

With the backing of Hearth's three Ember Keepers, Talmir had the white walls and the adjoining cliffs manned, braziers lit and oil stocked and boiling before the first line of dark men began scrabbling up the white rocks at the base. Garos Balsheer, arguably the most powerful Ember in the Valley—the folk of Last Lake being the arguers—took the front gate, while Misha Ve'Gah commanded the cliffs to the north and Creyath Mit'Ahn stood with Talmir along the South Bend.

"These are not Dark Kind," Creyath said, shaking Talmir from his private reverie.

"No," Talmir said, clearing his throat. "But the flames still put a scare in them nonetheless."

Creyath nodded, peering over the walls at the thick line of blackened char at the base. It should have made Talmir feel better that these dark men could no more readily threaten his walls than the formless creatures of nightmare that harried them throughout the Dark Months. But then he caught sight of that red-eyed commander, gaze unwavering across the field, and his surety evaporated.

"I want an arrow through that one's skull."

Creyath, ever the literal one, sighted the distant figure through the gloom, but shook his head as he lowered his bow.

"I don't understand," Talmir said.

"What?"

"Any of this."

He turned to Creyath, whose eyes were the burnt orange of sunset.

"Before word came up from the Lake last week, you were the only one in the Valley who had slain a Night Lord," Talmir said.

"I was also the only one to come upon one. Besides, those tales are exaggerated. I don't know what I fought. It is dark in the Deep Lands, and dark things wander there."

Creyath considered the Captain curiously.

"Why do you bring this up?"

"I remember you saying the thing that struck you most about it was the eyes," Talmir said, and a shadow passed over Creyath's already-swarthy features.

"Red like rubies," the Ember said. "Or blood. But it was not the color, Captain. It was how they moved, the way they considered. They were not the eyes of a beast, and they watched after the deed had been done."

"At the time, you believed them to belong to another," Talmir said and Creyath nodded, looking across the field toward the distant commander, who stood unmoving in the drizzle.

"The tales from the desert claim that the Eastern Dark unleashed greater powers from the World Apart, Night Lords and Sentinels, the latter of which could turn their victims. What's come against us now has nothing to do with the Dark Months or rifts between worlds. This army was sent, and I think we know who sent it."

"He lives," Creyath said, as if it had never been in doubt.

"Did the Runners go out?" Talmir asked, changing the subject.

"To Lake and River," Creyath said. "They took the path beneath the cliffs."

"If a force this large is already at the fields, I hate to think how our friends at the Fork have fared."

"Or the Scattered Villages," Creyath put in. "Perhaps the Faey managed to divert them."

"Most of the villages are in the woods to the far west," Talmir said. "Hopefully none besides that foolish old man and his daughter were out on the roads so early in the season."

The sickening thought that the army scraping at the base of their walls could be their own threatened bile.

"Have any of your men got a close look at them?"

"They appear to be foreigners," Creyath said, answering the unspoken question.

There was a lull in the conversation that matched the slowed press of the army, which had sent one wave to be doused in oil and flame, the next now milling about just out of bowshot. Talmir used the silence to take stock of his soldiers. He did not look at them, meeting eyes and sharing nods. Instead, he listened.

There were light conversations among pairs, triples and small groups. The subject could be easily guessed at, but it was the tone Talmir was after, and he sensed no panic therein. That was good. He heard Garos's booming voice echo down from the main gate, and even thought he heard the higher-pitched shouts of Ve'Gah carrying on the wind down from the white cliffs.

Still, Talmir was a realist—some would label him a pessimist—and the fact that the army arrayed before them had affected the watchful hunger of jackals had him concerned. They were not reckless like the usual Dark Kind. They were mindless, but there was a mind behind them.

"I think I'll go relieve myself before these man-beasts give it another go," Talmir said. "Think they'll give it another go?"

The question was rhetorical; of course they would, but Creyath shared his slow nod regardless.

Just as Talmir was cresting the top of the stairs, the blaring sound of horns nearly knocked the piss out of him then and there. He caught himself, spun and rushed back to his place. The air was already buzzing with Creyath's building heat, his brazier glowing as the Ember drank its contents in through his palm.

"What is it?" Talmir asked, eyes straining in the dusk—or was it morning? The storm clouds had redoubled, making the passage of the low sun difficult to judge. "My eyes are not as sharp as yours."

"You are younger than I, Talmir Caru," the Ember said. "Look beyond your red man. Look to the trees."

Talmir did, and though his eyes told him otherwise, what he saw he did not quite believe. It started as a vibration that shook the canopy like the surface of a lake. The dark green foliage became a blur of motion, branch and trunk joining leaf in the foreboding dance. He heard cracks split the sky, but saw no streaks of light to mark the thunder. There were sounds of great things moving in the forest.

"They may not have gone after the villagers or the Faey," Talmir said, realization dawning. "But there are some big things hiding in the Untamed Hills."

"Let us hope they are all equally flammable," Creyath said, looking much more like predator than prey in that moment. And when Talmir saw the first of the beasts break from the trees, he was glad he had a few of his own along the wall.

There were only a handful, but they ranged from bear-like to serpentine, and they were very, very large—an affectation of the Night Lords that had challenged the White Crest in the passes a generation ago, if not the real thing.

"You take the call here," Talmir said. His tone was even, no hint of the nerves writhing just beneath the surface.

Talmir moved along the wall, the soldiers parting to let him pass. The mood had changed, but he knew they would stand and fight no matter the circumstances. The Valley that was supposed to be their refuge had become something else entire; as a result, it was often the youngest among his men and women that displayed the most grit. It was a sad truth, but one he welcomed now.

Questions spun in his mind, and no matter the form they took, the core was the same, tying them to a single word that echoed like a lone piece of sanity in a world gone mad.

Why?

No matter the answer, the question remained. The dark was here, and it had to be stopped. Talmir had done it before. He and his Embers, and the men and women they led. All had played as large a role in stopping the extinction of their people as the great white walls themselves. Still, some part of him knew this time was different, that this was not just an attack, but a mission whose purpose was singular.

Talmir skirted the edge of the battlements as he walked, dodging archers and couriers alike. Once, he nearly tripped and took the two-story drop into the courtyard below. This caused him to break a rule he usually kept to, and that was not to look at the yolk in the nest he protected. But he saw. He saw faces young and old drawn tight with worry. They stood in the streets and milled in the doorways, caught between tasks as the horns sounded once again.

They were looking at him.

"Caru! What are you doing this close to my gate?"

A great shadow passed over Talmir, only this one leaked warmth in place of terror. Garos Balsheer's stern features broke into an easy smile as he pulled the Captain away from the edge.

"Thought the folk down here could use a real commander," Talmir said, earning a punch on the shoulder that promised to bruise despite the armor he wore.

"Wonder where these things've come from," Garos said as they stared out over the oncoming horde.

"Does it matter?" Talmir asked bitterly.

Garos looked at him for a spell and then laughed full-bellied. He took to shouting his orders and the men and women around him shaped up, faces hardening.

There had been a time not so long ago when Garos's mocking demeanor had been genuine. The First Keeper did not like being led by an upstart, especially one that was not Landkist. Somewhere along the way, that had changed. It was subtle enough that it had taken years for Talmir to notice, and even longer before he registered how much it mattered to him.

"The situation," Talmir said, and Garos made a great show of clearing his throat. The display sent ripples of stifled laughed throughout the assembled soldiers. It was the way Garos led, and Talmir had long ago stopped interfering.

"My lads and I've got this gate covered," he said. "Literally, actually. There's enough pitch in the gap there to fry the whole army, if they make for it. As for the cliffs, Ve'Gah and her man Dakken have it. Not many of the critters hanging around the north. No way in that they can see, so the White Guard have sent most of their own south along the bend to bolster our ranks. I assume the straight man has the South Bend?" He looked to Talmir, who nodded. "Splendid."

"It will have to do."

"It always does," Garos boomed, and Talmir saw the young soldiers—some of the boys too young to shave, the girls too young to have been kissed—glancing at the powerful Ember from beneath lidded helms. They searched for a source of strength, though they were all killers in their own right.

"I want all three Embers at their braziers at all times."

"Radius formation, eh?"

"Yes."

"That leaves you to cover the gaps," Garos said, trying to keep the doubt from showing in his tone.

Talmir smirked, loosening his father's sword in its scabbard. He turned away from Garos and made for the gap between the First and Second Keepers along the South Bend. Creyath would stay by his post, he knew, but he knew just as well that Garos would abandon his if it meant saving the lives of his soldiers. Garos's brazier had not been giving off much heat, which meant the lion's share was already coursing through the Ember's veins. Talmir almost felt sorry for whichever of the great beasts made for the gate.

"Captain!"

Talmir spun. He saw Garos standing on the edge of the gate, hands braced on the parapets. A banner woman was pointing to the southwest, where the titans approached at a run. Abominations and approximations of ape, boar and bear rushed forward, pounding the earth and sending the white stones in the fields flying like hailstones, glowing eyes throwing red trails. The shadows at their feet lurched forward and broke into a trot that soon became a sprint, and a hush descended on the assembled soldiers.

"Fires!" Talmir screamed, iron in his voice. "Light and let fly!" And the arrows lit the sky like tiny comets streaking beneath black clouds.

None here had been born in the heart of the windswept deserts of the north. None here had felt the sand sting their eyes and backs, the elements lashing like whips against hides tough as horned runners. These were Valley children, soft and green. But there was fire in their blood, and it shined brightest when things from the night approached.

Swords and spears raised, strings pulled taught on bows, banners slapped in the violent winds and a single clear note rang out from the heart of the Valley, from Hearth. It was a note that rose on the beating of stubborn wills.

The black swarm slammed into the walls with a savage force that told Talmir all he needed to know: there would be no retreating into the night this time, no hiding from the dawn. The dark army broke upon his walls like a wave with white-capped foam. The shadows scrambled up the uneven face, hands hooked like claws, pulling themselves up only to be flung back to the burning ground below.

Talmir saw the giant, ape-like beast break off from the rest, thundering toward Creyath on the South Bend. The Captain took off at a run, jumping over clattering shields and feeling the blistering heat of Garos's spinning staff even as he fled its arc.

He pulled up, skidding to a halt in sight of Creyath Mit'Ahn, who stood glowing like a firefly before a dark and wrathful god.

CHAPTER FOURTEEN

THE CAVE

"**H**ow is he?"

"How do you think?"

"I mean, how will he be?"

"How should I know?"

"Who would but you?"

"I wasn't speaking to you."

"Speaking loud enough for us all."

Baas rumbled the last from his place beside the fire. He poked absently at the dying embers with a charred stick, simmering and unsure, as they all were. Nathen frowned but otherwise made no response other than to withdraw from his place beside Linn and climb into his bedroll in the corner of the cave.

Linn felt a pang as she watched him go, but had to admit she did not mind the reprieve. How was she supposed to know? What was she supposed to do about it?

But then, hadn't this whole endeavor been her idea?

They were out here because of her. Larren Holspahr was out here because of her.

Linn peered through the hazy glow of firelight to the form laid at the back of the cave. She saw the telltale rise and fall that signaled life, but even those breaths were slow and labored. Larren had not appeared in tremendous spirits when she had first rejoined the group following her own battle on the trail, but his condition had deteriorated rapidly. Much like Kole, the Ember bore few visible marks from his tangle with the Sentinel, but it had done its work in other ways. Linn had been lucky.

Iyana and Ninyeva were nowhere close, and it appeared none of the Faey had a mind to lend their healers, even had they been watching from the trees.

The Second Keeper's ailing condition had done more damage than she ever could have imagined to the group's morale. Linn could not say she blamed them. In truth, she was probably the most disconcerted of the lot, other than Kaya Ferrahl, whose leg was in a bad way. They had one Ember left standing, and though Linn had certainly had her troubles with Jenk in the past, she found herself looking to him for guidance as often as he looked to her. So far, the extent of their leadership had been finding them a deep cave in which to wait out the storm, perhaps to bury their dead.

She tried to shake the image, but it would not quit.

Kaya was scrunched up against the opposite wall with her head resting on Jenk's shoulder. Her leg was set in a splint Nathen had fashioned, and Baas had carried her most of the way here, half a day north of Hearth. When Larren had collapsed for the third time, he did not get up, and they had been holed up in this dank cavern ever since.

Try as she might, Linn could not entirely keep from placing some blame on Kaya for Larren's plight. After all, she had not minded her footing and it had cost them an Ember in the fight. To protect her, the Second Keeper had been forced to sacrifice his notorious footwork in order to fend off the shadows that made for her like jackals at a wounded bird.

They had first made camp along the banks of the Northwest River, which joined up with the Fork and Baas's people further east.

There, they were set upon for the second time.

Linn had spotted them first, black specs that must have caught their scent on the breeze. There were no Sentinels among them, but they were dangerous nonetheless. Baas and Jenk had done most of the killing, while Linn and Nathen assisted the injured Embers from the fray. Linn was sorely missing her bow, but it would be knife work from here on out.

Knife work, against the Eastern Dark. She supposed she had better turn her hoping to praying that the White Crest was alive.

Linn let a small laugh loose despite the circumstances, earning a glare from Kaya, a curious look from Jenk and something in between from Baas.

For the first few hours spent in the cave, they had jumped at every shadow—all of them but Baas. The Riverman had replaced his former enthusiasm for their trek with something more dour, but he was not afraid. Without his strength, they would not have made it this far. Linn hoped they could count on it to get them a bit farther.

Jenk might not be badly injured like their other Embers, but without a roaring fire to replenish his stores, he was running on fumes. Whatever work he might be able to do with his blade, she doubted if it would compare to the fight on the road.

Linn looked at Nathen as he curled up against the side of the cave. He was strong and hearty, but younger even than Kaya by half a decade. She felt sorry for how short she had been with him and considered going to him, but the rhythmic hiss of steam rising from his mouth told her he had found sleep where the others could not.

Another crack of lightning illuminated the sheets of pouring rain outside and set Linn's head to buzzing as it collided with the rocky hillock above. Larren coughed and murmured in his sleep. He sounded in pain and it reminded her of Kole in his tower. She had visited shortly before setting out but could not bring herself to stay long. Iyana had cast her a strange look at that, but it could not be helped. Any further delay and Linn might have lost her nerve.

That, or her too-perceptive sister would have guessed the game.

Of course, things being as they were, that might have been the best outcome for all involved.

"Ahem."

Linn was so lost in her own thoughts that she had not noticed Jenk's shadow. He wore his customary smile as he sat next to her, but it masked an obvious worry. The gash on his brow seemed to be healing nicely, and the rain had washed the blood from his sandy hair.

Jenk shared a conspiratorial sigh as the two observed the silence of their heroic abode. And then the Ember croaked his own small laugh that cut the silence like a knife, jagged and crass. She understood completely, even if Kaya grimaced in her sleep.

"Enjoying the life of a traveling hero?" Jenk whispered.

"That's ever been your role, Ganmeer," she said, elbowing him in the ribs. "Something you always wanted." He gave her a strange look, but she shook her head. "Don't deny it. I'm not saying it's a bad thing, but that complex has followed you ever since you lit your first blade. Before that, you'd practice your rally cries to the mice in the meadow."

"You and Kole could be quiet when you wanted."

"Very."

Jenk was silent for a moment and Linn felt another pang for having offended him. He laughed again, this one a little louder. She felt lighter because of it.

"I guess we all played those games to some degree," he said. "Back when we could afford to. Back when there was such a thing as playing."

Linn's face darkened, though Jenk could not see it as the flames flickered and came close to dying. Her parents had been among the first to encounter the Dark Kind in the Valley. It had not gone well for them. It had not gone well for many that first year.

It was strange, but the distinction between Landkist and not had never mattered so much and so little at once. Everyone who could lift blade, bow or bucket became a value against the night, but the Embers took their preferred place as the true heroes of their folk. Jenk, along with Kaya and Kole, was among the last known Embers born in the world. It was no small wonder he had grown up with some piece of destiny in mind.

"Feeling any better?"

"Pain has given way to exhaustion," Linn said with a smirk. "I didn't love the former, but I'm not thrilled with the latter. How are you?"

Jenk opened his hands. She hadn't noticed before, but he had them clasped together. When they opened, she felt the warmth touch her face as the pile of burning coals tumbled over each other. No matter how often she saw the Embers fight, it was still amazing for her to see the little ways in which they communed with the fire. It was a part of them.

"Will that be enough to keep you going?"

Jenk closed his hands and leaned back, closing his eyes.

"A brazier would be ideal. But beggars cannot be choosers. I'll do my part. I just hope we can find a place in the mountains to get a real blaze going, away from those things."

"Might be more dangerous eyes up there."

"True enough. But then, an Ember with a full blaze is no picnic either. If it comes to that, they can try their luck."

Linn did not know if he truly believed it, but the words were comforting nonetheless.

"I tried to share heat with Larren," the Ember said, glancing sidelong at the prone form at the back. "I burned him."

As shocking as it was for Linn to hear, the effect on Jenk was tenfold. For an Ember as powerful as Larren to be hurt by flames rather than restored by them, he had to be in a state far worse than she had imagined.

"It was a brave thing you did," Jenk said, looking at her. "Going after that cart. I thought you were lost to us."

Linn looked away.

"Does Baas still want to turn east?" she asked, changing the subject. The Riverman had shifted to the back of the chamber, his footfalls impossibly soft for one as large as he—some trick of the Rockbled, no doubt.

"I think."

"But you don't think we should."

"We don't know where these Corrupted are coming from. Could be the Fork. Could be from the lands beyond."

"The ones in the woods didn't look like Rivermen."

"No," Jenk allowed. "But they were heading to Hearth. How many do you think there are if they're heading for Hearth?"

"The Dark Kind attack Hearth just as often as they attack the Lake."

"This is different. This is an army, with Sentinels and who knows what else? This is an army sent, an army controlled."

Linn observed Baas as he squatted over their fallen leader. His were a strange people to her. The Rivermen refused to label their Rockbled as Landkist, though they clearly were, choosing instead to mark them as having earned the title due to their deeds in battle. It was likely an attempt to sow a feeling of equality among their ranks, and also to nurture a fierce will among the Rivermen not blessed by the earth.

She found herself wondering where they had come from, before the Emberfolk found them in the passes a century ago. When the Rivermen had been displaced from the canyons and trapped in the Valley with them, the Faey had treated them as much like foreigners as her own people, though they had been neighbors for some time before. Knowing how Baas felt about the forest peoples, it was not hard to imagine his tribe avoiding the woods of the Valley and keeping to their caves, but where had they come from before?

She focused on Baas because she did not want to focus on the form beneath him nor the spear leaning against the far wall, black blade cold and wet.

"Blame is a poison," Jenk said next to her. "Don't drink it yourself."

Linn regarded him. She opened her mouth to speak, but nothing came out.

"No matter the path we're on," he said, "we're on it. And I mean to see it through."

Linn swallowed.

"Do you think he can help?" she asked. "If the White Crest is alive."

"I'm more concerned with the 'if,' but yes, I do. Either way, we need to find the source. We need to find out where the Sentinels are coming from, and we all know it's in the peaks or beyond."

"Why would he let this happen?" Linn asked, verbalizing what the Emberfolk of the Valley kept close and secret.

"I won't pretend to know the mind of a Sage," Jenk said, a hint of bitterness in his tone. "It was they who cast the world into the chaos it's in. Them that drove us from the deserts."

"One of them," Linn said and Jenk shrugged. "You're sounding like Kole."

He chuckled. "I suppose I am."

A shadow stole over Linn's face and for a moment she feared the dark men had crawled into their cave undetected until another flash of lightning illuminated Baas's hulking form. He was crouched before them, having moved from the back to the cave mouth in a silent blink. His eyes were pealed, one hand resting on the ground beneath him, fingers splayed in the mud. It looked like he was listening.

Silently, Linn and Jenk moved to flank him. Nathen was already up and moving, bow clutched in one hand. He moved in front of Linn, and the four of them peered out into the driving rain, Kaya still sleeping soundly behind them.

Jenk glanced at Linn and nodded toward the trees across the way, but she shook her head and then held up a hand. She thought she could see movement, but it was difficult to distinguish branch from limb in the drizzle.

"Larren?"

The four of them whirled, shocked to see Larren standing over a startled Kaya, his face illuminated as the last embers faded in the pit.

"Holspahr," Jenk said sharply, and the Ember's head swiveled toward him with a jerking motion that gave Linn the disturbing impression of an owl. She could not fully make out his eyes in the gloom, but she thought she caught a hint of ruby red in the black.

"Jenk?" Kaya said, scrabbling back in the grip of fear, her palms working in the mud, heat going up around her as she panicked.

Larren was working his fingers into fists, clenching and unclenching, his jaw working as he repeated something Linn could not make out.

"What's he saying?" she asked in horrified fascination as Baas tensed.

"Run," Nathen said.

And the night came alive behind them.

It was a wonder Linn was not killed immediately as the forest came in after them. If not for the shocking speed of Baas, she surely would have. He met the charge of the shadows with his great shield and greater chest, shattering one against the cavern wall and launching the other into the mud as he went.

Jenk's sword ignited, throwing the whole scene into chaos as he advanced on Larren. Linn ducked under a slashing arm and came up next to Nathen, knife in hand. He launched a shaft point-blank into her attacker and she took the next to the ground in a tackle, stabbing in a fury, thunder crashing with renewed gusto as she spilled out of the wide cave mouth and into the storm.

But for the orange glow of Jenk's sword, the only light came in the form of intermittent lightning and the flashing moon it made of Baas's shield, which rose and fell, swept and punched as the Riverman forged out ahead of her under a tangle of black limbs. It was impossible to tell how many assailed them, and the only intelligible sound above the din was Jenk's increasingly desperate voice as he tried to shout sense into Larren.

Linn realized her knife had done all the work it could—she was stabbing the mud now—so she stood on wavering legs and whirled toward the cave mouth. Larren loomed over Kaya, Everwood spear held aloft to set the whole chamber awash in the amber glow. His face was lost in shadow, but Linn thought she could see a wolf's grin. He took a step forward and Jenk did likewise, lit blade angled while Nathen's bow twanged as he tried to keep the beasts from flanking Baas.

The force of the Embers' clash sent a shockwave of heat and flaming trails that had Linn and Nathen diving to the mud. When Linn got to her knees, she saw the thing that was no longer Larren forcing Jenk back with sweeping arcs, gouts of flame flashing every which way that had the younger Ember blinded. Larren forced Jenk to duck a vicious swipe, planted one heel in the mud and spun, planting the other square into Jenk's chest and launching him out into the storm. Jenk came up spinning and slashing as the shadows fell on him.

"Back!" Kaya screamed, grasping wildly. She snatched the butt of her staff and dragged it toward her, its ignition stealing what was left of the air in the narrow confines and making it impossible for Linn to cross the threshold.

All the while Larren advanced, eyes glowing blood red and teeth bone-white.

"Ve'Ran!"

Linn spun to see Jenk being forced back under a surging press, his boots slipping in the slush. Dark forms lay smoldering at his feet, wounds still glowing. She brandished her knife and sped toward him, taking the first shadow in the neck, blood that seemed as black as the rest of it coursing out and making her hand slick. The second spun on her with a snarl and Jenk cut it down in a glowing streak that had her seeing stars.

A roar to her back drew Linn's attention. Baas warred with a pack of them, each flailing form the Riverman threw replaced by another. One clung to his broad back, claws rending through leather like paper and scouring deep gouges. Baas sprinted toward the tree line and spun, hurling his back at an oak trunk with a crack that rivaled the storm's latest retort.

"Baas!"

Jenk was screaming, but the Riverman was in a rage and beyond listening.

"Ve'Ran, tell him to go to Kaya!"

Linn exhaled and charged into the driving rain. She came up in front of the panting Rockbled, who now stood alone, waiting for the next pack to detach itself from the forest. He noted her presence and focused on her, pupils dilated, blood flowing from wounds that went from brow to neck.

"Jenk will hold them here, Taldis. Kaya needs you. Now!"

Even as she spoke, the Ember dashed in front of them and met the charge of the newest shadows. One went down under his fiery attack and one of Nathen's shafts took the other in the chest, Linn finishing it off as it writhed in the muck. Baas charged toward the cave mouth and Linn followed.

A high-pitched scream echoed into the night and a form hurtled past them. Nathen tumbled and rolled unceremoniously in the mud. Linn spared a backward glance as she ran and took heart that the hunter was already trying to gain his feet. When she turned back, she nearly ran headlong into the wall formed by Baas's back.

Linn skittered to the side and froze. The cave was dimmer than it had been when the Embers clashed, but fires ate hungrily at the cavern walls. Larren stood in the center of the cave, the twisted form of Kaya Ferrahl beneath his boot. If he noted their presence, he made no move to show it, nor did he seem particularly distressed about the arrow sticking out of his shoulder, its feathers blackened and curled by the heat. His red eyes roved over the corpse of the young Ember at his feet like a lizard, her fair skin taking on a macabre glow.

Some part of Linn worked to reject the scene before her; it was the same part that had denied the death of her parents in those early dark days. But the rest of her, that which was fire-forged even if she lacked Ember blood let it all in and fanned the smoldering coals into a fresh blaze.

Kaya Ferrahl was dead. A demon had killed her, just as it had killed Larren Holspahr before her. And they had harbored it, wrapped it in covers and brought it warmth and trust, offering themselves up as lambs to the slaughter. The Sentinel before them wielded the heat of an Ember, but it was no less cold than the black ghouls at her back.

A similar sort of cold enveloped Linn now. It numbed her. It was the feeling of steel shining in starlight, of being perched on an arrowhead.

She was in a killing way.

"You must go."

Baas, in the grips of rage just moments before, now spoke with an eerie calm. The hawk's eyes of the corrupted Ember darted up and took them in, sized them up.

"Go," he said again, more insistent this time. But Linn's hands were closed into steely fists. She scanned the cave and noted Nathen's bow close at hand, his spent arrows strewn in the mud.

She looked back, and her icy resolve shattered when the thing that bore Larren's face smiled at her, white teeth shining like a ghost. She heard a low growl and traced it to the deepest parts of Baas's chest. His boulder of a body tensed, blood flowing freely from his many wounds.

The Sentinel, seemingly amused, leaned its weight more fully onto Kaya's lifeless form, sending up an audible crunch that resounded off of the close walls and low ceiling. Linn knew she would hear that sound in her dreams for the rest of her life, but the animal roar of Baas Taldis quickly rose to supplant it in the moment.

The Riverman charged, covering the distance between him and the Sentinel in a leaping stride as Linn dove for Nathen's bow. Sure-handed, she snatched it in a roll and came up with a feathered shaft nocked. She cursed, heart pounding as she fought to train the missile onto Larren's lean form as it grappled with Baas. Even possessed of whatever supernatural strength it was, the Sentinel was giving ground, white teeth gleaming as it fought for purchase, spear igniting and setting Baas's shield to glow as the weapons came together in a shower of sparks.

Baas's shield protected him from the worst of the flames, but Linn worried about that Everwood blade. The Rockbled were only impervious to weapons made of metal, one of the major reasons they had fallen in numbers against the Landkist among the Emberfolk generations before.

Suddenly, the Sentinel withdrew from the press and Baas stumbled forward as the flaming spear slashed low, cutting deep into one thigh and sending the Riverman stumbling. Linn saw her opportunity and seized it, bowstring humming. The Sentinel saw the shaft at the last moment and Linn was shot back out into the rain as the chamber erupted into an inferno.

Nathen pulled her up and she peered into the cave, seeing the Sentinel and its spear silhouetted in the blaze. Her arrow had found its mark, but the missile had already burned up, the wound on Larren's chest now a smoldering scab. Those red eyes flashed her way and her hands worked of their own accord as she fell to one knee. Arrows lanced into the cave, most batted aside from the whirling wall of flame put out by the Everwood spear, but several found their marks, and Linn saw Baas's shield glowing white hot as the Riverman charged in from the back of the chamber.

Baas was a roaring comet. He collided with the Sentinel shield-first and slammed it into the wall, stone breaking off on the impact. The Sentinel snarled and turned the flames on him, but the Riverman would not be cowed.

"Go!" Baas screamed as he brought the rim of his shield up to shatter the Sentinel's nose. They battled in a pocket of hell, and just when Linn thought Baas was caught dead to rights, he punched the wall of the cave itself and the earth responded, sending a crumbling spur to pin Larren's foot in place. Now it was forced to stand and fight, and the spear sent a torrent of fire at the glowing shield, Baas growling behind it.

"Go!"

Nathen snatched her by the wrist and they ran, the animal hisses of the shadow men mixing with the steady patter of rain. The brilliant light of Jenk's blade stood out in the woods. He had been forced away from them and Linn saw the fire's dance slow, the yellow trails growing sluggish.

They broke into the clearing and Nathen was forced to fall to his back as Jenk's blade found new life, shooting toward him with deadly intent.

"We need to go!" Linn shouted over the storm as the branches clashed above them.

Jenk was panting. His face was pale, skin hissing and sending up steam that mixed with the smoke emanating from the burned bodies at his feet. More shadows raced through the trees, timbers cracking and bending as they approached.

The Ember nodded and ran in the opposite direction, Linn and Nathen following the bouncing glow of his blade as they lost the moon to the clouds and canopy. Jenk yelped as his blade was extinguished with a splash, but they could not slow, so Linn let out a shout of her own as they broke through the brush and crashed into the fast-flowing swamp.

They paddled and Linn lost sight and feel of the others. Her strength flagged, and that was when she realized how strong the pull was, dragging her unerringly forward. A great shelf of jagged stone loomed ahead, breaking from the canopy and standing vigil like a silent titan. She heard the screams ahead, and then the darkness took her in a rush as the mud beneath her boots gave way to open air.

CHAPTER FIFTEEN

TWO PAIR

The rain had relented, fading for the first time since they had set out. Occasional cracks of thunder still punctuated the sky to the north, but on the borders of Last Lake, all was quiet.

Shifa splashed into the stream, lapping at the cold water before crossing to the opposite bank, and Kole followed. He held his boots in one hand and closed his eyes as his bare feet hissed upon contact with the flowing water. He felt the steam rise, tickling the hair on his shins, enjoying the battle his body fought with the cold for equilibrium. It was a battle he knew the water would eventually win.

The hound barked and he waded across with a sigh. Taei and Fihn should be near. The fact that he could not hear them was only a testament to their uncanny woodlore. Normally, the forest would be teeming with game, with birds and beasts of every persuasion lending their voices to the canopy, but not now. Now it was as silent as it was during the deepest parts of the Dark Months.

Kole found a moss-covered boulder and climbed it, settling at the top. He patted the spot next to him and Shifa hopped up, her pack rattling as she did. Kole checked it, ensuring the pitched arrows were wrapped and secure before pulling the map out of a pocket in the leather. The twins claimed to know every inch of the Southern Valley. Kole did not doubt them, but Tu'Ren would not let them leave without the parchment, so he had taken it.

The guilt at having left the Lake still gnawed at him, but it was a distant thing when compared to the need that drove him on—the need to find Linn, and the need to reach the peaks. Kole knew the defenses would hold. Tu'Ren had assured him, but there was no telling how long. If Hearth was besieged to the degree Ninyeva said, then Last Lake would be next.

As it turned out, he was not the only one feeling guilty: Kole had originally intended for Shifa to be his only companion, but the Kane siblings had insisted on accompanying him. Whether they felt more guilty for not having gone north with Linn's group or for failing to tell the First Keeper until it was too late to affect change, it was impossible to say.

Being honest, Kole could not say he particularly enjoyed Fihn's company, but the deeper they got into the woods, the more assured he felt that their presence could only be a good thing. Taken separately, Taei and Fihn were two of the more formidable swords in the Valley. Together, he doubted if anyone was up to the task. Though only Taei was Landkist, his sister had made it her singular drive to prove to the World that it had chosen wrongly. From what Kole had witnessed, she had a point.

As he waited, Kole turned over his final conversation with Ninyeva. The Faey Mother had been uncharacteristically intense, even nervous.

"Even if you do not find the White Crest—and I pray you do not come across the Eastern Dark—your journey can still bear fruit," she had said. "The red-topped keep lies in a cloister in the spurs. Whatever drives this darkness is in its bowels."

"Was that not the White Crest's abode?" Kole had asked, skeptical.

"Once, maybe. Either way, there could be power there, Kole. Power for the taking."

"You would wield the tools of Sages."

"I would wield anything to save our people," Ninyeva said harshly. "Unless it has the touch of the Eastern Dark. If so, purge it. But Kole," she had looked earnest, younger even. "The White Crest was a being of wind and light. If any of his power remains, it would be a boon, not a curse."

Linn Ve'Ran's face popped into his mind. He knew how she felt about the White Crest. He knew she was convinced he still lived. There was the guilt again. Did he know it? He felt it in his bones. He saw it when he closed his eyes at night. But did he know it? Or had he simply assigned his anger, his rage, to a being that had protected them simply because it had failed to protect his mother? Perhaps that rage had blinded him to the true threat, to the threat his people had fled the northern deserts to avoid.

Kole did not hear their approach, but Shifa bristled beside him, issuing a low growl that quickly morphed into an excited bark. Fihn greeted the hound at the base of the boulder and Kole jumped down beside them.

Taei emerged from a patch to the east a short time later. He seemed hesitant, but Kole had a difficult time reading the other Ember. Fihn, however, mirrored his concern.

"What trouble?" she asked.

"Nothing," Taei said, shaking his head slowly. "The woods are silent."

"How far did you go?" Kole asked, and Fihn nodded at her brother to continue.

"Farther than I had planned. Even the trees seem fearful."

"Ninyeva said there was a great host before the walls of Hearth," Kole said. "That's where they all are."

"Maybe," Taei said. "Maybe it's this cloud cover that's got the woods quiet."

He looked up and the others did as well. The canopy was dense, but sunlight should have filtered through the gaps in the leaves. Instead, there was only a lighter gray streaming in like moonlight through ash.

"Do you think they tried for Hearth?" Fihn asked.

The twins stared at one another, concern evident.

"If Linn Ve'Ran thinks like I know she does, she went around," Kole said. "West would bring them to the pines and up toward the peaks from the woods. She would not have risked the mission by stopping at Hearth."

"Who says she was in charge?" Fihn challenged. "Larren Holspahr—"

"Is a powerful Ember," Kole said, "and an incredible warrior. But this is not his mission. They went around."

Kole adjusted his blades and re-tied his boots before heading onto the northern trail, unwilling to let the twins further the argument. After a time, he heard their soft footfalls drifting through the trees to his left. They would follow. And he would hope that he was right.

CHAPTER SIXTEEN

ENDURANCE

When Talmir awoke, he was in a suffocating darkness. For a panicky spell, he thought he was dead and raised again as a small part of the black ocean that assailed the walls of Hearth. He imagined the white walls as little more than an eggshell whose innards shook and quivered with each attack.

He cursed himself a fool when he sat up and swept back the black curtains, memories half-formed but flooding back in a rush. His body ached, but he was largely unhurt. His mind felt stretched, and judging by the marks on the melted candles on the ledge of his chamber, he had rested long enough.

It had not been Talmir's idea to take a respite with his city in such dire straights, but rather that of his three Keepers and their lieutenants. They had repelled the titans that had come against them from the west: three had been slain and one—the serpent—had not been seen since it had snaked its way into the tall grasses beneath the White Cliffs. Relatively speaking, they had been safe when he took his leave.

As he had meandered down from the battlements, head swimming through the fog brought on by witnessing Creyath's short, tempestuous battle with the Night Lord, he had come upon Karin Reyna, First Runner of Last Lake. The man had made it in before the first charge and was now cut off from his own, with his own. Talmir had met him before, and though others held him in high regard—Garos Balsheer chief among them—he had done little to distinguish himself in the Captain's eyes.

If ever that was want to change, Talmir thought these might be the circumstances.

Talmir rose as quickly as he dared, stooping to buckle on the sword and belt that he had dropped unceremoniously to the floor. His joints reminded him in no uncertain terms that he would never possess the supernatural endurance of the Embers. Then again, he was in much better condition than Creyath. The Second Keeper had acquitted himself well, putting all of his power into a single strike to the crown of the great beast's skull, but that had not saved him from its dying throes. He would be in the Red Bowl now, and Talmir hoped he would mend as quickly as Landkist usually did.

The booms, claps and clangs of battle echoed in the cold stairwell as Talmir took the steps two at a time into the guts of the barracks below. The sounds had become so constant over the last few days that one could mistake it for the steady drone of rain on clay and tile.

The breeze dried his face and stuck the sleep sweat to his skin when he threw open the door to the mess hall. The shutters were blown open and the wind howled outside. Bone-weary men and women craned their heads and leaned up from their cots to glance his way. Some saluted. Most fell back into what sleep they could.

A young, mousey-haired lad stared at him from his place beside the fire. He was stirring a black cauldron of stew. Behind him, an old woman worked in a ledger, taking turns between scratching lines on parchment and candlewick. These men were on a timer that the Captain was not, and he felt the familiar pang of guilt over it as he straightened and strode toward the street beyond.

The air was an odd mix of fresh and peppery, the smells of pitch and flame stinging his nostrils. He breathed it in and exhaled a sigh of relief as he noted the walls still standing and still-manned, Garos's great brazier glowing atop the gate. The twang of bowstrings mixed with the guttering of torches. Since the Corrupted made no sounds but for the scrabbling of nails on stone, it looked from this angle as though his soldiers battled the storm itself, their flames having dried up all its water.

"Captain Caru!"

The shout came from closer than Talmir had expected. He put his head on a swivel but did not see the speaker until he felt a tug on his sleeve. A child no more than ten looked up at him, dark features and even darker eyes peering through a face caked with smoke and resin.

"You're a bit young to be a Runner," Talmir said, and the child adopted a look so professionally perturbed he felt foolish for having said anything. He tousled the boy's hair, which only served to amplify his annoyance.

"A joke, lad," he lied and the boy's brows drew up. "I take it you were chosen for your sharp eyes and ears. What news to report?"

"Captain Caru!" he restarted his address. "First Keeper Balsheer has held the wall with no untow—" his features screwed up in confusion, swarthy cheeks going a deep red before the light went on. "With no untoward!"

Talmir nodded encouragingly, waiting for him to continue, but the boy appeared finished.

"No untoward ..."

"Happenings!" the boy shouted, remembering himself and pleased that he had. The rest of his address went more smoothly.

Garos, together with Third Keeper Ve'Gah and her partner Dakken Pyr, had repelled three more salvos from the host. The Corrupted had only gained the walls once and had been thrown down in short order. Although there were several wounded, there were no casualties to report.

The calculations ran and resolved in Talmir's mind. He nodded stiffly and squatted to meet the boy at eye level.

"You've done well," he said, smiling. The boy did not return it, only stared at him through those dutiful browns. "Now, I want you to take a message to First Keeper Balsheer. Tell him I've gone to the Bowl to check on Creyath and that I will return to relieve him as soon as I'm able. He'll get a kick out of the second part."

The boy nodded curtly and started toward the gate, but Talmir caught him by the crook of the arm.

"After you've seen to that, I want you to make your way to the mess and have them fill you up with something hot. I'll not have one of my best operating on an empty stomach."

The boy looked grave, deadly serious. He ran toward the sound of battle, and Talmir tried not to think on it.

It struck Talmir as he walked quickly up the sloping cobbled streets of Hearth how disparate the faces he passed under the awnings and milling behind the stained windows truly were. He saw the very old and the very young, but very few occupying the space between. Those were at the wall, or under their feet.

How far had his people come? Had it been worse in the deserts?

They had been fighting the Dark Kind for a generation. Why, then, did this feel so different?

If nothing else, Talmir knew the answer to the last question. Strange as it might seem, the Dark Kind were a force of nature, though they emanated from another world. Fighting them was akin to battling landslides, quakes and even storms on the water. It was a fact of life.

But this was different. What assailed them now hearkened back to the worst stories from the northern deserts, when the Eastern Dark had opened the doors to the World Apart a bit wider in an attempt to claim the Embers as his own.

As far back as he could remember, this was the first time Talmir actually thought they could lose. He only hoped his people would live to tell this tale.

The streets further in were choked with traffic. When the cobbles leveled out, Talmir turned to look back toward the white shell protecting his city and the small fires protecting it. He was struck by how small and fragile it looked from here, just as he was struck by the vastness of the roiling mass beyond its arc, like a black sea.

He shook his head, turned and picked up his pace, the city transforming from the gray and burnt orange of stone and tile to a kaleidoscope of vibrant colors as he entered the Red Bowl. This was the city's central market and the driving force of all trade in the Valley, from the Lake to the Fork and the forests beyond. Great sheets of blue and white silk dripped their colors, clashing with the bright reds and oranges of the canvases that sheltered the merchants and their wares.

Today, the market was as busy as ever during the Bright Days, but for all the wrong reasons. In place of the usual vendors and carts, Talmir noticed makeshift sick tents. In the place of lavish carpets were great sheets of cloth and bedrolls, laid out and waiting for occupancy.

Talmir pushed his way through the buzzing throng and drove to the center, where the tables and crates had been arranged to make alcoves and halls through which healers walked with their wounded. Candles flickered on benches and in sconces in the beams overhead, casting the scene in a ruddy glow. The canvas flapped at its zenith, the sound like death's wings, and Talmir felt suddenly very cold in the warm surroundings.

He felt this way until he entered the alcove that had been reserved for his closest friend, and though Creyath Mit'Ahn slept, the heat hit him like a wall. The Ember's bare chest festered with black and purple blotches where the Night Lord's barbs had struck home, but his breathing was steady. The flames in the nearby candles grew and shrank in time with his breast.

A young-looking man stooped over the Ember, his palms roving. He looked up when Talmir's shadow fell over him and the Captain noted the bright green that marked one of the Faeykin, striking in the gloom. His lot were rare among the Emberfolk, though common among the Faey as the Rockbled were among the Rivermen. In recent years, their births had far out-stripped that of the Embers, something not lost on their peers, for better or worse.

"His condition?" Talmir asked.

"Stable. He asked to be woken when you came."

The green eyes flickered as he looked Talmir over, making it all-too-clear what he thought of Creyath's request.

"We are thankful for your gifts," Talmir said, sounding stiff and feeling wooden.

"Yes," the Faeykin said. "Though the Embers do not respond as well to our touch. The fire burns out most wounds, but we assist where we can."

"Unfortunately," Talmir said, looking at Creyath, "I think your gifts will be needed on many more before this is done. How many of you are there in the city?"

"Faeykin? Perhaps a dozen. But only a select few have actually trained in the Eastern Valley under the Faey themselves."

"I see," Talmir said. "I trust you are one of them?"

His look was answer enough. He bent back to his work, but paused.

"Captain," he said, hesitant.

"Yes?"

"Can we hold?"

"Precisely the question I'd like to ask," a reedy voice carried on the back of a cool blast as the tent flap was thrown open.

Talmir sighed and turned. A diminutive man wrapped in gaudy blue with gold trim strode forward with a confidence that stood at odds with his stature. This could be owed to his company, a pair of tall, burly guards Talmir would much rather have seen atop the wall. Behind the trio was a modest gathering of entirely immodest men and women bedecked in everything but steel.

"Well?" the small man demanded, jewels jingling like the bell on a goat.

Creyath groaned and shifted in his sleep, and Talmir patted the physician on the shoulder and left them, forcing the small retinue to follow him to the edge of the tent. As he walked, the Captain counted in his mind, eyes closed. It would not do to throttle the Merchant Captain of Hearth in the midst of a siege. Perhaps later.

That was reason enough to win.

He forced a tight smile as he turned. The act was akin to chiseling solid marble with a stick.

"Merchant Captain Yush," Talmir said, looking down at the man before sweeping his gaze to encompass the flanking guards and nobles, "and esteemed members of the Merchant Council." He affected the poorest imitation of a bow he could muster. It did the trick. "To what do I owe …" It was too much. "This?"

He finished without a shred of the force humility he had intended to project. Yush Tri'Az had the beady eyes of a rodent, but he was a sharp one with a long memory. Talmir knew he factored a little too heavily into said memory, and he had likely just carved himself out another spot. To Yush's credit, he swallowed the slight best he could.

"How long, Captain Caru, do you expect this storm to last?" he asked through gritted teeth.

"As long as it takes, I would expect."

Yush looked him up and down as the merchants flanking him fell into hushed deliberation.

"Where have they come from?" Yush asked, accusation dripping. "The Dark Kind have never attacked during the Bright Days."

"The army here now is of the same world," Talmir started.

"The World Apart," Yush waved his hands, ridiculous sleeves bouncing. If Talmir were a hound, he'd have torn them apart, tassels and all. "Where else would they come from? I've heard the whispers in the streets, Captain. They say these are men at our gates, not beasts."

"A bit of both," Talmir admitted, flashing a smile that had Yush unsettled. "You're welcome to take a look for yourself, Merchant Captain," he said, emphasizing the modifier to his own title.

The silence that followed was stunning to the gathered merchant nobles, humiliating to Yush Tri'Az, amusing to the various physicians bustling about the tent and entirely welcome to Talmir.

When next Yush spoke, he nearly spit the words.

"Have they no leaders?"

"They have," Talmir said, the red eyes flashing in his mind.

"Then why have we not sent riders out to challenge them?"

Talmir shook his head and blew out a sigh.

"I am charged with defending this city."

"And I am charged with ensuring that in continues to run," Yush said, cheeks red.

"Your trade roads are not my concern."

"They will be," Yush said in a harsh whisper. "When the fish stop coming up from the Lake, the venison from the woods and the steel from the Fork. Those roads will be your concern then, and the concern of every living person in the city as the Dark Months fall."

Talmir was silent, fuming. He met Yush's stare as the others looked away.

"What of the Lake?" Yush asked.

"They would be foolish to try for Hearth."

"What of their mission? A number of their Embers were spied heading north through the western woods not a few days past."

Talmir bristled.

"Where did you hear that?"

"From the daughter of the old man you watched be cut down," Yush sneered. "She met them on the road. Larren Holspahr was among them."

"Holspahr," Talmir breathed.

"Some fool's errand from the witch Ninyeva," Yush said, whipping around as Talmir's thoughts spun of their own accord. He came back to himself.

"I'll let you and yours worry on the particulars of blame," Talmir said, shouldering past the group. "I have a city to defend."

And a certain Runner to confront.

CHAPTER SEVENTEEN

DUEL NATURES

The power to see.

That was what Ninyeva had. That was the true power of the Faey and the Landkist of the Valley dubbed their kin.

Faeykin had come to be synonymous with healing, but the trick was in seeing the hurt, feeling it. But the sight could go far beyond hurt and the ways around it. Her teachers could pierce cloud and canopy with theirs. Some could make a tool of time itself. Ninyeva was not so adept at navigating the Between, but she had made a go of it, and what she saw there she feared to believe.

After her most recent trip, the sky had turned black, turning dream to premonition.

The Emberfolk held her up as the best of their own, though the sands had not blessed her. The same Rivermen that cast stones at her in those early years later begged her to heal their children when the sick came. Their songs had followed her back to her village as she left on her uncle's bouncing wagon.

Of course, the fighting had continued, had even increased for a time, but it was Ninyeva who first sowed the seeds of peace in the Valley's core. Relations between the Emberfolk and the Riverman had improved drastically over the next two generations, and even the Faey had grown less scarce, their wilder tribes less prone to violence.

This was just one of the reasons they referred to her, simply, as 'Mother.'

And what sort of mother was she? She, who had sent her children, her bright stars, out into the night on a fool's quest. She had planted those seeds as well, and how quick they had grown, first in Kole and then in the hearts of others who now found themselves in the wilds as the black river of Dark Kind flowed unabated into their world.

Ninyeva felt the sting of the cold as a particularly violent gust threatened to tear the shawl from her shoulders. She gripped it tighter and leaned against a post under the eaves, waiting for the worst to pass. She felt the cold as despair. But more than that, she felt a simmering of rage, and it was the same rage that gripped the whole of her people each in their own hearts. It was the rage of a people with a fallen king and an absentee guardian.

Where was the White Crest? Where was their savior when they needed him most?

Not since burying the Night Lords of the Eastern Dark in the fissures of the Deep Lands had he made his presence known. And now here they squatted, huddled in the cold and dark, waiting for the Dark Kind to finish the job the Eastern Dark had begun a century ago on the red roads to the north. The peoples of the Valley would die in the shadows, their Embers spirited away to serve one they despised.

The Eastern Dark was their enemy, but she knew the power she had felt in the peaks, and it did not match the dark storm that had come against them. The White Crest had been killed by that same enemy.

Or had he endured? If only her people knew how she railed against the very visions she used to guide them.

"Mother Ninyeva?"

She opened her eyes to find a gruff man with white stubble staring at her through the eaves.

"Don't worry on me," she said, straightening and smoothing the folds from her robes. "Headed down to the Long Hall."

"I'll take you," he said in a tone that broached no argument. He took her by the crook of the arm.

A decade earlier, she'd have refused him. Now, she only sighed and let him guide her down the way, through the slipping stones and tiny running rivers the storm had left behind.

He left her by the door with a warm, good-natured bow, though his look said to her, 'You are old and weak.'

Ninyeva showed him her smile, canines and all, and climbed the short stair. At the top, she twisted the copper handle and entered without knocking.

It was warm inside but not pleasant. Doh'Rah and his son were here. The First Keeper slouched against the far wall with arms crossed, unwilling to grant his father respite from the withering attention of the crows in the chamber.

"Faey Mother," the tallest of them said, her stare baleful. "Did the storm harry you?"

Ninyeva only smiled at Doh'Rah, whose gaze softened under her own. His color was high and his face weary, the scavengers having been at him a while.

No matter. Ninyeva was far older than they, half as frail and doubly cunning. Their shadows were loping things and hers was a tiger. The Seers of Eastlake were all too aware of this, and they parted to make room for her beside the fire.

Ninyeva sat and the crows—Kita, Virena, Maeg and Rusul—met her green eyes with their own quarrelsome beads.

"Now then," Ninyeva started. "What have you to say?"

The others shrank and fumbled, but not Rusul.

"The storm outside has quieted, Faey Mother," she said. "But not in the north. Corrupted walk the green fields of Hearth; we have seen this and so have you. They are thick about the walls, and soon they will break through."

Ninyeva made no move to correct her and Tu'Ren shifted uncomfortably, averting his gaze.

"In this time," Rusul continued, "we are left without some of our stoutest defenders, Larren Holspahr chief among them. And now Kole Reyna has followed them fresh out of nightmare. He has taken the Kane twins with him."

"And you hold me responsible?" Ninyeva asked, unable or unwilling to keep the challenge from her tone.

"Ninyeva has nothing to do with the whims and fancies of would-be heroes," Doh'Rah cut in.

"I want to know where they've gone," Rusul said, ignoring the old man. The red in his face deepened.

"North," Ninyeva said, drawing a mirthless laugh from Maeg, whom Rusul silenced with a glare. The eldest of the crows tried to project Ninyeva's sense of calm, but it was a thin veneer.

"And what do they hope to find there?"

"The truth, as it were," Ninyeva shrugged. "Whatever form that takes to the young and restless."

"Your truth, you mean," Rusul said more than asked. "You planted the seeds in Reyna and his ilk after the Night Lord came."

"Think what you will," Ninyeva said, looking at them each in turn, "but I do not profess to know it completely, no matter what I have seen. I do not cast bones and entrails to see ends. Our youngest and brightest have taken charge of their destinies, and ours as well. Whatever they find in the north, they will be the engineers of its reckoning."

Doh'Rah cleared his throat.

"Our children and their children have bled and died in darkness for a generation," he said. "Our leisure time is spent in preparation, and we have no time for mourning; it is a chore, another cold thing to be buried next to the dead. The World Apart sends its denizens and we blame a faceless terror from the desert days. The Eastern Dark fell, and now perhaps he has risen, but we should lay the blame at our own feet. Too long did we let the waves break upon us."

"Too long did another watch the tide rise," Ninyeva said.

"You would blame the White Crest?" Rusul asked. "Who fell to protect us from one of his own?"

Ninyeva swallowed, her confidence wavering. And then she saw the light snuffed out in the passes as a Sage watched on. She saw Kole Reyna sobbing in the rain for a mother lost and a father just as well for the impact it had.

"If it is the Eastern Dark returned," she said, "why has he sent a force to purge the Valley, where before he wanted to control, to wield? The guilty burn alongside the innocent when the fire is wild. Each flame carries its own truth, and there are a few heading north to see what catches."

Something in Ninyeva's tone—the honesty, even the uncertainty— gave Rusul pause as her sisters shifted and mouthed their complaints.

"Our gifts are for more than casting old bones and seeing where they fall," Rusul said. "And we have not come to the same conclusions."

"You have not come to any conclusions," Ninyeva said. "Watching has virtues all its own. We now find ourselves in the roll of observer."

"So it would seem," Rusul said, eyes roving. "Only take care your strings don't catch fire, lest your fingers burn with the rest."

CHAPTER EIGHTEEN

HUNTERS HUNTED

The farther north they trekked, the more agitated Shifa became. Once or twice they had glimpsed shadows moving beneath distant branches. They were spared from sight only because of the hound's low warnings. These were not the typical forms of the Dark Kind, but rather the shadows of men all twisted.

The Corrupted were easy enough to dodge, but it was the Sentinels Kole feared. He felt it in his bones that it had been luck more than fire that had saved him among the roots, and he kept alert for the telltale glint of ruby red amidst the black.

Kole had explained the Sentinels to the best of his ability—their strength and speed, as well as their cunning. While Taei nodded curtly, Fihn had adopted an attitude that bordered on curiosity, as if she wanted to test herself against the Captains of the World Apart. Part of Kole wanted to disavow her of that notion by letting her try, but the greater part hoped she would be able to keep her smug disposition until their journey was through.

"They're bees," Fihn said, polishing her slender sword for the second time that day. "The Corrupted are their drones, the Sentinels their messengers and the Night Lords their Queens."

"What does that make the Eastern Dark?" Taei asked.

"A Sage," Fihn tossed back. "One who meddles with powers not his own."

"Who says it's the Eastern Dark?" Kole asked over his shoulder. He had his head on a swivel as they checked gear and waited for Shifa's return. He turned when neither of the twins answered and found them staring at him as if he were daft.

"Forget it," he said, bending to strap on his pack, ensuring the handles of his blades were not obscured. He went back to his scanning. The forest was thinner here in the central Valley, with more spaces between the trees. Though it was day, the light was gray through the smoky cloud-cover, which had not lifted since they had set out. He shuddered as the black images from his dream flooded back.

"What's got you all out of sorts?" Fihn asked pointedly.

It was a profoundly stupid question to Kole and his look said as much. Fihn rolled her eyes.

"You killed it, didn't you?" she asked. "Now you know what it takes, and you know you've got it."

Kole shook his head, but a snap in the brush had him whirling, the twins fanning out around him. Shifa came bounding into the clearing and greeted him eagerly, tongue lolling. They relaxed.

"Whatever I found," Kole said, patting the hound behind one ear, "it's either gone or buried so deep I haven't been able to call it up since."

"Before we reach whatever end you're dragging us into," Fihn said, "you may have to. Hopefully my brother can do the same. You'd think the Ember twin would have the edge in a spar, but I give him bigger fits than I have any right to."

That was a rare enough admission.

"Perhaps we Embers just have the courtesy not to light you on fire during a spar," Kole said and even Taei smirked. "Now, what's the word?"

It was impossible to see the horizon from their vantage and the sky was awash in shadow. Still, through it all, Taei had managed to orient them with rare skill. He was no Nathen Swell, but he was the best they had, navigating by the occasional break in the clouds at night and the direction of filtered sunlight by day.

"We're closer to Hearth than I'd have liked to be," he said soberly.

Kole noted the look of concern Fihn turned on her brother. The other Ember looked pale, and Kole was reminded of his own flagging reserves. They would still be formidable in a pinch, but with no brazier of stone or sky to bath them in its glow, they would have to tread carefully.

Shifa complained even as the prickle started up his spine. It was as much the sting of the Sentinel's probe as it was realization dawning.

Had they been corralled?

Noting the tension of Ember and hound, the twins drew their weapons, Taei an Everwood blade and Fihn her steel.

"We bear west," Kole said, grabbing Fihn before she could sprint away. "And always north."

"How have they found us?" she asked in a harsh whisper.

Kole shook his head slowly. It was as much a mystery to him as it was to them, and while Taei was more versed in the wilds than he, it was Kole once again who felt the pull of the enemy, the constant threat. The sensation was not as strong as it had been before his first clash with the Sentinel—fainter shadows of the same source.

"I'm going to cut far out," Kole said. "I'll angle north before the river widens. Slow at the pinch and I'll catch you at the crossing."

Fihn nodded and the twins were across the narrow brook fast as forest elk, forking off into the brush at chaotic angles that belied their poise. Kole knew the diverging paths were near to illusion. The twins would never let each other out of earshot. Their seeming solitary paths created attractive opportunities, for their enemies first and for them last. Kole would only disrupt the pattern.

Shifa whined again, nuzzling his hand with her wet nose. He closed his eyes and tried to wade through the chemicals warring in his blood to trace the kernel of pulsing alarm. He attempted to locate its origin, but he was no Faeykin. His sensitivity seemed more a happy accident than a gift of the land. Perhaps all that were hunted by the Sentinels felt it.

Kole squatted and met Shifa at eye level, staring into the deep browns. The hair on the nape of his neck smoothed in the wash of heat he released, the cold ridges flattening as he sighed.

"Good luck, girl."

He drew his blades with a dull ring as he rose, the fire scraping at his veins like metal on worn sheaths. He tensed and shot into the neighboring clearing to the west, cutting a swerving line along the narrow river, and Ember and hound carved their own intersecting trails in the trees. Shifa barked and Kole ignited his blades. This was no time for silence. They had been found. Now all that mattered was making sure the finding did not.

The canopy thickened in patches and Kole saw the shimmering ribbon of orange on the horizon shrink and narrow in the reflection of the rushing stream as the clouds stole back the sky. When the last specs of light faded, Kole heard Shifa howl in the enveloping blue-black curtain. Clutching the Everwood hilts tightly, he sent heat cascading into his legs and felt the muscles bunch and stretch, propelling him onward in great, leaping strides.

The forest grew eerily silent around him, with nothing but the babbling of the stream and the occasional snap of wood as his feet landed. The babbling soon morphed into a dull roar and creepers crowded the spaces between trees, the white mist of the rapids filtering between the sheets of dry scrub.

Kole felt the pulse just as the tree line ended. He skidded onto a small rocky shore, sending pebbles up in a cascade as he spun, wavering blades up and ready, the heat washing his face in its amber glow.

The forest before him was still, and he held the opposite shore in his periphery. A shadow detached itself from the rest and he saw Shifa, tail straight as a rod as she splashed into the shallow water. She stood in the center of the river, rigid and pointing toward the trees before him.

A familiar blur and the Sentinel came from the side. He was ready.

In a flash of red-orange flame, Kole met the charge with his blades framed out, stopping the first lashing limb and ducking the next. As he ducked, he rolled under, scoring a blistering slash across the black midsection, which bubbled and spat. This one was smaller than the first and noticeably weaker. It had those same ruby reds, but stood a full head shorter than him. It sported the twisted braids and slender frame of the Valley Faey.

Ember and demon circled each other like spitting cats. Shifa passed into his field of vision. She made no move to enter the fray and instead stood stock still, looking past the circling pair and into the deeper woods beyond. Kole was glad she did, as the next shadow that came for him would have skewered him on the end of its arm if she hadn't leapt to intercept it.

Hound and shadow went down in a tangle and Kole used the distraction to press his advantage. He lunged forward and his quarry took the bait, darting in with another slash. He took that arm off at the elbow as he backpedaled and then used the momentum to spin, burying his other blade into the creature's skull up to the hilt. The only sound made in its dying was the sizzle of whatever had been in the shell. He flared and made a torch of its head and tried not to think of what it had been before the Sentinel had taken it.

He moved to assist Shifa, but she had already finished with the other, and Kole sighed in relief as he realized only one of them bore the red glint that marked the Captains of the World Apart.

"Come," Kole said, and they splashed into the river.

No sooner had they crossed to the opposite shore than his fears were realized, the forest coming alive with black pursuit as the fallen Sentinel's pack descended. Shifa barked as she outstripped him, so Kole pulled some of the flame from his blades, dimming them to a dull blue and sending the energy to liven his legs once more. His blue scythes carved a path through the winding trails left by summer boars.

Shifa's barks turned to yelps and had Kole tearing up a rise thick with brambles and lashing spines. The Ember cleared the crest, bursting into the embattled clearing with a brilliant flash. These were the Dark Kind he knew well, the gnashing beaks and whipping tails eclipsing the white patches in the center as the hound fought amidst the talons. His blades knew them as well, and they fell smoking before the next pair of humanoid shadows approached.

He carved these as well, racing into the next thicket and trusting Shifa to keep up. The forest thinned as narrow rivers became more plentiful, interrupting the mossy plateaus, and he knew before he cleared the final copse that he had erred. Even without the Sentinel to guide them, the Corrupted had herded him farther east than he had imagined.

The rush of the river before him betrayed its size even before his eyes had mapped its contours over the white foam. The snarl of the Dark Kind mixed with Shifa's baying as she worked to keep them off Kole. In the distance, across the black and white mix of frothing water, Kole thought he glimpsed the glow of flame. He squinted, recognition dawning as the pale white of Hearth's walls resolved.

The image was stolen as quickly as it had arrived, as a much closer glow lit the opposite bank. An Everwood blade announced itself and the shadows there turned in. Shifa streaked into the open air trailing a warning and Kole spun, dodging enough to avoid claw but not bulk as he fell in a tangle, the cold hitting him like a blow as he plunged into pitch darkness.

He came up hacking and managed to snag the long grass of the opposite bank between his fingers and the steaming hilts of his doused blades. He hauled himself up an embankment and peered over the top. There, he saw twin shadows warding off a swarm of others in the light of Taei Kane's sword. Shifa scrambled up a smaller rise to the east and raced to join him.

As Kole rose and worked to reignite his blades, he heard his pursuers clawing their way up the bank. They could not win out.

There was only Hearth, with its white walls and glowing braziers, its stout defenders and roaring Embers. And the army massing at its base that made their desperate plight seem a skirmish.

CHAPTER NINETEEN

FIREFLY

A s the black head tumbled down from the spurting stump, mouth agape in that silent scream, Talmir knew they could not win.

He knew this just as he knew the sun would rise behind dark clouds again tomorrow. He knew it just as he knew the wars in the other lands would continue unabated until there were none left to tend the gardens of the World but fox and vole. He knew this, and still he fought.

Down below, huddled behind the timber-and-steel gate on which he stood, the great grandchildren of the desert peoples pressed back at the storm that assailed them. They were his children, mothers, grandmothers. They were his tinkers and greedy merchants, his grizzled smiths and moody cooks.

The dead had begun to pile on both sides of the wall, though the mounds without still far outstripped those within. It was something to be grateful for, but Talmir did not feel grateful.

They could not win. They would not win. They had to try.

The rain had long since abated, but the Captain was still drenched, some red mixing in with the salt that ran off his skin in rivulets as he rushed to and fro behind the great brazier of Garos Balsheer. The First Keeper roared his challenges and made good on every one, but even he was beginning to flag, and the swarm showed no signs of relenting. The distant Sentinels watched from their place along the tree line.

Talmir felt a tug on his sleeve and spun to see the small boy that had become his messenger frowning up at him.

"Jakub!" he yelled, glancing around wildly to make sure none of the Dark Kind had gained the walkway. "I swear, if you stood a head taller you'd be missing a head. I told you to pass reports up through Massen."

The mousey-haired boy frowned and pointed down to the base of the stair. Talmir saw a pair of soldiers hauling a twisted form—presumably Massen—away from the stonework and up toward the Red Bowl.

The macabre image did not have the sobering effect it might have just a week earlier, but Talmir let loose an involuntary sigh nonetheless and closed his eyes to offer a silent prayer.

"What is it, Jakub?" he asked, smoothing the edge from his voice as he squatted to the boy's eye level. A shadow gained the wall and a sword took it in the neck and sent it tumbling back before Talmir could react. He dimly recognized his savior as Karin Reyna and made a mental note to speak with him soon, his third such note in as many days.

"… his bed."

"Come again?" Talmir shook his head to clear the cobwebs.

Jakub favored him with a withering glare. He was quite adept at those.

"I said, Second Keeper Mit'Ahn is giving the healers trouble. He won't stay in his bed and is asking where his Everwood is."

Talmir chuckled despite himself.

"Thank you," he said. "No, I need—

"That's not all," Jakub said, indignant.

"Be quick about it, then," Talmir clipped, some of the edge returning. "It's not safe up here."

"Third Keeper Ve'Gah reports that it's quiet on the North Walk," he said. "She's asking to come here."

"You were on the North Walk?" Talmir asked, unable to hide his anger. "Jakub, I told you to stay below. The cliffs are steep and the White Guard isn't quite as accommodating as my men and women here."

Jakub only stared.

Talmir sighed again. It seemed he had one of those for every word now.

"I need Ve'Gah to keep her section. We knew the North Walk wouldn't be pressed, but we can't afford to leave the crags unguarded. The Dark Kind are stout climbers. These Corrupted even more so."

"Corrupted …" Jakub tasted the word. "They were like us?"

Talmir swallowed, trying not to think of the way the ink bled away when they cut the shadows down. Trying not to think of the pale, innocent flesh beneath. He shook the thoughts away and gripped Jakub's shoulder, his boney collar feeling like a bird's wing under his hand.

"After you've delivered the message, get yourself to the Bowl."

Jakub rolled his eyes and turned to leave, but Talmir spun him back around.

"Jakub," he said, deadly serious, and the boy's brown eyes widened slightly. "I mean it this time."

He gulped, turned, and sprinted toward the steep incline that marked the path to the North Walk, dodging the defenders as he went and teetering uncomfortably close to the edge on several occasions.

"He'll be fine," a voice said, and Talmir rose and turned to see Karin. The black-haired man was leaning against the parapet and wiping the ink from his blade, a short length of steel that seemed paltry compared to the spinning Everwood staff of Balsheer, which acted as their proxy sun in the gloomy chaos.

Talmir nodded and approached, looking out over the fields. The Dark Kind were pulling back, but it was merely the swell of a tide before the next wave broke. Still, it gave them precious time to change lines, exhausted soldiers being helped down from the South Bend as their moderately fresh replacements rose to relieve them.

The momentary respite allowed him to take stock of the First Runner of Last Lake. Although he had youthful features and long, healthy hair, the marks of tragedy were undeniable. Talmir knew the stories, and although everyone in the Valley had lost, Karin Reyna's loss had been something more. Without closure, there could be no healing. The man before him looked like a good man who'd been sipping poison for a decade and more.

"I had meant to speak with you sooner," Talmir said, extending his hand. Karin shook it firmly, displaying more strength than he had expected. "As you can see," Talmir swept his hand out to encompass the crowded fields beyond the walls, "I've been somewhat indisposed. As have you, it would seem."

"As far as excuses go, I suppose that one's as good as any."

"And you fishermen say we're the stiff ones," Talmir said. "Come, let's speak away from the battlements. We're getting in the way, though I know my soldiers won't dare say it." He guided Karin away from the crenellations and winked at a young woman moving past with a fresh cache of pitched arrows.

They stood at the base of the stair, keeping out of the way as wall hands rushed up and down, carrying weapons, water, oil and fuel for Balsheer's brazier. The sounds of battle were constant. Still, after a week or more of anything, Talmir supposed you learned to adjust.

"I must say," Talmir said, leaning in conspiratorially, "I never thought to see the walls tested like this. The people of Hearth like to cling to the fact that they've never fallen like it's some great thing. The truth is, we've never truly been tested, not by a force like this."

"It is said the white walls were constructed to withstand the Sages themselves," Karin said, his tone unreadable.

Talmir smirked and issued a laugh.

"Said, no doubt, by its architects. Well, our enemy has not made himself known, but we can guess easily enough. I suppose those claims will be put to the test soon enough."

Karin nodded and they both looked out over the tents in the courtyard, the torches guttering in the wind.

"It was easier to kill them before I knew what was beneath," Talmir said, earning a sympathetic look from the other man. "Before they were, well, us."

"Perspective," Karin said. "It's everything, and it's the one thing we can't perfect. The Emberfolk have largely come to think of this Valley as something of a prison, a hole to die in. But this is a grand place, with life teeming to the brim. It's more full than the northern deserts ever were, but ask any here where they'd rather be."

The main gate shuddered under an impact—a barrel of oil dropped too close—and the iron chains rattled and sent splinters down to wake the soldiers in the tents below.

"I know it isn't easy," Talmir said after a time and Karin turned those watchful, tired eyes his way. The Captain regarded him with sincerity. "Fighting away from your home, cut off from your loved ones. You came to warn us, or to report back to the Lake in case your warning came too late."

"We are all Emberfolk," Karin said. He looked as though he wanted to say more.

"And we're running out of Embers," Talmir said, his tone shifting in a way that caught Karin off guard. "I've heard, Karin. I heard about the expedition to the peaks—a fool's quest with most of the Lake's brightest stars. And I heard about your son."

"When I set out," Karin said, voice barely above a whisper, "he was improving. The Sentinel's barbs were no longer entrenched so deeply in his mind. He will endure."

"He's made of strong stuff," Talmir said.

"He is his mother's son."

There was a silence between them, and even the din of battle seemed to fade, a restless ocean in the background.

"The seeds were sown with her death," Karin said, his eyes faraway. "She made for the passes, gained the Steps and sought out the White Crest. She died there, and Kole saw her fall in his dreams, the flames snuffed out in her only to awake in him soon after. For a time, I doubted him and pushed his dreams aside, too lost in my own grief. But then Mother Ninyeva shared her visions with me. They matched his."

Talmir waited for him to continue. He had only met Sarise A'zu in passing, but her reputation was well earned. When the Dark Kind had first come spilling into the Valley in force, hers was one of the brightest flames holding them back.

"I think," Karin continued, "I think something changed in Kole after she died. Something changed in all of our children. They've grown up in war."

Talmir could not help but glance at the rushing soldiers under his command, reminded once again how much their stern visages clashed with the soft skin of youth.

"They want something more," Karin said. "And they want to take it for themselves, even if it means challenging the Sages. Sometimes I think Kole and his own would take on the legions of the World Apart if they could."

"They may yet get the opportunity," Talmir said with a bitter laugh. "This has to be something close."

Karin regarded him, eyes clearing as the haze of memory passed like a spirit.

"The group you speak of must have left shortly after I did."

"By accounts, Larren Holspahr leads them."

"No," Karin challenged, shaking his head slowly, brows knitting together. "No, Holspahr leads in name only. Kole may have inherited something like his mother's fire, but Linn Ve'Ran is the closest thing I've seen to her will."

"And what of us?" Talmir asked, as much to the swirling gray skies as to the First Runner. "Do we merely sit idle, waiting for our roving band of heroes to bring us the head of one Sage or another and end this blight?"

"There is only one who flirts with the power of the World Apart."

"Yes," Talmir said. "I know. And it's one they have no hope of defeating. If he's truly come for us in earnest, then our only hope is to endure."

"Endure," Karin mouthed.

The silence had no space to settle this time, as a horn sounded, ripping Talmir from his contemplations and sending icy shards through his blood. They were completely besieged and in the direst of straights. What could possibly be cause for alarm? Could Tu'Ren have come? What of the Rivermen and their Rockbled, or perhaps the Faey?

The horn sounded again as he made his way up the stairs, Karin passing him in two leaping strides. The Captain's heart was gripped by a sickening combination of dread horror and that more deadly poison: hope. He reached the gate panting and stopped the young lad from putting horn to lips for a third blow. The Dark Kind scrambled up the walls with renewed vigor, the Corrupted souls opening their black maws in those noiseless wails as the clear, echoing notes whipped them into a frenzy.

"What is it, son?" he shouted at the startled scout. "We're having a hard enough time as it is. What could possibly—

"Oh."

At first, it looked like a firefly, dancing and buzzing at the edges of a meadow with darkness all around. There were two lights lashing back and forth in sharp arcs, the Dark Kind parting before them before closing back in behind like whirlpools.

"What is it?" Talmir asked, knowing the answer even as he asked.

"Embers," Karin said. "Embers in the fields."

The ice settled in thick around Talmir's heart. There were Embers in the fields. And he could not open the gate.

———◆◆◆———

If Kole was the prow of the ship then the twins were his sails, Fihn's silver blade the lightning strikes amidst Taei's red storm. Kole's twin Everwood blades were a single, whirling thing. He parted the sea of Dark Kind and left the remnants to the allies at his back like flotsam.

Taei and Fihn Kane moved as if in a shared trance, while Shifa was Kole's constant shadow, the only one not seeking to part his head from his shoulders. When he began to slow, his blades drawing much of his strength, the twins bore him up in their wake, Taei's flames augmenting his own. They came to a shallow depression in the middle of the field, a trench formed by a dry riverbed, and when they came up on the other side, the twins were in the lead. Kole turned to form the rear guard.

He dared any of the shadow men to make a try for him. Many did.

They splashed into one of the myriad shallow streams and it almost ended there. Taei lost his footing, his blade going out as he fell in a torrent of foam and steam. Fihn reached in to pull him out, cursing all the while, and Kole put his flames into a spirited defense, his legs burning, hands working in a violent blur.

They came up on the other side of the trench and although Taei managed to get his blade going again, it was clear that he was tiring. Shifa was the only one whose pace never slowed.

A horn sounded up ahead. It was a bright, clear note that clashed with the permanence of the ruddy night. It sounded again, and Kole spared a glance. Through the hazy blur of his blades he glimpsed the white shell, silver-tipped spears glittering on the battlements and red-roofed buildings cloistered in their nest. He saw the great black gate that stood stark and knew it could not be opened to them.

Another note sounded, but this one was a yelp of pain. Kole spun to see Taei clutching his side. Blood flowed freely, splashing and bubbling on the torn turf. Fihn stood over him as he dropped to one knee, silver blade going up like a crescent moon.

"Down!" Kole screamed. "Down!"

Fihn lost her sword and clutched her brother in the chaos. Kole shot toward them, his blades sending great arcs of flame out that burned black flesh like birch. The scar Linn Ve'Ran had left him burned on his cheek, and the pain drove him on, his vision blurring red and indistinct. His veins bulged and formed ridges along his arms and neck, the flames dancing along his black blades turning from orange to deep red flecked with crackling blue. The fire spread to his hands and curled around his elbows as he fought.

Some distant part of him heard Fihn crying out, her shielding of Taei changing hands as the wounded Ember wrapped her up and turned away from Kole's whirlwind. They cowered there before an elemental, and Kole later thought he heard the laughter from his dream. He thought it might have been his own. He tore through the Dark Kind and through the innocent flesh of the Corrupted like a tornado through a fallow mire.

His head swam as he heard the twins retreat at his back and he was dimly aware of the sound Shifa's claws made on the timber and chains as the gate began its protesting ascent. The smoke spread but would not clear, the flames eating hungrily on the field of corpses he'd made. He thought the black-pitted eyes beyond stared at him with something approximating fear, and the telltale glint of the Sentinels' blood reds faded back into the distant trees when he chanced to look their way.

Hooves clattered and clomped on the cobbles within and squat steeds, brown and white, issued forth from the city. The twins were pulled up, Fihn sobbing silently as Taei cooed, and Kole turned his back on the black tide and let the flames go out as he passed under the arch.

The gate shut behind him with a strange echo.

CHAPTER TWENTY

POWER

"He has been waylaid at Hearth."

Rusul said it and then took a long drag on her bone pipe, some product of a horned runner of the Untamed Hills. She held it in for a spell before releasing the milky vapor in a billowing plume.

Ninyeva wrinkled her nose. She was well versed in pungent odors and so she did not complain, but the Seers and the Faeykin produced their sight with contrasting methodologies and that was doubly true for the ingredients they used.

The Faey Mother stood in the dimly lit common room Rusul shared with her sisters in Eastlake. Outside, the establishment was a strange tangle of ramshackle brick and mortar. Inside, what some might describe as cozy, others would consider stuffy bordering on stale. The floorboards were bent and sloping and the walls peeling due to the constant presence of moist vapor. Worst of all, the ceiling was low and no fresh air snaked its way in from stack or pane.

More so than the confines, however, it was the underlying smell that insulted Ninyeva. It was faint, but deep and pervading, seeping into everything like a rot. It was the smell of old blood and it made her want to scrub her pores.

"Apologies," Rusul said, tipping the pipe and spilling the ashes into a ceramic bowl. "I need something to settle."

Ninyeva raised a corner of her mouth and nodded.

"You don't seem surprised about Reyna's whereabouts."

"It's been a month full of surprises. Each is more mundane than the last."

Rusul searched her face and shrugged.

"Reyna's location may not be surprising," Rusul said, setting her pipe down, "but the manner of his arrival was … something."

"Something."

"Indeed."

It was clear that Rusul was trying to gauge how much Ninyeva knew, which—at least as far as scrying was concerned—was very little. The Faeykin could travel the roads of the Between. They were not limited by time or space, but the desert Seers like Rusul and her sisters had an edge where it concerned seeing as most understood it.

"The Seers of the Sand—Oracles, as they used to be known—have long held themselves apart from mortal affairs, as you know," Rusul said.

"You are mortal, and you are a far cry from the Oracles of old," Ninyeva clipped as she settled down on the dusky carpet.

Rusul's lips formed a tight line.

"What have you to tell me?" Ninyeva asked without pretense. "What was the manner of Kole's arrival to Hearth?"

"My words have relevance," Rusul said without humor. Ninyeva motioned for her to continue.

"The Oracles were wiped out in the wake of an Ember King's blind rage," Rusul said, wincing at the imagined memory. "King Kaizul. Do you remember why he did this?"

"His son Mena'Tch visited the Oracles," Ninyeva droned. "They told him that no Ember living or yet to live would possess his power—no Landkist in the wider world, for that matter."

"And in exchange for their prophecy, what did they ask?"

"For Mena'Tch to kill the Sages. Every one. It did not go well for him."

"But not because of the Sages," Rusul said, leaning forward. "He never got his opportunity to test himself against them before his father, the king, came for him."

"Some believe that. Others believe he failed in his first attempt, falling to the Sage of Balon Rael."

"The latter is the popular telling," Rusul said. "Something passed down from those who believe in the power, if not the goodness of the Sages. The former is the truth. It was Mena'Tch's wife who betrayed his plans to the King of Ember. To save his people the retribution of the Sages, Kaizul committed a grave sin. After killing his son in his sleep, he took out his anger on the Oracles, my forebears."

"I fail to see the relevance," Ninyeva said. The crows were more verbose than their namesake. Ninyeva was not a patient woman; she merely played one when she wanted to.

"There are any number of ways to find relevance. For instance, the Oracles saw their deaths in the flames, so they hid away their young."

"A line from which you and yours claim to descend."

"That was the smaller of Kaizul's mistakes," Rusul said, ignoring the barb.

"The greater was in eliminating a power capable of challenging the Sages, as no Ember Keeper was before or has been after."

"Our own King of Ember was more formidable than you know," Ninyeva said, bristling.

"And he fell to the Eastern Dark."

Ninyeva grumbled, but it was the truth.

"The Seers of this Valley have long subscribed to the notion that the White Crest was an exception among his kind," Rusul said, her eyes taking on a glazed quality. "Now I wonder."

It was a surprising admission.

"And your sisters?" Ninyeva asked and Rusul's brows turned up.

"Do you see them present?"

Ninyeva settled back and the two eyed each other with something approaching respect.

"I know I've been rambling," Rusul said, and her seeming vulnerability made Ninyeva at once suspicious and touched. She searched out the feelings, her eyes glowing faintly, and found not a hint of deception therein. "I only wished to preface the scene we witnessed with the information I felt most pertinent."

"You feel the Legend of Mena'Tch is a pertinent story to Kole's having arrived at Hearth?" Ninyeva asked, eyes widening.

For all her faults, Rusul was a strong woman. Seeing her in such a compromised state was unsettling. Ninyeva had not noticed how haggard she looked upon entering. Now, it was impossible not to see.

"What did you see, Rusul?" she asked. She almost wanted to reach out, but refrained.

"I do not know what Mena'Tch looked like," Rusul said, "but I now think I know what power he possessed. I saw it in the fields of Hearth, in one of our own. I saw it in Kole Reyna."

"Tell me," Ninyeva whispered, images from her own travels in the Between playing out in her mind's eye.

"We saw much. My sisters are still recovering. We saw the dark army—yes, an army, not the faceless and formless packs—surrounding the walls of Hearth. We saw the broken husks and homes of the Rivermen along the Fork, but no bodies. We saw Night Lords or something like them sheltering in the trees and sneaking among reeds in the swamps near the Deep Lands. We could not penetrate the peaks with our sight, and just when we were about to withdraw ..."

She hesitated.

"Yes? Go on."

Rusul looked up, eyes wide.

"We thought it was the sun suddenly returned, breaking through the black clouds. It was that bright. It was him. It was Kole Reyna, fighting his way through the Dark Kind as if they were dried weeds to be burned out. Virena thought it was Mena'Tch himself, or the King of Ember returned. But it was Reyna."

An image of Sarise A'zu.

Had it been concern for her people that had driven her to the peaks in search of the White Crest those years ago? Or had it been something in her blood? Something of prophecy. Ninyeva saw much of her in Kole, much more than his father Karin. She remembered that vision in the rain. She remembered the shadows that had come against her, and how long she had stood. She remembered thinking the flames had been augmented by the viewing glass of the Between, but now she wondered.

And another image sprang into her mind, one from the same night. When she had gone to Karin, Kole had been overtaken by thrashing nightmares, turning his entire bedroom into an approximation of Towles' Steam House. She had never seen anything like it.

"Bloodlines do not guide the awakening of Landkist," Ninyeva said, trying to convince herself as much as Rusul. "Not in these lands or any other. Not in the desert."

Rusul merely relit her pipe, her decorum lost in the stress of their exchange and the strain of reliving her travels.

"Do you think this a bad thing?" Ninyeva asked, surprised at the question. "This power within Kole?"

"He's on our side," Rusul said with a shivering shrug. She breathed the pipe weed in deeply and exhaled threw her nostrils, the tendrils forming a fading dress around her crossed legs.

"But ..."

"For a long time," Rusul said with a sigh, "we looked to the White Crest as an exception among his kind. Perhaps he was. Either way, he was a power we could look to in the absence of our king. We have powerful Embers, more powerful than any of the Landkist in the Valley, but their Everwood blades would be pale candles to the Eastern Dark. Perhaps Kole could challenge him. But I cannot pretend that what I saw was a comforting thing. I don't think power like that is meant to bring comfort."

"Only change," Ninyeva said, nodding.

"You are hiding something from me," Rusul said, a bit of the familiar ice returning. "What is it?"

"My own sight works much differently than yours," Ninyeva said, choosing her words carefully. "I see shadows half-formed out of place and time. It takes time to separate the superfluous from the true."

She rose and brushed the lint from her robes.

"There is a power in the north," Ninyeva said. "That I know, but I am not ready to say it is our enemy returned. At least, not all of him. Now," she continued, cutting off further inquiry, "you say you saw much. Did you see Holspahr and the others?"

"We could not be expected to scan the woods themselves. Wherever they are, they're keeping quiet. And wherever they are, let's hope they keep it that way. None in that company has the power to stand up to a Sage, assuming it is one of the Six come against us."

Ninyeva nodded and turned for the door. The air outside was cool and fresh, though ozone still tickled the tip of her nose, the threat of storm returning.

CHAPTER TWENTY-ONE

THE RIVER F'RUST

There had been a heavy blackness—a rushing that enveloped her completely. It dragged her down and guided her over jagged spurs and smooth knobs, which tore at her skin and clothes and set her muscles and bones to ring. She was acutely aware of the air that remained in her lungs and guarded it like a jealous drake.

The water dragged her down into the guts of the mountains, where it no doubt thought to kill her. The pain was blinding as the air burst out of her of its own accord, and the panic gave way to a dreamy sort of dying. Her head swam. Linn had never surrendered, but she considered it then.

She felt open air and gulped hungrily before the river tossed her unceremoniously into the guts of some primordial stomach carved from long-ago liquid fire. This time, the current slowed, and her feet touched down on rock and silt. She rocketed up and broke the surface, gasping and crying, and it felt like a second birth.

Linn could see, and that surprised her. Treading weakly at the surface, tired legs churning beneath her, she saw dim shafts of filtered light spilling in from a place out of sight. Something brushed against her arm and she yelled out before she recognized the creature to be none other than Jenk floating facedown in the black water. She worked to turn him over, but the river was not done with them and the current was picking up again, purchase impossible to find.

The lake narrowed ahead and it looked like blown glass dipping down as the current ate hungrily, forming small eddies and hills in the glittering obsidian surface. With a heave, Linn turned Jenk over, his light hair falling in tangles around a pale face, and together they rode the growing swells helpless and hapless. She pumped her legs furiously, but white caps formed on the water now, the river's strength redoubling as hers faded.

The roar of the impending falls drowned out her cries, both echoing and mixing as they bounced off of the cavern walls. To the right, a great length of smooth stone leered at them like a savior just out of reach, its surface dry and promising salvation. Her heart sank as they shot past, until she saw the drenched and worried face of Nathen Swell bracing to meet them on a lonely slab cut from the same piece further ahead.

"Push off!" Nathen screamed, likely for the tenth time, bloody hands cupped over his mouth to be heard over the rush. Linn tried, but her kicking found no stone and only served to send them into a chaotic spin.

"There!" he screamed, and Linn came back around, her heart catching in her throat as she saw a steep swell up ahead. It looked like the fin of some great leviathan, and though it could just as easily kill them, it marked their only hope.

Live.

The thought was a small, glowing thing at her center—the same that had compelled her to fight back against the Sentinel on the road. She had then and she would now.

The frothing spur shot toward them—or they toward it—and Linn braced, extending her legs forward and preparing for the shock of impact. When her feet struck, it was all she could do to keep Jenk from being torn from her grasp. She heard Nathen yelling, heard the roar of the falls and she despaired.

Until she heard Jenk breathing. As the current buffeted them on the near side of the stone, she pulled the Ember close and felt the heat of his breath on her ear, the rattle of phlegm in his chest. She concentrated on her legs, judging the distance between her and Nathen's promontory.

Hers were legs that had run down bucks under the trees. They were legs that acted as unmoving beams that rooted her to the wall as she fed slicing shafts to the Dark Kind. These legs did not shake when she learned of her parents deaths or saw the sheet fall from her father's face.

She met Nathen's eyes, and her steely look had him swallowing, his feet shuffling forward as he crept to the very edge of the plateau.

One moment to erase all others, and she shot across the breach. The current caught her around the knees and tilted her awkwardly, Jenk's prone form acting as an anchor she tried to drag with her. But Nathen caught her hand, his seafaring muscles bunching sickly at odds with his boyish features. He heaved and brought them both up, and she felt the cold obsidian rush up to meet her as she fell coughing onto its surface.

The panic took time to settle, and Linn pulled herself away from the rushing river as if it were a beast deprived of its prize. She squeezed her eyes shut, willing the spinning and throbbing to stop. When it did, she pushed herself up onto her knees and turned to see Nathen working over Jenk, his palms pressing furiously on the Ember's chest as water bubbled from his open mouth.

She thought Jenk lost, and the look on Nathen's face nearly confirmed it, until that look turned from horror to discomfort. The air shimmered around Nathen and the prone Ember like liquid. It bent and twisted like a mirror, and then the steam began to rise from him as the water was burned out of his lungs. His chest rose and fell at even intervals.

"Jenk," she choked, struggling to her feet and dragging herself forward. She kept a wary eye on the black current. Though its roar now seemed dulled, they were still far too close for her liking.

"Ve'Ran," Jenk wheezed, smiling up at them both. "Swell. I see the two of you made the trip in one piece."

Jenk appeared none the worse for wear, but the gash he had suffered on his scalp was a nasty thing, his hot blood doing little to close it in the chaos and exhaustion. Nathen drew a needle from the drenched pouch on his belt and tore a blue thread from his shirt, setting to work as Jenk winced.

"Now, now," Linn said, settling down gingerly onto her bruised tailbone. "You're an Ember of the Lake, Ganmeer. Don't let a fisherman's hook scare you when demons cannot."

"Fair enough," Jenk said through gritted teeth.

A short time later, Nathen pulled his shoulders back in a stretch. He stood and wrung out the remnants of the river from his shirt, a thread of which now adorned Jenk's bloody blonde hair with a streak of blue. Jenk sat up, and the three were silent for some time, the drone of the river the only conversation.

"Where are we?" Nathen asked. He looked to Linn and she to Jenk.

Jenk had his dark Everwood blade drying in his lap. Somehow, his sheath had held where theirs had not. Aside from a long knife Nathen had beside him on the stone, Jenk's was the only weapon between them.

The Ember raised his arms to encompass the view behind him. The high ceiling was lost in the filtered gloom that had now grown darker than before. The lake shone like a glittering black gem and the white spray of the river lapped hungrily at the glass shelves before tumbling down into the winding depths. To the right, there was something approaching a natural staircase, framed away from the curving river by a natural pillar that spanned the space from ceiling to floor.

"My children," he said, blowing out a sigh. "Welcome to the River F'Rust."

Nathen looked confused, while Linn's eyes widened.

"The river that was broken during the White Crest's battle with the Night Lords?" she asked, looking around in awe.

"The very same that feeds the waters of the Fork. Though, you can never truly break a river, only redirect it. Looks like this one retreated down. Our great grandparents likely walked along its shores when they first entered the Valley."

Nathen looked embarrassed.

"I wasn't raised on the Lake," he said by way of apology. "The folk in the Scattered Villages aren't much for history lessons."

Linn nodded. She knew the folk in the villages, though Emberfolk by blood, had largely cast off their histories. She could not say she blamed them.

"We need to get moving," Jenk said. "This is the River F'Rust, or some spawn of it. If we follow it, we should be able to find our way to the Steps above."

"It's no wonder," Linn whispered, and the others regarded her. "It's no wonder Baas and his own fear the Deep Lands. There aren't any Night Lords lying in wait for us—no Sages prowling the depths. But think of how many of his folk must have fallen in the battle. The Rivermen weren't named by mistake. The passes were their lands before the Breaking of the Valley."

The caverns took on a new light, the echoing sounds of the water crashing discordantly, like voices. Nathen shivered and Linn felt foolish for having said anything.

She rose and checked herself over, noting few cuts but myriad bruises that had purpled her flesh. As she turned, she noted Jenk's roving look and strange expression.

"Nothing like that," Jenk said, holding up his hands as he gained his feet. "It's just, seeing the state you're in, I can only imagine how I look."

"I'll manage," Linn said. "I imagine you will too."

Nathen rolled out his pack, revealing their meager stores. They ate the soggy bread immediately, since it would not keep another day, and distributed the thin strips of dried meat. In the silence of preparation, Linn could not help but replay the scene in the cave. She heard Kaya's breaking and wondered how long Baas could have lasted against the Sentinel wearing Holspahr's skin. Judging by their expressions, the others were thinking along the same lines.

"Where to next?" Nathen asked. It would have been funny if his easy demeanor was not just a pale mask. Linn smiled at him anyway. If ever there was a time for masks, this was it.

"For starters," Jenk said, "it looks like we're going down."

He pointed behind the two of them to the sloped chute that carved half a hollow from under the pillar. Jenk took the lead, but kept his blade doused for the time being. There was still enough of the filtered light to see by, spilling down through the cavernous heights and following them into neighboring chambers that broke off from the guts of the subterranean lake.

"That light has to be coming from somewhere," Nathen said.

"I'd imagine the sky," Jenk quipped.

"The sky is black," Linn said, and the three of them stopped dead in their tracks. "Wherever it's coming from, it has to be above the clouds."

The revelation propelled them onward, and they took comfort in each other rather than dwelling on what might lie in wait above or below. They walked for a day and more, and the light faded, the sloping caverns traveling down along the thickest sections of the river rather than up. For the most part, they managed to keep their course, following the flow by walking on shelves alongside or crossing the river. Linn never looked at the black water for long.

There was nothing soft in the Deep Lands. No moss grew along stalactites or stalagmites. No animals skittered in the darkness. Their journey was beginning to remind Linn of being on the inside of a massive nest of coral, only one devoid of life. It was place for ghosts and bones. She thought of Iyana and how her younger sister would collect the dried pieces of white and pink from the shore and line them on her windowsill.

If there was one benefit to the exhaustion they all felt, it was that it let them sleep anywhere and at any time. She could not speak for Jenk and Nathen, but for Linn, the fatigue also served to keep the nightmares at bay, picking at her from the edges but rarely stepping into the light. She hoped it would last and felt guilty for it, the faces of Kaya, Baas and Larren passing like shadows behind her eyelids.

She woke to the sound of rushing and the furious beating of her own heart. Though it was cool, she was sweating. This rush was not the sound of gentle running they had followed for hours the previous day, but the concussive roar that had swept them along its thrashing currents and nearly drowned them. For an instant, Linn thought it was the confusion and haze of waking, but as she stilled her breathing, she listened closer.

It had not been long, but Linn felt as though she knew the River F'Rust as if it were a living thing. She knew its moods and dispositions. This was a drum of anger, the steady pounding of the river against the bowels of the broken peaks that formed its prison.

Linn rose and drifted toward the back of the small cavern in which they rested. She reached the back wall and placed her palm on the black stone. It was slick with wet, soaked through and thrumming like a bird's wings. It was pitch dark, Jenk unable to keep his blade going without wasting precious reserves, so she navigated by touch.

She yelped as her right hand passed through the space where the wall should have continued. Luckily, the fall was not far, her hands scrabbling for purchase as the bottom of a small tunnel reached up to greet her. The sound was magnified here and the air less stale.

Nathen and Jenk were up in a rush, their feet slapping on the stone. A flare burned up the darkness and had Linn yelping again, this time for the shock as the light hit her eyes.

"I'm fine," she said, holding up a hand to ward off the yellow light. "More than fine, actually."

"What is it?" Jenk asked. "What did you find?"

"The way up."

CHAPTER TWENTY-TWO

A Cold Hearth

As it had so many times before, the dream marked his passage into sleep just as it ushered his way into waking. It was the same dream Kole had been having since he was nine. It was a dream of his mother.

Sarise A'zu was surrounded by shadows in a strange, wind-swept land of rocky crags and misty peaks. She bled from a dozen wounds, weakened from a hundred slashes and bruised from scores of staggering blows. But she fought, drawing the flames from the air itself when her twin blades broke and tumbled into the swirling clouds below.

The dream had grown clearer as of late, the shadows resolving themselves into forms more distinct, more horrible. Even his mother's face, which he had never forgotten, grew lighter. It was stern and beautiful. Just as she always did, Sarise burned all of the shadows away, the Dark Kind fleeing before her wrath. This was where the dream usually ended and the confusion set in.

She had killed them all. They were ashes in the wind and rain. But there had been another. Until now, it had been a presence, like a feeling on the edge of seeing. Now, he saw the white robes fluttering like wings, and he saw Sarise standing at the heart of her flames, her eyes piercing and chin up. She looked like defiance, mouthing words he could not hear.

For a long time, Kole thought the flames she conjured from her bare hands were an invention of his subconscious. Now, he was not so sure. Not after what he had witnessed before the walls of Hearth. Not after what he had done.

Did all Embers possess such latent power? Did Tu'Ren? Larren?

It seemed impossible, but seeing that his body felt like a burned-out husk and his head pounded like he had drunk nothing but mulled wine for a week, he supposed there were reasons to keep from finding out. There was another, but it was beyond his reckoning at present, dangling just behind his conscious mind.

He swept his legs over the edge of the cot, his feet touching the cold stone of the barracks floor with a shock. Captain Caru's chambers were sparse and modest, the light limited to the blue nightglow issuing from a lone square window and the dull red flicker of the dying embers in the grate. He crossed to the fireplace and dug his fingers into the ashes, communing with the burning nuggets within. Though they were loath to give up their heat since it meant their deaths, they did so for the Landkist of the deserts.

Kole breathed deep and rose, feeling stronger than before. He felt his blood run hotter as it passed through his heart and into his aching limbs, where it warred with and ultimately annihilated the pain. He put on the clothes that had been laid out for him and tied his harness, eyes widening when he noted the scars and cracks along his Everwood blades. It was said such weapons, properly treated, could survive a thousand battles. How hot, then, had those fields become? It was all too hazy for him to remember.

There was a stairwell—stone, like everything else in the barracks—and Kole took the winding way to a pine door at the bottom. He passed into what had been the mess hall two days before, which now resembled a makeshift infirmary. It surprised him to see the wounded soldiers belting on swords by the wall, checking over their weapons. These were not the grievously wounded, then, but merely those taking their rest between shifts.

They glanced but did not stare. Only one, a small boy with eyes darker than his hair, watched from the doorway, gaze unwavering. He followed Kole out onto the street, where a light mist greeted him along with the bravest hound in the Valley. Shifa jumped at him, whining enough to draw eyes.

"There, girl," Kole said, patting her wet flanks as the boy watched. He supposed he was some messenger working on behalf of the Captain. He certainly lacked subtlety.

Kole made his way west, his two followers taking up his gait at waist-height. The braziers still burned, casting their red glow onto everything, the armored soldiers resembling rubies in the dusk. The clouds had rolled in even thicker than before, blanketing the skies to the far horizon.

Talmir Caru was not at the gate, nor was he on the battlements. Kole walked them, the boy dogging his heels determinedly. The Dark Kind still churned en masse below, black shapes pouring indistinct from the distant trees. There would be no end to them, Kole knew, but Hearth's defenders threw them back, wave after wave, faces matching the steel of their helms.

"Looking for the Captain, boy?" a booming voice that he at first mistook for Tu'Ren's shook him. He turned to see a man that stood a head shorter than the First Keeper of Last Lake, which still made him a head taller than Kole. His broad chest nearly doubled Tu'Ren's.

"First Keeper Balsheer," Kole said, extending his hand, palm up. He had never met the man, but who else would it be? Who else carried a weapon that was more fallen oak than staff? The ends had been dipped in iron and still glowed a dull red.

Garos switched the mighty weapon to his left shoulder, soldiers nearly diving out of the way as the hot stone passed overhead, and extended his right hand, grasping Kole by the wrist. They each flared a bit during the embrace, and Garos smirked, raising one brow.

"No wonder," Garos said, releasing him, and Kole did not ask what he meant.

"You're holding, then," Kole said, looking out over the field and taking stock of the wall as it sloped up toward the cliffs.

"Well enough," the First Keeper said. "Not that it matters much."

They considered one another, and Kole was acutely aware of the black, broken earth leering up at them from the space below the gate. Garos noticed.

"You've given the lads on the gate a reprieve, at least," he said, all good humor. "That was some light show. Your flames nearly took down the gate. I had to put a bit of my own stuff into them to keep them off." His look changed then. It was only for a moment, and then the easy humor returned, but Kole thought it was something like fear.

"The Captain will want to see you," Garos said, color rising to his cheeks.

"My companions—

"Healing," Garos clipped. "Right now, you'd best meet with the Captain. Were you not supposed to tell him so?" he asked, looking over Kole's shoulder to where the dark-haired boy stood by the top of the stair, Shifa sitting near. The boy bristled and started forward, and Garos raised both brows at Kole.

"That one's a spitfire," Garos said, "no matter what he looks like."

"What would pull Captain Caru away from the wall at such a time?" Kole asked as the boy began tugging at his sleeve.

"I've heard it said that in other lands, war is profit," Garos said. He turned and swept his free arm out to encompass the dark ocean before the walls, which stood like the caps of waves. "Not this sort of war. You folk of the Lake have your fish. You keep to the old ways. I respect that." He turned back, his smile falling to one less enthusiastic. "Hearth is the engine that makes the Valley turn. Here, the man who wields the quill is more influential than he who wields the flame."

"I imagine he thinks so," Kole said, spitting and drawing a throaty laugh from the barrel-chested Ember.

"Off with you then," Garos croaked out, waving his hand as if he were shoeing a fly. "Jakub, off with you. Take him to see the wielders of ink and parchment. Take him to the Merchants, and do bring back our Captain if he still lives. Your father is there as well."

Kole only remembered flashes of having spoken with Karin when he first entered the city with the twins. He had to get north, but seeing the state Hearth was in, it seemed as though that road was closed to him. As First Runner of the Lake, perhaps Karin would know a way.

Of course, there were other reasons to want to speak with his father. The dream had yet to fade from his mind. It had stuck there like a jagged stone in a mire. But father and son rarely spoke of such things. If there were to be a time, however, Kole thought it might be now.

Kole allowed himself to be dragged away. As they walked, he reflected on how strange it was that he knew so little of how Hearth worked despite living in the Valley his entire life. But then, traveling the roads and ways was only safe in the Bright Days. In the distant past, the Dark Months had merely held the small possibility of encroachment as the World Apart drew closer to their own. As the packs had turned to swarms and now the swarms to armies, the Bright Days had changed from periods of celebration to preparation.

The Emberfolk were tribal by nature, Kole knew from the tales from the desert. According to Ninyeva, Hearth and Last Lake were actually more intertwined than the various tribes had been in the north. The Scattered Villages of the Valley were a more apt representation of their former communal habits. Kole wondered how those villages were faring right now. He wondered how many of the army come against them carried the blood of the Valley peoples and how many had been victims from other lands.

An image of the burned and broken earth before Hearth's gate came up like bile. He noted now what he had skimmed over during his talk with the First Keeper: the twisted limbs poking out from the ash and dirt, black paint all washed away to leave pale skin where the fire had not reached.

And then he heard it. Fihn's screaming amidst the flames. He heard it as if for the first time, and it made him double over in the middle of the courtyard, struggling not to retch as soldiers watched him and made their private judgments. His vision blurred, clearing a bit as Shift moved into his line of sight, whining softly. He noted the boy's muddy boots.

"Jakub," Kole said, straightening a bit. "I need to see my friends. Take me to them."

The boy known as Jakub frowned, shaking his head slowly.

"Captain Caru," he said in a rough voice at odds with his appearance. He could speak, then.

"Yes," Kole said, standing up straight and wiping the drool from his bottom lip. "In time. But now, take me to the sick and wounded. Take me to my friends."

Jakub shook his head again, looking panicked this time, as if he feared retribution. Kole thought he might fear the Captain, but everything he had heard of Talmir painted him as a thoughtful and kind figure, if a little stern. Was it Kole the boy feared?

"No," Jakub said, repeating it several times as he shook his head back and forth.

Kole sighed.

"Very well, then," he said, closing his eyes. "Lead on. First to Captain Caru and my father, and then," he emphasized the last, "to my friends."

Jakub almost smiled then and took off at a walk that bordered on a run. This caused Shifa great stress, as she doubled back continuously, barking at Jakub to halt for a spell as Kole strode through the cobbled streets, staring in wonder at the city he had only been in as a child and held no memory of.

They walked a wide street that sloped steadily upward, as all roads in Hearth did. Unlike the rural brown roads of Last Lake, those here were inlaid with flat stones that grew slick in the mist. They allowed for the easy passage of carts and other wheeled contraptions, many of which now sheltered under dripping awnings.

Where the homes and buildings of the Lake were largely horizontal, Hearth's confining walls had forced new construction up. It was like a forest of odd replicas of Ninyeva's own tower, one leaning in on the other, the orange and red tints of the candlelit windows flashing their own brand of beauty.

"Where is the meeting place?" Kole called out, and while Shifa's white tufts perked up, Jakub's barely twitched. Kole sighed.

As he walked, his thoughts could not help but turn back to the dream, and, curiously, to the Faey Mother. Kole had stated his intention to venture north to the peaks after the great ape had breached their timber walls. Ninyeva had not openly championed him, but she had certainly not stood in his way. He remembered the night his mother had died. It was the first night he had the dream, and he woke to find the Faey Mother in their home, consoling a father gone mad with grief.

Did she know of the White Crest's presence? Did she know what Kole planned to do if he found him?

None of it had ever made any sense to Kole. After all, the White Crest was thought to have fallen in battle against the Eastern Dark. Even if he hadn't, why would he turn against the people he had sworn to protect? Perhaps it truly was the Eastern Dark he saw all shrouded in light.

Kole tried to cast the thoughts away like a rotted cloak, but they would not quit. He tried to turn his mind to Linn and the others, but his heart simmered, calling for the same thing it had for over a decade: revenge.

Kole felt a tug on his sleeve and looked down to see Jakub, his expression irate. He had slowed too much for the boy's patience, whose tugging only ceased when Shifa tested a growl low in her throat. Jakub's worst fears of dalliance were about to be realized, as a figure broke the plane from road to sky, his profile framed in the light of a neighboring tavern.

The figure stood a bit shorter than Kole, but he may as well have been looking at an aged mirror. Karin's face broke into a broad smile, white teeth showing. He came down the slope in a gait lighter than matched the mood of the city, but for now, all that mattered was their embrace. Shifa wagged her tail and barked excitedly, while Jakub was the picture of frustration, his arms crossed as his mission experienced an unexpected delay.

Karin pushed his son to arm's length.

"You're looking none the worse for wear," he said, looking Kole up and down. "I know he's late," he tossed over his shoulder to Jakub, "but I thought it important to catch him before he entered that pit of vipers." He smiled at Kole, but now it was the strained look he knew so well. "Come," and he took Kole by the shoulder and turned him east, continuing up the rise.

Jakub skipped off ahead, weaving in and out of passers-by with Shifa close at his heels. He never let Kole out of his sight, but their forward progress seemed to have appeased him some.

As they crested the rise, the streets grew thicker with traffic. Men and women very young and very old went about their business, but there was undoubtedly a note of panic to their movements. Karin watched him.

"This attack is unlike any other," Karin said. "They go about their days as if the dark tide will recede, as it always has."

"It won't," Kole said.

"No. It won't."

They walked in silence for a spell, watching Jakub and Shifa disappear and reappear in the snaking crowds as the land began to slope steadily downward.

"I'm wasting time," Kole said.

"You're lucky to be alive," Karin answered, more sternly than was usual. "I did not make for Hearth until I was certain you were on the mend. Even so, I never thought you'd be fool enough to leave the Lake in the state you're in—in the state we're all in."

"I'm fine. You said so yourself."

Karin stopped dead in his tracks and Kole turned to regard him. His father had closed his eyes, squeezing them tight and clenching his knuckles at his sides. Jakub and Shifa paused farther ahead, but they held their peace.

"Kole," Karin started. "Which one is this for, this quest of yours?"

"Which one?" Kole asked, incredulous. "It's for all of us."

"What is?" his father sounded exasperated, desperate even. "You're going to take on the Eastern Dark yourself? You're going to fight the Sages?"

"I'm going to fight whoever's responsible," Kole said, his tone a challenge.

From their position on the hill, they could see straight to the walls, Garos's glowing brazier lighting the crenellations, the churning fields beyond alive with movement. Kole swept his hand out.

"This isn't the Dark Kind," Kole said. "This isn't some random incursion from the World Apart." He pointed up at the sky, at the roiling clouds overhead. "That is the work of them," he said, nearly shouting.

Some of the traffic slowed or stopped around them, but he did not care. "You know it is."

As he finished, he felt a pang of guilt. His father's anger had blown out, leaving him barren. He looked at Kole with nothing but love and the fear that came with it.

"Linn, or your mother?" he asked, stepping closer. "Which one are you going for?"

Kole's mind worked, steam rising from his skin as the mist grew thicker.

"Linn," he said, not knowing if it was the truth. "They're out there now. Out there," he pointed beyond the walls. "And I'm here."

Karin nodded and took his son by the shoulder. "They need as many as can be spared here."

"I can't be spared," Kole said.

"I know."

There was another pause, but Jakub was relieved to see them continue on, taking the slope down into the Bowl that made up the central market of Hearth.

"You looked like an Ember of old out there," Karin said, keeping his voice low. "Even the Dark Kind, or the Corrupted—whatever the wretched things are—seemed stunned. They backed off from the walls for half a day, and none have tried for the gate since, something that's been irking Balsheer."

"The twins, father," Kole said past the lump in his throat.

"Taei is fine," he said.

"And Fihn?"

"Less so, but she will recover."

"How bad?" Kole asked, a hint of desperation in his voice. "I should see her."

"No. Not now. There are several Faeykin here. Some trained under Ninyeva at the Lake and others under the Faey of the Eastern Valley. They'll have her back soon enough."

"Would that Iyana were here."

"If she were, do you really think you'd make it out of Hearth?"

Kole found himself chuckling despite the mood.

"I take it that means you won't try to stop me?"

Karin paused.

"I doubt very much if I could. But I have to be honest, Kole. I don't know if the answers are in the north."

"They're not here."

"No, they aren't. But some are starting to see you as an answer, Kole. And they have more sway than I."

"This Merchant Council?" Kole nearly spat the words.

"The very same. You've been at the center of some bright events in all this darkness, son. People are starting to take notice. The leaders of Hearth have noticed, and they wonder if keeping you here might not serve our people better."

Karin continued to talk, telling his son of the Merchant Council's various members— what he knew of them, at least. His father was probably the most well traveled person in the Valley. It stood to reason he knew much and many. He seemed to have a great deal of respect for Captain Caru. It was strange, Kole thought, that he had no memory of meeting the man whose bed he had occupied the previous night. And there was another kernel of guilt, that Kole had slept once again as the Captain had defended his people.

As his father spoke, Kole was split between listening and seeing. Even now, in the midst of a siege out of nightmare, the central market of Hearth bustled with activity, and not all of it was concentrated on the wounded that occupied the great billowing tents. When compared to the open air of the lakes and forests to the south, the Red Bowl was a confused press and jumble, people rushing to and fro. Normally, they would be peddling their wares, but now, merchants were replaced by physicians, some of them sporting the glowing greens of the Faeykin. Instead of baubles, they carted the wounded, groaning and grasping.

On the battlefield, the scents of rot and mess were masked by ash and ozone, which covered the slow horrors beneath the fighting. Here among the sick, the rusted smell of blood covered the sweeter odor of infection. Where the Faeykin were too few to purge it, they used flame to burn it.

In all the years of war with the Dark Kind and in the sorry conflicts before, a sight like this had never been witnessed in the Valley.

Jakub's expression did not so much as quiver throughout their walk, the sick and wounded seeming apparitions to him. For some reason, it made Kole pity him for the childhood he had lost. In that moment, Kole felt thankful for his own, however fleeting it might have been.

After a time, they came to a looming structure carved of white stone. It was same rock that ringed the northern section of the city. Its gate was adorned with gold reliefs, and a bronze dome capped its central tower, albeit one caked with green decay as if it, too was wounded beyond saving.

As they passed the gates, which sat on the borders of the market, Kole studied the depictions. They marked an obvious attempt to pay homage to the Emberfolk of the desert, but they came off gaudy and strange. The interior was no better.

In Kole's experience, there was nothing in the Valley that could be considered ornate of a scale to match the stories of old. An antique tea set, perhaps, or maybe a carpet designed in the old way. Ninyeva had some of these things, as did Doh'Rah. Even Karin had an eye for art—silverware and the like. But the truly magnificent was reserved for the desert palaces that had passed into legend, where jewels adorned every handle on every door, the only things shining brighter than the sun above being the structures of its desert children below.

The inside of the Merchant Council's shared meeting place was not one of these structures, but he recognized an attempt when he saw one. If the myriad artistic styles on display—from the carpets ringing floor and wall to the murals on the flat ceiling—matched the egos he was about to endure, facing one Sage or another would seem nothing by comparison. In its own way, there was a sickness here that ran deeper than that festering in the tents outside.

Kole tried to lose the thoughts as they crossed to the bottom of a spiral stair. Mahogany steps ringed by a black rail curled up into the light of too many lanterns, and he bade Shifa sit at the base. Jakub glared at him, daring him to try the same.

Kole did not, but the boy stayed with Shifa anyway.

At the top, Karin opened a door that seemed older than the rest and ushered Kole into a shockingly modest den. In place of the lanterns ringing the stairwell, the whole affair was cast into a strange light from twin hearths on opposite walls. Faces turned to regard him that may as well have been masks for all he could read from them at a glance.

"Karin Reyna," a middle-aged man standing at the head of an oval table said. He carried himself with the bearing of a man at arms, and though he wore no formal mark of rank, Kole remembered him as the Captain of Hearth's white walls. "And his son, Kole Reyna."

Talmir Caru did not wait for a response from the assembled merchants and approached Kole with his hand extended.

"Welcome again," Talmir said in a low voice, sharing a conspiratorial smirk. "I know our first meeting may have been lost on you."

"There was a lot going on," Kole said, trying to sound more sure than he felt, which was distinctly uncomfortable. "Thank you for your hospitality."

Someone at the table scoffed, and Kole craned his head around to see a woman in white shaking her head, bemused, her raven-black hair swaying. She met Kole's stare and winked.

"If you think those chambers hospitable, my boy, you'd think mine were fit for the gods," she said, all silk.

"And how would you know the difference?" a peevish-looking man asked from her left. He wore a crooked lavender hat and no small degree of irritation.

The woman offered him a smile, though Kole noted a subtle shift in her eyes, a steeliness that seemed to make the older man squirm ever so slightly. Just as quickly as it appeared, however, the look was gone, replaced by a burst of girlish laughter.

"Oh, come now, Yush," she said. "We are all progressive here, are we not?" She looked back at Kole—looked him up and down. His martial mind attributed the roving of her eyes to an attempt at sizing him up, and his masculine side came to the same conclusion. "Though I am more progressive than most."

If the Captain was at all embarrassed by his sometimes-lover's display, he covered it well, leading Kole and his father over to the table, where Karin took the woman's proffered hand and offered a kiss.

"Rain," she said, reaching for Kole. He took it and gave it a squeeze, injecting a bit more heat than usual. She withdrew with a sharp yelp that turned into a chuckle.

"Rain Ku'Ral," she finished, shaking out her hand. She watched Kole with intense interest as Talmir made the rest of the introductions.

There was Yush Tri'Az, he of the purple hat. He was flanked by two female council members. Kole noted the way the three of them watched he and his father with keen interest, if not outright suspicion. He also noted their standoffish attitude toward the Captain.

Kenta Griyen was a thin man who looked as though he bore the collective weariness of all those gathered. He was the head physician and his eyes kept darting toward the door. Kole knew he would rather be helping his people than basking in the formality of a council meeting.

Aside from them, the final member of the council—or perhaps just an observer—was a man whose skin was darker than any Kole had seen, painting a stark contrast to irises that bore the burnt amber hue of overripe honey. Kole wondered if he was the exotic result of Emberfolk mixing with the Faey. Even from a distance, Kole could feel the heat radiating from the alcove in which he sat. He was an Ember, and a strong one.

"Allow me to introduce one of Hearth's staunchest defenders," Talmir said, indicating the quiet fellow. "Second Keeper Creyath Mit'Ahn. Without him, it is quite possible—probable, even—that the wall would have fallen a week ago."

One of the council members beside Yush scoffed, but it sounded not far off from a choke when Creyath flashed his too-white teeth in her direction. The low fire in the grate nearest him flared for a moment, and in the light, Kole could see that the Ember was wrapped around the chest in bandages. That explained his absence from the battlements, then.

"Yes, yes," Yush said, waving his hand, fingers waggling. "We're all very grateful we have brave men such as you to defend us, Mit'Ahn. Now let us get on to more pressing concerns."

"What concerns press more than the safety of our people?" Talmir asked, an edge in his tone, and Yush sputtered, his cheeks going red. "Besides, I only meant to introduce one Night Lord slayer to another."

Kole and Creyath considered one another once more, and Kole thought he saw the other man offer a slight nod. He returned it.

"Night Lord?" Yush whined. "Night Lords?" He held up his hands, looking from one face to the next as if he were at a loss. "The last of their ilk was slain by the White Crest in the passes a generation ago."

"Are you telling two Embers what they fought?" Talmir asked. "When you weren't there?"

"I needn't have been there!" Yush shouted. "Those were abominations. We are thankful you felled the beasts, but they were just that: beasts. They were not Night Lords. Not true ones, in any case."

"Perhaps not," Kenta said, his tone even as he considered Kole. "But formidable nonetheless."

He could not be sure, but Kole thought he had the room mapped out well enough. Yush and his lackeys made up one triangle, while Captain Caru seemed to have the respect, if not the open support, of the remaining pair. He was not sure if Creyath held sway here, since he did not appear to be a member of the Merchant Council. Now it only remained to be seen how Kole fit into the groups' respective plans, and how he could keep from fitting.

"We are gathered to make decisions," Talmir said, moving on from his spat with Yush. "The Valley is currently in the midst of the darkest storm it has ever witnessed. Take it literally or take it any way you like it. There it is. We've had no word from the Fork since the siege began, and we've seen strange faces amidst the Corrupted once the ink has drained away. Some are undoubtedly victims from the Scattered Villages, but many are foreigners."

"I fail to see the relevance—

"The relevance," Talmir cut in, "is that we have no way of knowing when this tide will end. Or if it will."

Kole could use that to his advantage.

"As for our brothers to the south," he glanced at Kole and his father, "Karin's report is the last we've received, but their position is decidedly more positive than the view from our balconies would suggest."

"Get to it, Talmir," Rain said, her tone more solid and resolute than it had been before. She stared at the Captain hard enough to make him flinch and swallow.

"I was standing on the gate when Kole Reyna, the young Ember you see before you, cut his way through the swarm to reach it," he said.

"I was not alone," Kole said meekly.

"No," Talmir allowed, looking at him before turning back to the table. "But he may well have been, for all the good it did the Dark Kind. I've never seen anything like it. That power. He was more an Ember King than a Keeper."

Kole blushed despite the mood.

"Forgive me," Yush started, raising his brows at Kole before switching his challenging stare on the Captain, "but how is he any different, any more potent, than First Keeper Balsheer, or even Mit'Ahn over there? What about Misha Ve'Gah? No doubt she'd have something to say about it."

"She wasn't there," Talmir said. "If you want the most accurate account, ask the earth before the gate, which is broken and scorched beyond anything I've seen. Truly, we are lucky he didn't bring the timbers down around him. He surely could have."

And now it was Kole's turn to swallow. This was the sort of talk he had been dreading. He began to steel himself for the inevitable argument. He would make it a short one. Direct.

"No," Talmir said, disgust evident. "Seeing that would bring you too close to the fighting."

"If Talmir Caru says it," Creyath spoke from his corner, "then it is so."

"Take my word or leave it," the Captain said. "But the truth remains. I have not seen a force so powerful in all my life."

"I saw," Kenta said. "I saw the white rocks spilling up from the broken earth like bones. I saw some of those besides. It was … a sight."

"He is cut from the same stuff as his mother," Karin said, and all eyes turned to regard him. "Sarise A'zu."

A hush descended. Many had died in the Valley. Many had fallen to the Dark Kind. But none quite in the way Sarise had. It was a reminder both of the void she had left and of the fact that most in the chamber had not connected Kole with her. It made him angry. His heat rose.

"Well?" Yush broke the silence. "What have you to add, Kole Reyna? What of your power?"

Kole cleared his throat.

"I don't know what I can add that hasn't already been said. I don't remember much from the fields, save for the fact that I called to the flames and they answered. It was the second time I've felt power like that in near as many weeks."

"Does it frighten you?" Kenta asked, his voice calm, considering.

"Fear has no place in it," Kole said, voice projecting confidence he did not feel. His mother's name still echoed in his mind, her face blurry but for in dreaming. "There is a time and a place for power."

"And where and when will that be?" Rain asked.

It surprised Kole how much her demeanor had shifted in the space of minutes. This new woman was authoritative and direct. Apparently he was not alone. She earned a few glances for the question.

"I thought we were speaking plain, here," she said, ignoring them. "My boy, we all know you did not come here to rescue your brothers and sisters in Hearth, noble as that may have been. We know of Larren Holspahr's quest. We know what he would seek to do."

"Enlighten me," Kole said evenly, and his father gave him a warning look.

"If the White Crest lives, they will beg his aid like children come before an absentee parent," she said, mocking the very thought. "If they find something else, something decidedly more sinister—a source for this scourge—they will burn it out."

"You have a problem with either scenario?" Kole asked, unable to help himself.

"Not necessarily," Rain said, sitting back and raising her brows. "Though, I wonder if you share the same goals. I wonder if you do not have designs of your own in the peaks, no matter what you find."

"That is completely beside the point," Talmir intervened before Kole could mount a response. "The question on the table is whether or not Kole should stay here in defense of the city or venture north on some fool's errand."

"Should that not be Kole's to decide?" Kole asked. He was tiring of the games. The reminder of Larren—in actuality Linn's—journey reignited the spark of urgency within him. He tried not to think on Rain's unspoken implications.

"And what sort of designs might this Ember pup have with a Sage long dead?" an older, raven-haired woman asked from her place beside Yush. She was bedecked in gaudy jewels and wore far too much paint.

"Please, Sister Gretti," Rain said, earning a hateful glare from the other woman. "Just because you play the pious one in your fortune telling doesn't mean we're going to buy the act now."

"Pious?" Kole asked, sounding as disgusted as he felt. "For a Sage?"

"What of this group now?" Kenta asked. "Do we know where they are? Do we even know if they live?"

"No to both," Talmir said flatly, eyeing Kole.

Kenta nodded and steepled his fingers. He was a calculating man, and he calculated now, working over the implications and possibilities. Where the others in the chamber were free flowing with their emotions, Kenta was reserved, controlled. His brow crinkled, as if a sudden thought had occurred to him, some conclusion that Kole was not at all eager to hear.

"You wish for this young man to aid us in the defense of Hearth, no?" Kenta asked, cutting in before the Captain could respond. "And yet, by accounts, he cannot even control the power he wields. Tell me," he turned his eyes on Kole, "have you been to see your friend? The one your flames nearly consumed?"

The words clattered around the chamber like thrown stones, settling in the deep corners of Kole's heart and leaving him heavy and speechless. He heard the shouting as his father, Captain Caru and Rain Ku'Ral took

Kenta to task. Sister Gretti and Yush came to Kenta's defense, but even they did so weakly and without fervor.

"Kole," Talmir said, and Kole did not hear it until his father nudged him in the side. "Kenta has apologized. Do you accept?"

Kole eyed the physician intently. He did not seem sorry; however, he did not seem smug, only resolute.

"It is I who is sorry, Captain," Kole said, letting his stare linger before switching to Talmir. "But I am not the hero you're looking for. I still could be to my friends. And I promise you—I promise all of you," he swept his gaze to encompass the gathering, "that I'll do my best to bring my flames to bear against whatever has sent this threat against us. The answers may lie in the peaks. They may not. But they certainly aren't here. Here there is only death. It just hasn't settled in yet."

Their expressions ranged from serene to reassuring to suspicious, but it was Captain Talmir Caru who truly looked at a loss. His brow worked, lips moving to form words that would not come. Finally, he blew out a reserved sigh and let his palms relax on the oak table.

"I understand why you would have me stay," Kole said. "But the city is in good hands. Hands far better," he glanced at Kenta again, who nodded slightly, "and far more steady than mine. It's time we stopped enduring. It's time we started living."

"You risk much," Talmir said.

"I risk myself," Kole answered as his father looked on. Creyath raised his chin, eyes glittering in the dim-lit alcove. "I risk much more by not going. I risk everything. They will not stop," he swept his hand out at the walls. "Not this time."

"Young Ember," the speaker was the other woman beside Yush. Her hair was long, white and tied in a braid. Her eyes had a milky sheen, and for most of the meeting, he had assumed her to be dozing, or else pointedly ignoring the other exchanges. "What do you know that draws you so unerringly toward the peaks? What do you see in the passes?"

"Forgive Sister Piell," Yush started, but Rain silenced him with a sharp look. It was a stark contrast to the respect she had not afforded Gretti. Perhaps there was something to this old woman after all.

"Whatever it is," Talmir put in, "let us pray he sees it up close before we're all dead and gone." He turned for the door, his steps heavy. Creyath watched him go as Karin turned a look half-pride and half-heartbreak on his son.

The Captain opened the heavy door and pulled it in on oiled hinges that emphasized the silence. He turned and nodded to Kole, who followed without a backward glance. Karin assisted Creyath to his feet and helped him to the door. None of the esteemed Merchant Council of Hearth made a move to stop them, verbal or otherwise.

They took the winding stair silent as shadows, and took up Jakub and Shifa in their wake once they reached the bottom. Kole marveled at the loyalty and patience of both. As Shifa dogged his heels, so did Jakub skirt those of the Captain. Once they were outside and safely out of earshot, Talmir turned, his looked strained, brows furrowed.

"I am no fool, Kole Reyna," he said evenly. "Though she lapses from time to time, that old woman up there isn't either."

Kole tensed and his father did so as well, but the Captain held up a hand.

"I will not stand in your way," he said. "If you wish to make for the Steps and the peaks beyond, I cannot stop you. But I can ask what you're really after, besides your friends and fellow Lakemen."

Kole swallowed. He looked at his father, but Karin's expression told him nothing. When he turned back to the Captain, he was resolute.

"The White Crest lives," Kole said. "I have seen it."

"And yet you are an Ember, not one of the Landkist of the Valley. Were you one of the Faeykin, I might believe you more readily. What could you know that they do not?"

"I can't explain it," Kole said. "But I know what I feel. I know what I saw that night," he looked at his father, whose eyes took on that faraway ghost light. "I don't pretend to know what the White Crest once was to the Emberfolk, the Rivermen or the Faey. I know what he is now. Whatever's left of him, that is. He is not our protector. He is our jailor. Now, our executioner."

There was a silence but for the trundling of carts, the shouted orders and the unsettling drone of the wounded in their tents.

"The Eastern Dark is the Sage we have long counted as our enemy," Talmir said, speaking slowly, directly. To his credit, he waited on Kole's response, taking his measure.

"Perhaps he still is," Kole said. "He is a Sage after all, just as the White Crest is. They are brothers of a sort. Not much to distinguish one from the other."

"Then why focus on one long thought dead?"

"Are they not both thought as much?"

Kole nodded to the west, toward the sloping roads of Hearth's Bowl and the unseen walls beyond.

"There are no natural rifts this large to accommodate such a force," Kole said, his patience wearing thin. "The Dark Months have ended, or hadn't you noticed?"

"I had," Talmir said. "The Eastern Dark is the only one of the Sages known to flirt with the World Apart. What makes you think—

"It doesn't matter. If I'm wrong, I'm wrong. Either way, I'll find whatever's causing this and put an end to it." He was breathing heavy, heat rising. Creyath smiled as he limped before him to stand shoulder-to-shoulder with the Captain.

"But I know, father," Kole said, turning to Karin. "I've known it since the night Ninyeva came to our door in the rain."

"Be careful of the truth, son," Karin said. "Sometimes it can burn you more readily than the flames."

Kole said nothing.

"Captain Caru," Karin said, and the Captain turned to regard him. "My son needs a way out of Hearth."

Talmir sighed and Creyath chuckled.

"Let me see if I can help on that account," the Ember said with that toothy smile.

Kole returned it, but the beating of his heart felt like a violent drum in his chest.

CHAPTER TWENTY-THREE

THE FIRES OF HATE

The day was wet and dreary. All the days had been since the sky had darkened. It was scarred, now. Burnt beyond recognition, and what was normally a time for growth and plenty had become an unending nightmare.

Iyana Ve'Ran walked the muddy streets alone, wearing cotton britches in place of her robes. She navigated the puddles nimbly, finding small patches of soaked earth to traverse. The pressure of her passing left the tiny mounds unstable, to be swallowed up by the groundwater.

It was a miserable experience, but it jogged a half-pleasant memory. Iyana saw Kole and Linn hopping from one stone to another in the deep streams of the wood. She had tried to follow, but she was small and clumsy. She had fallen, floundering in the shallows and sure to drown if Linn had not come back for her.

Her light mood lasted as long as it took a worried soldier to rush past, red-faced and panting, a reminder of the precipice on which they all rested. It was the waiting that was worst of all. Waiting, while Hearth was besieged. Waiting, while Linn and Kole were out there.

Iyana felt vulnerable. Worse, she felt helpless.

She sighed and continued to pick her way up the slope toward the northern section of town. Halfway up, the road split and she turned left, avoiding even a glance at the other road, which led to the leaning tower of the Faey Mother, her teacher. The tower loomed out of the milky haze at her periphery, a reminder that while she hopped between puddles, Ninyeva worked through her dreams and visions, trying to be of use.

Normally, Ninyeva would include Iyana, but things had been different ever since Kole had gone north. She had stopped making sense, at least as far as Iyana could tell. She babbled about a power in the north, one whose face she could not see and whose lair she could not penetrate. And she spoke of a figure wreathed in flame. He was an Ember, but one possessed of a dark and frightening power. Iyana guessed this to be Kole, but when she had said as much to Ninyeva, the Faey Mother had merely waved her away. Iyana wondered if she even noticed her absentee apprentice these last days.

Iyana had been angry at first. But now she knew that the anger had merely been a cover for the fear. Never had she seen Ninyeva so embattled, so confused. She had even taken to meeting with Rusul and the Seers of Eastlake, something Iyana would have scoffed at even a month before, during the deepest days of the Dark Months.

Desperate times, indeed.

Iyana shook thoughts of her teacher away and continued on the northern road. It was strange, she thought, how all paths seemed to be pointing in that direction of late. She supposed it made sense, seeing how their corner of the World was as far south as south went.

She reached the crest before the refinished gate and looked down over her the town that had been her only home. Gray smoke rose from the brick chimneys, mixing with the unnatural fog to form a pleasant curtain that looked far less foreboding than the one hanging over their collective heads night and day.

She turned back toward the gate and noted the gatehouse off to the left, the first puffs of smoke just starting to curl from the bent pipe in the leaning roof. Iyana had not set out with a destination in mind, but she always wound up in the gatehouse with Tu'Ren when she was upset.

The First Keeper eschewed the comforts of his own home, the protection of his people taking precedence over everything else. It was likely that, as agonizing as the waiting and uncertainty had been for her, it was doubly worse for Tu'Ren. As far as she knew, he had not received word from Hearth for a week and the decision to withhold aid was not one he had made lightly.

The worn pine door was shut and latched, so Iyana knocked and then rocked from foot to foot under the dripping slats. An archer heard and peered down at her from the raised platform above. Iyana could not make out her features from under her hood, but they were no doubt familiar, as all faces at the Lake were. The guardian lost interest quickly and went back to her bored survey—bored, but disciplined. A wall hound rested at her feet, panting in the humid air.

Linn's face flashed in her mind's eye, bringing with it a pang of longing along with the now-familiar stabs of fear. There was even a little anger she could not quite bury. All of this was forgotten as the door swung open to reveal a grizzled stone of a man squinting down at her.

"Yani?" he said. "What are you doing out in this mess?"

Iyana shrugged meekly and blinked up at him.

Tu'Ren shook his head in the way a disapproving uncle might, but he moved aside and ushered her into the stuffy gatehouse nonetheless. He took the soaked shawl from her shoulders and grumbled as he fished around for a fresh one, settling for a wool rug he had mistaken for a blanket. She accepted it anyway, stifling a laugh as she followed him to the center of the tiny structure.

Iyana sat on a worn couch as Tu'Ren busied himself arranging fresh tinder in the smoking fireplace. It was a little game they played, seeing who would speak first.

Tu'Ren was not a quiet man, but he had taught Iyana more of patience than even Ninyeva had. She had long since forgotten when their games had first begun, but she guessed it to be around the time Linn and Kole had begun their training for the garrison. Where Linn went, Iyana followed, and the stern Ember could not help but be smitten with her girlish charm.

Years later, Iyana had been shocked to learn that Tu'Ren had lost a daughter shortly after birth. She often wondered if she reminded him of her, and sometimes felt strange because of it. She never asked, even though their silent game depended on questions as the only source of consequence.

Tu'Ren had a miniature mountain of white pine shavings piled in the hearth and now begun the painstaking process of laying a foundation of split oak about it. He would build the framework of a tiny house and continue from there. Iyana knew this because she had watched him do it a hundred times before.

"I've always wondered," she said, and his ears perked up, "why you insist on building fires the old fashioned way."

"Nothing old fashioned about building a fire the proper way," he grumbled. "If there's a better way to do it, I've yet to meet the man who's found it."

"Perhaps you should ask a woman, then."

He smiled.

"Perhaps," and he went back to his work. He was tense, but less so than he had been when she arrived. Even if her Faeykin abilities did not allow her to perceive emotions as plainly as others perceived the wind, she'd have seen the hard set of the First Keeper's shoulders and the haggard look behind those icy blue eyes.

"You know I hate it when you do that," he said

"Do what? Oh, sorry," she said, color coming to her face. It was a hard thing to turn off.

Tu'Ren smirked and Iyana cursed, knowing he had tricked her into asking the first question.

"You would think that famed intuition you women speak about would be enough. But no, you need to go and be chosen as the Valley's own, blessed with powers of knowing and sight the rest can only guess at. Or maybe you're all fakers who like to sound right."

"A bit of both," Iyana clucked.

Tu'Ren grabbed a flint from the windowsill and knelt to strike it.

"Why do you build it that way?" she asked, her tone shifting.

"I never asked my question," he said.

"Very well," she said with a dramatic sigh. "Ask away."

"This seems an important time for the Valley and everyone in it," Tu'Ren said, looking at her over his shoulder as he balanced a sharp piece of tinder on the brick.

"Is that a question?"

He struck the flint and the spark took, blazing the fire to healthy life in a heartbeat, washing the chamber in its moving glow. The flames licked and curled at the white pine almost as eagerly as they reached out for Tu'Ren. He reached one hand into the blaze, and no matter how many times she witnessed an Ember do it, it never lost its novelty. He closed his eyes, and she saw the veins bulge and pulse. After a few moments, he withdrew and left the longing fire to its business, crossing to sit next to Iyana on the couch, his heat radiating pleasantly.

Iyana curled up in her rug-turned-blanket. She remembered touching his bare forearm for the first time as a girl. It had given her the sensation of a black stone left in the sun. Though they were both Ember, the First Keeper's heat felt different from Kole's. It was steadier, more frequent but less likely to burn.

"You haven't asked your question," she reminded as they stared into the dancing elements beneath the chute.

"Ah, yes," he said a bit absently. "I only thought, in this time above all others, wouldn't Ninyeva need your assistance? She has much to ponder. Her visions and sights," he finished, waving his hand in a way she might have found silly if the subject were not so frustrating.

Iyana frowned and turned away. It was a bad habit and one that made her look so much like the sulky adolescent she had tried for years to leave behind.

"I think I've discovered your reason for coming today," he said with a smile.

"If I tell you," she said, "will you tell me why you build your fires that way?"

"That is how the game works."

"I've asked before," she said without hesitation, and then she turned those piercing green eyes his way. "You've never told me true."

Tu'Ren blushed and looked away, and Iyana felt shame for the second time that day. After an awkward moment, however, he recovered and boomed with laughter that shook them both.

"I used to think I had trouble getting anything past my wife," he said, wiping a tear. "Would that she could have met you."

Iyana smiled up at him, feeling his longing like a stab in the heart. It was a sweet thing and not at all bitter.

"In fairness to her," Iyana said, "you've kept this one so deep even I took time to suss it out."

"I'll tell you true, Yani," he said, using the rare pet name. He was the only one that could get away with it, and even then on sparing occasion. "But I'm curious. What stands out to you about the way I build my fires?"

"It's not the fact that you don't use your flames," she said, "though it is odd. For a while, I just assumed you preferred it that way."

"And what changed that opinion?"

"There is something in you when you build a fire that way," she said, her eye shifting like emerald pools as she looked up at him. "It's important to you. It awakens something in you, or else keeps something asleep. I feel sorrow and solitude. Most of all, I feel regret. It seeps from you like storm waves from a far-off cove."

Iyana came back to herself. She had begun to drift off into a trance. When she looked back at Tu'Ren, the Ember was staring at the flames, his face unreadable and emotions masked, even to her.

"Even without your gifts, you are wise beyond your years, little Yani," he said, smiling wistfully. He looked down at her and gave her a small pat on the head before standing and moving to tend the fire.

"I build fires this way," he said, leaning on the mantle and staring down, "because it reminds me that I control the flame and not the other way around."

When he looked back at her, there were tears gathering round the rims of his eyes.

"The price some had to pay for me to learn that truth is something I can never forget. And every time I build a fire, every time I stock my brazier on the wall, I remember. I let it linger. I let it burn."

Iyana swallowed as the First Keeper looked away from her, gathering his thoughts as he ploughed the waves of memory.

"I am a powerful Ember, Yani," he said. There was no boast, just truth plainly presented. "But whatever Linn, Kole and even Larren have witnessed of me, I can honestly say they have not seen the truth of it. Had Kole and Larren not taken down that beast a moon past, I daresay they may have."

Tu'Ren looked at her, his eyes sharper than before.

"You are studied in the early conflicts of the Valley, are you not? Those between the Emberfolk and the Rivermen?"

Iyana nodded, enraptured.

"Those conflicts ended some time ago, long before you were born and long before I became the man I am today. Shortly after they ended, groups cropped up like sullen weeds. They were victims, of a sort—those whose parents or siblings had lost their lives in the battles. They wanted what all victims want: revenge. Closure. When they came upon a group of Faey in the eastern woods during a hunt, they took it, though the woodsmen had done nothing but protect their borders as we clashed with the Rockbled."

Tu'Ren shook his head at the memory, the knuckles of one hand going white and the fire below him burning a little brighter.

"The young hunters said the Faey attacked them. Once, I might have believed them, but not after Ninyeva had returned from her time beneath the branches. She learned much from the original Valleyfolk. Enough to know the hunters were lying."

Now when Tu'Ren looked at her, she felt the pain coming off of him like fresh agony.

"You see, Yani," he said, "something had to be done."

Iyana said nothing and Tu'Ren turned back to the hearth.

"The decision was made by my father and First Keeper Croen Teeh, Jenk's grandfather. As newly appointed Keeper, I set out with Croen and First Keeper Vennil Cross of Hearth. That was a big deal, since my father's separation from Hearth was still fresh by a generation. We were to find the runaway hunters and bring them back for a joint trial before the twin Ember settlements and the Rivermen of the Fork. They were a formidable group. Nine hunters, three of them Embers."

He paused.

"Why did only three of you go?" Iyana asked.

Tu'Ren laughed a bitter laugh.

"We did not expect them to resist. Alas. Fort'U Reyna, Karin's mother and Kole's grandmother, helped us track them. Lucky for her, she largely excused herself from what happened next."

The Ember swallowed. He was now deep onto the paths of memory, and Iyana was swept along with him, her eyes glowing almost as bright as the fire in the hearth. She was not there, not truly, but she hovered on the edges with the three Embers as they followed Fort'U through the forested lands skirting the edges of the Untamed Hills. The Dark Months were in full swing, but in those days, there was nary more than a shadow or two to be burned away. Things watched from trunk and burrow, but the Embers kept their blood up and nothing challenged them.

Tu'Ren continued to speak in the present, but Iyana was in some version of the Between. His younger self—white hair tied back to frame strong, youthful features as he brushed the branches away from his face—mouthed the words. Their direction was staggered and uneven; it appeared to make as little sense to the Embers as it did to Iyana, but Fort'U led them on, and the darkness soon gave way to a ruddy glow.

The tracker waved them forward and they entered the clearing, looking over what Iyana at first took for the scattered remnants of a camp hastily abandoned. And then she saw the bodies, burnt and twisted, and all of them bearing the pale moon faces of the Faey. They ranged from the very young to the very old, the flames still eating hungrily in places. It was nearly enough to make her sick, and she knew that young Tu'Ren felt the same way.

The company picked over the scene, finding the body of one of the hunters. Iyana shuddered to think that a Faeykin had done that to him, turning him inside out in a stark reminder of how the healing powers of the Landkist of the Valley could shift to the stuff of nightmare out of necessity.

Could she do something like that?

Iyana could still hear Tu'Ren's words, but they were far away now, much farther than the scene before her. His younger self was in shock, and though Croen and Vennil felt the same way, the older Embers did a better job at hiding it.

There was something else welling up inside of Tu'Ren, however; it was hotter than the flames in his blood, hotter even than those burning in the clearing and over the mangled bodies of the Faey children.

It was something much like rage.

The company moved further west in silence, and Tu'Ren had killing on his mind and in his heart. The scent of ozone tickled Iyana's nose.

"Quell your fire, young one," Vennil said, catching Tu'Ren by the crook of the arm. All she received in reply was a stare like death and she withdrew.

There was a smaller clearing further ahead. This one had its own fresh flames, which looked gaudy in the unfiltered moonlight. Iyana followed in Croen and Vennil's wake. Tu'Ren stood within the circle of trees, Fort'U beside him. Below them, the tiny chest of a female hunter heaved and shuddered past the arrow stuck through it. Her eyes quivered with fear and pain, but Tu'Ren did not see it. He only looked past her, seeing the charred remains of the Faey who had sent the shaft.

Croen put out a hand, but it was too late. Tu'Ren incinerated the girl so quickly she died without issuing a sound.

"Kadeh!" the First Keeper shouted, turning Tu'Ren around forcefully. "She was to stand trial. As are the others."

The young Tu'Ren looked at his mentor with an odd mix of disgust and confusion.

Croen opened his mouth to speak again, and an arrow sliced through the night air, parting his tongue and sinking with a squelch into the back of his throat.

The sudden violence shocked the other three into action, as they spun to meet the charge of the rogue company, which crashed into the clearing with blades held high, spears leveled and flames shooting forth in deadly brilliance. Tu'Ren took a gash in the side, broke the spear at the shaft with a slash of his Everwood blade and snatched the sharp end before it tumbled to the ground. He sank that into the swordsman on the left and grabbed the spear-wielder round the throat, lifting him into the air with ease.

This one did have time to scream, and he made it count as Tu'Ren's bare hand burned through his windpipe to the bone.

Vennil unloosed twin black Everwood axes from her back, ignited them and spun to meet the charge of the Ember triad. Her blades worked furiously, dealing back threefold each wound she received. One of the three died gurgling before the other two could mount a more measured attack on Hearth's deadly tornado of fire.

Iyana lost track of Fort'U in the chaos, but a scream that was cut short from the surrounding trees let her know that the tracker had found the archer.

Through it all, Croen Teeh pitched and rolled on the ground, clutching at the bubbling wound with eyes wide. Somehow, he managed to light his sword and sink it into the calf of a female hunter that got too close to him while circling away from Tu'Ren's deadly arcs. She fell with a pained yelp and Croen finished her off, sinking his burning blade into her chest and pinning her to the forest floor. Then he lay still.

Iyana was breathing fast. She knew she was in no real danger but could not help but skitter to the edge of the clearing, putting her back against the trunk of a tree as she watched Tu'Ren advance like a force of nature. His blade glowed so bright she could not make out the wood at its core, blue lines spilling off at the edges.

He went to work like one of the Embers of legend. Metal weapons seemed to dull and bend as they came into contact with his own. Their wielders fared no better, as Tu'Ren sent flares far wider than Iyana had known possible, the rays shooting out from the edges of his blade as if shot from a bow.

Soon enough, only the two young Embers remained of the rogue company. Vennil battled both, but a slash to her thigh put her down in a tangle, one axe spinning from her grip along with three fingers.

Iyana was sickly fascinated watching the Embers battle one another. Though they were effectively immune to each other's flames, they still made use of them, sending flares and crescents to blind and confuse as they danced their deadly dance. It was a tense battle while it lasted, but Vennil had lost, and she would have been cut down for good had Tu'Ren not moved to stand before her, eyes shining like a god's.

The young Embers withdrew and paced before him like jungle cats. By their movements, Iyana thought them to be brother and sister. By their poise, she thought it obvious they were the leaders of the rogue brigand, the ones most responsible for the trail of garish sights. And now they had slain the First Keeper of the Lake and maimed the First Keeper of Hearth.

The pair came at him mid-stride like bolts fired from a crossbow. Tu'Ren repelled them with a violent gust. The male lost his blade, which embedded itself in the trunk of a nearby tree. As he moved to retrieve it, his sister renewed her assault on Tu'Ren, forcing him back with a blitzing attack. Her fury only served to highlight her desperation.

Her brother had nearly pried his burning blade from the scorched trunk when she was launched into him so forcefully that he was impaled on the dull end of his weapon. The impact resulted in a sickening crunch that ended with a sorry gasp as he died on the still-burning length of Everwood.

Tu'Ren was standing over her when she came to. There was a storm in him, and Iyana knew beyond a shadow of a doubt that it was far from spent. The Ember—no more than a child, really—glared up at him through dirt-caked tears.

"I can still remember the way she looked at me," he said, raising his glowing blade and the burning palm behind it. "There was accusation in her eyes. As if I was wrong. As if I was evil. A thing to be feared."

Despite the circumstances, the girl was beautiful, her face lit orange and blue. Iyana wondered whom her parents had been, if she had loved or been loved. She tried not to look at the prone form of her brother leaning sickly above her head.

"I felt like a passenger to the flames," Tu'Ren said, and as he did, the girl finally broke, her body wracked with sobs. She looked down at the ground.

Iyana heard rustling and turned to see Fort'U helping a woozy Vennil to her feat, the tracker keeping a weary eye on Tu'Ren all the while. The First Keeper of Hearth reached her maimed hand out toward the still form of Croen Teeh as Fort'U whispered words of comfort, dragging her onto the paths beyond.

"I wanted to ask her why she had done it."

Iyana turned back to the deadly scene. Tu'Ren's fist was all blue now, his eyes the yellow of sunlight.

"I wanted to ask if the children of the Faey had whimpered as she did now before she burned them up. Most of all, I wanted to ask how either of us could ever be forgiven."

The blade became a beam that became an inferno, engulfing the girl, her brother and the tree that marked them in a flash of light so bright in rendered Iyana blind. She screamed for what felt like minutes, the image of the kneeling girl imprinted on the backs of her lids. She was shaking. Or being shaken.

"Yani? Iyana?"

She opened her eyes to see a face lined with care, worry … and regret. It was a face so at odds with the one she had just seen it almost seemed alien.

"I'm … okay," she said weakly, allowing the Ember to help her into a seated position.

Tu'Ren put a cold cup into her hands and she drank deeply, the shock revitalizing her. Neither of them spoke for a time as the fire turned to coals in the hearth.

"You were there, weren't you?"

Iyana nodded and Tu'Ren looked as though his heart might break then and there. She laid a hand on his arm, surprised at its coolness.

"Thank you," she said, green eyes shining. "I know how hard that was. Truly I know."

Tu'Ren nodded and sighed. He stood and crossed to the window, looking out at the gate beyond.

"I need to get back up there," he said without turning. "Need to keep up appearances. Make it look like we're doing something, after all. Something aside from waiting."

The Ember retrieved his cloak from the rack. He wore no scabbard and instead strapped his great Everwood blade—a different one than that he had burned up in the memory—to his back.

"The reason I build my fires the old fashioned way, little Yani," he said, standing over her, "is because it reminds me that, though I hold the flame within me, we are separate things. It is a gift from the World. That does not make it a good thing or a bad thing. Just a thing."

He put a hand on her shoulder.

"The Embers may be more overtly powerful than many of the other Landkist," he said, "but the World does not bestow any of its gifts lightly. I have to believe that. Explore yours, Iyana, but never let them explore you. Do not become lost from who you are."

"You never have," Iyana said. "I know who you are."

Judging by the look on the First Keeper's face, it was exactly what he needed to hear.

After he had left, she wrapped the rug tighter around her, watching the sputtering flames in the hearth.

"I know who I am."

CHAPTER TWENTY-FOUR

A Light in the Dark

A s it turned out, the air got no fresher the higher they climbed, the appearance of another arm of the subterranean river proof of how violently and how deeply the River F'Rust had delved in its decades of captivity.

The three of them knew the river completely now: the smell of its waters—metal and gravel mixed—and the cool kiss of its spray. They knew its taste—tin and copper—just as they knew its sound as the roar of the earth itself.

The feeling of elation Linn had experienced upon finding a tunnel that moved up instead of down days earlier had entirely dissipated, leaving her struck with the helpless reality that they were hopelessly lost. Their food stores were nearly depleted and their bodies bore the scrapes and bruises of creatures unused to the darkness of the Deep Lands.

Linn hated the river. She hated it as she had never hated another person. She hated it as she had never hated the Dark Kind. She hated its indifference, most of all. Even as it provided her its lifeblood, she accepted it grudgingly. It felt like drinking poison.

"I think we should rest here," Jenk said when they came to a particularly wide berth of the same featureless black rock they had come to loath.

Nathen dropped the small pack that represented their combined possessions and sank in a slouch against the tar-colored wall without a word. His eyes were vacant and his stomach spoke louder than he did.

"Works for me," Linn said. She leaned against the same wall and watched Nathen out of the corner of her eye. His breathing was slow, deliberate. She worried about him.

Sighing, Jenk stripped off his boots and went to the edge of the platform, sinking his feet into the flowing black water with a sigh. He did this each day they stopped to rest, and each day, the hiss the water made upon contact with his skin grew fainter. He needed light. Needed it badly.

Watching him, Linn had to admit that Ganmeer had surprised her. She had never much liked him at the Lake. But then, she had never truly known him as a separate thing from Kaya. Perhaps he had played at being a hero in the vein of his grandfather long enough in youth that it had come true. His face bore the haggard look of exhaustion, but, unlike Nathen and, perhaps herself, there was no defeat to be found in the Ember.

It was ironic, in its own way. Linn knew that men and women showed their true colors when pushed to the limit, and those colors were rarely bright. Though his heat had cooled, Jenk seemed to be the exception.

A sound that was keener than the low rumble of the river and more muted than the echoes of splashes among the black rocks snaked its way through the chamber. It was a pitiful sound, Linn thought, squeezing her eyes shut. She did not realize it was coming from her until Jenk put his arm around her shoulders and it stopped.

Linn struggled past the lump in her throat. When she finally did, she opened her eyes and saw that Jenk's own glistened with dew in the darkness, two more sparkling surfaces in the slick caverns.

"I'm sorry," she said, and the echoes magnified the words. Jenk regarded her with a mix of sympathy and confusion, while Nathen merely adopted the latter.

"I can't imagine what for," Jenk said. It could have been a joke for the sharp irony, but he said it with conviction. He meant it.

"All of it," she said. "For bringing us out here. For Larren. For Baas. For," her voice broke. "For Kaya."

"What else were we to do?" Jenk asked, letting his head fall back against the wall with a thud. "We were waiting for our deaths at Last Lake. Might as well take control and choose a place for it."

"You'd choose here?"

"I don't plan to die here."

There was a pause as they all digested the words, worked them over and held them close. Nathen looked a little more awake now, a little less sullen.

"What do we do if we find him?" Linn asked, more to herself than the others.

"The White Crest or the Eastern Dark?"

"Either. They're both Sages."

Jenk turned a curious look on her.

"I would hardly compare the one with the other," he said.

"Kole would."

"Our people are dying."

"And we are here, in the Deep Lands."

"That is why we are here," Jenk said. "We've all become good at killing and better at dying since the Dark Kind started coming in earnest. It's time we tried something else."

The Ember sighed as he finished, and Linn was suddenly conscious of how cool it was in the close chamber despite his presence. He looked pale in the gloom. If not for the light trickling in from faraway chutes and chimneys, they would have had to spend him more by relying on his blade to navigate.

"How are you?" she asked softly, putting a hand on his bare arm. He pulled away and tried to affect a smile.

"I'll live," he said. "Someone has to answer for all this."

"That someone being a Sage, most likely," Linn said. "Unless it's some general from the World Apart holed up in these mountains."

"No," Jenk said. "That's not how they operate. The Night Lords are their generals, the Sentinels their Captains of corruption. Only the Eastern Dark communes with them, organizes them like this."

"What if Kole is right?" Linn asked. "What if the White Crest lives?"

"Then I'll have my answers from him," Jenk said, the threat of violence lingering. "If he hasn't intervened on our behalf, as was his agreement with the King of Ember, he's in no position to stand up to us."

"To you," Linn corrected. "Nathen and I are capable, but we are no Landkist. He'll answer to you."

Jenk shrugged as if it did not matter, but Linn could feel the atmosphere swell and collapse as he flared.

"Jenk?"

His breathing grew heavy and his eyes fluttered.

"Fine," he said, but the word drifted as he slumped.

"Nathen!"

The other man was up in a flash that belied his exhausted state. He pulled Jenk away from the wall and laid him down, the Ember's breaths coming short and fast. Linn rested a hand on his forehead, which was pulsing, alternating between hot and cool before settling to something close to normal. That was not good. Linn had never heard of an Ember dying from lack of sun and flame, but prolonged deprivation could make them seriously ill.

"I'm … fine," he whispered again and Linn shushed him.

A blanket of calm settled on her. There was something to do and she'd see it done.

"You're fading, Ganmeer," she said. "We need a fire."

"What about his blade?" Nathen asked. "Why can't he light that and use the flames to charge?"

"Everwood blades are conduits. I don't understand it completely, but I know they don't burn so much as come to life. He needs a fire with real fuel."

"Nothing," Jenk started, but Linn spoke over him.

"There is," she said, turning to Nathen. "You remember the last pool we passed? The slow one with foam at the edges."

Nathen nodded, eyes widening.

"There was debris. Bark or lichen."

"I remember," he said, rising to his feet as Jenk tried to grab at him weakly. "It won't take long." He walked to the back of the chamber, where the path curved around the river. Linn followed.

When they were comfortably out of earshot, she turned him around.

"You know the way?"

He nodded, looking to their right, where the pathway spiraled down into the deeper darkness. Jenk had been forced to ignite his blade shortly after passing that pool, but Nathen was an experienced hunter; mapping the paths was second nature to him.

"Don't worry," he said. "Back before you know I'm gone."

Linn watched his silhouette melt into the shadows. She sighed and went back to Jenk.

"You'll be thanking me when we reach the Steps," Linn said, trying to ignore the pointed look Jenk managed despite his delirium. "You'd have done the same." And that quelled him.

Jenk struggled against it for a time, but he eventually succumbed to sleep, leaving Linn to her thoughts in the dark. She thought of the twisting pathways through the woods to the south and how much she missed them. She'd even take them chock-full of Dark Kind over the maddening maze of tedium they found themselves in now.

She thought of the cave. No matter how hard she tried, however, she could not help her thoughts from turning toward home. Toward the waters of Last Lake, which would never ignore her in the dark and deep as the River F'Rust did. She thought of Iyana. Finally, she thought of Kole. Surely he had awoken by now to find her gone. She only hoped he had not been as foolish as she.

There was a dry snap that jolted Linn into a crouch, the long knife Nathen had left her held out horizontally in her hand. She did not flinch. She never did, eyes piercing the middle distance like few could match. Jenk stirred beside her but did not wake.

She exhaled, all relief as Nathen's broad shoulders broke the black canvas. He kicked a dried tangle forward. At first, it looked like a bundle of branches clutched in his arms, but as he neared, Linn noted that the material was an odd mix of purple and blue. It was some sort of fungus.

"Think it's safe to burn?" he asked, dropping the bundle. "Dried fast." His bare chest was still slick from a mixture of water and sweat.

"We'll find out. How did you get down there so fast?"

"Took a shortcut," he said, and something in his tone made Linn look up from snapping the dried pieces into kindling.

"You didn't," she said, shocked. He smirked. "You rode the river down?"

"I'm a strong swimmer," he said and she shook her head.

Nathen looked at Jenk.

"He looks like a corpse."

Linn gave him a sharp glare and he held his hands up.

"Think he can get a spark going?"

"He'll have to."

Together, they lifted the Ember into a seated position. His eyelids fluttered but he gave no sign of waking. It struck home then just how depleted Jenk must have been. Linn wondered how she had not noticed it sooner. Her respect for him had already multiplied since setting out from Last Lake, but now it soared to new heights.

"Jenk. Jenk ..."

Finally, the Ember woke with a start, eyes darting around as he attempted to orient himself. Linn took hold of his temples and looked him dead on. He settled.

"Ve'Ran," he breathed.

"A spark, Jenk. We need a spark."

She indicated the pile of scrap before them. It would burn quickly, but Nathen had gathered more than she would have thought possible. It had to be enough.

Jenk did not look entirely convinced, but he squeezed his eyes shut tight and leaned forward under his own power. For a spell, he was still as death, and then the veins stood out on his neck, their swelling forming ridgelines that snaked their slow way down his arms and tunneled like worms on the backs of his hands. His light hair moved as if stirred by a breeze only he could feel.

His eyes flashed opened, and Linn thought she caught a hint of bright amber before the blues returned. A spark took, igniting the cache in a flare that rendered Linn and Nathen blind and yelping like pups. After what felt like a searing eternity, Linn opened her eyes to a scene so at odds with the sudden violence of the burst that she nearly laughed.

Jenk sat cross-legged before the crackling flames, his eyes closed and his face a picture of serenity that bordered on communion. Judging by his own expression, Nathen must have been thinking the same thing.

"Thank you," the Ember said, and though his voice was distant, it already sounded stronger, steadier.

"My pleasure," Nathen said nonchalantly, scooting closer to the flames now that his eyes had adjusted.

Linn moved to join them, watching curiously as Jenk drank in the heat from the darkening coals that broke off from the pile.

"Will it be enough?" she asked, concerned at the rate at which the scrub was disintegrating. The fire was already losing its life.

"Plenty," Jenk said, and the blaze flared up again before settling back down.

"You're controlling it."

"I can slow the flames," Jenk said. "Get as much heat out of it as possible."

They sat around the fire like children waiting for a tale. Linn had not been aware of the chill in her bones, but it evaporated and left her feeling warm for the first time in weeks. Her stomach growled as the scent of burning reminded her of food, and they split the last shreds of salted meat between them, softening it in the flowing river before setting to chew.

"Why did you both come?" Jenk asked, and Linn felt as taken aback as Nathen looked.

The Ember opened his eyes to regard them.

"I mean no offense," he said. "But since we've some time to kill, I thought I'd know. I asked Baas the same thing before we set out. His reasons were quite simple: the Rivermen have no love for the Sages—any of them. He knew that playing any role in the death or surrender of one of them would plant him firmly in the lore of his people."

Neither Linn nor Nathen spoke. Jenk sighed and continued.

"Kaya's intentions were never verbalized, but I knew her better than most."

Jenk's expression changed, a shadow passing over his face. He swallowed.

"She sought to prove herself. To me, to you." Linn rocked back, uncomfortable. "To everyone, I'd expect."

He cleared his throat.

"Larren Holspahr set out under a sense of duty, I expect. I don't know if he believed in the validity of our trek, but he certainly didn't think we'd get far without him."

"There's irony," Linn said, staring into the flames.

Nathen sighed and gripped his leggings so tight his knuckles went pale.

"My mother is sick," he said, unable to meet their surprised eyes. "The waste is in her. She doesn't have much time left and neither Ninyeva nor Iyana could help her much."

"Iyana said she wouldn't accept help," Linn said, trying to keep the challenge out of her voice.

"That too," Nathen said. "I've never believed in the White Crest, but she does. I'm not sure what I expected. That I'd find him, fall to my knees and beg his help. Now, I don't feel much like begging. I don't feel much like asking, to be honest."

He looked up at them, face set and stern, a look that clashed with his youthful features.

"If he does live, then he abandoned us," he said. "Or something much worse."

Neither of them argued with him.

"There's nothing wrong with hoping," Jenk said.

"Plenty wrong with it," Nathen said, but there was no fight in him. He stared back into the flames, which had sunk lower.

Linn reached out and took Nathen's hand, turning a sympathetic smile on him. She was not her sister, but empathy was not exclusive to the Faeykin.

"There is no shame in what you've just said, Nathen," she said. "I know it doesn't seem like it. I know that I have a hard edge. But I believe in the White Crest."

"Still?" he asked, eyes shining.

"I think," she said uncertainly. "At least, I believe in what he was. I don't truly know if Kole is right. I don't know if he's still up there. But if he is, I have to believe he'll help us. I have to believe there's a reason why he hasn't."

"This is the path we've chosen," Jenk said and they turned to regard him. "No matter what waits at the end of it, we need to act together."

They nodded and spoke no more. The echoing rush of the river soon regained dominance over the crackle of the fire as the Ember replenished himself with its dying. Linn laid down to rest on the hard stones, which, for once, were warm against her cheek. Soon enough, the others dozed as well.

Some time later, Linn woke and wiped the sleep from her eyes. There was a flicker of movement ahead and she froze, waiting for it to come back. After a time, it did, and she could not believe what she was seeing.

The firefly—green and pulsing—was the first living thing she had seen in the Deep Lands. Linn rose slowly and the light darted toward her. It was impossibly bright, and just when she was about to cup her hands around it, it shot back and vanished into the next sloping tunnel.

Linn followed.

CHAPTER TWENTY-FIVE

ROCK AND REED

As he stood under the unyielding orange stare of Creyath Mit'Ahn, Kole sought out the calm provided by his father's steel-gray eyes. But Karin Reyna's gaze was far off, looking through the fogged, torch lit glass of the west-facing window. His expression was unreadable, but Kole knew he was afraid—afraid of son joining mother.

Still, there was nothing to be done.

Kole bit back the sting as a pair of elderly smiths—a husband and wife who spent as much time arguing as they did fussing with the leather straps and brass fastenings—worked to adjust the black armor.

"Still, my dear," the woman cooed as she worked to force the seams of his greaves under the shifting shoulder plates.

Kole was bare-chested under the armor at the smith's request, and the gruff man pulled his hand back sharply when his knuckles brushed against the Ember's skin. He shot Kole a glare and he responded with a shrug.

"He is a hot one," Creyath said with a laugh by the door, his pearly whites glowing in the gloom.

The smith pointedly ignored the Second Keeper and stepped back to look Kole up and down. His nod, like everything else about the man, was curt, stiff and without warmth, but he seemed satisfied.

"By Man," he said with an exaggerated eye roll. "Leave the boy be, Berta. Pull that shell any tighter and it'll melt to him."

Berta gave the final strap a sharp tug in response, cutting off Kole's breath for a panicked moment before the invisible seams shifted to accommodate his lungs. He looked up to meet the penetrating twin gaze of the smiths. They stood shoulder-to-shoulder and studied their handiwork.

Truth be told, Kole did not see the need for armor, but the Merchant Council of Hearth now saw him as an investment, one to be protected.

The smiths grinned simultaneously, the only thing they had done together near as Kole could tell.

"That'll do," the man said.

"Aye," his wife responded. "I'd like to see someone try to put a dent in that, Night Lord or Sage beside."

"Well?" Karin asked, coming to stand beside him. "How does it feel?"

"Honestly," Kole started, glancing sheepishly at the smiths, "It doesn't feel like much."

"That's the point, boy," the smith said. "Give it a twist."

Kole did. At first, he doubted the armor would move, since it appeared as a solid piece of worked obsidian. As he rotated his hips and shoulders, however, the metal broke into myriad glinting scales and grooves to accommodate his form. He could feel the polished metal sliding across his skin, but there was no chafing. It was as if he wore a silk gown rather than a suit of armor.

"Brilliant," Kole said, glancing down at the shoulder plates, which narrowed to blood-red tips. He still wore his thin traveling pants, but the smiths had fastened separate three-piece plates that ran from knee to instep. He tested a few lancing kicks and exhaled in satisfaction.

"Right, then," Berta said, holding out her hand. "Onto the matter of payment."

Creyath moved forward, his steps slow and halting. He deposited a mesh pouch into her hand.

"I trust you'll have the decency to wait until we've left to count it."

"It's a small enough town," she said with a wink and a wag of her finger.

The three men stole out onto the street, Kole marveling at the way his armor moved like a second skin. His twin blades rested comfortably across his back, freshly oiled by Talmir's personal doctor. It was the Captain's last favor to Kole before he made his way back to the gate.

Shifa barked and twined around his legs, starved for attention. She yearned to be back on the road with him, he knew, but Kole had decided the loyal hound had done enough. He would not take her to the peaks.

It was dark outside and the streets were largely empty in this section of town. The pale blue light of the moon was losing its battle with the growing legion of black clouds that now assailed the sky like a swath of drifting smoke. The sounds of battle could not be heard, but Kole could see the red-orange halo hanging to the west, the light of the braziers and the burning pitch below giving the impression of a sun not yet risen.

Creyath had moved off toward a street cook, the steam rising from a grill laden with fresh vegetables from the window gardens above, leaving father and son in the middle of the street.

"Amazing, isn't?" Karin asked. "Even in the midst of all this, our people carry on."

Kole nodded and the silence resumed.

"I'll make it to the peaks, father," he said. "I'll find out what happened."

"Your mother made it, Kole," Karin said. "It's the making it back you need concern yourself with."

Kole did not turn to face his father. He steeled himself.

"Just try to make sure I have something left to come back to."

A boom sounded in the distance that was too short for thunder—likely one of Balsheer's casks going up on the other side of the wall. As if on cue, Creyath removed himself from his perch and waved for Kole to follow as he set off toward the north.

"I don't think Creyath is the type of man to wait twice," Karin said. "You should be off."

"Where will you go?"

"I have business with the Merchant Council," he said, some ice in his tone that made Kole turn.

"What sort of business?"

"I have it on good authority—my own, actually—that our mercantile friends have been hording supplies that would prove quite invaluable to Captain Caru and the troops."

"Seems to be plenty of food in Hearth," Kole said, indicating the street cook, who was now pointedly ignoring them, since they had not deigned to make a purchase.

"Hearth has never wanted for food," Karin said. "Nor has the Lake. For all the nightmares this Valley has thrown against us, we have never wanted for resources. No, their hording is more of the martial variety."

"Weapons?"

"Arrows, mostly. Caches stalked in their palisades on the edges of the Bowl. And I'd like to see those personal guards put to better use."

They stood there in awkward silence once again. As impenetrable as Kole could be, Karin was doubly so. It did not make for a warm relationship, but it was not one without love.

"Goodbye, father."

"Son."

Karin reached out and placed three fingers upon Kole's brow, sending tingles of memory racing down his spine. The gesture recalled a meditation technique Karin had taught him when he was young, when the fire was still difficult to control.

The First Runner of Last Lake moved off toward the east, toward the Red Bowl and all its horrors, and he took Shifa with him. Kole stood rooted in place for a time. Remembering himself, he moved off toward the north, following in Creyath's limping footsteps.

He caught up with the other Ember in an oval intersection where six streets met. Though drenched in sweat—it was a hot night—Kole marveled at the fit of his armor and the way it allowed him to move without restriction. Now all that remained was to put it to the test, but that would come soon enough.

His blood felt hot as the white cliffs loomed above him, his legs itching to be set free in the fields separating Hearth from the Fork and the peaks beyond. Creyath was silent as they walked, so Kole matched him. The houses were more separated here and shorter, though of finer make than those on the interior.

As they neared the cliffs, they slipped from the blue shadows of the leaning buildings and crossed into a brightly lit area of white stone cobbles. At first, Kole thought the lighting to be the work of street mirrors, but then he noticed a sliver of moon peaking out from the clouds to the east. Shafts of lunar light hit the northern cliffs, lighting their face in a way that reminded Kole of Last Lake. He nearly had to shield his eyes before the smog took back the sky and plunged them into shadow once more.

The houses grew more spaced and more lavish the further north they traveled, undoubtedly the abodes of the Valley's wealthier inhabitants. Kole wondered if the caves of the northern deserts had seen such displays of luxury. He supposed all cities did, if given long enough to ferment—to rot.

There was a sound like rushing, and Kole saw the white froth of a river up ahead struggling to rise over the cut stones that lined its edges.

A small bridge spanned its width and they crossed, the cliffs looming larger with each stride.

Kole examined the white face, noting the guard towers poking out along the precarious expanse at the top. He was beginning to wonder if Creyath's genius plan involved him simply rappelling down the sheer cliff face into the marshes beyond and swallowed.

"What's the plan, exactly?" Kole asked.

"To get you out of the city," Creyath said, guiding Kole toward a path to the northeast that brought them to a jagged expanse of stone that jutted out over the river they had just crossed.

Kole looked back at the guard towers, picking out the rough-cut stairway that led up to the heights. Was there another way to the top?

"We're not going up," Creyath said, noting Kole's confused look. "We're going under. Well, you're going under. I can't afford to get these bandages wet."

"Wet? I thought this river passed underground. It's too far to swim, and against the current."

"If we can help it, you won't be swimming."

They stopped at the base of white stone where the grass ended. The outcropping was half again as tall as Kole and it shone like translucent marble in the spray from the surging current that passed under it.

"Took you long enough," a female voice called down.

She was perched at the top with her shock of red hair tied back in a tail that hung down across her waist in the front. Near as Kole could tell, she wore the same black-red armor as him, and there were brightly colored sashes tied at each bare elbow—one green and the other yellow. Across her lap she held a spear that must have stood taller than Larren Holspahr's, its butt held firm in a worn groove in the stone. The weapon, too, had colored streamers tied just under the head.

"Kole Reyna," Creyath said, sweeping his hand out in a mock bow. "Allow me to introduce the most … colorful member of Hearth's forces: Third Keeper Misha Ve'Gah."

"If I could kick you from here, Mit'Ahn, I most certainly would," the Ember said, and Kole was not entirely sure she was joking.

She switched eyes that shone near as green as Iyana's toward Kole. She did not seem impressed.

"This is the hero, then?"

Kole shrugged and she mimicked him.

"I saw the aftermath of your little fit before the Western Gate," she said, standing on long legs. "Don't get me caught up in something like that."

Kole looked askance at Creyath, but the Second Keeper merely smiled the smile that never seemed far from his face. He had been under the impression his mission would be undertaken alone. To send help, especially help in the form of one of only two uninjured Embers remaining in the city, Kole wondered if Misha was there to assist him or to babysit. Perhaps a bit of both.

He cleared his throat.

"If we come across a Sage in the north, I suspect my power will be the least of your worries," he said. Misha did not answer, just looked at him, considering. She stretched and eased the tension from her joints. "Besides," Kole was growing impatient, "I'd wager my 'little fit,' as you call it, did more to the Dark Kind than you've managed up in your towers."

Creyath smiled again, but this one was strained. As for Misha, she froze mid-stretch, her expression shifting from sudden fury to what he sincerely hoped was surprised and grudging respect, and not an eventual promise to murder.

"Very well, my Ember Prince," she said, dipping her own bow, her red hair brushing against the stone beneath her feet. She reached down and Kole took her hand, allowing her to pull him up onto the outcropping.

Together, they watched Creyath cross back over the river, each step looking decidedly more labored than the last. Instead of turning back toward the infirmaries to the east, the Second Keeper turned south, toward the red glow of battle.

"I knew it," Misha said in a harsh whisper.

"Should we stop him?" Kole offered, earning an amused look from the other Ember.

"At least he'll have other soldiers about," she said, dropping down onto a small patch of grass on the opposite side of the ledge. "That's more than I can say for us."

Kole dropped down next to her, the white-foamed current raging to his right and the cliff face rising up to his left. There was a jagged pathway cut directly into the cliff face. It started just before the place where white rock merged into the frothing river, which was as violent as the mouth of a sea drake, and Kole shivered despite his warmth.

How were they to get through that?

"Does the current slow deeper into the spur?" he called ahead. He saw Misha's red tail bobbing in the trench.

"In a way," she said and Kole sighed.

"What of the North Walk? Who will defend it?"

"Dakken Pyr," she called over her shoulder. "He's no Landkist, but he's the most violent man I know, and I mean that in a good way." Kole did not doubt her. "Besides, those poor things have been at the gate for weeks. They won't try for the cliffs. Too steep."

"Should be smooth sailing, then," Kole said under his breath, but his voice carried in the sloping tunnel, the black skies being lost as the trench closed overhead and admitted them into the bowels of the spur.

"So long as the Night Lord doesn't find us," Misha said.

"Night Lord?"

"Four came against the walls. We killed three and the fourth went into the marshes."

"Perfect."

The Night Lord, or whatever it was, would come again. The Dark Kind had made Hearth their singular purpose. They would not retreat, no matter the cost.

The walls thrummed with the vibrations of the nearby river, and Kole could not tell if they were passing under it or beside it.

"Is there no other way?" Kole asked.

"Not unless you want to try for the gates to the west and south. This is the best way, so long as it still works."

Kole did not bother asking what that meant.

As soon as the tunnel became dark enough for Kole to think about lighting his blades, it opened up into a large, hollowed out chamber that sparkled bright white with the reflected light of hung lanterns. Here, the sounds of the neighboring river were even louder, the bass echoing and growing in strength as it rebounded off of the steep and cavernous walls. The floor underfoot was smooth as polished glass, and around them stood a full complement of soldiers, most of which held arrows nocked and pitched. A fire blazed in their midst and none looked pleased to be there.

The floor of the chamber was roughly circular, and Kole noted what appeared to be a jagged trench running along the outer edge that looked to be almost as deep as he was tall. Most of the soldiers turned to look at them as they entered the chamber, and most quickly turned back to the far wall, where a gray slab of stone stood out plainly against the white marble backdrop. On the right-hand wall, Kole saw a rough-cut opening that marked the entrance to another dark tunnel, much like the one they had entered through.

"What is this?" he asked in a tone that approached genuine awe.

"Don't look too shocked," Misha said. "The chamber is mostly natural. It was discovered generations back when a small child fell into one of the vents atop the spur. When they dropped someone in to find her, they both came out speaking of a chamber that sparkled like a thousand diamonds in the torchlight. The powers that be decided it marked an opportunity."

"A means of escape," Kole supplied as they came to stand before a stern-looking man in a bronze helm. He nodded curtly to Kole but his attention was firmly focused on Misha. Much to his chagrin, she ignored him and turned back to Kole.

"Tensions with the Rivermen were high at the time," she said. "Ironically, it was one of their own that supplied the plans for the drain."

Kole shook his head. He was through asking questions.

"Ahem," the soldier grunted, color rising to his cheeks. He and the rest of his party were glistening like the white walls surrounding them. Kole could not tell if it was sweat or the invisible spray that seeped through the translucent stone.

"Apologies, Degan," Misha said, not meaning it.

The two engaged in a discussion concerning releases, levers and drainage that made less than no sense to Kole, so he stayed out of it. The drone of the river was stronger here than inside the walls of Hearth. It took their words apart and sent them careening back into his ears like mutants of their former selves. He moved closer.

"What if it's waiting on the other side of the cog?" Degan asked, clearly unnerved.

"Then your men will have something to do," Misha said easily and Degan grimaced. Kole wondered at their history.

"This is a Night Lord we're talking about," he said, and several of his men and women nodded hurriedly, apparently eager to support any argument that might stop the mission in its tracks.

"It's a beast," the Ember answered. "As dumb as any other."

"My man Brettin saw it just last night, questing for a way inside."

A broad-shouldered man in the company—presumably Brettin— glared daggers at them, daring them to challenge him.

"Do you follow orders, Degan?" Kole asked, earning a surprised look from Misha and a furious one from the soldier. He looked about to answer when one of his own—a young woman—interrupted.

"The fire's waning," she lamented, clearly not for the first time. "It's the damn damp. We can't keep it fed."

Misha looked at the girl as though she were daft and Degan looked as if he were about to strike out when the fire flared violently to life, sending soldiers skittering and spears bouncing off of the marble floor.

Degan whirled toward Kole, who stood staring at the blaze with his hand outstretched, twin fingers rising and falling at a steady cadence with the flames. Misha's look had changed from curious to decidedly shocked. The hint of a smile played at the corners of Kole's mouth even as his brow furrowed in concentration.

"How are you doing that from such a distance?" Misha asked, fascinated as the flames swayed to imitate Kole's hand.

Kole let his hand fall to his side, and the flames lost their luster, going back to their fuel.

"Sorry for the theatrics," Kole said, ignoring Misha's question because he had no answer. "But I need to be getting north. I was under the impression you could get me there."

Degan had managed to regain much of his former composure, which is to say, not much, and stood taller, adjusting the straps on his breastplate. His bronze helm was still askew, but he did not seem to notice and neither Kole nor Misha pointed it out. He looked to the Ember of Hearth.

"Seems you've dug up quite the firebug," he said. Misha glanced at Kole, her expression still caught somewhere between concerned and excited. She shrugged.

"The lever?" Misha asked.

"Moars!" Degan shouted and the same young woman from before snapped to attention.

"Right away, Third Keeper Ve'Gah," and she spun on her heel and made for the trench along the back wall. She turned around with a blush and lowered herself into the channel like a child might.

Misha sighed and handed her spear to Degan before making her way to the lip of the trench. She hopped down and Kole saw her hair bobbing as she walked along its length in search of the lever that would permit them passage into the marshes beyond.

Kole felt eyes on him and turned to see Brettin, the stocky man staring with a look that could only be described as hostile.

"Something on your mind?" Kole asked. He had tired of the entire venture and was keen to be off. Keen to be north.

"You think you know better than the White Crest," Brettin said, his voice oddly high-pitched relative to his imposing size. "You think he's against us."

"Most think he's dead. I'd say my stance is an improvement."

Brettin did not look amused. In fact, he was seething.

"Calm yourself, Brettin," Degan said, though he eyed Kole sternly. Now he was readily itching to see the Embers out into the marshes and out of his hair. "At least they've got the stones to find out what's going on."

Brettin grumbled and moved back into his place.

He and the rest of them rocked back onto their heels as a boom echoed throughout the chamber. It was followed by a sound like sliding plates. Ahead, Kole picked out the bobbing tail of Misha. The Ember pulled herself out of the trench and hauled the young soldier up with her.

"Clever thing," Misha said, coming to stand beside Kole and turning to look back wonderingly at the gray slab of stone, which had just begin to shift on its bearings. "How did they build this?"

"Rockbled," Degan said.

"Ah, yes," Misha said. "A powerful one."

"Why don't they build such structures along the Fork?" Kole asked.

"Modesty, I suppose," Degan said and Misha shrugged.

"Maybe we just don't know about them," Kole put in, answering his own question.

"Strange," Misha said, "that one of their own would help design the mechanism meant to help us through a feared siege by his people."

"Siege never came," Degan said. "They certainly thought it would."

"The city was not well established at the time," Misha said. "The walls only half built, and the Emberfolk recently split with the separation of the Lakemen." She glanced at Kole. "There were sober minds on each side of the conflict."

"Aye," Degan said as the gear shifted and the water began pouring in on the far wall. "Far as I know, they never had cause to use it."

"What would be the point of draining the river?" Kole asked.

"To move supplies in by a back way in the case of a siege," Degan said.

The gear jerked and groaned in protest as it rolled to one side. The dark water sparkled in the torchlight, turning from a geyser to a steady fall as the opening grew.

"Won't the chamber fill up?" Kole asked, feeling woefully uninformed.

"I don't pretend to know the particulars," Degan said. His soldiers had their bowstrings pulled taut, eyes trained on the growing gap between gear and wall. "This stone is porous. It sweats. The trench will drain into the earth beneath the spur, given enough time."

The gruff soldier looked on nervously as the water splashed into the chamber at an alarming rate. To their right, the torrent sloshed by, the fire hissing behind them as a questing spray rose from the moat to challenge it.

"Now," he said. "The trench is half full. The river should be low enough for you to cross into the tunnel. Be quick about it. Once it's full we need to shut it down or we'll be swimming."

He sounded far from convinced, and Kole and Misha exchanged nervous glances. Kole looked at the black waterfall, half expecting some great beast out of nightmare to come crashing through the foam.

By the tension in the gathered soldiers' faces, they were thinking along the same lines.

"Half!" Moars called out from the lip of the trench.

"Off you go, then," Degan said tersely, and Misha broke off at a sprint, Kole fast on her heels as they rushed toward the tunnel to the right.

Once they were inside, Misha called up a spark and lit a small hand torch she pulled from her belt. The light played off of the glimmering sides of the tunnel in shifting patterns that would have been alluring if they weren't so unnerving. It was a longer path than Kole was expecting, the floor slick and steep. They relied on carved footholds to find purchase and propel them upward, and all the while the river roared from both ends.

Finally, mercifully, Misha found the edge and slipped over it, her feet landing with a small splash in the shallow water. Kole was over in a flash and they cut left, running through a much larger cavern with all speed.

"Some system," Kole said harshly as they bounded around a bend in the cave. "Obviously not meant for this."

The bend straightened and a grinding sound like rock against rock set their teeth to chattering. There was a fork in the tunnel and Kole saw the current being diverted up ahead, but the gear was closing faster than he had expected. They hugged the right-hand wall as they ran, the water rushing near to waist level before they were safely through into the reeds. The water was slower moving here.

Before the river could have a chance to sweep them back into the filling passageway, they used the choked root system to climb a nearby bank, stopping to catch their breath and check their gear at the top. Kole was surprised to learn that his chest was completely dry, another marvel of his new armor.

"It's a wonder they don't stock the whole garrison with these," Kole said, checking the grooves along his torso.

Misha was busy emptying the sludge from her boots.

"The couple that made them work on their own time and certainly not for free," she said.

"I can imagine."

Kole tried to survey their surroundings, but they may as well have been in a forest, the reeds were so tall and closely packed. Below them, the river had regained much of its former strength and the cave opening was completely submerged, invisible to prying eyes. The sky above was gray as ash, but some of the brighter stars were still visible through the veil. To the west, the great white spur curved out of sight, bordered by the twisting network of streams and rivers that were the spawn of the River F'Rust to the north.

"Shall we?" Misha asked.

"Lead on," Kole said. "I want that spear between us and whatever else is out here."

CHAPTER TWENTY-SIX

DRUMS IN THE DEEP

Ninyeva had not attempted to travel the Between since being cast down the first time. It was folly. She knew this without a shadow of a doubt, knew that whatever power she had provoked was well beyond her.

And yet, she had to do something. She had to get answers.

She pulled her hood low and began the arduous trek from the Long Hall to her cramped abode. Nervous faces tracked her progress, and she was dimly aware that her frantic mood of late was doing little to ease tensions along the Lake.

As she walked, Ninyeva thought of power and all its permutations. The Faey had no word for power in their native tongue. They thought power came in the seeing, but she wondered what they called it when they turned their gifts of healing to those of destruction. She wondered what they would think if they could have seen Kole Reyna set the fields of Hearth ablaze.

There was a power in sight, and that was the power of knowledge.

What good was knowledge without action?

According to Rusul and her sisters, Kole had set out from Hearth with Misha Ve'Gah just hours before. Near as they could tell, Larren and the others were well into the Steps by now, though they could not penetrate the peaks to see. If she was to be of use to any of them, she had to know what they were up against. She had to know which Sage waited for them, if any.

There was one constant that had unnerved her above anything else, even more so than the power she had felt among the peaks. It was a sound like drums, and it was a sound beyond hearing. The very peaks themselves thrummed with dark energy. It was not a rift, but something like it. She would find the source, and then, somehow, she would warn them. She knew some of her teachers were capable of projecting their spirits great distances, but they had long since passed on.

"Faey Mother?"

Ninyeva turned. Cooper Rhees stared at her from across the lane. He sat bow-legged on a small stool as he leaned over the rim of a barrel. A small boy sat on the front step next to him, looking as bored as unbuttered bread.

"Yes?" she asked, forcing a tight smile that had all the effect of curdled milk. The boy grimaced and looked away. "What is it?"

Rhees covered his embarrassment with a smile much more genuine than hers.

"It's just," he started, rubbing the back of his head with the hook of his hammer, "I wondered why you were heading toward the pens."

Ninyeva's brows arched. He was asking if she knew whether or not she had lost her mind. She did.

She nodded with a curt smile, spun on her heels and spied the shingled roofs further to the north, picking out her lonely leaning tower and its painted balcony. Rhees shrugged and bent back to his work. He had the courtesy not to say anything further.

Now, she kept her thoughts more focused as she walked, careful not to let them guide her. She thought of the drums and the invisible tethers she felt snaking out of the peaks like tendrils of darkness. Rather than reaching up into the black skies, however, these coiled about the walls of Hearth. She was sure it was the driving force of the Corrupted at the city's gates.

As she rounded the bend and picked her way up the slick and rounded cobbles at Westhill, she thought of sending for Iyana, but dismissed it as soon as it surfaced. She would not involve the girl in something so dangerous, no matter the cost to their relationship. Iyana was smart as a streaking star, her healing powers second only to Ninyeva herself—and that was a gap fast closing. But the Between was something else entire. It was a burden to be endured, not shared.

As it was, Ninyeva was likely the only soul in the Valley—the World, for all the difference it made—capable of navigating those shifting roads.

Ninyeva was nearly out of breath when she reached the faded blue steps of her tower. She leaned against the worn railing post, the chipped paint rubbing off on her robes, and tried to calm herself. From here, she could see clear down to the docks despite the fog, the sails of the fishing boats bobbing on their moorings.

With a sigh, she stole into the tower and climbed the creaking, narrow stair to her chambers. The preparations were already made and she settled into her place. She reminded herself that the roots, pastes and powders were aids, not crutches. She brought the mixture to a bubble over the coals in the grate before pouring the thick concoction through a mesh screen. When she was finished, she eyed the translucent purple liquid and steeled herself.

She unwound a black cloth and dipped it into the hot mix, careful not to soak her skin. When it was suitably damp, she wrapped it around her forehead, tying it tightly in the back and settling onto her pillows. She pulled the cloth down over her eyes, letting the sodden material touch her lids, and exhaled long and slow.

The effect was almost immediate. Colored lights played across the black canvas like lightning strikes absent thunder. A steady buzzing started at her temples and set her head to ring. Her skin tingled as her nerves ignited, the sensation moving between pain and ecstasy.

She hummed to orient herself, and soon the lights faded, to be replaced by the contours of the Valley as seen from the black clouds above. She glided on the currents swift and silent as a crane. She felt the familiar beating and angled up, piercing a particularly dense section of cover and coming out the other side in a swirl of gray smoke. There, she saw a coil like nesting snakes, all red and black. Tendrils reached down through the gray canopy and streaked toward the fields below—the fields of Hearth.

Ninyeva skirted the edges of the mass and swept around to the back. There, she saw four thick bands angling to the north. These were darker with only the faintest flecks of red, and their pulsing was slower, deeper and more rhythmic.

She kept her wings close and sharp, diving below the clouds only long enough to glimpse the ground below. The Steps passed beneath her, the great plateaus stretching out like a giant's staircase. The black tethers drew closer together above the peaks and shot down, and she shot with them, swirling into a cyclone of wind and energy. It was all she could do to keep from brushing against the strands, like a fly fearful of the spider's web.

The rushing of wind and buffeting of electricity ceased, and she found herself in a chamber of hewn stone. She was high up, but deep underground. Orienting herself was difficult. Already she felt the pull, saw the edges of her room at Last Lake shimmering on the corners.

She felt the buzzing overhead and peered up. The black tethers hummed angrily, snaking forward where they separated and disappeared into a series of alcoves that glowed faintly red.

Ninyeva moved closer, and as she neared, her heart beat faster. A ruby light spilled from the shapes, which she now recognized as great hearts half again as tall as a man. There was a stone slab directly before the alcoves with a shape resting on it, its chest moving up and down. The black tendrils tinged with red snaked around the stone like vines, and now her heart froze.

She felt it. The same presence from before.

Ninyeva was held between beats, caught between the urge to flee and the need to edge closer. As it turned out, the prone figure chose for her, as a blue-white light illuminated its chest. The eyes lit in a blinding flash before resolving into a serpentine figure that floated with crackling energy above the slab. The hearts increased their tempo, the sound of drums echoing off the black walls.

In place of the majesty she had felt upon entering the Valley all those years ago was a hawkish and misplaced fury, erratic and formless. Red light leaked from the corners of the diamonds she took for eyes and the serpent swayed back and forth like a snake readying to strike.

She thought to ask it something, anything, and then she seized upon its dark intent and knew she must go. Ninyeva streaked away and the wraith followed, encasing her in an atmosphere of its own making. But it had underestimated her strength. She tore through the casing and in that moment saw the consciousness of the Sage arrayed before her, an ocean of power whose waves crashed black with red foam, all anger and discord.

Ninyeva felt the Lake pulling her, calling her home. She pushed on, and in the passage between the shattering she glimpsed a strange horizon: there was a figure clad in white and blue—the White Crest as she remembered him—and before him stood a dark man wreathed in flames. Above them both, pulling strings that called back the red-black tethers was a figure blacker than the skies. The peaks collapsed and she was thrust back into herself, the fields passing in a blur below her and the stink of corruption screaming for her blood.

Her return was violent, and she fell back on an invisible current, her chambers coming back to her with sudden ferocity. She retched, all the while trying desperately to hold onto the vision and its portents.

She remembered the Sage, rotting and resting on his slab. She remembered the Dark Hearts drumming in the alcoves, and the red-topped citadel she had witnessed upon fleeing the dark keep. She remembered the sun, which she had not seen in weeks, burning like a half sunk fire over the lands beyond the Valley—lands from which she had come and never returned.

And there was one emotion that followed her faster and farther than any of the others. More than the rage and insanity, she had sensed fear from the being once known as White Crest. Not fear of her. She had been a meadow vole in the gaze of a hawk; this was fear of the other, of the figure wreathed in flame.

It was fear, she thought, of Kole Reyna.

Ninyeva attempted to reorient herself to the World, but it was an agonizing experience, like a star had exploded behind her eyes. She let the veil fall from her head and cast about the chamber, grasping wet roots that she chewed hungrily, squeezing her eyes shut and wishing the pain away.

She had lingered too long. The phlegm had built up and she could not concentrate enough to shift from gifts of sight to healing. Her consciousness was fading, and before she lost it completely, she saw what looked to be a fairy light, green and shimmering. It spoke to her through the veil.

Ninyeva shook her head and the light resolved into the soft visage of Iyana Ve'Ran. Her apprentice helped her to sit with hands far stronger than they appeared, and she felt the warmth of the Faey light moving through her blood, bringing her back.

"I found it," she said through a cracked throat. "Found him."

Iyana eyed her with a wild and fearful expression.

"He was so pure, once," Ninyeva whispered.

"Who?"

"Kole was right. He is not our ally. Not any longer. There is another in him. Infected. Rotten."

She was rambling and she knew it, but it seemed that Iyana had taken the point.

"He has betrayed us, after all," Iyana said. She did not sound shocked, but rather resigned.

Ninyeva reached out and took Iyana's soft hands in her weathered ones.

"He is as much a victim in this as we, I think," Ninyeva said. "The dark comes for us all."

"The Eastern Dark," Iyana offered.

"I can see no other possibility. It seems he has begun his war on the others, starting with our own guardian."

Iyana stood abruptly and moved to fill a cup with cold tea. She handed it to Ninyeva and adopted the stern, motherly look she wore so well.

"You should not have flown so far, and for so long."

"And how did you know I had?" Ninyeva asked, amused.

"I felt it," Iyana said, eyes going distant. "But that's not why I came." Her eyes refocused.

Ninyeva took a swallow and looked at her pupil expectantly. Iyana met her gaze, her emerald eyes glowing brighter than usual.

"I found them," she said. "I found Linn."

"Where is she?" Ninyeva asked, thoughts racing.

"In the Deep Lands," Iyana said. "And I saw others. I saw dark figures following them, tracking them from above. One of them looked like Larren Holspahr. But it couldn't be."

"Iyana," Ninyeva said. "You must find her again."

CHAPTER
TWENTY-SEVEN

---◆---

SISTERS

W hat at first Linn had taken for a fairy light out of dreaming soon morphed into something else: a feeling that she should follow. The green bulb buzzed faintly, moving about in circular patterns that alternated between alluring and frantic. Its movements were far too measured to be wild, and the part of her mind given to suspicion wondered if it might be some trick meant to tempt her into the sheltered cove of some deadly denizen of the Deep Lands. She imagined the gnashing beaks and razor claws but knew in her heart that she was safe.

She was taken on a short and winding climb, and she kept the river always on her right. There was a natural stair of sorts, which led to a small plateau. The air here was fresher, more alive. The light flashed and darted to the space between her eyes, causing Linn to reach up instinctively. Before she could grab it, the light streaked into another chamber, and there it stopped.

Linn guessed her position to be directly above the sleeping heads of Jenk and Nathen.

"What now, little bug?" Linn asked, feeling immensely foolish. Maybe she was beginning to lose her mind in this place of ever-present darkness.

The light burst in a shower of green and white sparks. There was no sound, but Linn was rendered blind in the searing bright. She fell to her knees, feeling about for purchase, and the throbbing slowly ebbed away from the backs of her lids. Had she not already fallen, the sight that resolved itself before her now surely would have done the trick.

Where the fairy light had been, Iyana now stood, her brows turned down in the concerned way only she could manage. Tears stung the corners of Linn's eyes and left their tracks in the pits of her hollow cheeks.

A sensation like touch but fainter tickled her shoulder as Iyana reached out, but Linn knew she was not there, not truly. The green glow was faded now, but it hung about her younger sister like a curtain. Iyana's eyes shone like burning emeralds, brighter than ever before.

"How?" Linn managed to choke out between wracking sobs. She had not realized how much she had to give until it had been given, collected in her own salt pool in the crevices between the stones beneath her.

"Landkist," was all Iyana said in response, her face strained with the effort, as if uttering a single word was akin to lifting a mountain. Perhaps it was.

Linn had never heard of the Faeykin projecting themselves, but then, the Landkist of the Valley were not well known to the Emberfolk. Only Mother Ninyeva knew their secrets, and even she doubted if she had them all.

"Linn," Iyana said, her mouth moving at odds with the words, her voice coming as if from a great distance. "You are not well."

She had to laugh at that, looking down at arms that had lost much of their color and more of their sinew. Arms that could previously draw the stoutest war bow were now faded to fish bones.

"It has been a hard road," Linn said, unable to meet her sister's eyes. Her own glassed over now, recalled to another dark place on the edge of a storm—a cave at the edge of a forest.

Iyana reached out her hand, and though the sensation was only a little more than nothing, Linn's chest heaved and wracked again, but her salt was all spent. When she was done, the old stone that marked her as Ve'Ran returned, pebble upon pebble filling her breast as she bent back from the breaking.

"Kole is on his way to the peaks," Iyana said.

"For me?" Linn said, unsure if she was furious or relieved.

Why would he? How could they let him leave Last Lake? Why had she?

"Ninyeva says the White Crest still lives."

There it was. The truth Kole Reyna had always known, that had driven him in singular purpose as nothing else had.

"I see."

"But he is not himself."

"Who is she to judge whether a Sage is or is not himself? Where has he been all this time?"

"Asleep."

"Asleep?"

It sounded ludicrous.

"He has fallen to the same corruption that plagues the Valley now. There are hearts beneath the keep. The plague is in them, from them."

Linn looked up, noting something else in her sister's face, now that they had both settled some.

"What is it, Yani? What else?"

Iyana's moon face flickered, her energy shifting as she drew a breath from wherever she was—Ninyeva's leaning tower, most likely.

"There is someone," she paused, "someone tracking you."

"I see."

"But it doesn't make any sense, Linn."

"Yani ..."

"He can't be."

"He is. We were attacked in the western woods. Larren is under their sway now. He is one with the Dark Kind."

"He's up above," Iyana said. "Waiting."

"Figures," Linn said, a sardonic laugh escaping her chest.

"Larren is powerful," Iyana said.

"He is. But he is not himself either." Linn smiled, trying her best to project a sense of confidence she did not feel. "Lucky for us, we still are."

Iyana smiled her sweet, knowing smile, and Linn almost hugged her, or tried to.

"I almost forgot you're not really here."

"I am here, Linn. And Kole will be, but you cannot wait for him. You won't last."

"Wouldn't want to spend another day longer than necessary here anyway. I assume you've found the way out?"

Iyana hesitated. She was growing more faint, as if she were fading.

"Yani?"

"You can find a pathway through the Steps and come back home," she said. "Back to the Lake. Back to me."

Linn frowned.

"Kole can do what he likes. We came here to find the source of the scourge. We're not turning back now. Not after what's been lost."

Linn expected Iyana to argue, but she was silent.

"What's it like up there?" Linn asked. "Above the peaks, I mean. Are the fields golden like the ancestors say?"

"Clear as glass," Iyana said. "Too high for the wind to reach. But the sun is there, Linn."

"I know someone who will very much enjoy hearing that."

Iyana smiled, but it was tinged with sadness, a knowing that Linn did not want to know.

"The Lake still knows peace?"

"For now."

Linn nodded.

"They'll need you before the end. Don't come back looking for me."

Iyana's brows drew close together, her lips forming a tight line, but she offered the slightest of nods. She flickered and nearly went out, and Linn's heart caught in her chest. She did not want her to leave, though she knew she must.

"This tether is failing," Iyana said, her voice even softer and more broken than before. The tiny firefly could be seen near where her heart would have been, its wings buzzing softly, weakly.

"Show me the way," Linn said, her resolve strengthening, mind bending to its purpose. She would find the White Crest. She would discover what he was about. And she would do it all before Kole had a chance to become what he most hated and feared.

She hoped.

CHAPTER TWENTY-EIGHT

THE WORM

They moved as quickly as the sodden terrain would allow. At first, they did so quietly, but now they made all haste, the booming percussions from the battle to the south punctuating the night and covering their progress. It was becoming increasingly apparent that the vast majority of the Dark Kind were massed outside of Hearth's walls.

Kole felt the guilt welling up like acid, the one fire to which he was not immune. Misha Ve'Gah, however, was a pragmatic sort, and though he kept pace with her evenly, she often as not took his silence for dawdling.

"Since I'm doing all of the navigating," she said, "the least you could do is keep up."

Kole said nothing. He knew the other Ember was merely covering her anxiety. In some ways, she reminded him of the Ve'Ran sisters, albeit a bit more brash. And though she carried her spear with a steady hand, he wondered if she knew how to wield it. He wondered why she had been positioned along the white cliffs, where action was sparse during the Dark Months.

In truth, Kole said nothing because he was tense, and that tension rode them all the way through the marshes in the shape of reed, rock and root. One great beast was unaccounted for. And it had last been seen in this region. Kole knew the Night Lord had not given up. Misha knew it as well. It had both of them peering around every bend in the slow-moving waters and twitching at shadows between the stalks. Though the land would have been difficult for her, Kole regretted leaving Shifa in Hearth.

Misha seemed to sense it before he did, her measured strides morphing into a trot that became half run. She looked back, eyes wild to see if Kole was behind her.

"Go," he whispered harshly, the back of his neck prickling.

The spear wielder broke into as close to a sprint as she could in the slop, cutting through swaths of reeds in the choked alleyways. Less experienced soldiers might have felt foolish for having been spooked by something unseen and unheard, but these Embers trusted their instincts.

Sooner than Kole would have hoped, the whistling spear separated the furry cattails from the final stalks between them and the river, and they let the current help them along as the way grew less choked. They waded forward, not turning back, and Kole could pick out the rough bank ahead by the way the silver light filtering in from the clouds carved stones from the darkness.

Misha grew taller as she gained purchase on the gravely river bottom, and she must have heard the sound before he felt it. The ripples and waves could have been natural, but he felt the coming of the beast in the undertow, the river pulling at him like an indrawn breath. The loose pebbles underfoot began a rapid slide that threatened to suck his feet out from under him.

Up ahead on the shore, Misha spun, her bright hair indistinguishable from the flaring tassels on her spear. The air around her grew hazy as she set her weapon into a slow spin that soon became a blur. Her features were obscured behind a whirring of green, red and yellow as the atmosphere turned liquid.

Kole flushed heat into his legs as he struggled up the cascading shore. He was chest-deep and slipping. One final lunge brought him up to his naval before he heard a hissing streak along the water's surface. He spun, the bottom betraying him once more in a lucky stroke that spared his life. As he fell, a spray of water hit him like shards thrown from the prow of a windship. The black mass was indistinguishable from the foam, but the red eyes glowed their ruby glow, and he knew the beast had come as he went under.

The river was cold and black. It enveloped him completely and he tumbled in the wake of the snake's passing. His fingers scored gashes in the rough sand and he fought to gain a horizon. He did not dare to surface, but rather clung to the bottom and waited.

A weight like a tree trunk slammed into his side and sent him careening end over end. Again, it was luck that saved him. Instead of the beast's razor teeth, the shallow stones met his brow, leaving their scrapes but sparing him a more ugly fate. Again Kole managed to dig his roots into the sliding silt, scanning the deeper darkness for signs of movement. Just when his lungs were about to quit on him, two red stones appeared in the inky black, and the serpent shot toward him with frightening speed.

Embers rarely ran from fights. They were more than worth their weight in water, unless they were in water. Kole swam toward the surface. The instant his head broke through, his eyes were stung by a brilliant kaleidoscope of amber, yellow and red.

Heat that would have killed any other buoyed his lungs and charged his blood with power. He set his feet in the rolling rocks and ran toward the blazing shore, where Misha Ve'Gah strained in the cyclone of flame. Behind him, the crash of the beast breaking the surface was drowned out by its roar of pain as the flames set to eating.

Kole reached the shallows and spun, drawing his blades as he did and setting the air around him to shimmer as Misha's flames died out. The serpent surfaced again, its head a smoking ruin, its cry more rage than pain now. It looked like no creature Kole had ever seen, though its body recalled the great burrowing worms of the Untamed Hills, docile creatures that met most challenges with swift retreats.

The fire distorted the Night Lord's form, the horns atop its head and the frills of its mane a melted and moving mass of coiling black.

"Reyna, down!"

And Kole put the fire in his legs, shooting backward as the serpent lunged for him. A comet in the form of Hearth's Third Keeper hurtled over him, spinning shaft in hand. The monster was so intent on Kole that it spared Misha no heed, its maw a frothing mess that smelled like death.

Kole lit his blades and angled them sharply, fearing he would be crushed in the collision. There was a whistling as the spear whirled and then a sharp sound like metal on marble.

The river stilled.

As the spray dissipated enough for Kole to see, the beast's head appeared directly before him and reflex had him stabbing out. He speared one ruby eye, which burst in a shower of hot blood that sizzled along the haft of his blade and coagulated into syrup as it rang along his armored forearm.

There was no cry as the beast died, no animal roar to rival the distant din of Hearth. It had died the instant Misha Ve'Gah's spear made a hilt of its skull.

Misha pulled her weapon free with a sucking sound and the Embers walked to the shore as the shallows stilled. Kole marveled at the sinews standing out along the backs of her arms, which were bare, her own armor ending at the shoulders.

They both looked at the dead creature in silence. As had been the case with the ape Kole had wounded at Last Lake, the ink sizzled and spat, draining into the river and coating the surface in a slick that shone like ice. The worms of the Untamed Hills had no bones, just cartilage beneath their shifting skin. This one's was gray and very near to rotten, its stench overwhelming enough to compel them onward with nary a backward glance.

"Not a true Night Lord, after all," Misha remarked.

"None of them have been."

"Then what are they?"

"Same as the souls before Hearth's gates: victims."

They followed the river's snaking progress north, and as they did, Kole thought of the serpent's eyes. It had the same glint as the ape, the same murderous, intelligent glow as the Sentinels in the woods. He thought he'd like a closer look at whoever had been staring back.

Though expected, the sight of the abandoned homesteads along the Fork hit Kole like a physical blow. As they crested the rise that looked down on the stout stone structures, he held out hope that they might find some resistance. There was none.

Kole tried to tell himself that many of the Corrupted before Hearth's gates were from lands beyond the Valley, but the desolation before them was impossible to ignore. Still, he could not help but feel some modicum of relief that Last Lake still stood, and that ever-present kernel of guilt glowed brighter in his gut as they walked among the empty husks and homes of their Valley kin.

"They fought," he said, as much to fill the wind-swept silence as to distract him from the few dead they passed. He could tell which had turned—their eyes were misshapen, limbs elongated—and which had died before the change could take hold. Death was a mercy in this war. How defeating, to wish for the Dark Months in place of this madness.

"They lost," Misha said after a time, but her voice had lost much of its solidity.

"There."

They were passing an alley when Misha noted a particularly dense collection of former persons strewn about a northern square. Carts had been overturned to form some semblance of a defense, and they could see the spires of a guard tower that stood in the shadows of the mountains.

Coming closer, they saw deep grooves in the earth that stretched like snails' tracks before coming to rest at the bases of great boulders—telltale signs of the final stand of the Rockbled. Kole did not know how many of the stone-throwers remained among the Rivermen, but he knew there were more of them than there were Embers in the Valley.

He wondered how many had fallen here. He wondered why they had chosen this gate as their final ground.

And then he saw the tracks leading north, and his heart swelled despite his mind's warning.

CHAPTER TWENTY-NINE

NUMBERS GAME

Talmir did not see Kole Reyna off in person because he knew he would regret letting him go.

Now, the guilt that had burned at his center had morphed, questions about whether or not he should have allowed the Ember to leave replaced by those demanding to know why he had not done it sooner.

Looking out over the roiling black waters of the Dark Kind, Talmir knew he had chosen right. He knew that, no matter how brightly Reyna may have burned, all fires would drown in the face of this darkness. Had he not sent him north, the questions would have haunted him unto his dying breath. The more he thought, however, the more he knew that questions over what the Embers would find might do the same.

In any case, he was resolved not to die. At least not while his city bled.

Talmir stood on the parapets and looked out over that black sea. The Dark Kind still attacked en masse, but the alleys and trenches were soaked with pitch and oil, the fields burning in defense of the city. Any of the sorry creatures lithe enough to crest the wall were dispatched in short order. But the defenders were only men. And men tired.

Whenever the Captain needed a morale boost, he would cast his gaze to the north, where First Keeper Garos Balsheer stood vigilant before the stonework, his broad arms soaking in the glow of his brazier.

Of the Corrupted, Talmir had taken close account of them. While they still approached in a fervor, their bodies had lost much of their substance, their shoulders sagging, chests sunken. Their maws hung ever open as they slogged forward and their black skin cracked and peeled. They seemed to be unending, pouring out of the trees in an endless stream that would make the River F'Rust blush.

Hearth's defenders were stronger of body and mind, but the sickbeds had been overflowing for days. Talmir did not know how many soldiers he had lost, but it was too many. He thought of sending for aid from the south, but he knew it was folly, knew that if he were in the position of Tu'Ren and Doh'Rah Kadeh, he would be loathe to send his own to certain death. The Dark Kind would find them soon enough, if they hadn't already.

How many arrows did they have left? How many casks of oil?

"You going to count the rain drops as well?"

Garos regarded him through half-open lids beneath a half-tilted helm.

"I really have a counting face?"

"A man has a face for everything," Garos said, looking out over the swarm. "Long as you know the man. Women have two faces for everything, and a man can never know both."

The hulking warrior bent and stretched, his groans swallowed in a small cacophony of creaks and cracks. Talmir morbidly wondered how much of the miniature concert emanated from the Ember's armor and how much betrayed the war between tired bone and sinew. The thought that even Garos was beginning to wear down under the steady onslaught was disconcerting, especially with his brazier so near.

The First Keeper likely guessed the direction of Talmir's thoughts, as he replaced his strained look with one of the usual bravado.

"To tell you the truth," Talmir said, turning toward the field, "I hadn't noticed the rain until now."

"It's too big a thing for you to notice, I suppose."

"Pardon?"

"You're a man of detail, Captain," he said. "Sometimes the big picture becomes lost."

Talmir regarded him.

"And the big picture is rain?" Talmir asked. "I could be excused for thinking the siege to be more ..." he swept his hand out.

"Pressing?" Garos supplied. He was adjusting the straps on his plate armor, an early model from the same metal smiths Talmir had contracted for Kole and Misha. The First Keeper's was less flexible than theirs, but unyielding as the walls upon which they stood, much like the man himself.

"Pressing. Yes."

A skirmish along the South Bend had been quelled, the soldiers there now falling back into the steady rhythm of poking down at their attackers with rod and spear.

Talmir surveyed the broken field before the gate, his eyes picking out movement among the wreckage. He tensed, fearing another Night Lord come crashing through the rock-strewn earth. He relaxed when he picked out the diminutive form of a sorry ghoul crawling amidst the char, its progress slow but unerringly forward.

"You've got to admire their determination, if nothing else," Garos said.

Talmir could not bring himself to smirk.

"Never thought I'd live to see the day where I longed for the unthinking beasts we fought in the Dark Months."

"Don't think there's all that much going on in that one's mind, Captain."

"No," Talmir allowed. "And even still."

"Aye."

And Talmir knew the Ember felt it as well. The defenders of Hearth had taken to calling them various names: ghouls, creeps, shades, Corrupted. It all meant the same thing: these had been men and women once. Deep down, they still were.

The occasional ting of water had increased to a steady patter, painting the white stonework something closer to gray. A thought occurred to Talmir.

"When was the last time we had rain?" he asked.

"Ah," Garos huffed. "Now you're back on the point."

The older man looked toward the sky and Talmir followed his gaze.

"Notice anything different up there?" Garos asked.

The sky was still dark enough to feel like the beginnings of dusk or the hunting hours of early dawn. And yet, the clouds were rougher, more patched and less solid. The black was now streaked with gray. It was a silent battle between ashen smoke and swirling vapor.

"Haven't had steady rain since the day the dark came back," Garos said.

"Sister Gretti told me the clouds were unnatural things."

Garos shrugged.

"The stuff of Sages," he said, as if no further explanation were needed. Perhaps it wasn't.

Could the dark be breaking?

Talmir rarely dared to hope, but something was happening up there, something that was disturbing the unnatural storm in favor of one from the skies above. The hissing sound picked up as the rain increased, burning up as it touched down on the Ember's skin next to him.

"I don't think those things will fancy a shower in their current state," Garos said. "Otherwise why cover the sky in the first place?"

"To block out the sun, I'd guess."

"They don't burn up any more or less readily in my flames than anything else," Garos said, unconvinced.

"The sun is a whole other fire. Magic's a strange thing, especially that which was taken from the World rather than gifted by it."

"Magic."

Garos heaved an offering of spit over the walls, his bullet landing within splashing distance of the crawling thing beneath them. If it noticed, it paid no more heed to that than anything else as it reached the rough-hewn stones at the base of the gate and started climbing.

The Ember placed his palm on his stone brazier, the heat building in the atmosphere around him as he drew it in.

"If only we had more," Talmir said.

"More what?"

"Landkist. Embers in particular."

Garos paused.

"You give thanks for gifts," he said. "You don't lament their absence, only what you might've done to bring it about."

"And what might that be?" Talmir asked a bit more forcefully than he had intended.

"We left the desert," Garos said, his tone fatherly and without judgment. "We never went back."

The sound of falling pebbles announced the presence of the climber, its brows furrowed in hate or pain. A bowstring went taught, the sound of stretching yew grating on Talmir's fraying nerves.

He held up a hand.

"Don't waste the shaft, soldier," he said without turning and the bow relaxed.

Garos placed a hot palm on Talmir's shoulder. He could feel the heat through his armor.

"Don't pay any attention to me, lad," he said. "It's true our people were stronger in the bosom of the desert, but we weren't strong enough to stop this darkness then, otherwise we'd still be there. Our Ember King fled and took his people with him. This war was a long time coming. Everything up to now has just been testing. Don't know how I know, but I do."

The climbing thing had left gouges in the stone that marked its steady progress. Flakes of black skin had peeled from its fingers, leaving the tips red with fresh gore. They could see bits of white flesh through the cracking mask on its face, which was now soaked through with the falling rain. As it drew closer, they saw the angled teeth and the pale tip of a sharp-angled ear that revealed it as one of the Faey, the only one Talmir could recall having seen amongst the horde thus far. He could not help but wonder who she had been, and he was doubly resolved to ensure that none of his soldiers would suffer the same fate.

It seemed that the Sentinels needed to be close to affect their magic. So far, none had strayed from the trees to the west, making it impossible to guess their number.

"I'm tired," Talmir said, low enough so that only Garos could hear.

Garos grunted.

"If it's any consolation," he said, "she looks dog tired herself."

The Ember lifted his great Everwood staff overhead and the air around them grew hot and liquid. The spiked iron ends took on an amber glow.

"Thing I've always loved about fire," Garos said as he sent his staff into a slow spin, "so long as you feed it, it'll never run out on you."

"Aye to that," Talmir said, the familiar stone encasing his heart.

The butt of the staff came down just as the Faey's head crested the rise, and the angry, sorry visage exploded in sparks that erased the gore, the singed corpse falling away to join the rubble below.

Talmir was not often accused of being an optimist, but one could be forgiven when standing beside the might of Garos. He drew his sword, curved and folded steel that stood just a pair of hands below his full height. It was an heirloom from his hero father he had never grown into. He signaled the archers along the North Walk and the South Bend alike.

A streak of lightning split the sky to frame Talmir in a moment that could have been carved into the cavern walls of the northern deserts, his father's sword lighting up like a rod. He slashed down and the miniature comets streaked out onto the field for the tenth time that day.

Talmir grinned an animal grin, all full of teeth, his face tightening against the lashing rain, which now came down in buckets.

This is where we turn it all around, he thought. *The sky is reclaiming its domain from the dark, and we'll follow suit.*

His soldiers took up a cry for the Emberfolk and resumed their slaughter with a gusto that would have disturbed Talmir had it not been exactly what he wanted from them, what he needed from them. The creatures below seemed to respond to the emotional spike, hurling themselves at the walls with renewed vigor, skin flaking away like wet ash. More climbed the gate only to be smashed by the god's lantern that was Garos's staff.

Talmir was about to add his lungs to the chorus along the South Bend when a voice like a flute lilted up from the stairs behind him.

"Captain Caru!"

Talmir spun to see Jakub standing at the top, two guards huffing as they caught up with him. They turned sheepish expressions toward the Captain as he stared balefully. The boy had apparently tossed out the satin shirt Rain Ku'Ral had provided for him and replaced it with his usual rags, and Kole Reyna's hound was at his feet, framing herself between the boy and his would-be captors.

"What is it, Jakub?" Talmir asked gruffly.

"I came to help," the boy said in a tone that suggested Talmir was denser than the walls on which he stood for asking. That earned a bark of laughter from Garos that was well timed with the crack of a splintered skull as another enthusiastic climber met its end.

Talmir edged closer and squatted down with a sigh. He placed his hand on the boy's shoulder, setting his blade down across the stones with the other. The hound watched him intently but made no move to intervene.

"I put you in a position to help at the Bowl," Talmir said. "You were to look after the girl from Last Lake."

"The one that Kole burned," Jakub said.

"Yes," Talmir said with a swallow. "That one."

"She doesn't need looking after. Her brother won't let anybody touch her. Only the Faeykin."

Talmir sighed again, trying to keep his emotions in check.

"He sounds like someone that might need looking after as well."

Jakub's frown deepened, if that were possible. He had a gift for mixing suspicion into nearly every face he made. All of them Talmir had yet seen were of the same mould, but what an expansive mould it was.

"He's a coward," Jakub said, his decision made. He crossed his arms as Talmir rocked back, brows rising.

"Taei Kane, a coward?"

Jakub nodded.

"Why would you say such a thing?"

"He won't come out to fight," Jakub said, accusation dripping.

"His sister is hurt badly," Talmir said. His patience was wearing thin. "Besides, this is not a time for judging others. Does Karin know where you've run off to? Creyath?"

Another shrug.

Talmir nodded. Another climber lost its head in a flash of heat that momentarily dried the skin and armor of all atop the gate. The din of battle intensified to the south, the discordant sounds bouncing off of the Talmir's skull as he grappled with a child's problems—unsuccessfully.

He put a hand to his forehead.

"Listen, Jakub. It's not safe here."

"It's not safe anywhere."

"Hearth is safe."

"Nowhere is."

Talmir looked into the boy's dark eyes. Really looked. After a time, he nodded to the guards and tried his best to ignore Jakub's screaming protests as they ripped him away from the gate.

"Caru!"

It was Garos.

"What is it?" Talmir asked, running up beside him. He craned his neck to look down before the walls. There were several creatures making their way up one precarious handhold at a time, but not so many as to cause him alarm, never mind the Ember guarding the top.

"Their faces."

Talmir looked closer. The sight before him, coming clearer with each struggling reach, was enough to make his skin crawl. The black masks had begun to fall away in the wash. They looked horrible, the gray skin of death mixed with the rot of decay, flesh peeling and purple with frozen blood. Others looked fresh and powdered as though they were slumbering in moving shells not their own.

Garos nudged him on the shoulder and Talmir looked toward the South Bend. He heard the gasps and cries and saw the horror etched onto his soldiers' faces. How soon bravery and bloodlust could turn to terror.

It seemed that sinking was the only feeling Talmir had time for these days, the former rush having all but gone out of him like a blown match. The fear and disgust grew along the wall like a living thing, a parasite nestling inside the hearts of his soldiers.

"Jakub!" Talmir called, rushing to the top of the stair.

To his relief, the guards had only managed to drag him to the bottom, the hound barking as the boy scraped along the stones and tried to root himself in place.

"Let him go," he said, and they did, sharing confused and annoyed glances.

"I have a job for you after all," Talmir said, crouching down as the boy reached the top of the steps in bounding leaps, the hound following after.

Talmir pointed to the north, where the snaking white walls gave way to quartz cliffs. There was a tunnel carved into them that burrowed up to the towers at the crest.

"Run to the white cliffs. Find me Dakken Pyr and his men, and bring them here. And hurry, Jakub."

The boy was off at a sprint before he had finished.

Talmir closed his eyes and breathed long and deep, loosening and tightening his grip on his father's blade. He rose, spun toward the south and walked with measured steps.

It could not be said that Talmir was all pessimism. As he walked the white walls, he knew the elders that had seen them built had been correct. The walls of Hearth would never fall.

Its people, however, were doomed.

CHAPTER THIRTY

DEEPHOME

L uckily, they stumbled upon the tracks before the storm did. When the clouds finally opened, they did so with a sudden fury, the lashing rain making hissing pans out of the Embers' hot metal suits. The shallow depressions they followed turned to tiny pools, which were soon lost in the wash, indistinguishable from the muck that was all the northern Valley counted as pasture.

"What I wouldn't give for the rocky fields of Hearth," Misha said as her boots squelched through the sodden terrain.

As was often the case since their meeting, she was annoyed at Kole, although this time she had the decency to blame it on the elements. For the early part of their trek, she had used bursts of heat to dry the land they crossed in order to make the tracking easier. Soon enough, they had discovered other tracks. These were unmistakably human in origin, but they were lurching and accompanied by scores and scratches. The Embers were not the only ones following the Rivermen, and that had put an end to the Misha's flares. Kole did not want them walking into an ambush.

It seemed that not all of the Dark Kind were massed before the walls of Hearth. Some were here, and if there were Dark Kind, there could be Sentinels. Kole could not help but think of his own battle with the Sentinel, both beneath the roots and in the realm of nightmare. It had taken all his willpower and the help of two of the most potent Faeykin of the Valley to stop the change. Most were not so fortunate.

"Easy," Misha whispered from behind him.

Kole looked up. No more than a few strides ahead, there was a pile. Kole's stomach churned.

The Embers moved forward cautiously.

"I know you're a hunter and all," Misha whispered. "You Lakemen all are, but don't let what's in front of you get lost in what's below."

"Linn was always the hunter," Kole said. "I just followed along."

An odd mix of relief and horror flooded Kole as they reached the pile of bodies. The forms at their feet belonged to Corrupted, their skins newly-acquired and not yet near to flaking in the mud, though the pools were stained dark around them.

"They don't look like Rivermen," Misha said.

"Hard to tell. Could be Faey."

"They took their chances in the woods," Misha said a little disdainfully

"It's not like we made them feel entirely welcome."

"Speak for yourself, Reyna," Misha said, lifting one of their heads with her boot before letting it settle back down. "This happened too quickly for us to send out warnings or for the Faey to heed them. Besides, they've always fared well in the Dark Months. Better than us some years."

Kole only half heard her. It was strange, looking down at the mangled forms at his feet, their bodies twisted as if a great weight had come against them, pressing them into the mud. Misha put a hand on his shoulder and turned him around.

"This isn't all on you, Reyna," she said, her tone—if it were possible—empathetic.

She moved off, and after a few awkward, blinking moments, Kole followed.

The black peaks loomed out of the ever-present dusk ahead, their caps lost to the swirling skies. Now, packs of gray disturbed the black in the clouds, and they could just glimpse the faint orange hues of the sun in the north. The light had the tinge of blood to Kole, and he found himself relieved when the mass of stones ahead blotted it out and sank them back into the gloom they had come to know so well.

They were in the Deep Lands now, cracks in the earth expanding into crevices. These took chaotic, nonsensical routes until they came together to form the bottomless trenches that gave the land its name. These wounds were eternal, and all who crossed them knew they would never close or fill. Kole had grown up with tales of the Night Lords stalking their depths. He doubted they were true, but could not help but wonder how the true generals of the World Apart would stack up to the sick imitations of ape and worm he had battled these last weeks.

The further they moved, the more apparent it was that desperation had forced the Rivermen this way, a desperation that Kole hoped was fueled by the promise that lay at its end.

With the scarred earth, the path of the refugees was becoming more difficult to follow. The memories of violence done to the land here in the titanic clash between the Sages discouraged growth, and the soil morphed into a thick clay that harbored no tracks. In the place of grass and weeds, only moss and the occasional scrub brush sprouted. Soon enough, the Embers followed intuition more than sense, following the path of least resistance over and around the gaps and plateaus.

A gray-black mass of stone rose before them to mark the base of the Lower Steps. Kole had never been here, though it was not so very far from home. The Steps marked the beginnings of a place out of memories that should not have been his, a place where Kole had lost much.

"Reyna."

Kole was standing still.

"Sorry," he said, making to move off, but Misha hooked his arm and yanked him back roughly.

"Wait," she hissed, eyes wild.

They stood on a steel-colored slab that narrowed to a point ahead. At its tip, just a few strides away, a larger mass of bodies was tangled together on the edge.

"Listen," Misha whispered, and Kole did, attempting to sift through the wind and rain.

There was a faint scratching sound, and his eyes adjusted to the haze, picking out hints of shadows ahead. They worked at something on the opposite ledge. There were no sounds of struggle, and as the Embers split off in opposite, circuitous routes, Kole saw that this pile did not contain Corrupted alone.

He felt the familiar warmth seeping into his blood from the white-hot core that all Embers carried. He sent it down into his legs, the sinews there flexing and pulsing. His armor creaked and groaned in protest as the heat built, black scales sliding over one another to expose tiny gaps that hissed like kettles.

There were close to a dozen of the creatures clustered across the gap. They were huddled on a narrow ledge with their backs to the Embers, and they scratched at a man-sized slab of stone that stood out fresh against the darker rock surrounding it.

Kole's experience with the Rivermen was limited to Baas Taldis. But he knew the Rockbled's way with the earth. It should have come as no surprise that his people would have had a way into the mountains in case of a mass exodus.

The thought of Baas reminded him of Kaya, Larren, Nathen, Jenk … and Linn. The tangle of bodies on the ledge swelled up in his mind's eye.

Some part of him saw the colored tassels of Misha's spear spinning to his left, attempting to signal him, but his blood was up. With a lunge, he was airborne, hands flashing to the Everwood blades across his back. He timed his draw with his landing, carving two of the creatures down the lengths of their spines on impact and ignition. Their flesh bubbled and sealed under the scorching blades, and they died with hisses that rang like the screams of demons to his ears.

The others fell on him.

Kole heard Misha shouting, but his concentration was forward, twisting and turning, deflecting and scoring as they came for him with a hunger.

"Jump!"

And Kole sprang back, the ghouls following in suit, several to their own demise. As he landed, skidding across the smooth surface of the slab, the beasts readied themselves as cats would and leapt across only to meet the fires of Misha Ve'Gah.

Her furious press sent another tumbling in short order, while those remaining ducked and darted like jackals. Kole was on them an instant late, allowing Misha to skewer one while he took the next under the ribs. On they came and down they fell, Misha's whirling attack forcing them into non-action while Kole skirted the edges of her blaze like a wolf at slaughter. They left the Corrupted in smoldering ruins, extinguishing their flames before the last of them had finished dying.

"That was bold," Misha said, scarcely out of breath as she adjusted a strap.

Kole did not respond. His blood would be a long time cooling. He leapt back across the gap to inspect the makeshift door and Misha followed after.

"Bluestone," Misha said, running her hand along the once-smooth slate where the Dark Kind had scored gouges into the surface. The stone was hewn in the rough shape of a door, and it stood nearly half again as tall as Misha's spear. The rain was breaking and a sliver of moonlight poked through the clouds. In the faint light, the door shone with a silvery blue shimmer that was entrancing, if conspicuous.

"It's the lightest stone in the Valley," Misha said.

"Doesn't seem it," Kole said, testing the give with his shoulder. It didn't budge. Judging by its proportions compared to the gap they had just crossed, it was only now serving as a door because its use as a bridge had run its course. Kole could still make out the muddy boot prints on its face.

"It's slightly ajar," Kole said, noticing a child-sized gap on the lower edge that betrayed a hasty retreat.

"Grab a handhold," Misha said, and Kole rewarded her with a blank stare before she nodded toward her spear.

"Really?"

"Really. Unless you want to call up that power you used before the gates and shatter the stone yourself."

Kole looked back at the stone. He ran his fingers along the lichen-choked face and over the grooves left by the Dark Kind. He closed his eyes and sought out the fire. He did not know if it would be there, but it assailed his mind with a sudden ferocity that had him spinning.

Something that felt like a pane of glass broke in his mind, and the door shattered in a stinging shower of blue-white dust. Misha yelped and Kole reached back reflexively, grabbing the Ember by the wrist as she fought to regain her balance, face ashen.

"Sorry," Kole said as Misha sat and dangled her legs over the chasm, panting. Her face was pale and covered in the dust that had made up the door moments before.

"I'm not sure I was serious," she said.

"That makes two of us."

She looked at him, eyes wide.

"Where?" she asked. "Where does such power come from?"

Kole swallowed.

"Rage, I would guess."

Misha's face worked through myriad emotions before settling on something Kole could not read.

"Hope there's more where that came from," and she was up and moving into the dust-choked doorway.

"Wait."

Kole lit the edges of his blades with a faint blue outline, highlighting the passage in an iridescent glow. They were in a spherical antechamber made of the same bluestone as the entrance he had just destroyed. It seemed that the hard rock encasing most of the cliff was just a shell protecting a softer underbelly.

"I guess the Rivermen found the yolk in the mountains," Misha said.

The chamber widened slightly ahead, and Kole had to blink as he noted what looked like stars winking at him from a faraway exit atop the rough-hewn stairs. Kole listened for the steady drip of water from stalactites, but the passage was dry as milled flour. The edges of the tunnel vanished into the deeper darkness, the tiny stars at the end twinkling with the reflected light of Kole's blades.

The Embers encountered nothing untoward during their climb, which must have lasted half a mark. Kole kept expecting to trip over a tangle of bodies or to hear another pack scratching at a distant door, but there was nothing.

Soon enough, the blue-blackness and all its glittering stone faded, washed out in the pale light spilling in from above. They crested the top stair and found themselves shielding their eyes from the light of a moon they hadn't seen in its full glory for weeks.

Before them, ringed on all its distant sides by sheer cliffs of black and gray rock was a dark green field infested with white daisies. In the distance, Kole could see the ruddy glow of campfires clustered at the base of a rise.

"We're in the Steps," Misha said, nearly at a loss.

They both looked up at the sky, noting the way the black clouds and swirling grays had moved off to the south, leaving the fields before them clear and fresh.

Kole wondered if his mother, father and the other Runners of the Valley knew of this place. He had always known the Steps to be inhospitable—barren lands of ash and choking dust. But this one was a veritable paradise.

As they moved toward the camp, the darker peaks beyond loomed like angry giants.

CHAPTER THIRTY-ONE

FIELD OF SUNS

Despite Iyana's help, it had still taken a day and more to reach what they hoped was the final in an unending series of tunnels beneath the peaks. They could just see the yellow rays bouncing off of the black, glass-like surfaces of the cavern walls ahead. The light sent pleasant lances into the backs of Linn's eyes. Whatever was on the other side would have to waits its turn to disappoint her. For now, she was relieved, if not happy.

Linn knew the sun would do wonders for Jenk, but Nathen seemed almost overcome upon seeing it, his gaunt face lighting up. Their rations were gone, but it was the dark that had been killing them. As they rounded what must be the final bend, Nathen took hold of Linn's shoulder.

"Thank you," he said, water gathering in the corners of his eyes. Linn shared a smile with him. He looked young then and it sent a pang through her heart. Jenk smirked and moved off ahead.

"Now we can die in the sun," the Ember said.

"We won't be doing any dying," Linn said. "Not now."

The cave had rocked each of them to their core, but it had changed Jenk most of all. His usual easy confidence was laced with something darker, something full of intent that reminded her of Kole. He saw Kaya's death in the reflections of the River F'Rust and heard it in the crackle of his own flames. If any of them was to have a true weapon remaining, she was glad that it was him.

As the tunnel brightened and the air grew fresher with every stride, Linn thought it funny that they had not entirely believed her about Iyana's visit. To their credit—and for lack of any better ideas—they had followed her through sloping pathways that curved downward as often as up, Iyana having mapped the path in Linn's mind as a series of impressions. Their collective mood had not begun to shift until they caught the scent of grass and soil, two things alien to the Deep Lands.

As she left the terrors of the tunnels behind her, Linn could not help but feel the anxiety attempting to renew its vice grip on her heart; how quickly one threat could replace another. She had not told them of Iyana's warning. Foolishly, she still hoped against hope that the White Crest, if he truly lived, was not beyond salvation. Or redemption.

Pure sunlight hit them, and what they at first took for the great orb itself eventually resolved into the tunnel's jagged mouth. When Linn's eyes cleared enough to draw colors again, she saw the bright blue of the sky. There was not a hint of storm on the horizon.

Nathen nearly sobbed beside her, while Jenk hesitated for only the faintest of instants before running to the opening. He stood there with arms out, chest facing the distant blaze as he drank it in.

Together, Linn and Nathen followed, walking shoulder to shoulder. Roots and vines snaked their way into the black mouth and purple flowers dotted a curtain of moss that framed the hole. But it was the view beyond that took their breath, just as it had yet to relinquish Jenk's.

It was a field of green with orange fire. From up on their rocky hill, they could see it all: a field of suns—clear pools that drank up the oranges, reds and blues of the sky to create wells of startling beauty. They came in all shapes and sizes and dotted the narrow landscape to the east far as they could see. The ground between them was covered in a carpet of green and purple with black stones jutting up to form a pretty sort of violence.

To the north, the ground fell away, revealing a gorge leagues deep, brown earth with ridges framing the horizon, white clouds snaking around their peaks. In the middle was a great divide, and the silver flow of the River F'Rust slithered through, looking like a tiny serpent in place of the dragon they had come to know so well. Far beyond the natural gate, at a distance only Linn could see, were rolling hills and lush trees melting into the distance.

It was the World, and it was not covered in the darkness that assailed their Valley home. It was nothing like she had expected and everything she had hoped.

"There," Jenk said, pointing east.

Across the pools, framed against the dark clouds to the south that spilled into the Valley, was a cloister of mountains small enough to look like stalagmites from their vantage. They formed a semicircle around a rocky cliff whose bottom dropped away. Below the tallest stones but above the black cliffs, they could see a ruby-red roof glinting like blood. The structure beneath it was half in shadow. It looked as though the mountains were taking it back.

The mood shifted the moment they spied the keep, and that was fine to Linn. She knew they had grim work ahead.

"If anyone's home," Nathen said, "I'd assume we've been spotted already."

"Keep to the shadows just in case," Jenk said, and they moved off, following a grassy depression that sloped southeast.

"Feels like being an eagle," Linn said, peering down into the Valley that had ever been her home. "It looks somehow bigger and smaller than I imagined at once."

There was a labyrinth of smaller, jagged peaks below that framed the ceiling that had hung above them throughout their hellish climb, and she could see the cracks and fissures of the Deep Lands even from this height. Between were the Steps, great shelves of rock that might as well have been plains. Linn could see a glittering lake on the lower-most one and what looked to be green, standing at odds with the barren shelves above it. The clouds had thinned in the north, but darkness still swirled thick in the distance.

Straining, Linn could just make out the white jewel of Hearth standing alone in the Valley's center. It looked to be choked by black, rotted fields, but she knew the truth of it. She looked to the south, but even her eyes failed to pick out the forests before Last Lake.

"Perhaps we've become giants," Jenk said as they picked their way along the rockier ridges. "Maybe these pools are vast oceans and that keep a house of gods."

"I have a feeling its occupant thinks so," Linn said without humor.

"Who's to say he's not," Nathen put in.

"Doesn't mean we can't have a chat," Jenk said.

"We should wait for Kole Reyna," Nathen said, and Jenk's expression shifted as Linn watched him. She had told them both of Kole's approach. Nathen thought it represented a grand opportunity, but Jenk seemed to equate it only to another delay before an inevitable confrontation.

"We don't know which of the Sages resides there," Linn said. "If any."

"Look around," Jenk said bitterly. "I'll give you a guess."

"And if it's our Sage?" Linn asked.

Jenk was silent for a time.

"Then we'll talk, and see what he has to say."

That ended it, and they walked until the cloister loomed above them.

"Damn."

"What is it?" Jenk and Linn asked in unison.

"No way we make it up there without being seen," Nathen said from under the next rise.

They moved up behind him. Over the ridge, they could see the keep clear as day. It rested at the top of a crisscrossed series of pathways carved into the steep hillside. They looked like cart paths overgrown after decades of neglect. Linn could make out a wall of green-flecked marble in front of the structure, and the gate in the center of the yard was broken and leaning at the hinges.

"Well," Linn said, "if it is the White Crest, we probably don't want to surprise him anyway."

"Assumptions," Jenk cursed. "Power corrupts, and it corrupts the mind most of all."

An image of Kole Reyna was called up in Linn's mind. She shook the thought away.

The three moved off, wending their way up the zigzagging path as casually as goatherds out for a graze. The dark stones of the citadel loomed overhead, another dark cloud to replace those they had climbed above. Closer now, and the red tiles looked less like jewels and more like rusted, spiteful things full of growth, the curved towers and gaps leering like something sick.

But the nightmare was down below, Linn reminded herself. The nightmare her people were living through, dying through. Whatever she might face in the dusted halls of an old Sage's keep, she would give as fine an account of herself as she could.

Nathen was the first to see him, sitting on a rounded boulder that must once have been part of the keep but had since broken away. His upper body was stiff, back straight and gaze locked on them as his legs dangled in the wind.

Even from a distance, Linn could see Larren's bearing, but something had changed about him, seemingly for the second time. In place of the red eyes of the Sentinel from the cave were stones of piercing blue. They tracked their progress with the glacial calm of one who has seen mountains grow and slowly crumble into dust.

None of the three spoke, tensing as if they expected him to leap down on them at any moment. His spear was not in hand, but it leaned against the boulder, and they had all seen Holspahr wield it firsthand. At his peak, he was one of the most formidable warriors among a people whose children now counted themselves as players in a generation of war with the Dark Kind. Though the Larren they knew was clearly gone, Linn did not expect him to be any less potent now.

As they neared, the details of the keep resolved themselves in vivid detail, carved beaks and piercing gazes of birds of war adding their own stone scrutiny from behind their former ally.

They reached the sloped ground before the crumbling gate, the boulder and its keeper seated to their left. Across a small courtyard, the maw of the keep opened wide, doors long since rotted away, the hints of cold statues bedecked in armor that glinted molten in the late afternoon rays of the sun.

It took Linn a moment to register that Nathen was no longer beside them. She tried not to alert the thing on the boulder as she cast about, eyes wide, but the creature wearing Larren's skin laughed a laugh that boomed like faraway thunder and whistled like the wind between ridges.

"Missing someone?" it asked. "He slinked off into the rocks midway up your climb." It leaned over the rock and crooked its head, neck contorting in an odd way that gave the impression of an owl. "I must admit, even I lost track of him, and these eyes see quite far."

Neither of them answered, and that looked to annoy the creature. It sat back with a sigh.

"Come," it said, "Do not let us be burdened by the loss of friends … however recent their departure."

Beneath the discordant layers of melody in his voice, Linn could hear Larren bubbling through. She wondered if there was anything left of the Ember.

As if he could read her thoughts, the creature smiled at her in an exaggerated way that exposed teeth whiter than marble, canines filed to points like the Corrupted they had fought in the Valley.

"I like this vessel," it said. "I sent that other beast out. What have you taken to calling them? Sentinels. Yes."

Jenk spat, his fingers twitching toward his sword.

"We can't allow those princes of darkness to ride around in our precious Ember shells, now can we?" it asked, looking at him pointedly. Its smile dropped to a hard hawk's stare.

Linn remained quiet. She glanced about for signs of movement along the ridges. There were plenty of hiding spots about, but the creature did not seem concerned.

"Are we speaking with the White Crest?" Jenk asked. "Or merely a servant?"

"Both, in a manner of speaking," and the smile returned. The blue hawk's eyes swiveled to Linn, making her feel very small. "I wonder if you are the ones I sensed approaching. My Sentinels lost you in the Deep Lands. It is no small thing to come through those catacombs unscathed."

"Do we look unscathed to you?" Linn was trying to mask her attempts at stalling, but the creature's ease gave her the distinct impression that they were merely rats in a cage at that moment.

"Are you not the White Crest?" she asked.

"I am a being of light, wind and air," it said, leaning back and spreading its arms out wide. It breathed in deeply, and a breeze stirred around them, tickling their tattered clothes in an embrace that was part caress and part threat.

"Why?" Linn asked. "Why have you turned against us?"

For all the fury she had built up, she felt somehow deflated upon the realization that Kole had been right, that their Sage was party to all that had come against them. She hated the child's voice that escaped her, asking questions where no answer could serve.

The creature turned those blues on her, its smile shifting for the barest moment into something that approximated pity. As soon as she saw it, however, the look vanished and turned cold.

"There are many powers in the World, children," it said, voice melancholy. "Some have been here a long time. Some would seek to challenge the others."

"We grew up on tales of the White Crest's bravery," Jenk said, voice rising. "That you withdrew from the affairs of your kind."

"That does not mean the others removed their attention from me," it said, sneering. "One has mistaken my dalliance for weakness. He sent those foul creatures here weeks ago—or was it a generation? Those black beasts, titans from the World Apart."

The creature tilted Larren's head.

"No matter," it said, settling back. "I sniffed out his plan, and now his weapons are my own." It examined Larren's hands, calling up a tiny flame between thumb and forefinger that had Linn and Jenk stepping back warily.

"The Embers are not yours to wield," Jenk said, anger mounting. His hand moved ever closer to the hilt of his Everwood blade.

The flame disappeared, as did the smile behind it.

"All Landkist are weapons," it said, "put here by the World to challenge us, or to be used. I've already teased out more power from this husk than Holspahr could in a lifetime. Would that they still made your kind like they did when I first happened upon you—or when you happened upon me and my Valley—all those years ago."

"Perhaps they still do," Linn said, and the blue eyes shifted to Jenk.

"I was your shield," it said. "Your shield from the terrors out in the World."

"Until you brought them here," Linn said.

"The Dark Kind were not my doing. At least, not at first."

The creature wore a curious expression as its thoughts traced their way back in the far reaches of memory. It looked as though it were fighting through a constant fog. Linn had seen elders possessed of such mannerisms, but she had not expected it from one of the Sages, creatures of immeasurable power and limitless wisdom.

"I ..." it paused. "I am not so easily controlled. I found myself in the same darkness as you, and now I'll fight back with the light. Your light, to be specific."

It stood Larren up, straight and tall.

"I did not ask for this fight," it said. "The Eastern Dark thought I could be used, controlled." It curled Larren's fists, and Linn winced when she saw the blood running between the Ember's fingers. "But no longer. I am awake, thanks to one of your own. His plans are nothing but wisps on my winds, now."

The blue eyes softened, fists relaxing as the blood went dry with a faint sizzle.

"It's all a bit dark, yes. But then, all magic is." The blue eyes turned on Jenk. "Even your gifts, born of the land, have a dark bent when led by a vengeful heart. There is nothing separating us in this."

The veins stood out on the side of Jenk's neck. His muscles tensed, thickening with fast-flowing blood. The air around them shimmered and Linn broke out in a sweat.

"What of your bargain?" Linn screamed as the wind picked up. "What of the King of Ember?"

"It is forfeit," the White Crest said. "My hand has been forced. He'll not have the weapons in this Valley. I'll no longer be his Keeper. Now then—

A form slammed into him from behind, spearing him over the lip of the boulder and tumbling down the steep ridge. Linn and Jenk sprang into action, sprinting toward the edge of the cliff where the two wrestled. Nathen struggled and spat, hands clamped around Larren's throat.

Linn was fast, but Jenk shot past her, sword out and catching fire as he leapt high into the air. His arc brought him down, sword angled sharply, curved point lancing toward the skull of the Sage's host.

A sound like the shriek of an eagle rang in Linn's ears as she ran. She saw Nathen launched backward, his head cracking in a spray against a nearby spur. He slumped, blonde bangs plastered over unseeing eyes.

"Ahh!"

Jenk's sword came down in the same instant, but the sudden burst of wind had pushed him off-course. His blade split a rock just behind the prone Ember's head, sparks flying up around them.

Larren rolled away, came up in an animal crouch and shot directly toward Linn with inhuman speed, horrifyingly fast even for a charged Ember. It took all she had to send Nathen's hunting knife spinning while she dove to the side. She heard the metal ring as it struck armor, and then she hit the rocky terrain at an odd angle, ribs shaking as she tumbled. She stopped her roll dizzy and disoriented, one arm dangling into the open air above the Steps.

The clash of weapons had her struggling to turn and she saw Larren's spear alight and locked in a bitter and spitting embrace with Jenk's own blade. The young Ember had managed to trap the other near the boulder on which it had stood, but he was already losing ground.

Jenk gave way, relaxing his push and ducking under the spear to cut low, but his strike was blown off course by some unseen current and Larren spun away, hopping and slicing. The Everwood spearhead thrust straight, but the flames curling off its end carved at odd angles on crescent gusts. The flames could not hurt Jenk, but they interrupted his vision and slowed his stellar swordsmanship.

Linn knew that Jenk was fighting a losing battle. The thing wearing Larren's shell could not recall the Second Keeper's technique fully, but it fought with an alien quickness, its mastery of the very air in which they fought making it impossible to predict and harder to harm.

She struggled to her feet, her hand reflexively closing around an errant stone as she did. She rolled it around in her fingers and shook her head, attempting to clear her vision. The Embers ducked and rolled in their deadly dance. Larren backpedaled onto the edge of the far cliff, where the ground fell away steepest.

It was a feint. Linn knew the instant she saw it, but Jenk was too caught up in the exchange to notice. He charged, sword stiff and steady at his hip, aiming for Larren's gut. He ducked a lazy swipe and thrust forward, but Larren was not there; instead, he hopped back, dangling for the barest of moments in the open air before rocketing up and over the young Ember in a somersault.

The Sage landed lighter than a feather and streaked forward with that inhuman speed. Jenk could not turn in time.

Linn's throw prevented him from being skewered where he stood. It took the Sage in the cheek, opening a deep gash and knocking him off course, but it was not enough. He slammed into Jenk shoulder-first and Linn watched him fly off the precipice, sword going wide and mouth open in a scream that was lost to the howling air.

The blue eyes wheeled on her and another freakish leap brought the White Crest face-to-face.

"I know who sent you," it said, spitting and wild. "The same old bird that woke me. I think I'll pay her back the visit."

"You should fear her," Linn said, but much of the fight had gone out of her. Her knees felt weak. "You should fear us."

"Healthy fear is sometimes a boon," it said, grasping her around the throat and lifting her without effort. "She'll tell me who else she has out here."

"Know …" Linn choked out.

"What's that?" the grip loosened.

"You already know who it is."

The blue eyes flashed and then Larren held up a hand to Linn's nose and mouth. The air was pulled from her like a ghost. As her vision faded, she saw Nathen's sorry form leaning awkwardly against his stone. When the darkness took her, she saw a green firefly making its trails on the backs of her eyes.

CHAPTER THIRTY-TWO

BLOOD FROM STONES

K ole and Misha were on their third round of a circular argument concerning how best to approach the refugee camp when the Third Keeper of Hearth made a grab for her spear.

"We should just light our blades and call out to them," she said.

Kole put a hand on the haft, drawing a murderous look.

"After what they've been through tonight?" he asked, exasperated.

"We've all been through it," Misha hissed. "Besides, what are they going to do?"

"I'm sure the Dark Kind they left in their wake would've asked the same."

"We left a few of our own," she reminded.

"We don't even know if it's really them."

"What does that mean?"

"There must've been Sentinels about—at least one. Those Corrupted looked freshly-turned."

The mist had cleared somewhat and the field was cast in a ghostly glow from the light of the embattled moon overhead. The Embers were huddled under the eaves of a natural trench just a few strides from the nearest tent. They had seen little activity but for the occasional pass-erby—a woman carrying skins of water or wine toward the center of camp. No guards were posted, which had Kole jumpy.

A light, musical sound like the trill of a songbird lilted over the rise.

Before he could stay her, Misha was up, spear in hand and charging over the lip onto the grassy knoll. Kole scrambled after her, running face-first into her armored back, as she had stopped almost immediately. Kole backed off wincing and drew his blades, craning to see around her.

The source of the sound appeared to be a girl no older than seven. She had light features and dirty blonde hair, and she looked directly into Misha Ve'Gah's eyes as if the serrated tip of a six-foot length of sharpened Everwood was not angled directly between her own.

"Are you coming?" she asked, frowning slightly when neither of the Embers made a move to speak. Misha's eyes darted wildly, searching for signs of ambush. The girl asked them again, speaking more slowly this time, either to help them comprehend her thick accent or because she suspected them of being slow.

Kole placed two fingers on the haft of Misha's spear—the second time he had touched the weapon in as many minutes—and lowered it. The little girl turned another frown on Misha before she switched her gaze to Kole. She smiled warmly, her pale skin turning bright pink.

"What's your name?" Kole asked. He sheathed his blades and squatted down to meet her at eye level. "And where are your parents?"

"Undermiddle, with everyone else," she said in that child voice.

Misha planted the butt of her spear in the earth with a dull thud.

"And who sent you to get us?" Kole asked. "Did you see us under the rise?"

"No," she said. "Old Farsight saw you hiding."

"That a Seer?" Misha asked, patience wearing.

The girl stuck her tongue out at Misha before turning back to Kole.

"He always knows where anyone's hiding," she said.

Kole nodded. Though he did not know much about their Valley neighbors, the fact that they had something approximating a Seer surprised him, since they held no love for the Landkist among the Faey. Misha continued to scan the camp and the surrounding mist, the thought of being discovered so easily not sitting well with her.

"Lead the way," Kole said, rising to his feet.

"Karpi," the girl said, extending her hand. "That's my name."

"Kole," he said. He took the small white fingers in his own darker ones and squeezed lightly, causing Karpi to pull back with a startled shriek that soon turned into a bubbly fit of giggling.

"Hot," she said, bouncing up and down and shaking her hand out dramatically. "Your name fits! Follow me." And she was off at a skip.

Misha smirked at Kole, who shrugged and followed.

Their winding path took them through a camp that was much smaller than Kole had anticipated. There were plenty of tents, but the ones on the outer edges seemed deserted, no signs of bedding or cookfires within. The larger tents in the middle of the plateau appeared only recently vacated, flaps thrown open and pots and pans still dripping grease.

The only Rivermen they saw during their walk were either the very young or very old. All of them largely ignored the passing Embers and their fluttering guide, who talked excitedly in her harsh tongue while she bounced.

"No wounded," Misha remarked, scanning the makeshift settlement intently.

Kole nodded.

"Hard to get wounded over the Deep Lands," she said, and Kole did not argue.

"How can they be in such high spirits?" Misha asked, staring at the bouncing gaggle of children that had joined Karpi in front of them. Several of them tossed sour looks her way, tongues lolling out of tiny mouths.

"The Rivermen are supposed to be resilient," Kole said. "If Baas Taldis is cut from the same cloth, it doesn't surprise me."

"He act like this?" Misha asked, nudging her spear toward the joyful caravan.

"Not exactly," Kole admitted.

As it turned out, Undermiddle was an apt name for the structure Karpi led them to, if you could call it a structure—more a slab of slate that leaned at an awkward angle. A three-step stair was dug into the earth beneath it, along with a doorway absent frame. Though it looked as though the slab could collapse at any instant, crushing those beneath it, Karpi entered with a twirl while the other children milled about and made faces at the Ember pair.

They entered a chamber that was just as sparse as Kole had imagined. A fire burned in the center pit and the dirt-packed walls had benches dug out along the entire length. There were many open seats. The ceiling was low enough to force Misha to keep her spear level, something not all in the room seemed to appreciate.

As for the occupants, these were the fighting men and women the Embers had expected. There were perhaps two score, most holding axe or hammer—some a combination of the two. Kole noted that most of the weapons were carved from a solid piece of stone; it was a wonder they could lift them at all. Great shields of pitted steel leaned in the empty slots along the walls, reflecting the firelight like angry suns.

Misha nudged Kole in the direction of a far corner, where a particularly squat, barrel-chested man watched from the shadows.

"That one's staring at you."

"They all are."

"That one's really staring."

The brute was bandaged in so many places it was a wonder they hadn't wrapped him for burial. He stood slowly, unsteady, and shuffled forward.

"Kole?" he said, a sound like grating timbers.

"Baas?"

The initial flood of relief Kole experienced upon seeing someone from the Lake was supplanted almost immediately by the realization that Linn and the others were not with him. Given the state the Riverman was in, Kole felt his heart sink like a stone.

"I see you two know each other."

Kole and Misha turned to see an old man standing on the opposite side of the fire. He was adorned in simple skins in place of the leather and iron sported by most of the company, and he bore an unmistakable resemblance to Baas. Kole had not noticed him upon entering.

"You are?"

Misha, Kole was learning, was not one for first impressions. All in the Valley were used to conflict, but Ve'Gah seemed to breath it. He tossed her a look, which she pointedly ignored.

If the elder had taken any offense, he played it off well. Kole glanced at Baas, whose expression was similarly unreadable.

"I am Braden Taldis," the old man said, "and I am the grandfather of your fellow Lakeman there." He indicated Baas, who continued to stare at Kole.

"Old Farsight!" Karpi called from somewhere in the back.

Braden made a low rumbling that could have been a laugh, though it emanated as if from the walls themselves. He reminded Kole of Tu'Ren, and even of Garos Balsheer, whom he had recently met on the walls of Hearth. Apparently each of the peoples of the Valley had one great bear among them, a figure of strength and solidarity in the midst of ever-present chaos. He struggled to picture what such a man might look like among the Faey.

"Your borders are unprotected," Misha said, drawing a few more rumbles from the crowd, these ones decidedly less mirthful.

"They appear so," Braden said with an easy smile.

"You are a Seer," Kole said.

"What is sight but the colors of the mind, eh?" Braden said, stepping a little closer as he examined the Embers. A few of the more battle-worn warriors stepped forward protectively. Misha's spear swayed in their direction like a cat's twitching tail.

"You followed our trail," Braden said.

"Yes," Kole said shortly. He very much wanted to speak with Baas, his stress redoubling by the second.

"Ease," Braden said, holding up his hands in a calming gesture. The room breathed, Kole included. Misha fought the sensation, shifting from foot to foot, but she lowered the tip of her spear until it was even with the dirt.

"We must have our answers," Braden said, calm but firm. "You followed us here, but that is not why you've come."

"No," Kole admitted, ignoring Misha.

"You came to do what my grandson failed to."

He stated it as fact, and Kole saw Baas's broad shoulders slump. Braden stepped forward and placed a hand on a bandaged shoulder.

"Truth only has the power to hurt if we fail to recognize its power to lead," he said. There were nods and murmurs of agreement, but Baas still had the look of a whipped dog.

"I can't speak to Baas," Kole said, "but I'd say you've guessed the truth of it."

"To kill the White Crest," Braden said, and there were a few gasps.

Kole nodded hesitantly and then turned a look of earnest pleading Baas's way.

"Tell me what happened," he implored. "Tell me they're alive."

Baas shifted under the stare.

"I lost them in a storm," he said. "The survivors, in any case."

Kole did not know Baas well. The Riverman had ever held himself apart from the defenses during the Dark Months, a source of disdain among some of Last Lake's Emberfolk, Keepers chief among them. He did not know which member of the party Kole was most invested in.

"My grandson does not remember much from the encounter," Braden said. "He was found buried under a mountain of loose stone. Were he not Rockbled, there is no telling how many pieces he'd be in." He turned a prideful look on Baas. "He would have gone after them himself had we not dragged him back to the Fork."

"And the others?" Kole asked, more forcefully this time.

"Two of your Embers fell," Braden said, and Baas squeezed his eyes shut. Whether it was a look of sorrow, rage or pain, it was impossible to tell. "The others fled. We found no trace of them, though their path led to the Deep Lands, to the deepest and most rabid mouth of the River F'Rust. We could not follow."

"Two Embers," Misha said, breathless. "Not Holspahr." She looked to Kole, who nodded solemnly, thoughts racing.

"Larren was buried with me," Baas said in a voice barely above a whisper.

"The one that turned?" Braden prompted, and Baas nodded.

The elder looked back to Kole.

"Your Keeper was corrupted by a Sentinel. It was he whom the others fought, and whom Baas brought down in the cave."

"You beat Larren?" Kole asked, astonished.

Baas shrugged as if he genuinely did not know.

"He is Rockbled," Braden said, as if that were explanation enough. "There are few of us left, but more than enough to make our stand against those beasts. Many have forgotten the songs of the earth, but rock and river runs through this one's veins."

"I must admit I've never seen a Rockbled fight," Misha said. "But I find it hard to believe you bested Larren Holspahr."

Kole knew Larren had been of Hearth before he settled with a woman from Last Lake. He wondered if he had any connection to the Ve'Gah's. Or perhaps it was merely Landkist posturing.

"I did not fight alone," Baas said. "Jenk Ganmeer and Linn Ve'Ran were there after Kaya fell. The fisher's boy, too. Nathen."

The mention of Linn's name centered Kole, as did the realization that Kaya Ferrahl was dead.

"This corruption is a new thing," Braden said. "We have never known the Darklings to turn anything but rats, worms and the like."

"We've never had to face their Sentinels," Misha said. "This isn't just some rift like those that open during the Dark Months. This is an invasion, complete with Captains and all from the World Apart."

"A Sage's errand boys," Kole said bitterly.

Braden looked at him curiously.

"Strange, is it not, for one of the Emberfolk to question the White Crest?"

"I didn't say his name."

"No," Braden allowed. "I suppose you did not." His gaze lingered, searching.

"I have a question," Misha said, interrupting the exchange. She lanced a finger at Baas. "Why was this one raised at Last Lake, among the Emberfolk?"

Baas's look was steady, and Braden placed a hand on his shoulder.

"I often sent my son Aerek to the Ember towns and villages on errands," he said. "He was lean and handsome—much easier on the Emberfolk eyes than many of us." He smirked, as if the story need not go on. "The days of conflict between our people are long since past."

"Not so long," Misha said under her breath.

"My grandson is one caught between worlds," Braden said. "But we all are, us Valleyfolk, in our own way. Only the Faey can truly claim to come from here, and even they may be fallen leaves from far-off trees. We are all of us orphans in our own way. We are together in this darkness."

"Together?" Misha's mood shifted, anger boiling over as her heat rose. "I for one am no orphan. My mother and father are currently cowering behind the walls of Hearth along with the rest."

All eyes in the room shifted to Braden Taldis, awaiting his response— all, that is, except for Kole's, which were currently boring holes into the side of Misha's sweating temple.

"No Runners came to offer us sanctuary," Braden said, "though I have no doubt Captain Caru would have, had he the time. We made our own place. I would bid you point your anger where it belongs, to the Sage at the peaks. Magic such as theirs is nothing but an abomination. All of its roads lead only to corruption. To court the creatures of the World Apart." He spat.

"You won't try to stop us, then?" Kole asked. "Your people could earn retribution should we fail."

Braden studied him before switching his gaze to Misha.

"This one has followed you out here because she believes in ending the scourge of the Eastern Dark," he said. "But you and I both know that is not the Sage residing in the peaks, though his magic is thick about the Valley."

Misha looked askance at Kole, but he continued to look straight ahead.

"Prove her right, for following you."

"My mother used to travel these paths," Kole said. "She was friend to all in the Valley, Rivermen and Faey alike. She came to these peaks to plead with the White Crest. She did not believe he had fallen. I believe she was right."

He looked at the ground, where the orange glow of flame mixed with the dark brown earth to make something close to crimson.

"I've seen her blood mix with the rain every night since. I'm done waiting behind walls or hiding beneath rocks like worms in the garden."

He looked up, and noted that all eyes were on him. He did not try to read them.

"I knew Sarise A'zu," Braden said, and it was Kole's turn to look shocked. "In passing, maybe, but I knew her. My Rockbled will accompany you. The Sage has not left all his tricks down in the Valley—of that you can be sure."

He took a step closer.

"One stone can change the course of a river, no matter how strong the current," he said. "Only take care you do not presume that stone to be you, Kole Reyna."

Kole swallowed. Several of the Rivermen stepped out of the shadows, hands gripping stone weapons. There looked to be a dozen or more that intended to join the Embers, and Baas was one of them.

Braden noted his grandson's advance and made as if to speak, but a look from Baas silenced him.

"Very well," Braden said, leading the way out of the Undermiddle and into the cool night air of the Steps.

The Rivermen warriors moved off into the camp, presumably to gather what gear they needed, perhaps to say their goodbyes. It was difficult to tell which of them were Rockbled, but Kole thought a few seemed more solid, striding as if mountains might move out of their way rather than make trouble.

Kole and Misha stood alongside Braden, who watched Baas's slow steps.

"Do not worry on my grandson," he said. "The World chooses its guardians well." He looked up, his gray eyes seeming to pierce through the vapors of the Steps and the dark wisps of cloud above.

"Why did you never attempt it before?" Kole asked, and Braden regarded him coolly. "Your people have ever held a deep distrust of the

Sages, our supposed protector among them. Why not seek him out? Make him answer?"

Braden paused. He had an audience now as several of the warriors milled about, Baas carrying a huge pitted shield that looked to be made entirely of stone. Kole felt a fool for asking.

"Our people, like yours, came to this Valley to escape the wars of the Sages," Braden said. "We came out of fear. I suspect that to be the reason we have stayed. I do not presume to know the truth surrounding the darkness that assails us now, but I know it was not the White Crest's doing alone."

"How do you know it was him at all?" Misha asked, though her tone was now subdued.

"Ninyeva is not the only one to recognize the talents of the Faeykin," Braden said. "I have seen things. I have heard a beating like great hearts these last years. It has grown, like something dead now living. I cannot escape the sound any longer. It is a sound of ending, and now I have seen the source."

"Where?" Baas asked. "How?"

"A young girl showed me the keep just the other night," he said with a smile. "In dreaming. She had bright green eyes and hair the color of mountain caps."

"Green eyes?" Kole asked.

Braden smiled at him.

"I suspect you know the source," he said. "She told me to expect you, as well."

Braden took Kole by the arm and guided him away from the gathered warriors, as well as Misha, who looked on suspiciously. He leaned in conspiratorially, his breath smelling of ginger.

"It may sound foolish to say, but do not underestimate a Sage, no matter how dormant he may seem."

"I won't," Kole said.

"Some say they were the first Landkist," Braden said.

"Do you believe that?"

Braden paused and considered the field as it stretched out before them, ending abruptly at the base of the next shelf.

"Whatever they were, they have long since forgotten," Braden said. "That is what I believe."

"What could the White Crest gain from all this?" Kole asked, earning an amused look from the elder.

"You are beginning to doubt your conviction?"

"I've always doubted it. Vengeance is good motivation. It's rarely innocent, or all the way true."

Braden nodded, seeming impressed. He laid a hand on Kole's armored shoulder, and even through the black scales, the strength was immediately apparent. Kole felt very small of a sudden. He suspected there was a point to be made there, whether or not Braden had intended it.

"The Landkist may not be as potent as the Sages in power," Braden said, "but the Sages know we are the key to winning their private war. Quaint as this Valley must seem to the wider World, it represents a fine opportunity to horde such treasures as you away from the rest."

"The Eastern Dark," Kole said. "You think he wanted us here? The Embers."

"Embers, Rockbled, Faeykin," Braden said. "I do not know. I would not assume the White Crest to be himself these days. So many are not, even those who started as our friends. I suspect you'll find the truth of it soon enough."

Braden turned to stand square with Kole.

"Do not worry too much, Reyna," he said. "This burden does not fall upon you alone. Do not doubt the prowess of our sons and daughters, though the stones can seem slow and unmoving on the surface. Just the same, do not let the flame be too quick to violence. Be sure that yours burns in the right direction."

There was nothing left to say, so they said nothing.

Kole made sure to find Karpi and give her white fingers another squeeze before they departed.

They set off just before dawn, two cinders ringed by their dozen stones.

CHAPTER THIRTY-THREE

RECKONING

T aste was the first sensation that returned—saliva and the crusted, metallic blood of lips gone too long without moisture. Smell would be next, but before it came, she had to remember the path she had taken.

Ninyeva called it the haze of unreality, and Iyana was feeling it keenly as she came back to herself. She had let intuition guide her through the tunnels of Linn's dreaming and had spent longer than she should have navigating the milky roads of the Between. After years of being able to do little more than heal scrapes and ease the pain of the passing, Iyana had tapped into the true gift of the Faeykin. She was Landkist.

When she had run to the Faey Mother, Ninyeva was not surprised in the least. She helped to center Iyana and her ensuing tutelage had better prepared her for the trip she returned from now, wending her way back from the webbed dreams of the Riverman.

Build a net and tether, Ninyeva had said. *Find this and follow it down, from branch to root, until you come back to yourself.*

Iyana had set out to find Kole, but there was no tether she could feel, no connection to guide her to him. She saw him as if from a great distance, moving through the northern Valley with an Ember of Hearth. It was like following an echo. She traced the ripples and found them belonging to another Landkist. She had descended into his mind uninvited. It had been a far cry from steering the consciousness of a firefly.

The elder had ensnared her almost immediately, and she was caught fast in a prison of untold depth, encased in imagined stone so tight it squeezed the breath from her lungs. A man stood before her, squat and broad-shouldered, his sturdy outline stark against the black cave of his mind, his thoughts hidden away from prying eyes.

Iyana could not remember much from their exchange, but the man had released her. In truth, he seemed more concerned with how she had entered his mind than why. He knew of the Embers' approach, and he had promised to assist them on their road to the peaks. She trusted him, though she had little reason to.

Sage.

The pungent odor ripped her back to the stuffy room that was her teacher's attic. She felt the floorboards groan beneath her as the tower leaned in the billowing winds of storm. She heard singing, and her eyes snapped open, the low light of the fire in the grate burning like a thousand suns for the briefest of moments.

Rusul, her raven hair ragged and disheveled, eyes sunken, looked positively thrilled to see Iyana staring back at her. She had not been here when Iyana had departed, but Ninyeva said that time was a fluid thing in the Between, its meaning dubious and its hold tenuous.

Ninyeva seemed in a trance a hair above sleep. She was humming a tune that Iyana now recognized as a song from her childhood. She felt a pang in her heart when she heard the 'Melody of Wind and Willow.' It was a song passed from mother to daughter and from daughter to sister.

Together, Iyana and Rusul waited for Ninyeva to return. Iyana was not entirely comfortable with the Seer, but Ninyeva seemed to trust her of late.

Ninyeva opened the only eyes in the Valley greener than Iyana's own. She wore a pleasant smile when she noted her pupil staring back at her.

"He caught you prowling, yes?" Ninyeva asked, astounding Iyana yet again with her powers of observation.

"How?" was all Iyana had the wherewithal to ask.

"You are blessed with abilities far beyond what I had at your age," Ninyeva said. Rusul watched the exchange with something between respect and envy. "But I have healed thousands. Emotions tell their own stories. I merely tagged along with yours. They told me enough."

Iyana nodded slowly.

"Caught?" Rusul asked, concerned. "Caught by whom?"

"Someone old," Ninyeva said. "Someone wise."

Iyana nodded again, steeling herself for a verbal lashing, but Ninyeva turned those grandmotherly eyes on her, her smile soft.

"You must take care in the Between," she said. "It may seem like a dream, but it is all too real. A Faeykin is not the same as a firefly."

"It wasn't one of the Faeykin," Iyana said, shaking her head.

"No?" Ninyeva sat back, surprised. That was a rare enough thing.

"He was a Riverman, I think," Iyana said.

"A Riverman?" Rusul asked in disbelief. She raised her brows appraisingly, looking between student and teacher.

"Braden Taldis," Ninyeva said. "Rockbled. The oldest among his kind."

"He is to be trusted?" Rusul asked.

"Given that our girl is safely returned to us, I would assume so," Ninyeva said. She reached for a bowl set on the edge of the grate and handed it to Iyana. It smelled of lemon and lavender.

Iyana took a drink. The hot liquid shocked her throat, but after the initial burn, she felt better than she had in some time. How strange, that a journey outside of the physical could take such a toll on the body. It was no wonder Mother Ninyeva did not attempt the search on her own. Something had happened on her last trek, and Iyana still did not know what.

"Braden," Iyana said, seeing the shadowed face of the Riverman. "I saw Kole and another Ember in his mind. He knew they were approaching."

"Approaching where?" Rusul asked.

"Not the Fork. Somewhere farther. Somewhere beneath the peaks."

"It is a good thing that Braden escaped," Ninyeva said. "Wherever he is, I hope most of his people made it there with him."

"He will help Kole," Iyana said.

"What have the Rivermen to offer an Ember possessed of such power?" Rusul asked. "What can they do in the face of a Sage?"

"How do you think they warred with us in the early years of the Valley?" Ninyeva asked. "They are unyielding as enemies. That will hold true as allies."

"There was an anger in him when I mentioned the Sages," Iyana said, remembering. "It was seething just below the surface."

"The Rivermen have no love for magic or its consequences," Ninyeva said.

"None do," Rusul scoffed. "They appreciate having their Rockbled. No small magic in them."

The Seer switched her charcoal eyes to Iyana, her stare intense and penetrating.

"I want to know how you did what you did," she said, taking Iyana aback. It felt like an accusation. "Ninyeva has been around a long time. How did you go from mixing poultices to walking the Between in a span of weeks?"

Iyana made a move to respond, but Ninyeva cut her off.

"We are Landkist," Ninyeva said. "Our gifts are bestowed. The Ember-folk have put such a strong emphasis on bloodlines that we sometimes forget that."

Rusul turned to regard Ninyeva, her expression shifting strangely. It was a look that said more than she was willing to reveal in present company.

"Given recent events," Rusul said, "it is strange to hear you decry the import of blood or its effect on the World."

Ninyeva held her palms up.

"Blood has memories," she allowed. "But even blood comes from the land itself. My own powers did not awaken until my thirteenth year. That was a time of great turmoil in this land, before the Dark Kind followed us in. Before the White Crest fell. I think now would qualify as another such time."

Rusul looked about to argue, but seeing the strain on Iyana's face, she relented, her face coloring in shame.

"Apologies," she said, stilting. "It is sometimes difficult being a witness. Always a witness."

Iyana nodded and swallowed.

A creak in the floorboards alerted Iyana to another presence. She twisted, yelping like a pup when the knots in her back protested. She saw that Tu'Ren was standing at the back rail, his form outlined in gray through the thin screen.

"He's tense," Iyana said, turning back to the other women.

"He was tense in here," Rusul said, rolling her eyes, "so we told him to take it outside."

The screen was thrown open with unnecessary force and Tu'Ren stole in with a strained, tired look that softened a bit when he noted Iyana staring back at him from her place on the carpet.

"Well?" Rusul asked, impatient. "What news?"

Tu'Ren grimaced at the Seer's impropriety, but he stifled a biting retort.

"The hounds are restless. The wind's picked up."

"Those beasts are always restless," Rusul said, but Tu'Ren shook his head.

"Not these beasts. We cannot see the Dark Kind, but they're out there, hiding beneath the canopy. They've choked the trails. We've had one Runner back of the four we sent with Karin a week ago."

"And the Corrupted?" Ninyeva asked.

"No sign," Tu'Ren said, the admission seemingly more disconcerting to him than an open siege might be. The First Keeper of Last Lake was a man of action, Iyana knew. Waiting idle did not sit well with him, especially when their cousins in Hearth bled.

"I know it is diffic—"

"It doesn't make any sense," Tu'Ren said, interrupting Ninyeva. He was nearly shouting as he stomped around the small chamber. "Why do they assail Hearth and leave us alone?"

"Magic takes energy," Ninyeva replied calmly. "The legions of the World Apart are not easily guided. Our time, I am sorry to say, will come soon enough."

"But why?" Tu'Ren asked, exasperated. It made Iyana distinctly uncomfortable to see one so strong reduced to childish questions. "Why would the Eastern Dark come for us now, after all this time?"

"We don't know how their war is going," Ninyeva said. "We don't know who is winning. He has long coveted the power our people possess. The power you possess."

"Some power," Tu'Ren said softly, examining his hands in the dim light.

"None can be sent to Hearth, Tu'Ren," Ninyeva said, her voice hardening. "Not now."

Tu'Ren looked about to argue, but he never got the chance. In hindsight, Iyana wished that he had.

It started as a keen whistling that threaded between the storm winds, prickling at Iyana's ears. Soon enough, the whistle became a drone, like wind through a tunnel, strong enough to chip stones. As it grew, the sound morphed into something like madness.

Rusul looked up from her bones, glancing around the chamber worriedly. Ninyeva's brow crinkled, and even Tu'Ren, red-faced and hot, went ghost pale to match his tied hair.

"What is it?" Rusul was shouting.

Iyana went to stand, but Tu'Ren stopped her, casting about for his Everwood blade. It made her feel no better when he held it in hands more scarred than the blade itself. What use was a blade against the storm?

Ninyeva had her eyes closed, humming something that was like an anchor of calm amidst the chaos.

The noise was now a hurricane, rattling the windows in their panes and sending chips of spray from the lake below lancing through the canvas door to the balcony like shards. Of a sudden, the whole of it went quiet and deadly still. Ninyeva opened her eyes and they sparkled with something Iyana could only later recall as terror.

Shadows speared across the skylight, black comets in the shapes of crows. Tu'Ren set his blade alight, and the shadows it cast joined the maelstrom playing out along the leaning walls. There were no birdcalls, only the flapping of a thousand airy winds slicing the atmosphere with dark intent.

A horn went up in the distance—a signal to man the walls—and Tu'Ren cursed, making for the torn balcony. Iyana looked up through the shattered skylight, into the cyclone of shadow birds that rose like a chimney of thick, billowing smoke. In the center was an eye, glowing blue-white. In a horrifying instant, Iyana knew it was looking at her, and she knew their doom was at hand.

"Tu'Ren! No!"

Ninyeva was shouting above the wind, but the Ember could not hear her.

The First Keeper whipped open the tattered canvas screen and it broke apart like a puzzle, splinters slicing through the bottles along Ninyeva's many shelves. Iyana shielded her eyes and felt the skin on her forearms tear, but the Ember stood in the midst of the storm and cried his challenge to the heavens, flaming sword held aloft.

The heavens answered.

Iyana only remembered bits and pieces of the destruction. She remembered the blue-white eye lancing down toward the Ember like a bolt that became lightning. It struck him and sent him tumbling along with the remainder of the timber frame, half the chamber breaking and falling with him. She remembered clawing her way to the space where the floorboards broke and fell away, Rusul dragging at her heels as she screamed down to the wreckage on the street below.

She saw Tu'Ren's hand sticking out from the debris, blood trailing. Tears stung her eyes as much as the spray from the salt lake to the south as Rusul dragged her from the precipice.

There was a sound lighter than thunder but as percussive, and it took Iyana a few moments to discern the words swimming in its fury.

"You sent the Runner to me!" it bellowed, and the paper tore from the walls of the chamber, which had broken like an eggshell. "You sent the Runner whom I slew. You flew in dreams of my dreaming, a lamb in the dreams of a wolf."

Iyana's head began to clear as she focused on words that held no meaning to her. She screamed for Tu'Ren and made for the broken floor again, but Rusul pulled her back.

"Faey Mother!" Rusul yelled.

Iyana turned to see Ninyeva, her face cut by a hundred tiny splinters of wood and rain sitting with her back against the far wall. Ash from the grate coated her gown. She looked sodden and frail, eyes wild as she stared slack-jawed at the maelstrom beating around them.

"The stairs!" Rusul shouted at Iyana, who nodded. Together, they seized Ninyeva by each arm and hoisted her toward the door. The tower swayed precariously and Iyana feared it would collapse at any moment.

Rusul shouldered the door open and the three of them affected something of a controlled fall to the landing below. Ninyeva was trying to say something, but Iyana could not hear her. Downstairs, the windows had all been blown out and the breams were cracking like the glass underfoot. Looking up, Iyana saw the ceiling swaying like the bough of a tree.

Another crack sounded that was almost too loud to hear, the impact ejecting them through the splintered web that had been the front wall. They landed in the street, mud pooling around them, hands and knees scraping on rock and debris.

Iyana could feel warm blood coursing down her bangs. People ran to or from the destruction of which they were the center, screaming and crying. A pair of lads—smiths, she thought—dug desperately at the wreckage of Tu'Ren's balcony, heedless of the danger swirling above.

The horn sounded again and the baying of the hounds was drowned out in the voice of the White Crest. How could they ever have thought to question such a force—to challenge it or its ilk? How could they ever have been so arrogant to call it ally, protector?

Iyana felt then that the Landkist were merely ripples along the waves of the Sages.

A streak of green and brown passed by Iyana as she groveled in the dirt. She looked up to see Ninyeva, standing straight as an arrow, walking toward the mouth of the storm. The White Crest resolved itself into a cyclone of blue and white, something like a hawk's face coalescing in the chaos, lightning orbs for eyes crackling as it tracked the old woman's approach.

"Ninyeva! Faey Mother!" Rusul, her red robe clinging to her in a manner that made it impossible to judge her wounds, reached toward the old woman.

Iyana's heart leapt when she saw Tu'Ren, white hair coated with red, gaining his feet and casting about dizzily for his blade, whish still burned brightly in the wreckage on which he stood.

"Why have you come against us?" Ninyeva railed against the storm, her voice carrying impossibly well on the air of the Sage's making. The great head swung and pivoted, a mix between serpent and bird.

"I was to be a tool," the beast boomed, each syllable sending rain from the ground to challenge that falling from the sky. "I was to be his tool, used to cull the chaff from the wheat, to separate blessed from doomed. You were the crop and I the scythe."

Ninyeva moved closer, standing just below the creature's shimmering beak. Her robe swung and danced violently in the storm, but her face had dried in the wind, hair unbound and flowing in an approximation of what she must have looked like in youth. She was strong and noble—dauntless. Behind and around her, Iyana could see archers gaining precarious perches, lighting arrows on ungainly roofs and pillars.

"Who?" Ninyeva asked. "Who guides the strings of one so strong as you?"

This sent the beast into another undulating fit, but Iyana thought the storm had lost some of its fury.

"None control me," it hissed, those crackling eyes drawing closer to Ninyeva's face. "He sent his Night Lords and I took their hearts. I wield the darkness of the World Apart now. I own this realm and all in it."

"The dark has made a blade of you," Ninyeva said. "You, who we counted as ally."

"The King of Ember was my ally," it said. "My weapon. He failed to kill the Eastern Dark. You Embers were my charge—fireflies lost at sea with no reed on which to land. I was to cultivate you. That was my charge.

But I am awake, now. I am myself. I am, and I will cull his fields to draw him out. I will turn his darkness upon him. You sent your Embers to me and I have turned them or thrown them from the cliffs."

And suddenly Iyana knew that Linn had failed. She felt cold hands interlaced with her own and turned to see Rusul kneeling beside her, staring ahead with the rapt attention of one kneeling at the foot of some terrible god.

Perhaps they were.

"There is another you have sent," it said, head menacing. "One whose power I have felt from a long way off. A power I have not felt in a long time. He will be my sword remade against the darkness. My Ember blade. I have seen him in her mind. He will not come against me while I have her."

Ninyeva stood even taller than before. Blood leaked down her cheeks like the paint of the Faey tribes.

"I had hoped against hope that we might find you dead or gone," Ninyeva said, spitting with disdain. "And here you are, a thing used. A thing corrupted."

The beast's form grew indistinct—all wind, rain and lancing light. The bright orbs dimmed under Ninyeva's scrutiny and Iyana felt something like shame emanating from it in waves that made her nauseous.

It remembered itself and the orbs brightened once more, the dam breaking. The wind picked up and the water, charged as it was, transformed into tiny arrows. Iyana scanned the rooftops, where the scattered archers were prepared to loose. But what could they do?

An orange blur lit her periphery, and Iyana swiveled toward the wreckage of the Faey Mother's tower. Tu'Ren stood, his skin set to a pulsing glow, sword held alight before him.

"You know nothing," the beast said, but its roar turned from fury to pain, and Iyana saw the atmosphere around Ninyeva warp like heat in a clear sky. The Faey Mother's eyes took on a glow so bright that Iyana could see it even from behind, and the Sage twisted and writhed.

"What is she doing?" Rusul asked in a horrified whisper.

"She found an opening," Iyana said. She could not explain the battle that raged before them, but she knew of the Faeykin's darker gifts. It was said they could turn their empathy to whips and lashes, as Ninyeva did now. She remembered the twisted corpse of the hunter from Tu'Ren's memory.

Ninyeva's knees began to shake. Lightning split the sky, arcing down and sending the roof of the smithy up in cinders. The archers loosed their burning shafts, which were blown away like matches. The Faey Mother screamed like Iyana would not have thought possible. She collapsed as the White Crest roared.

Iyana broke free from the hands that tried to hold her back and ran. The hounds howled in the darkness, driving her onward, and the air grew thick with water, wind and flame as she waded through the maelstrom, eyes focused on the pile of green and brown crumpled at the foot of the storm.

When she reached her, she was shocked to see that her teacher's emerald eyes had lost their sheen. They had faded to white, and though Ninyeva still breathed, it was labored, her chest wracking.

"A Landkist seeking to enter my mind!" the beast roared. It sounded manic as the storm it created. "This is not the world of dream, you retch. You escaped last time. Now you lay broken and scattered. Your power is nothing to us."

"Our power …"

Iyana turned her challenging stare from the maelstrom to her teacher, who struggled to speak. She laid a hand on her cheek and nearly recoiled for the shock of pain she felt. She anchored herself to it, tried to ease it. But there was too much to take. She wept.

Still, Ninyeva breathed a little easier, her voice growing more solid. Iyana pulled her head from the mud, cradling her like a babe.

"Our power," Ninyeva croaked, eyes unseeing, "is a gift."

The great break swung toward them, making Iyana flinch. Tears streamed down her face as the White Crest laughed its maniacal laugh.

"A gift," it mocked, words popping like logs in a hearth. "We brought magic to the World. You and yours are nothing but leeches."

"You took it," Ninyeva said through a sigh. "It belongs to a World of which you are no longer part."

At first, Iyana took it for a grimace of pain, but Ninyeva smiled a strained smile and the Sage's lightning eyes widened once more. The Faey Mother's eyes were blank, but she stared directly into the storm.

"Your keep lies unprotected, fool," she said, laughing a witch's laugh. "Your Dark Hearts will be cured, and then yours will be the only one that remains in this Valley. Soon enough, that will be cured as well. Burned away. Ash on your own winds."

The storm reared back and unfurled great wings of debris.

"Your Ember hero is still a day's march from my keep," it gloated, but there was an edge. "I threw the other from the tallest peak with the hands of one who called him ally. Your sister," its eyes blinked toward Iyana, its victory infecting her to the marrow, "sits in chains. The woodsman," it continued, "I shattered his head on the back of a stone. His bones will bleach in the sun you will never see again."

Ninyeva smiled.

"He lives."

And Iyana knew that Ninyeva could see him even now. Nathen Swell, alive against all hope and reason.

The beast roared and made as if to take off, its form shimmering in the spray it sent up.

"Tu'Ren!" Ninyeva screamed.

Iyana saw only white like the brightest snow and felt the wash of heat as the First Keeper leapt over them, trails of swirling gold curling in his wake. He slammed into the avian head and their meeting split the atmosphere with a crash not unlike thunder. Although insubstantial, the White Crest roared as Tu'Ren sunk his burning blade home, bringing the storm down in a shower that only flew in one direction.

The Sage gathered itself and hurled its energy back at the Ember, but Tu'Ren Kadeh stood his ground, the wind seeming to feed the flames of his blade.

Iyana was forced to squeeze her eyes shut tight against the clash, and soon the crackle of lightning, the roar of flame and the howl of the wind faded like a memory. The hounds still cried in the distance, and she could now here the echoes of shouts along the walls, bowstrings twanging like harps as the Dark Kind came at them.

She opened her eyes to see the closed lids of Ninyeva, curled in her drenched lap like a sleeping child. Rusul stood on unsteady legs and moved off, swaying like a tree in the breeze. Men, women and children emerged from the shadows of broken frames and leaning piles.

Ahead, Tu'Ren knelt in the mud, his great back heaving with long pulls, smoking sword hissing in the rain beside him and causing a puddle to froth and boil. When he turned toward her, she saw tears mixing with the rain.

"I tried," Iyana said, holding herself just above the surface.

Tu'Ren rose with a groan and moved to her. All signs of the Sage had passed.

"We all did," he said, laying a hot hand on her thin shoulder that warmed her to the bone.

"He's gone."

"Back to his roost," Tu'Ren said. "Whatever she did," he looked down at Ninyeva, "it rattled him enough for me to strike."

"He is weak now. He spent too much energy coming here."

"We gave them what chance we could."

Iyana nodded, wiping the droplets from Ninyeva's face.

"Now let's hope they do the same for us," Iyana said.

The horns went up again along the walls, calling the First Keeper to his brazier. A scout screamed down the road from the north, waving a torch and bellowing.

"First Keeper! You father requests your presence immediately."

The scout looked at the chaos along the lane that was now a causeway and blinked like a dog.

Tu'Ren lifted Ninyeva's prone form and stood to face him. Iyana's thoughts turned to Linn, sitting alone in the dungeon of a Sage's keep, her closest hero a woodsman whose head had been dashed upon the mountaintop.

CHAPTER THIRTY-FOUR

THE DARK HEARTS

Linn woke in the cold and damp, feeling the moss-covered stones beneath her.

She was cold. She was tired. And everything hurt.

The Sage wearing Larren's skin had fled and left his shell behind, and the sudden fury of his passing had drawn her from the depths of unconsciousness.

He was heading for Last Lake, she knew. For Ninyeva. For the leaders of the Emberfolk. He was heading for Iyana, and there was nothing Linn could do about it. She would outlive them all in spite of her every foolhardy effort to get herself killed in the mountains.

Once her eyes adjusted to the gloom, Linn was somewhat surprised to see that her cell was barely a cell at all—more an old wine cellar, broken crates long since rotted to sludge. The barred door was missing most of its bars, and those that remained looked as though a light breeze might crumble them to dust.

She may as well have been at the bottom of the River F'Rust, for all the good it did her. Just at the edge of sight, through the toothy bars and across the dank hall, two red eyes glowed dully in the gloom.

The White Crest was gone and Larren had once more become the shell for a Sentinel, a ghoulish hound set to preside over the damsel in distress.

How strange it seemed to Linn. She had spent most of her life fighting the denizens of the World Apart, but never their Captains. When she was a girl, they told her the Sentinels would never come through unless the Eastern Dark returned. How sickening, that it was a Sage they thought to be their own that had set the beasts on them.

Linn spat, and she could see the hint of a smirk pulling at the edges.

She pulled herself up against the wall, hugging her knees in a futile effort to gather what warmth remained in blood and bone.

For a spell, she assumed the Sentinel was staring at her; perhaps it was, but it was also looking through her, its focus away. She saw those ruby reds pulsing with an odd cadence, a rhythm that matched the beating of drums she had felt since waking. The walls thrummed with it, and the air around her—sticky with age and rot—buzzed on the edge of an explosion.

She looked back at the Sentinel. With each passing hour, it looked less like the Second Keeper of Last Lake. Iyana had told her of the White Crest's corruption. She had told her of the Dark Hearts. With each pulse of those red orbs, she became more certain they were beneath her, buried in the deep stores of the keep. She wondered if Larren Holspahr still lived in some way, if he was present for what his hands had wrought against Kaya, Baas, Jenk and Nathen—all those foolish enough to follow her.

Linn considered making a run for it, but where would she go?

It was then that her heart, strong as it was, truly broke. It was then that Linn realized she only wanted to run so she could die in the company of those she loved. In a delirium forged by a mixture of pain, exhaustion and starvation, she cried, not caring that the demon watched her from its shadows.

Perhaps Kole would arrive in time to bury her, or else to add his bones to hers. Perhaps he was already dead. All told, Linn thought it might be better that way. She did not want to see the look on his face when he realized he had been right all along. No matter the reason, it was clear that their Sage was now the same as all the rest.

Even after Iyana had told her the truth of it, she had clung to a false hope. How ironic, that Linn—ever the pragmatic soldier—would be proven so naïve.

A small laugh escaped her chest and the Sentinel twitched.

She was so tired.

But she was a Ve'Ran.

"Do you take pleasure in being the Sage's dog? Even your master has a master."

Her voice sounded strange to her ears in this alien place, cutting through the constant drone from below. There was a crinkle along Larren's brow, but the Sentinel made no move.

"Do you have any power of your own? Or must your kind steal all they have?"

Now the Sentinel leaned forward, teeth bared in a wolf's false smile.

"Have you no voice?"

"Aye," it said, and though Larren's throat made the sound, there was an odd croaking that was macabre to listen to. It was as if the spirit was unused to the machinery within.

"You are a slave," Linn said. "A slave with no shell of your own."

A frown. It had worked those out well enough.

Linn clutched the sharp stone she had secreted in from the yard, the edge digging into the heel of her hand. She had thought to use it on herself, and then she saw Iyana's face, her lips forming a tight line, green eyes framed in the pout she knew so well.

Linn's thoughts turned.

Could a well-placed throw do what an Ember like Jenk Ganmeer could not?

"You are nothing," Linn said, not having to reach to call up the disgust she felt as close as the damp.

"I am," it hissed.

"Tell me," she said, ignoring it. "Where did you go when your master took the shell you're wearing."

Confusion replaced anger and the creature leaned back, face working.

"Where were you when the White Crest had him?" Linn pressed.

"Apart," it said sharply.

"You don't belong here," she said. "You are nothing. You belong nowhere. You are less than the rot in this cell."

The creature growled and Linn gripped the stone tight enough to bleach her knuckles white. She could feel the heat pouring from Larren's body even from this distance.

"I am—

"Nothing," Linn said, settling back in her corner and partially closing her lids, though she kept vigilant, taking in every detail, the obsidian throbbing as she tensed.

The darkness was dispelled as tongues of flame crept from Larren's torn leather.

"Your power is a loan," Linn said, shielding her eyes as if annoyed. "Your debt will be called in soon enough, and you will return to nothing."

"After," it was seething, boiling. "After I tear you apart. We are darkness. We are many, and we are powerful."

"No," she said, opening her eyes and looking at the imposter with all the hate she could muster. "You are nothing. You are from nowhere. And once the Sage is through with you, you will return to nothing. You will be displaced yolk."

"The White Crest is ours," it hissed. "There are no strings but those that bind him."

"Then he is as much a slave as you," Linn said evenly.

She was certain the Sentinel would leap upon her and rend her limb from limb then. It leaned forward, teeth flashing and flames sprouting on Larren's skin, something she had never seen an Ember do. The demon was destroying its mortal coil. She felt the drumming intensify, the vibrations running up her spine and setting the bones to click like plates.

As quickly as its anger had boiled over, it cooled, the Sentinel settling back, flames withdrawing like snakes in a burrow. It flashed a smile at her, red eyes wide and manic.

"If he takes this one, I will find another," it said, grinning sickly at her, head tilting.

Linn felt sick at the thought of the Sentinel taking her, but she turned the acid to a liquid fire that welled in her stomach before infusing her breast. A stretched calm fell over her. Her fingers relaxed around the stone before closing back on the myriad grooves she had quested from her dexterous study in the dark.

"I think I'd rather die," she said, her muscles flaring painfully to life as she brought the lever of her arm forward to throw. The Sentinel's eyes widened, red bulbs sparking as it caught the movement.

A scream that sounded like one of the silver lions from the Untamed Hills cut through the dark, freezing Linn mid-throw. The demon whipped Larren's head around as the echoes crashed and cascaded around them, bouncing off the low ceiling and sinking into the floor.

Now was her chance. Linn tensed to throw again, but before she could, the Sentinel darted into the murk, leaving her as it haunted the darkness for whatever beast had wandered in.

From the left, soft footfalls could be heard, and Linn was sure the beast had brought company. She cursed, settling in a tense crouch.

When it entered her view, she hesitated for a moment, and she was glad she did. The sight before her was no lion, nor was it another demon from the World Apart. Blood caked light hair, turning it pink, and one eye was crusted over with fresh scabs. His shirt hung in tatters, and his feet were cut and bleeding into the stagnant pools.

"Nathen," Linn whispered, dropping the stone with a clatter that echoed as if from the bottom of a well. In the distance, the Sentinel shrieked, enraged at its lost quarry or aware of the ruse.

Nathen, wounded and woozy as he was, exploded into action, smashing down the rusted bars and snatching Linn by the wrist. He dragged her out into the low hall and they took off at as close to a run as they were able. After a few strides, it was Linn doing the dragging, each corridor growing brighter with the promise of the sun.

The cries of the Sentinel drove them on like hares before a hound.

"How?" Linn asked, nearly breathless, but Nathen was in no state to answer. He kept his head low and trudged on.

They came to a cross section with a sheer wall in front, and the panic set in.

"I've had enough of tunnels," Linn cursed, whipping her head around. "Do you remember how you came in?"

"There," he said, pointing weakly down the right hall.

Now that she looked closer, Linn thought it looked brighter down that way. She made as if to move when something prickled at the back of her neck, the steady cadence filling the air around them like a broth. The dark engine called to her, beckoning with intent, its bass hypnotic.

"Linn," Nathen said, pulling at her.

"We must go down," she said, earning a look of disbelief.

Linn grabbed a hold of him by both shoulders.

"Whatever is feeding these beasts," she said, "it's in the keep. It's below. It could be the key."

Nathen did not look convinced, but another shriek pierced the gloom, this one sounding much closer than the last.

"Nathen, we have to try."

A short nod and they were off, the darkness growing thick around them. It was the sort of dark that was more than the absence of light; this darkness was something made.

Linn hoped it could be unmade.

There was a spiral stair, broken and crumbling from neglect. They followed it down, and the deeper they got, the slower they moved, as if something repelled them.

"The smell," Nathen wheezed, holding a hand over his nose and mouth to keep from gagging.

A scent like rotting meat hit Linn. The air was thick and humid, full of decay. The stones along the walls glistened with sweat and they navigated by touch, feeling their way down the slick.

The beating of drums grew deafening as they rounded another bend, the floor smoothing out as they reached the bottom. The darkness gave way to a red tinge, which set the floor to glitter like the ruby eyes of vipers. Great pillars loomed overhead, set into rows under a vaulted ceiling lost in the fog.

Linn felt dizzy. She rubbed at her temples as she moved forward. Nathen slouched, his broad shoulders leaning crooked.

A scream and Linn was sure the Sentinel had found them, until she saw Nathen collapse in a writhing heap. She ran to him, but the sound hit her next, buckling her in stride. She buried her ears in her hands and chanced a look. There, past a bare altar on the back wall, great slabs of meat lurched and bled in the shadows.

They were black with red blotches, which glowed molten in light of their own making. They were harbingers of death. Linn could feel their hunger and their hate.

She tried to turn it back on them.

Linn clutched the stone she had carried like a lifeline, gained her shaking feet and let fly. It pierced the center mass and an alien roar reverberated in her skull. A great geyser of red-black blood spewed forth, coating the nearest pillar in its stinking mess.

As the first bubbled and died, Linn felt the others turning their attention toward her. She spun and clutched the shaft of an iron sconce set into the stone and ripped it free from rusted hinges. That, too, flew straight, piercing the second heart. She could see they were hearts, now, and the second roar brought her to her knees, though another scream of agony from the halls above flooded her legs with need.

She cast about for another weapon, but the third had her in its sight and drilled a hollow of pain between her eyes that drove all thought from her. She fell a long way, and the moist stones greeted her arrival warmly. She saw lights dancing at the edges and fought the black that came for her.

"No!"

The drilling receded like a wave, leaving behind a well of aching that made it difficult to think, let alone move. But move she did, craning her neck to see.

Nathen had pulled her makeshift spear from the one and plunged it into the other. He drove it down with all the strength he could bring to bear, his feet sliding back in the spray, face coated and spitting. He yelled over the roar that must have been splitting his skull, and the heart groaned its last and stilled.

The deed done, Nathen turned and walked to Linn with ungainly strides. He looked like carrion.

"I wanted to believe," he said, looking down at his bloody hands, caked with rot. "I wanted to."

"I know," Linn whispered, standing slowly. She placed a hand on his shoulder. "But we've done something here, at least. Whatever power those things contained, it's gone."

Nathen nodded.

And then they heard the animal scream return, all trace of Larren Holspahr's voice torn away in a madness born of a pain that had given way to rage.

They ran faster than they had any right to, the glow of angry flames lighting their backs as they tore up the stairs and back into the twisting corridors. Sweat poured from them, evaporating before it could roll down their skin.

Finally, the light of day brought a welcome burn to Linn's eyes as they spilled into a great hall. The stone tiles underfoot were polished to a mirror sheen in the places that weren't cracked or overgrown. A white balcony ringed the chamber, and Linn could see avian faces leering at them from the shadowed alcoves above. The carvings were so lifelike as to appear real in the glow of their pursuit, great eagles and hawks with the bodies of men, all armed and armored.

Linn chanced a look behind and the sight nearly drove what breath she had left from her chest. The Ember giving chase was something born of fire and darkness, its hair a burning mass, spear a length of flame with no haft or tip. Behind it, seated on a turquoise throne, was the statue of a god whose carved feathers and razor beak put the rest to shame.

"Linn!"

Together, they cleared the gap and charged out into the open air, clouds wheeling overhead in a frantic and unnatural dance. To the south, the white clouds tore into the black in a battle of elements over the Valley basin.

Linn turned and fell to her knees as Nathen let out a hacking cough, spitting bloody phlegm onto the rocks.

The Sentinel stood before them, flames wild, ravenous and intent on them. Its red eyes darted erratically as it tensed to spring, and then it paused, eyes locking on something behind them.

Linn felt the kiss of heat on the nape of her neck and shuddered.

Her cry of anguish turned into a disbelieving laugh as Jenk Ganmeer stepped forward, shirtless and red as the rest of them, his sword held alight, flames dancing with poise and fervor.

The Ember of Last Lake took his stance and kept his eyes ahead as he prepared to face the ghost of Larren Holspahr a final time.

He could not hope to win, of course, but Linn felt happy to see him. She looked out over the roiling battle in the sky over the Valley below and knew they had done something here.

As for her, it looked as though she would not die alone after all.

She closed her eyes as spear met sword in a clash that heralded the beginning of the end.

CHAPTER THIRTY-FIVE

THE BREAKING

"**D**akken's boys know their way around a pike," Garos said as he and Talmir took a brief reprieve next to the Ember's glowing brazier.

Talmir did not disagree. For a group that had always been more about the show than the fight, Dakken's White Guard had made a difference, bolstering his flagging troops along the South Bend. While Dakken Pyr was somewhat notorious for being a concubine of Third Keeper Misha Ve'Gah, he was notoriously ferocious on the training grounds, and that ferocity was redoubled against the Corrupted. His twin hatchets spun in a constant blur, black limbs flying absent spray. Seeing him in action, one could be excused for thinking him Landkist.

Jakub had looked profoundly pleased with himself as he witnessed Dakken tear into the first climbers, and that look had turned to disbelief when Talmir sent him away. It was as if he was sending him to bed without milk. But what sort of place was this for an orphan boy?

Probably the sort of place that makes them.

"It's a wonder they were willing to get their armor dirty," Talmir said, coming back to himself.

"First time I can recall those boys on the front lines since Pyr's father fought against the stone-throwers," Garos said. "Even then, we had to put the lean on them."

"They are the sons of merchants, after all," Talmir said and Garos laughed and clapped him on the back hard enough to make him cough. The First Keeper walked the length of the gate, slapping the backs of the innocent the whole way.

Talmir studied the black sea before his walls. If it had a tide, it was high, though the Corrupted seemed to be slowing, their attacks guttering like a flame left too long at the wick. The bodies were piled on both sides of the wall, now, their black masks falling away in the rain. There were plenty of his Emberfolk among them, along with the squared jaws of the Rivermen, but most were foreign—pale or swarthy—all innocents in their own way.

The Captain hoped they were granting mercy. He had to cling to something and the anger had gone out of him. Instead of railing against the Sages and their war, his thoughts turned to questions of why rather than how. One thing had become clear: the army before them was one of endings.

What had changed?

It was no secret that the Eastern Dark had long coveted the power of the Embers, but the White Crest had been gone a generation and more. Why had it taken so long for him to come?

Talmir sighed. He supposed it didn't really matter.

The Captain unsheathed his father's blade and started south, following in Garos's booming wake, when shrieks that sounded as if from the pits of hell broke the sky. He wheeled toward the west and witnessed the approach of the Captains from the World Apart.

At the edge of the field, a small host of black figures advanced out of the tree line, the sea of Corrupted parting before them. The red jewels that made up their eyes glittered with a sentience the rest lacked. The one at their head, however, was not made of the same blackness. He sat astride a great black bear with long hair to match.

"Horns!" Talmir yelled, and the call was taken up the length of the battlements. The signal cracked the air even as a bolt of purple lightning did the same, casting it all in a ghost light.

The retort had the few soldiers not embattled—and even a few that were—chancing looks at the sky, where the heavens themselves seemed to be warring, white clouds storming in and colliding with the inky black swells that had hung over them for weeks.

Talmir sensed a quiet desperation, and it was not coming from his side alone.

There was a faraway sound, a keening wail that drifted above the shrieking of the Sentinels and the crash of thunder. It moved above the clouds, traveling from south to north. For a brief moment, Talmir thought he glimpsed the shadow of a great bird slipping in and out of the roiling vapors trailing static in its wake.

He had more pressing concerns.

The steady march of the dozen Sentinels seemed to whip the Corrupted into a frenzy. They scrambled up the walls with renewed vigor that the defenders tried to match, their arrows all spent. The White Guard had more energy than the rest, their halberds rising and falling with a steady and violent rhythm.

Dakken Pyr sent another falling in a silent scream from the ramparts and moved to Talmir.

"What is it?" he asked, wiping the sweat from his brow. He sported a fresh gash on his chin but was otherwise none the worse for wear.

"The cavalry," Talmir shrugged, looking down at the dark retinue and their beastmaster.

"Why not send ours out, then?"

"The ground before the gate is impassable for the horses," Talmir said.

Looking out at the approaching Sentinels, Talmir felt the sick swell of certainty that the Captains of the Dark Kind would be decidedly more difficult to add to the piles before the walls. The rider ceased his advance and the Sentinels stopped behind him.

Dakken propped his foot up on the crenellations, elbow leaning on his knee, the spike of one silver hatchet scraping absently against his front teeth.

"There is the path beneath the cliffs," he said. "The one Misha took."

"Aye," Talmir said as if he had not been tossing the possibility around for the last week. "Enough for a single-file retreat, if we divert the river fully."

"That would mean flooding a large portion of Hearth."

"I know."

"We would have had to start days ago."

"Yes."

Another kernel of guilt to add to the pile. Another mark of indecision.

Dakken straightened as Garos approached. The Ember had clearly noted the advance of the Sentinels, but pretended to pay it no mind, laughing his easy, booming laugh.

"These their champions, then?" the First Keeper asked loud enough for all around to hear. He held up his great staff, the iron-spiked ends going up in popping gouts that made the soldiers flinch back and the Sentinels below turn their ruby eyes up.

The wild warrior turned his head slowly. A darkness hung about him, obscuring his features, but his eyes were clear, tattoos swirling on his bronze skin. He raised a hand and pointed it like a lance toward the gate, his eyes never leaving the First Keeper. Talmir found himself wishing he still had three Embers at his back, but Misha was gone and Creyath firmly out of commission.

Talmir dodged an enthusiastic attacker—face melted to ruin—which Dakken dispatched without a backward glance, and examined the entourage more closely. The leader was undoubtedly human. Could he be Landkist? The foreigner was calm where the creatures flanking him were twitchy, mouths working, eyes shifting in agitation. These were not decaying husks like the Corrupted before his walls. These were creatures born in darkness, and made from it.

"From the Emerald Road, I'd guess," Garos said, following Talmir's stare.

"Done much traveling there?" Dakken asked sarcastically.

"Heard tell of the men there, is all," Garos said. "Fits the description."

"They all ride bears?"

Garos ignored him.

Talmir's mind worked. He thought of Kole Reyna and how he had supposedly slain two Sentinels, though one of those bouts had put him in a state not unlike death. But Kole was an Ember of rare power, and the Sentinels before the gates numbered more than two.

Garos bellowed down at the demons, while Dakken spun about, blades a silver blur as he released the Corrupted from their suffering, keeping Talmir free to think. The bear-rider switched his gaze to the Captain.

"Dakken," Talmir said as the warrior launched another from the walls. "Take your men and position them atop the gate."

"But the South Bend—

"It'll hold," Garos said.

"I want you in the courtyard with me," Talmir said to the Ember.

"The courtyard?"

"They're coming in, one way or another. I'd rather them come through the gate than over it. I won't have the soldiers on the walls flanked."

He turned to Garos.

"You have enough juice?"

The Ember smirked and gave his spikes a flare.

"Good."

Talmir looked back down, where the rider kept his arm rigid and pointing at the gate, his beast digging great furrows in the scorched earth. His compatriots looked fit to burst, hissing like a nest of snakes. The skies had them uneasy, no matter the mood their leader affected. It was growing brighter, the gloom fading as the sun struggled to take back its domain, and occasional rays of yellow burst through the canopy, splashing the white walls with color and setting the climbers to smoke and char.

"To join with the Dark Kind," Talmir said, shaking his head. Dakken spat and then moved off, the armor of his guards glinting in the intermittent beams. Garos headed to the top of the stair.

A climber crested the wall before Talmir, its skin popping and boiling, and he sent it back down absent head. He met the stare of the rider all the while, who smiled a white smile. He brought his clawed gauntlet slashing down and the Sentinels sprinted toward the gate, some on two legs, others rushing like beasts on the palms of their hands.

They were fast, and they were angry.

The great bear began its slow, rumbling, solitary march, and Talmir spun, moving to the stair as Dakken's soldiers arrayed themselves along the top of the gate, spears angled to throw.

As he made his way down the steps to the courtyard with a grace he did not feel, Talmir thought of the skies above. Could Kole have gained the peaks already? Could he have succeeded in discovering the source of the scourge? Had a Sage fallen?

No matter what was happening in the north, Talmir knew the battle on the ground would soon rival that in the air.

On cue, Dakken Pyr shouted his commands and the whip of missiles issued forth as the White Guard launched their volley. No cheer went up.

Had they hit a single one?

Talmir stepped back into the center of the muddy courtyard, leveling his sword alongside a host of displaced cavalrymen Garos had bellowed into loose ranks. The First Keeper brandished his staff of orange and blue, welcoming the coming storm as Talmir only wished he could.

The wall shook under a sharp impact. There was a sound like scraping, hoes and picks warring with the thick wood on the frame of the gate.

"Bring it down!" Dakken screamed, hurling a spear of his own. This one did send up a cheer.

Crashes echoed from the South Bend and Talmir chanced a look. He saw forms falling on the inside of the wall—the wrong side—armor and limbs clattering and snapping on the cobbles of the outer streets. Most of the populace had been moved inward, but a few remained. These took up arms and charged, more concerned with giving object to their rage on the stunned and dying Dark Kind than in assisting the fallen defenders.

Another crash and splinter and a black claw the size of a cleaver pierce the gate. Two soldiers took up swords and hacked at it, the strikes ringing out and sending up sparks. The claw withdrew and the scraping ceased, leaving the men and women in the courtyard to clench and unclench clammy fists.

There were screams from atop the gate, and then a White Guard fell like a stone, throat slashed.

And then it was chaos, black figures darting and slashing along the ramparts , some taking up weapons from the fallen. Whether armed or not, they fought like animals, and men and women fell screaming or choking in their fury. Talmir saw Dakken whirling in their midst, hacking at the speedy wraiths with his twin blades.

Talmir motioned to a squad, shouting at them to make for the stair when the gate shattered as if a ram forged by the gods themselves had come against it. The great black bear looked impossibly large up close. It tore into the first ranks like a badger at a mound. It was no Night Lord, but rather all flesh, fur and unbridled rage, and the shirtless warrior astride it laughed heartily as the gore flew.

Talmir shouted orders, but his pikemen were already surrounding the beast, corralling it with their halberds. Black blurs came pouring over and through the broken gate, ripping into the soldiers and freeing beast and rider to affect more carnage.

Talmir could see that his soldiers were caught unawares. They were used to the unthinking mobs they had been fighting for weeks and this was an enemy both fast and lethal, cunning and merciless. One of the Sentinels fell from the top of the wall, a spear stuck through its chest that served as a rod to root it to the courtyard below.

"See that, men!" Garos bellowed. "They die just the same as you and me. At them!"

Talmir saw. He raised his sword, silver edge gleaming in the shifting kaleidoscope of light playing through the breaks above. He cried a battle cry, charging into the fray heedless of the soldiers at his back. Corrupted had poured into the breach and made it a deadly press, and Talmir did what he could to tip the killing in Hearth's favor. He slashed and gutted until his sword rang out against a riposte, a spiked star clutched by a Sentinel that stood half again his height. He had not seen any of them use weapons before now.

They circled, Talmir prodding as the demon hissed and swung. A pair of female soldiers flanked the Captain, freeing him to focus on his private arena. The Sentinel's movements were erratic. It snarled, accepting hits and gouges in exchange for pure offense.

Talmir cut it to ribbons while dodging that streaking star that may as well have been a comet. His blade rattled off of the obsidian shaft and hooked under the glassteel head, and the two were locked in a spitting embrace. The Sentinel leaned over him, but Talmir let the dams break.

He raged against the World, for being the way it was. He raged against the cowardice of his ancestors, for fleeing the deserts in the north and sentencing their people to a Valley tomb at the edge of the World. He raged because he was angry.

The Sentinel buckled and Talmir used its momentum against it, releasing his press and letting it fall, shocked, on his sword, the red light leaking from its eyes like spilled wine as he added its shell to the mix.

A primal scream went up that was part anger, part joy and Talmir looked up to see the rider pointing his way, shouting a challenge in a harsh foreign tongue. The guards threw themselves at him, but the rider dodged their spears and launched himself from the back of his black mount. He soared impossibly high, landing before Talmir in a crouch that accentuated the bunching muscles of his legs and torso.

A pair rushed him and he left them choking and writhing with bladed gauntlets as deadly as the foot-long claws of the bear at his back.

Talmir charged anyway, bringing his sword down in an arc. The bronze warrior caught the blade with his jagged claws, polished steel scraping against fire-forged iron. Up close, the blades smelled of sap and rot.

"Brega Cohr," he said, spittle flying as he pushed Talmir back. He was shorter than the Captain, but strong as a jungle cat. Behind him, the black bear turned men to mud, its eyes glowing a fierce green that reminded Talmir of the Faeykin of the Valley.

"Brega Cohr," he said again, more forceful.

"Talmir Caru," the Captain said through gritted teeth.

"Caru," the warrior tasted the name.

Talmir felt a rush of heat and pulled back, bending at the waist in time with Garos's swing. A flaring arc of orange and blue passed inches above his chin, scorching his lashes as he ducked and rolled. When he came up, he expected to see the charred remnants of the warrior, but he had managed a dodge, squatting to the height of a child and slashing up to score a hit that opened the metal encasing the Ember's midsection.

Garos kicked out and set his staff to spin, sending licks of flame toward the feet of the bronze fighter, who leapt. Balsheer's staff was waiting for him, chopping down in an arc that he could not hope to dodge.

Only he did, twisting away and somersaulting over the Ember's head. He landed in a crouch and tensed to spring, but Talmir's slash had him rolling. Garos moved to join the fight once again, but a Sentinel cut him off and forced him back, heedless of the flames that ate at it.

Brega leapt for Talmir, faking high and cutting low, but the Captain parried and the two resumed their dance. Talmir was clearly the more practiced sword, but he knew he could not counter his opponent's speed for long.

One gauntlet flashed out to the side while the other drove straight in with its wielder behind it. Talmir sidestepped and brought his sword down in a chop that should have separated Brega's head from his shoulders, but again the other was away in a flash of spinning tattoos and yellow tassels, and the two came up eye-to-eye once again, the jungle warrior flashing a smile.

"Whom do you call master?" Talmir shouted over the tumult. "Who sent you?"

The warrior circled, cocking his head to the side like a dog.

"Slave," Talmir said, spitting in disgust. The warrior grimaced, his smile disappearing.

Around them, each pack of soldiers was locked in their own section of chaos, a series of miniature battles adding up to one bloody whole. Above it all, Garos's bellows rivaled the roaring of the black bear while Dakken's screams echoed down from the broken gate.

"Dark Kind nothing," the warrior said in halting speech, surprising Talmir. "Landkist needed. Ours." He nodded toward Garos Balsheer, who spun with his fiery staff, a deadly maelstrom at the center of the press.

"You'll have trouble convincing that one to join you," Talmir said. "You come on behalf of the White Crest? Has he betrayed us, truly?"

The warrior laughed heartily.

The Eastern Dark, then.

Talmir parried an attack the warrior timed with a bolt of lightning, but he lost his footing, sword flying from his hand as he tried to recover. The other was on him, but Talmir heard Dakken's shout and saw him leap from the stair, charging for Brega's back. His attacker's eyes went white as he froze, and then emerald leaked in from the corners to match the eyes of the thrashing bear in the background.

Brega whirled and caught Dakken's slashing hatchet in one of his claws, turning it aside as he twisted away. Dakken recovered and brought his lead back around, and then he disappeared in a hail of black fur and red blood with an audible crunch. The bear pinned him under a furious assault that had him screaming and hacking from his back.

"No!"

Talmir gained his feet and his sword. He charged Brega and the two dropped all pretense, chopping and slashing with abandon. The Captain's heart caught in his throat as Dakken's screams ceased while the rending and snapping of bone and sinew continued.

The beast's roar sounded like victory until Talmir saw a flash of black and white clutched to its reeling face—Reyna's hound tearing like a weasel on a hare.

Brega turned, eyes losing their glow as he witnessed the charge of a host of reserves. Talmir recognized the black-armored guards of the Merchant Council, but there were more streaming in, many of them armed only with torch or buckler. Karin Reyna was at their head and Creyath Mit'Ahn shouted at their backs. Talmir rewarded Brega's momentary lapse with a deep score across his chest, and the Landkist darted back, wading right into the path of the First Keeper.

The two Landkist came together in a tangle of violence that left Talmir wondering how he had managed to stand for so long against one.

Talmir shook his head and ran for Dakken, who had been dragged away by fresh troops. The fighter's fingers still twitched on the grips of his blades, but his eyes were unseeing, skin turning the pale complexion of death.

Karin intercepted a Sentinel that was angling straight for Talmir, tackling it to the ground and rolling away as the crowd set to hacking at the shrieking thing.

Talmir stood and swallowed the lump in his throat. He nodded to Karin, who nodded back, and the two turned upon the melee in the courtyard. The violence had slowed and the odds seemed stacked in their favor. The bear had managed to dislodge its passenger, but the spears had done their work. It soon sank down to join the dispatched flesh littering the ground, the emerald light fading from its eyes and leaving bloody moons in their place.

The Sentinels were dead or dying, the men taking torches to those that still writhed. A shield wall had gone up before the shattered gate, stemming the flow of the Corrupted as the emerging sun lit their backs and set their skins to burn.

"How soon we forget the protection the sun affords us," Karin said. "We call months Dark, but we've never lost the sun completely."

"The Dark Months are named for what they bring," Talmir said. "We'll rename them later. For now, I want to know how the Eastern Dark has managed to add Landkist to ranks that have only ever counted denizens of the World Apart."

And many eyes, including the Captain's own, now turned in toward the duel in the center of the yard.

Talmir stepped to the edge of a wide circled made of standing men and women. The circle had been made absent thought. The Emberfolk had been brought up on tales that theirs were the most powerful Landkist in the World. He supposed they would see now.

Watching the flaming hurricane before him, the fire fighting as a thing both of and separate from the Ember who birthed it, he had no reason to doubt it. It stood to reason that Brega was something special, else the Eastern Dark would not have bothered with him. The warrior of the Emerald Road had been intent on the First Keeper of Hearth. Now he would have him.

Talmir smiled.

Garos was a jovial spirit—a kind and gentle soul. But the being before them now was the Balsheer that had earned his place at the small table of Valley legends alongside the likes of Tu'Ren Kadeh and Sarise A'zu. Even Creyath, for all his poise, could not wield the flames so.

Brega knew he was outmatched. He moved like a tiger in the pit, lashing out desperately, unsure whether to dodge the metal spites on the end of the Ember's staff or the jets of blue fire that streaked from it in deadly crescents. He scored his hits, eyes widening as the Ember's blood burned away whatever poisons he had set to work.

Talmir looked down, examining the slashes in his armor and sighing in relief when he found no fresh wounds apart from scrapes and bruises.

He was about to give the order to advance and finish the trap when Reyna's hound started barking furiously. Sounds of abject terror went up in the back and Talmir saw the great black bear rise like a great shadow framed by Garos's flames.

Brega had been stalling, his eyes glowing bright green as they had before. He smiled and lashed out with a combination that put Garos on his heels, and the bear sent up a shower of bodies as it crashed into the circle, blood leaking from a hundred wounds.

The clatter of hooves sounded like thunder fast closing, and Talmir whirled to see a stampede of horses—most without bit or bridle—flying down the center avenue toward the courtyard, their eyes showing the same emerald sheen, mouths frothing with wild effort.

Talmir dove to the side, pulling another solider with him as the charging animals made the yard a sea of churning. He shielded his face with an arm after seeing Garos lay the bear low with a swipe that cracked with thunder all its own.

When the maelstrom passed, the animals scattered and reared, many coming up lame. But their eyes now showed red, white and brown. There was no sign of Brega Cohr.

As if on command, the sun beamed down in merciless intensity, lighting the macabre scene before them as the dark clouds melted away and revealed the startling blue behind.

Talmir was pulled to his feet.

"We won," Karin said.

"We survived," Talmir said, moving toward Garos, who leaned precariously on his smoking staff, the ends of which still glowed like fresh-doused matches.

"What do you reckon he was about?" the Ember asked as Talmir came to stand beside him. They looked through the yawning gap where the gate had been, over the mountain of black fur that once made up a giant of a bear and past the ruins of rock and stone in the fields beyond. The Corrupted were weak. Those that did not burn to a crisp fell to the renewed swords of the Emberfolk.

"Who knows?"

The Ember grunted as if it did not matter after all.

"You know," he said, "I'm loath to admit I actually thought we might escape the bastard's notice, here at the edge of it all."

Talmir only nodded.

"But why all the pretense?" Garos asked and Talmir looked at him quizzically. "Why not do this from the start?" He swept his hand out, but Talmir did not want to look just now.

"I suppose we have our protector to thank for that. The White Crest."

Another grunt.

"And who do we have to thank for that?" the Ember pointed up at the blue skies above, where the sun shone bright and beautiful.

Talmir smiled.

"Boy's got some bones, going up to them peaks," Garos said. "Suppose he's the one to thank."

"Some bones," Talmir said, and felt another twinge for having said it in such still company.

CHAPTER THIRTY-SIX

FIELD OF WIND AND FIRE

Kole did not know how long the duel had been raging, but judging by his physical state and the set of his shoulders, Jenk Ganmeer had pushed far beyond his breaking point already.

Everwood clashed against Everwood as sword deflected spear in another desperate parry, and Kole tensed from his place next to Misha Ve'Gah. They hid behind an outcropping just a stone's throw from the steep ground on which the Embers lunged and flared. Scorch marks scarred the ground beneath them, sodden mud and gravel turned to cracked char and glass.

The party's path had taken them by a circuitous route to the Sage's keep, which sat like a red-topped pearl in its black cloister below them, its shadowed door looming open. A winding pathway had been cut into the vertical slope to the west, and the Embers danced atop the precipitous shelf. The golden pools in the fields merged into the white clouds in the distance, lazy invaders that had come to dispel the pall hanging over the Valley skies.

Kole had wanted to rush out the instant he saw the yellow glow of Jenk's blade, but Baas Taldis held him back, motioning for patience as Jenk attempted to fend off the demon that had been Larren Holspahr. Kole looked to his right, frantic, where the hulking Riverman directed his compatriots. A dozen warriors snaked their way down the jagged cloister. They would set a perimeter around the White Crest's abode, but it was too long coming for Kole.

"So that's Ganmeer, eh?" Misha asked. She fingered the bright tassels below her spearhead, careful to keep it down.

"He was the second-youngest Ember in the Valley," Kole said. "In the World. Now he's the youngest. And I'm soon to be."

"He's got stones," Misha said approvingly. "He'll last."

"Last," Kole mouthed the word. He winced as Jenk let out a small cry, the burning shaft of Larren's spear slapping him in the temple and sending him reeling.

Much as he tried to stay focused, Kole could not help but glance behind the battling Embers to the figures on the shelf. There was Linn, her clothes hanging in tatters, dried blood covering arms and legs. She shielded Nathen Swell like a mother over her babe. Baas had spoken true: there was no sign of Kaya Ferrahl.

"Honestly," Kole said, shifting his eyes back to the duel, "I wouldn't have thought he had it in him."

"That's not the true Larren Holspahr he stands against," Misha said, sounding less impressed than she had before.

Kole nodded, searching the rocks below for signs of the Rivermen. They had vanished and the Embers twitched as they waited for Baas to receive his signal. The rock under Kole's palm began to steam, and Baas glanced over worriedly. Kole took the hint and tried to reign in his blood. The sun, which he had not seen this clear in weeks, imbued him with something close to the power he had felt in the fields of Hearth.

The northern skies turned from yellow to burnt orange as the great orb neared the end of its slow descent.

"Whatever's driving Larren now," Misha said, "it's burning up all of his stores. He's using fire too fast, burning too hot, and against another Ember. Useless."

"It'll last long enough to kill them, if we don't make our move soon," Kole said.

As he said it, Jenk drove the Sentinel back in a furious press. His advantage, however, was temporary, and he was soon back on his heels, ducking and dodging far more often than attacking. Misha was right about one thing: if that were the true Larren Holspahr, Jenk would have been killed three times over.

Still, Kole had to admit he was impressed. Some men, he supposed, are not who they wish to be. And some men are just what they claim to be. It was now apparent that Jenk was one of the latter.

Kole wondered if one could be both at once.

Misha shifted, dislodging a sheet of rock so thin it broke apart like paper and twirled in the breeze.

"Calm," Baas intoned, and Misha shrank down with a grumble.

The Riverman appeared the very picture of calm, but Kole could sense the need dripping off him. He wanted nothing more than to join in the fight, to right whatever wrongs had been done in the cave. If he could wait, so would Kole.

They had learned little of the Rivermen on their walk, though they seemed cut from the same cloth as Baas. Kole could pick out which of them were Rockbled by the stone bracers on their wrists. Baas did not wear them, but he carried the stone in the set of his shoulders and in the shield he bore on his back.

My mother died in these passes.

The thought crept up again. It was growing more difficult to suppress the higher they climbed. And now, at the zenith of the Valley that may as well be their world, it was impossible to shake.

Had she made it this far?

My mother died in the dark.

Had she felt any pain?

My mother died.

Kole's heart caught in his chest as Jenk bent back awkwardly to avoid a streak of flame he had mistaken for the spearhead, his heel slipping on a loose stone. The tongue of flame carried through, sweeping around the Sentinel and masking the approach of the serrated tip. Jenk cried out as the jagged edge tore into him, catching on some bone in his chest and spinning him viciously like a harpooned fish.

The Ember rolled when he hit the ground, dodging the deadly follow-through and narrowly avoiding being rooted to the mountaintop. He kicked out, his sword flying from his grasp and extinguishing as it did. The smoking matchstick clattered with finality at Linn's knees.

Jenk was a lamb and his blazing butcher sprang like a wolf with mange.

Embers were fast when they wanted to be—hot blood made hot muscles—but Kole and Misha were barely a third of the way down the slope when it looked certain Jenk's life would be extinguished along with his blade.

And then a bow sang in a baritone, a silver arrow half the length of a spear trailing on the echoes and shooting like a daystar from the northern spurs. The lightning shaft tore through the air and would have torn right through the Sentinel's spine had it not altered course at the last second, planting and leaping over the fallen Ember, tails of fire spinning in its wake.

The archer, a Rockbled male who stood half again Baas's height, emerged from his alcove and made ready to fire again, a great war bow standing tall as his target's spear planted in the shelf on which he stood.

The Sentinel wheeled and shot in his direction as Kole and Misha continued their descent.

The Ember pair leapt and darted around jagged spires, sliding as often as running, a hundred tiny avalanches of chipped slate flowing in their wake like obsidian rivers. Kole was shocked to see Baas's black hair dipping in and out of arches ahead; it was as though he rode the mountain rather than traversed it.

Three Landkist hit the ground running, a handful of Baas's warriors emerging from their places and joining in on the chase as the Sentinel closed in on the Rockbled archer.

"So much for waiting on the Sage," Misha said, huffing as she ran.

Kole put an extra burst in and shot ahead. They rocketed over the dirt road, passing within a stone's throw of Jenk, Linn and Nathen. Kole did not chance a look at them, though he could feel their eyes on him as he passed.

Ahead, the Rockbled warrior let fly another silver missile. The Sentinel dodged in a spin that make it look like a comet, and the shaft dug a trench a stride deep and three long, bits of earth ricocheting off of the shifting black scales of Kole's armor.

The leap had the Sentinel hurtling toward the archer's perch, but the Rockbled watched his approach stoically, making no move except to fall, crumbling with the spur beneath his feet and sinking in a cascade of black stone as the monster's spear carved the space his head had occupied moments earlier.

It was as if the spur itself had broken apart to avoid the demon's attack. Perhaps it had, as the Rockbled archer came up in a roll, unscathed as the stones tumbled around his feet.

Kole, Misha, Baas and the warriors of the Fork formed a semicircle around the rockslide on which the crazed Sentinel now stood, the last of the Rivermen emerging from their places, weapons trained on their quarry. The Embers flared their blades to life and nothing moved but for the flames dancing along Everwood blades of hunter and hunted.

Kole saw the red eyes shift imperceptibly toward his left; Misha must have seen it too, for the two of them darted to intercept the Sentinel's retreat. Their mistake cost the Rockbled archer his life.

Kole caught the ruse too late and the Sentinel slammed his spear into the ground, sending up a wall of flame that blinded his pursuers momentarily. He saw the dark form transfer the energy of its slam into an incredible jump that took it up and over. The archer let loose another singing shaft, but it made a tunnel in the shelf behind the demon. Larren Holspahr's spear, however, made one of its own in the archer's throat, and the big man went down in a choking spray, his bow clattering to the ground beside him as the party sprang into violent chaos.

"Contain it!" Misha shouted, tearing through the dissipating wall of fire as if it were a curtain of water. Kole followed after, blades leveled.

The Sentinel darted at Baas first, but the Rockbled was quicker than he looked, deflecting the fiery spear and cracking Larren's nose apart with a spinning strike with that stone shield.

Somehow, the Sentinel retained its footing, leaving Baas to ward off a jet of flame. A female Rockbled—bracers cracking along her forearms—stomped the earth, which responded by opening where the Dark Ember's booted foot fell next.

It went down in a tumble and the Embers were on it. What followed did not resemble a duel so much as a pair of wolves at a carcass, both Kole and Misha scoring punctures on their initial attacks as the shrieking Sentinel rolled up into a crouch, spear spinning, mouth agape and showing teeth that had blackened and chipped to angled points.

The beast did not fight like the Second Keeper of Last Lake, but rather like a cornered predator. The Embers drove it on, Baas occasionally filling the gap between them to deflect a wild stab as Kole and Misha absorbed the jets of fire, their own power only augmented by each blistering volley. Baas's warriors kept their distance, moving in a wide arc behind the three-pronged attack to cut off any chance at escape.

The Sentinel faked a stab at Kole only to lunge for Misha. It might have succeeded if not for a rock the size of a tortoise taking it in the chest and launching it backward to skitter along the edge of the cliff. The Rockbled that sent the stone was on his knees, bracers cracked like spider webs as he panted.

The Sentinel, spear low and flames guttering, rose on shaking legs and shot a look of wild rage to the east, where Linn watched with her charges. She stood, brown hair blowing in the wind, the maelstrom of white and black clouds battling in the far horizon over the fields below. Jenk lay unmoving at her feet, while Nathen cradled his head in his hands and knees, rocking.

"No!" Kole screamed, blades streaking forward in a two-hand stab as the Sentinel sprang across the gap. Kole missed by a hair's breadth and firm hands grabbed him round the shoulder and yanked him back—Baas preventing a fatal fall into the golden pools below.

The Sentinel streaked into the air in a bright arc, a meteor of death hurtling toward his friends.

Until Misha's thrown spear took it out of the air in an emphatic crash that flashed like the meeting of twin stars. Larren Holspahr's hands flew out wide, his own spear snuffed out like a dockside lantern, eyes melting to black even as he fell. His body landed in the golden wash below with a splash and sizzle, slow steam rising to punctuate his end.

Tiny motes of flame trailed out in a fairy path from the point of impact to Misha's outstretched hand. She stared at the liquid pocket of air with an expression of shock.

Kole approached.

"It wasn't him," he whispered, coming to stand beside her. He looked down into the pool below, noting the ripples that still played on its surface like tiny waves of molten gold. The sun was beginning to dip, framing the distant ridges to the north in silhouette.

Misha came back to herself and her expression changed, the usual color rising. She tossed Kole a look of mock disgust.

"My spear," she said, sweeping her arm out toward the quieting pool, though he noticed she would not look down.

Kole nodded and the Embers stepped back to where the Rivermen had gathered around their fallen comrade. The life had gone out of him quickly and Baas was set back from the others, his expression predictably unreadable.

Kole sighed and let his gaze drift back across the span, where Linn looked back with those piercing eyes, her own expression strained. He started toward her, and the walk became a jog, which quickly morphed into a sprint as he sheathed his blades, feeling the warmth of the Everwood against his back even through his armor.

A salt mist stung his eyes as his tears evaporated, the fire still high in his chest, and he nearly broke her in the impact of their embrace.

"You came," Linn whispered.

"Yes."

They broke off and locked eyes for an eternal moment before Kole noted Nathen staring up at them through his own curtain of tears, smiling weakly. Linn was gaunt, but Nathen looked the picture of death, his broad shoulders reduced to bony protrusions that matched their stark surroundings.

"Jenk," Kole said, squatting down. He had nearly forgotten the state of the other Ember in the flood of emotion.

"He'll live," Linn said, resting a hand on Kole's shoulder as he looked him over.

Blood caked the blonde bangs, but the ugly gash had been sealed by fire of his own calling. Self-cauterizing was very difficult for an Ember to do, given their seeming immunity to fire. But that immunity lasted only so far as the Ember allowed. The fire could be let in. The flame would always choose to burn if it could.

Jenk was in a state beyond sleep. He did not stir even as the distant booms of thunder rolled in from the south, the black clouds cracking apart, thrashing their death throes like gods made suddenly mortal.

"You must be Linn Ve'Ran."

Misha came over, extending her hand, which Linn took. She winced slightly, as the Ember's battle heat had yet to dissipate. Kole wondered if Misha had kept a bit of the sting in on purpose.

"Thank you," Linn said, nodding in the direction of the pool below, which had grown still.

Misha shrugged and studied the sorrier sorts at her feet. Nathen offered a sheepish smile; he seemed fragile enough that a single word could prove a titanic effort. The Ember's gaze lingered on Jenk.

"That one has some real fire in him," she said before switching back to Linn. She studied her appraisingly, looking her up and down and taking in the lean muscle and prominent ridges that stood out along her collar.

This is what we came for? The look seemed to ask.

This is what I came for. Or should have.

But the wind, which had been stirring all afternoon, picked up, and Kole looked back toward the hill and the broken gate at its crest. He stared into the darkness of the open keep.

"He's not at home," Linn said, following his gaze.

"Not dead, then?" Baas asked, coming up with a silence that belied his bulk. It was as if the earth itself went out of its way to mask his present. His warriors still stood apart, some chanting over their fallen comrade, others watching them calmly.

"No," Linn said with a shiver. "But we purged his Dark Hearts." She looked back down at the pool.

"Dark Hearts?" Kole asked, and Misha and Baas moved closer.

"His mechanism for controlling the Dark Kind—making them, perhaps. Iyana said they were taken from the Night Lords that came against the White Crest a generation ago."

"The skies," Baas said in his low rumble, nodding knowingly.

"The Sentinel," Misha said, uncomfortable assigning the term to the fallen Ember. "It continued to fight even after you destroyed them."

"They are not the same as the Corrupted that came against Hearth," Kole said. "They are something more pure. Captains from the World Apart."

"It did change," Linn said, her eyes glazing over. "After we bled them out. It grew wild. Erratic as the skies."

Kole examined her, the guilt for not having been there gnawing at him.

"Let's just hope it's happened to all of them," Misha said, looking down over the Valley, where the white jewel of Hearth glittered in the distance, smoke rising from the fields without.

A boom had all eyes looking up, and the orange glow at their backs cast a strange light on the skies, tingeing the white clouds gold and their fleeing adversaries bloody black, like coals left too long in the grate. Webbed patterns of lavender light arced between the breaches, which heralded a shockwave that scattered the vapors.

The waters in the pools below churned, flecks of spray changing to foam in the space of seconds as the winds took on a bite, ripping at the slopes. They whistled along the ridges and spurs and sighed through the open maw of the keep in a sound like a portent.

Linn shivered and Nathen drew his knees in. Kole felt a sudden coldness of heart that contrasted his blood.

"What is it?" Baas asked, squinting up at the shifting skies.

"Linn," Kole turned to her, and she peered into the distance, eyes widening.

"What—

"The White Crest," she said, nearly breathless. "He's coming back."

"Looks like he's bringing the sky with him," Misha said, hands twitching without her spear. Nathen handed her Jenk's blade, hand shaking.

"He is the storm," Linn said.

If anything, it may have been an understatement.

But though the heavens themselves seemed to move against them, Kole could not help but feel a tingling anticipation swelling up with the dread. It was a thing borne on the same tide. His was rising while those around him fell, particularly Linn. For her and for her alone, he would try to end it quickly, though his heart yearned for something longer.

What he at first took for the absence of clouds soon resolved itself into something apart from the air around it. It was a creature made of wind itself, and it was charged with crackling energy, reflecting the light of the setting sun with an undulating shimmer. As it drew near, Kole could see bright blue jewels glowing in the place of eyes. It was a drake, or an eagle.

It was the White Crest, and its tail left popping percussions in its wake.

"A weapon!" Linn screamed over the rising roar. "Hand me something!"

One of the Rivermen handed her the huge war bow that had fallen with its wielder, which looked comically large in her hands. Linn cast about for the silver missiles, and then the storm was on them, the great maw opening like a gulf.

Kole drew his blades and lit while Baas crouched down before Nathen and Jenk, raising his shield.

For a space of seconds that felt achingly long, Kole was sure they would all perish in a hail of cutting wind and stinging electricity. He cursed himself, certain that the only thing more foolish than believing a god might be on their side was believing it could be challenged. It was all he could do to keep his blades lit, glowing like twin lanterns in the maelstrom of dirt, grass and whipping water from the pools below.

The Rivermen stood strong, feet rooted in place. Some yelled into the wind, harsh sounds whose intent Kole could easily guess. Nathen clung to Baas's back like a toddler, and the Rockbled held the prone Ember down with his free hand. Jenk still did not so much as flinch.

And then it stopped.

Kole opened his eyes, and everything was still.

As one, they spun to the north. There, faint and fading, the great serpent floated, its bright eyes glowing like the pre-dawn sky. Its look was wild and hateful, and its features shifted chaotically from reptilian to avian and back.

Kole stepped forward, spreading his arms wide in challenge, his twin blades burning brighter than the golden fields beyond, the fading sunlight illuminating his black armor like a grounded star.

"Is this all your power?" he screamed. "We have taken the dark from you, monster! Now we take your life."

With a piercing shriek, the serpent wheeled and dived toward the keep, its passing churning up the pathway and shattering the marble gate in a rain of gray shards. Kole, Baas and the warriors of the Fork took up the chase, while Misha stayed back with Linn and the others, Jenk's crackling blade held uncertainly in her hands.

Kole felt the familiar heat light his veins like glowworms, his muscles charged and thrumming, aching to be freed into the beautiful chaos of battle. The flames along his blades streaked like razors, bouncing from tip to hilt and even engulfing his hands as he fed the fire.

He was first to reach the steps of the mock citadel and he plunged into the inky black, his blades flaring as he entered, tongues of fire whipping and curling. He cast about, wild, and saw nothing but the amber light reflected back from the cracked marble floors and sparkling soapstone pillars. Above, the light caught the glint of mirrored surfaces—armored figures with the stern, alien faces of birds.

"Sage!"

Kole shouted his challenge. He heard Baas and the Rivermen file into the hall behind him, spreading out among the pillars with practiced ease.

There were steps ahead, and Kole started up them. He had cleared half a dozen when the black shape before him resolved itself into a massive chair of carved turqoise. The glassy surface was slick with damp, but, unlike the broken floor, nothing grew here.

Seated upon the throne was a suit of armor twice Kole's height. His blood hot, he shot one blade forward and sent a jet toward the helmeted visage, and a blue glow flashed behind the visor. There was a sound like shattering stone and a great gauntleted hand stretched out with inhuman speed. Kole leapt backward and avoided most of the blow, but the impact still sent him skittering along the floor of the hall like a swatted fly.

The Ember kept hold of his blades and rolled to his feet, charging forward with Baas at his back, the warriors of the Fork flanking them. And then the chamber burst into a storm light that froze them all in their tracks. All movement ceased but for the hungry flicker of Kole's blades, which merged with the blue light of the Sage's making.

The titan stood upon its dais, glowing eyes looking down at them through slits in a polished helm that narrowed to an eagle's peak. Even from a distance, Kole could see black slits bisecting the blue eyes, giving impressions of lizard, cat and bird at once. The blue glow was not limited to the helm, but bled through cracks in the body of the armor, the molten scales shifting like feathers that struggled to contain the power within.

Another shriek carried a hurricane's wail and nearly brought the party to their knees. But Kole struggled forward, his steps lurching as his head wrung. The White Crest looked down at him balefully, great gold-tipped wings unfurling behind the armored back.

Kole heard a crack and something hurtled past him, flashing in the blue light. The Sage's eyes never left Kole's as one wing carved the missile from the air. White dust swirled as shards of marble flew in all directions.

"You destroyed them."

The voice carried a strange echo, but it was firm, strong and inhuman.

Kole shifted and began to walk forward again, Baas moving out to his left, the Rockbled female who had launched the tile on the right. Shadows shifted and metal glinted in the gallery above, making the gooseflesh rise along the nape of Kole's neck, but his heat was up, and the fire needed feeding.

"We did," Kole said, the flames on the tips of his blades dancing.

The Sage traced his path but stood unmoving.

"You know not what you've done," it said, its focus singular, unconcerned.

Baas raised his shield before his chest, gearing up for a charge.

"I could have killed her. I let her live so I could strike a bargain with thee."

"You are a scourge on this land," Kole said. "We are the folk of the Valley. We are the cleansing fire, come to purge you away. I will not bargain with you."

Kole ceased his advance at the foot of the dais, doing his best to match the blue stare.

"You have doomed your kind," it said, wings rising in an arch, spreading like an angel of nightmare.

Kole spat, the wet dart evaporating as it passed through the burning gate framed by the blades in his hands.

"You were supposed to protect us," he said, anger rising, flames settling into a low growl, turning from orange to red with flecks of blue. "We counted you as ally, and you turned the weapon of our enemy against us. This is your reckoning, and this is the place we'll have it."

The Rivermen began to emerge from the shadowed pillars, and the Sage's eyes flickered as he took in their approach.

"I've seen your eyes before," it said in that haunting melody, its head tilting in an affectation of owl or dog. "When I slept. I saw eyes like those."

"You saw them in another," Kole whispered, his heart turning from fire to cold stone. "She came to you for help and you cut her down. She came to you."

"You mistake me for your enemy," the Sage said. "But I am merely the object of your vengeance. Tell me, what will you do against the Eastern Dark when he comes for you without me? Without your protector?"

"You would have us all dead before then!"

"Only the weak," it said in a voice full of pity, or something like it. "You do not see things from outside of yourselves. I did not turn the dark against your mother. Yes, I remember her face. No, I harnessed the dark after waking. I turned the hearts of his generals to my own ends. He would have used you against me. Against the World. There is no other way to defeat him than to use the same fire. My brothers and sisters do not see. I would have been the end of him."

"You would be the end of us," Kole said.

"I would have been the sword to carry out your vengeance."

"What good is vengeance if none of us are here to see it?"

"A question I have long pondered, mourning the loss of my people." The blues flared to life. "Though I do not have their souls for companionship, their forms are always with me."

The shadows in the alcoves above shifted and a dull glow came down from the corners. The warriors at Kole's back spread out in a ring, backing into the center of the hall, weapons raised.

"I have sensed your coming for some time, now," the White Crest said, stepping down with a clack. "The Dark Hearts are no more. Your people are safe. It now falls on us to face him directly. To dispel the darkness, once and for all."

The Sage's feet were great metal talons, spread out and tapping.

"You fear us," Kole said, holding the blue gaze. "In trying to prevent your rival from using us against you, you've spelled your own doom. Your fate is sealed."

The blue eyes widened ever so slightly.

"He's weak," Baas said, tone firm, and the blues shifted to him. "It's why he's confined himself to this form. He's weak. Something's changed."

The titan took another deliberate step down, talons clacking. The blue glow in the gallery above brightened as he neared.

"What will you do?" it asked.

"Find a way," Kole said, and he launched himself forward, blades-first.

A great wing slashed down from the left that surely would have sliced Kole in half had Baas's great stone shield not intercepted in a shower of sparks. The blues flashed behind their armored slits and the titan bladed its body, shifting so that Kole's blades only scored gashes in the armored midsection rather than piercing clean through.

A clawed gauntlet flashed out. Kole took a hit in the ribs as he twisted and lunged back with a counter, flames flaring hungrily. A force like a lightning strike smashed Kole in the chest—the titan's foot, talons splayed—and sent him tumbling from the dais as Baas swiped low with his shield, taking the behemoth from its feet with a crash.

Kole came up in a roll next to the female Rockbled. She had her eyes closed in concentration as her brethren surrounded her, staring up into the alcoves with weapons bared. Cracks split and raced along the floor around her, and her eyes flashed open, arms extending in a push that sent shards of marble lancing toward the grappling pair on the dais.

The projectiles struck them both, bouncing harmlessly off of Baas and doing little more than distracting the armored Sage. One gauntleted hand closed around Baas's throat and Kole screamed as the other streaked toward his stomach, launching Baas back with incredible force. But the talons came away bloodless, the Sage's attack doing little more than ripping the Rockbled's leather armor and knocking the wind from him.

Kole shot to the top of the dais as the titan regained its footing. Another Riverman came up in a two-hand spin, axe a whirling blur aimed squarely at the armored chest. In a flash of blue light, the axe fell with a clatter, the warrior's head with a thud.

Kole leapt onto the armored back, wrapping his legs around the torso as it thrashed, spiked ridges ripping his cheeks and digging into his black shell. One gauntlet interrupted his Everwood blade, but he stabbed the other down at the crease between neck and shoulder, the flames glowing a deeper blue than the light beneath the armor as Kole drove in with all his strength.

The seam parted and the Sage unleashed an animal scream, arms thrown wide as lighting ricocheted throughout the chamber, bouncing off of Baas's shield and striking several of his kinsmen. One went down in a smoking husk, but the others found themselves and regained their feet.

Kole was launched forward, tumbling, his back slamming against a pillar near the entryway. White lights joined the blue and red as he struggled to right himself.

The titan was in a rage now, and another Riverman went down in a mess of blood and thrashing silver wings as he moved to guard Kole. The stone bracers of the Rockbled droned as they summoned strength from the stone underfoot and the earth beneath it, setting their feet for the clash.

The rails above shattered and came down in a rain of stone and dust, and a score of armored warriors taller than the tallest of the Rivermen streaked down on armored wings, duller approximations of the titan's form. The hall came alive with the screeches of hawk and the challenges of man and woman as the two sides came together in a blur of chaos.

"Draw them outside!" a voice shouted and then gurgled as a pack of winged assailants covered her in thrashing talons, her bracers shattering as her concentration broke and the razor weapons found homes beneath her flesh.

"I knew you would come for me!"

An uppercut took Kole in the chin and blasted him out into the open air. He landed in a crunch and rolled across the rocks in the ruined courtyard, blades nearly coming loose from his hands. He struggled to rise, and then another staggering blow landed, this one launching him into the crumbled ruins of the marble gate.

Kole felt something crack and hoped it was armor, though he tasted blood.

"Kole!" Linn shouted from behind. He could hear Misha shouting as well.

"No," Kole coughed. He set his feet on the moss and used the loose stones to help him up into a hunch. His veins felt cold, but he forced all of the fire he could into his blades, which deepened their color once again.

A bladed wing the size of a horse lanced down in a crescent shaped like the moon. Kole ducked it and scored a long slash, turning silver to liquid metal as he slid by. He spun and made to stab forward with the other blade, sending a fan of flame from the first up into the titan's visor, but a gauntlet knocked him away and one blade went spinning.

"I could have killed you at any time!"

Another blow landed, and this time Kole knew it was not just the metal of his suit giving. He turned the wracking cough into a strangled growl and sent a gout of flame from his remaining blade that scorched the armored visage and sent the titan stumbling.

"You took the Dark Hearts," the Sage circled, blue eyes flickering as it wiped ash from its helm. Behind, Kole could see the melee spill out into the yard, human warriors parrying and smashing apart an armored flock that wheeled and dived, prodding with spear and halberd and making mad screeches as they died.

"I offer you the chance to help me," the White Crest said. "Kill him. End his scourge."

Kole spat, breath wheezing out of him as he circled, blade guttering.

"You are a part of that scourge," Kole said. "You could have come to us first. Trusted us. But you feared us. You let the Eastern Dark guide your hand."

The Sage's silver hand glowed with energy. Though each circled the other, only one was the wolf, and they both knew whom it was.

"He'd have turned you against me, just as he turned your Ember King."

Kole stopped dead in his tracks.

"What did you say?"

A ball of lightning drove into his chest and a blast of wind from the other palm sent him crashing through the gate. He hit the ground with a thud, loose rocks scoring scrapes as his shell split. He tumbled down the slope before coming to rest in a heap a few strides from the lip of the ledge where Linn stood watching.

He could hear her yelling, pleading. But Misha held her back in an iron grip, her other hand leveling Jenk's glowing blade as a ward. The avian warriors fell on them and Misha released Linn as she did all she could to keep the lancing spears at bay.

There was a weight on Kole's chest, and he looked up to see the hawkish visage of the Sage glowering down at him like molten ice. He hacked a bloody cough as the titan's foot pressed, folding him up in a haze of pain and phlegm.

"Yes," he said, easing up so Kole would not expire. "I honored the alliance with the King of Ember. We rode out and met my dark brother in the east. Your king was struck down. I saw the corruption leaking into his eyes even as I made good my escape."

Kole wheezed again as he tried to speak.

"Coward," he spat through bloody teeth. He tried to infuse strength into his ailing limbs, but none came.

"You call me coward?" the Sage scoffed, beaked helm leering down. "I fought the Eastern Dark. And when your King was thrown down, I fought off the Night Lords that would have razed this Valley and everything in it. It was my battle with them that made the Deep Lands, which broke the River F'Rust. I took their hearts, and though they sank me into a poisonous sleep, I have awoken, and I had control. I had power over the Corrupted, over the legions of the World Apart."

"You left him," Kole said, accusation dripping. "You left him to die."

"As he would have left me."

The weight eased from Kole's chest and he was sent into a violent fit of coughing. The Sage swept his gaze out to take in the melee before the keep. Kole craned his head, seeing Misha put Jenk's blade to good use, carving into any beasts that drew too near. Linn worked at the huge bow the Rockbled had dropped. She had dragged one of the great silver shafts to the ledge, her teeth gritted as she forced exhausted sinews into the effort of pulling.

Baas was at the center of the battle on the hill, his great shield knocking flying beasts from their paths and shattering those that attempted to stand too long and challenge him. Only half a dozen Rockbled stood with him, but it was enough, and none looked to be slowing as the Sage's army dwindled before his eyes.

"I lost my people once," the Sage said, strange voice lilting. He watched the melee with a distant expression that was the most human that Kole had yet glimpsed in the immortal's façade. "I know what it is to lose."

When the blue eyes looked down at him, they hardened.

"The Dark Hearts spoke to me in that long darkness. I saw the corruption they sowed in the Valley that was my charge. The Dark Kind attacked each year, their numbers growing steadily for a generation. It was a strategy meant to strengthen the Landkist residing therein—the Embers most of all."

"My heart bled for the losses, but I could do nothing. But you fought back, and you fought well. There are braziers in the hearts of your people that will not be put out easily."

Flickering.

"The Eastern Dark was too preoccupied with finding his champions in other lands and making his wars on the other Sages to pay any real heed to the goings on in his Valley at the edge of the World. And that is where I saw my opportunity."

"To destroy us," Kole rasped.

"His darkness would have taken you all eventually," the White Crest said in a tone that approached sorrow but came up wanting. "I learned of the Sentinels. I invited them in. Better you be used by me than him."

A pause.

"But you surprised even me. A few of you, that is. Some not even counted among the Landkist. Together, we can stand up to him. Without the denizens of the World Apart. Without the Dark Kind and their dark gifts."

"Horrors," Kole said.

"Yes."

Kole sat up, his face coming within spitting distance of the armored visage.

"Why take down one evil just to prop up another?"

The blues flashed dangerously.

"For vengeance. For your mother."

Something snapped in Kole, and the Sage sensed it too late. He called to them, and the flames answered.

Kole's eyes peeled back to expose the fire within, and the flames from his discarded blade leapt of their own accord and traced a path to his waiting palm. The fire coiled there like a disc of sunset. The titan shrank back, blue light arcing up through the feathered contours in the silver armor, but Kole was the quicker. He thrust his palm forward and drove the disc into the sharp visor, and the sound of it was thunder.

The Sage roared and keened as it lit amber, its head thrown back in a violent retort, the armored body following as it twisted, wings flapping as it careened through the air like a meteor, smashing through the wall of the keep across the way. Fire sprang along the newly made entrance, and Kole was up and charging, his hand glowing, the orange outline spreading along his form until his body held a sheen that matched his blazing eyes.

Some part of him heard Linn screaming for him, but he kept on, eager to carve the darkness of the gap with his own burning.

Just before he reached the smoking stones, he saw the blue glow flaring to life within, outlining the silver form, which was now topped by a half-melted helm that glowed a dull red from Kole's attack.

Kole launched himself, wisps of flame trailing. The wind hit him like a hurricane, sucking the air from his lungs, but his rage only redoubled and he smashed down in the gallery, his landing making a crater where the Sage had crouched seconds before.

A bolt struck Kole in the shoulder as he charged again. He shrugged it off, along with the next gust of supernatural wind. He shot forward, slamming into the titan's armored chest with a crack like heat lightning. They locked hands, Kole's fiery glow muted by the blue and white of the storm.

The power of the skies flowed through him and set his teeth to chatter, his spine to quiver, but the Sage's gauntlets began to glow. They morphed from orange to red before warping to match the pitiful helm that stared at him now through one open slit. Kole glimpsed fear within, and the fear fed him, building his heat to a crescendo as his armor split, his bare skin reflecting the colors of their clash, all amber and blue.

The loose slate and marble from the broken floor and gallery spun in a cyclone as the titan called the air again into its service, its great wings thrashing in the maelstrom.

"The dark has made a weapon of you," Kole said.

The White Crest recognized its death was close at hand, and the wind became a tornado. Black tiles ripped loose from the walls and pink light spilled in from the newly opened skylight. Overhead, the stone supports creaked like timbers.

One metal hand shattered like ice in Kole's palm, and the Sage screamed something that sounded the cousin of rage and pain.

"You are all the same. I've known it all my life. You all need to go."

Their embrace was a torrent.

And then, just as quickly as it had come on, Kole's blood went cold, the flames evaporating from his skin and leaving motes and fireflies in their wake. He flew back, the remainder of his black shell shattering against the soapstone. He slumped, the blood in his throat drying to a thick paste.

And the White Crest approached, his footsteps halting.

"Fool," he said, blue sparks jumping from the one good hand to match the glow behind the melted helm. The storm quieted, which only served to heighten the sound of popping as tiny bolts built to their lethal charge beneath the armor. There was not a seam that was not lit.

"If you cannot defeat me, what hope have you against him?"

Kole struggled to find his voice.

The Sage stood over him, blue hand raised in the premonition of a god's smiting.

"I sensed your coming," he said. "I sensed your power in the fields of Hearth as you turned the dark army to ash. As you killed hundreds."

"Your army," Kole croaked.

"I still sense that power," the Sage said, tone curious, head tilting in a disgusting comedy. "And yet, here you sit, all but spent and at death's door knocking. Tell me, what tricks have you left?"

Kole doubted he could have lit a candle at that moment. His look said as much, and the White Crest sighed as if he were disappointed.

"No matter, then. Thanks to you, I must go into hiding, never to return. I cannot hope to defeat the Eastern Dark now."

"You never could."

And the voice that issued from the shattered sky above was not Kole's. The White Crest wheeled, and Kole felt his fear keen as a knife's edge.

The Eastern Dark had come.

CHAPTER THIRTY-SEVEN

LEGACY OF THE FLAME

Linn Ve'Ran had fought creatures of dark from the time she could hold a bow. Now, those had given way to beings that shined golden in the dying sun—angels of silver and red that streaked before her like harbingers.

They struck with spears and raked with talons, gnashing beaks never still. But the worst of it were their screams; they screeched like eagles riding the winds of death.

"Run!"

Misha had yelled the order three times now, but Linn would not heed her. The Ember wielded Jenk's Everwood blade better with each passing beast, slashing and stabbing from the shifting balls of her feet. Winged assailants came for her by the dozen, and many of them fell. But she could not keep it up forever.

Linn's knuckles were raw, lips cracking as she strained the corded band of the war bow back inch by gargantuan inch. It was a weapon unlike anything she had handled before, made of some mixture of earth and wood. It felt as though it would only yield to a giant's strength and Linn was fresh out of that. But she was a Ve'Ran. She struggled, and each creak the cord made was a small victory in the face of overwhelming defeat.

Kole had disappeared into a gap of his own making, and the lights that issued forth bleached the stones themselves, drenching the rocky slope in a splash of orange and blue that challenged the sunset and won out. The howling of the wind merged with the sharp retorts of lightning, and at its center, the maelstrom within the keep expelled its chaotic sounds and smells, all ash and ozone.

Linn cried out as the cord snapped back and nearly took her thumb, her concentration broken by a boom louder than the others. She looked up and through the mess of avian beasts and the warriors of the Fork to see a rain of red tiles that littered the slope like frozen blood. A swirling tornado of spinning clay speared its way through the roof, tongues of yellow flame climbing free.

"Argh!"

Misha staggered and nearly went down, her blade flashing out to parry a hawk's spear that nonetheless came away red with the Ember's blood. The Third Keeper of Hearth clutched her side and growled.

Nathen struggled to rise, but he was too weak, his bout with the Dark Hearts having sapped what remained of his strength.

Linn cursed and rose, bow in one hand, silver shaft held like a spear in the other.

Misha whirled to meet a second attack, turning the lancing spear aside and striking back in a shower of sparks, but her left was unguarded and the first hawk dove back in.

Linn shouldered the Ember out of the way and intercepted the spearhead with the front of the bow. She spun, dipping down and lifting her hips as she slammed into the armored chest. The arch of the bow caught the barbed spear under its head and Linn used the anchor to send the creature flying over her back and toward the ground, the razor wings gouging lines along her back and shoulders as she heaved.

They finished face-to-face, Linn and the white-eyed hawk. Before the beast could right itself in a furious flapping of wings and armored limbs, she released her hold on the bow and brought the silver arrowhead down with all the force she could muster. It was enough, shattering the metallic visage and cutting short the painful echoes of its dying.

Linn retracted the shaft from the earth and was surprised to see that it remained intact, none the worse for wear after passing through metal, magic and the face of the cliff itself.

Something flashed and Linn fell back as the shadow of another winged beast angled toward her. She dove to the side, the ground rushing up to meet her, but she needn't have. The hawk fell dead, its midsection ripped open and dripping molten, eyes losing their sparking light soon after.

A hand reached out and Linn took it, wincing as the heat scalded her palm. She pulled it away with a curse and came up to see Misha with her shock of red hair staring, her face broken into a savage grin.

"That was some work you did," the Ember said, head bobbing. She looked maniacal, and Linn was glad they were on the same side. "Sorry about the hand. Bit of a rush going now."

"No worries," Linn said. She nodded behind the Ember as another hawk dove in.

Misha ducked and Linn darted, dodging the thrust and bringing the arrowhead around point-first to take the beast in the eye. It went down in a heap and Misha came down on top of it, flaming sword going to work and tearing from torso to wing.

Linn bent to retrieve the shaft, and now it was she helping Misha up. The Ember's face looked suddenly pale and her breath came in short gasps.

"You're not looking too well," Linn said and Misha favored her with a withering glare. She made to rise, gasped again and sank back down to one knee, the point of Jenk's blade buried in the earth beside her, tongues of flame lapping up toward the hilt. The Ember shrugged.

"Seems a shame for me to be the one taking a knee after what you've been through," Misha said, panting.

"Not from where I'm standing," Linn said seriously. "I've done enough of nothing."

She looked back toward the keep, where the Rivermen had rallied around the whirling dervish that was Baas Taldis. His shield struck out with savage force, shattering any metal not baked in the hot furnace of the earth. The armored wings cracked like eggshells as the remaining Rockbled took up his flanks and sent spears of obsidian rushing up to the circling hawks. All told, they were giving more than they got.

Another boom wracked the grounds around the keep and Misha struggled to her feet, the flames along the length of her blade guttering and turning from deep orange to pale yellow as she completed the effort.

Linn looked at Misha and then down at Nathen, who covered Jenk's prone form like a mother bear over its cub.

"You mean to enter," Misha said, following her gaze.

Linn nodded.

"The Rivermen have the creatures occupied for now, but it'll only take one of them to finish these two."

Misha blew out a long sigh, the blood leaking down her armor like oil.

"Please," Linn said, her look one of stone. It was the look of a Ve'Ran, and even Misha Ve'Gah, Ember of Hearth, looked away.

"I'll do the thing," she said, waving Linn off.

Linn spun, but felt a hot pain on her wrist. She turned back toward Misha.

"You make sure it gets done," Misha said. "Whatever needs doing." And she released her.

Linn nodded. She clutched the bow in her right hand, shaft in her left. The sun had dipped low, painting the broken keep in red shadow. The lights had faded to a dull orange glow within.

And then an explosion sounded, the hole Kole had made erupting with a mix of flame and lightning. The force was so severe that it knocked Linn from her feet. She scrambled back up and saw that several of the fliers had gone down. The warriors of the Fork took advantage, hacking the fallen apart with their deadly tools.

Flames lapped hungrily in the miniature pools of fire that now littered the slope, a microcosm of those in the fields below. Wind howled through the peaks, drawn by the White Crest's call as the torrents streaked into the blasted roof. The air buzzed with energy and the ground shook with a sudden staccato of quaking bursts.

Was all this power directed at Kole? How could he hope to survive it?

What could she possibly do to help?

Linn took a steadying breath and took off at as close to a sprint as her starved and ruined muscles would allow.

She skirted the edges of the melee, Baas shouting for her as she passed, his shield shattering another of the gnashing beaks. The slope leveled as she climbed over the ruined gate, and the hellish mouth of the keep beckoned her, red and blue flashes interspersed with streaks of amber.

Linn closed her eyes as she took the cracked stone steps two at a time, plunging into the house of horrors she had so recently fled.

And the sight before her defied all sense given to those of mortal birth, even one raised among the Embers and their ilk. She wondered what the gods would say of this. She wondered if the beings throwing themselves at one another on the currents of violent magic counted themselves among them.

This was a battle between Sages, she was sure. Just as she was sure that she had no place in it.

No one did.

Kole lounged like a broken thing against a far column that had half melted, its black surface reflective as mirrored glass. He watched the titanic clash through half-closed lids.

Linn ran to him, screaming his name over the blasts of flame, roar of wind and scream of lightning.

━◆◆━

The White Crest, Kole had learned, was one who had a propensity to mince words. It was a bit shocking, then, to see him attack the intruder without pretense or preamble. He shot a howling bolt as he whirled, blue orb flaring in the half-melted helm, warped beak gleaming in the bright.

Kole was sure the visitor was none other than the Eastern Dark. Though the figure was not cloaked, a darkness hung about him that seemed a separate thing from the lengthening shadows of dusk.

He was sure of it right up until a torrent of red-orange flame erupted from the stranger's palms, absorbing the wind and burning up the lightning like a snuffed lantern.

This was no Sage, then. This was an Ember, and as the clash was joined in earnest, Kole knew he was witnessing a battle between the White Crest and a man out of place and time.

This was the King of Ember. None other.

Kole struggled to rise, but his body hurt all over and his palms were slick with his own blood. His lungs burned and displaced ribs stabbed. He wondered with a detached sort of interest if he was dying.

Mostly, he just watched.

The White Crest raged, but the dark Ember, his face wreathed in shadow and flame let his fire do the talking. The roaring flames transformed the keep into a furnace, and the Sage's winds did nothing but act as a bellows. The heat had the effect of nourishing Kole, filling him with a slow and aching vitality, and his senses began to return as if from a great distance.

He thought he heard a voice calling to him. It was familiar, echoing with pain and fear.

Kole craned his neck, rotating his torso best he could. A gout of flame shot up and blanketed the vaulted ceiling and all its arches in liquid fire that billowed like clouds. It cast an amber light on her hair, and for a moment in his daze Kole was certain his mother had come for him in his final hour.

He could almost see her green eyes shining under the shock of hair, which was tied back in a braid, but then she hid them behind an upraised arm, the force of the tumult knocking her back toward the entrance.

This was not Sarise A'zu.

Kole bent onto his hands and knees, willing life into his ailing legs. They felt heavy as cast-iron. He glanced up at the ceiling and saw that the black stone had warped around the hole, and he glimpsed a panicked image of himself encased in the very glass he leaned against—a tomb no light would ever penetrate.

The titans streaked before him, the silver armor of the White Crest glittering, chest plate shattering as a fist of flame came against it with inhuman speed. The Ember warrior carried no weapons, dark hair waving in the heat and face hidden in the black shadows that rose from his red armor like ink as he sent the Sage reeling.

"Kole!"

The welcome face of Linn Ve'Ran smoothed the hurt from having lost a mother twice.

"Linn," he rasped, legs tingling as they leeched heat from the stonework.

Her face was a mask equal parts determination and fear—fear for him, he realized. She looked in that moment to be a thing of beauty. Perhaps it was the way a streak of lightning framed her. Maybe it was the tiny stars of amber and gold that stood out on her brow and set her plastered bangs like tiny chandeliers. Past these, Kole knew it was the impossible way she pushed compassion to the front of all her hurt.

Landkist or not, Linn Ve'Ran would not be cowed by flames. Even as she bent over double in the midst of what seemed the glowing belly of a drake, she would not break.

She helped him up, supporting him, but his legs failed and they fell to the ground, Linn yelping as the stones burned her skin.

The image of the black tomb rose again, and this time Kole saw Linn embedded with him. His legs flared to life in agony, the fire in his blood sparking.

"What is this?" Linn gasped, looking around.

"The King of Ember," Kole said, pulling her up with him. He saw a length of silver sticking through the strap across her back, the bow across her shoulders making a trail through the sweating stones as they lurched toward the entrance.

"How?" She shielded her eyes from a blinding flare.

They turned.

When the smoke from their latest clash faded, the White Crest was on one knee, streaming palm glowing blue. His wings dipped, scraping the floor and scattering motes of golden ash as he struggled to rise. The lone blue orb flickered weakly, fear and anger leaking from him in equal measure.

His power was all but spent, and the King of Ember strode toward him, burning hands at his sides and a look of disgust etched onto the contours of his impossibly young features. Truly, he looked no older than Karin. The red sash around his torso fluttered in the Sage's dying winds. He was unhurt and unconcerned.

"We could have used Holspahr, you fool."

He spoke with a clear voice that reverberated through the crumbling, melted galleries and the flames that burned absent fuel.

"Is he our enemy?" Linn whispered.

"Ask me again once he's finished."

The White Crest laughed and the sound was a broken thing.

"We, is it?" he cackled, hawk voice piercing and shrill with all authority driven from it as he knelt before the King of Ember in a throne room wreathed in flame. "You're no different than Holspahr was at the end—a Sentinel. A slave. I was fighting fire with fire, but he's done some work on you, I see."

As he finished, he gave a grand flourish, wings undulating and gauntleted hand sweeping out to encompass his burning cathedral.

The King of Ember did not look impressed.

"I am no slave," he said.

"And yet," the half-melted helm tilted in that inhuman way, "here you are, come to tie up loose ends before they come calling."

Linn saw it before Kole did. She tackled him to the ground behind the nearest pillar, his back screaming in protest as the air was forced from his lungs. Blue light filled the chamber as the White Crest attacked and another primal shriek rang out, this one long and keening. The glow faded, as did the echoes of thunder.

They sat up in a tangle and saw the two figures in much the same position they had been, only it was the King of Ember who stood with glowing palm pointing down. As for their Valley's great protector, his head was bowed, remaining hand clutching at the melted and dripping mess of his other limb.

"Our battle is done," the King of Ember said, his tone broaching no argument. "This is your ending."

"You," the White Crest said, recognition dawning. "You were the one I sensed. You were waiting this whole time."

The Ember's eyes—orange like the sun—swiveled toward Linn and Kole for half a heartbeat before settling back on his quarry.

"Opportunity takes time. Little did I know how weak you had truly become in your slumber. Or was it the woman at the Lake that did this to you?"

"The Lake," Linn whispered, horror coating her voice.

Kole remained silent, watching the exchange. It was difficult to glean anything from the Ember's expression. The darkness that seemed to hang about him was not the same as the inky black paint that the Sentinels and Dark Kind counted as skin. This was a magic that followed.

"Did you really think you could turn the darkness against him?" the Ember asked. The flames in the chamber shifted with his mood, losing some of their hunger and shrinking back to set a softer glow over the scene.

The blue orb dulled to a sorry glow and Kole almost felt pity.

"I have to admit," the Ember said, "you surprised him by coming out of the sleep as you did."

The Sage looked at the melted marble at his knees, all defeat.

"You cast down the Night Lords he sent against you," the Ember continued, "never supposing there was more to them. That you were meant to win. That your heart was meant to be corrupted by theirs." He spat. "That you would turn that corruption on the people you once swore to protect ..."

The King of Ember took a step forward and the chamber brightened, the flames reacting hungrily to the mounting tension.

"We are here to clean up the mess you've made."

"We?"

The Ember laughed, full-throated and cruel, reveling in the Sage's cowardice. The blue orb flickered with intent.

"Fear not, puppet," he said. "The Eastern Dark has not deigned to come see you off. As always, his sister in the north has her watchful eyes on him. He sent us in his stead, and we will be enough."

It seemed that the Sage would be killed no matter who did the killing, but it was a sobering thought to Kole, that the White Crest much preferred the fire over death at the hands of the Eastern Dark.

"Are you ready, then, great Sage?" the Ember King raised his glowing palm again, and the flames throughout the chamber danced like snakes. "Ready to face your fate?"

The White Crest said nothing, only looked away, the anger—even the fear—having all gone out of him.

That look stirred something within Kole, and even as Linn worked to pull him away, he rose on legs that felt steady enough and walked toward the gods at the heart of the burning throne room. He picked up his discarded blade on the way—the other was still smoking on the slope outside—and guided the flames out of their path as Linn followed in his wake.

"You come here now," Kole said, stopping a few paces from the kneeling Sage and his would-be executioner. Both regarded him with curious expressions, the White Crest with suspicion and the Ember that would be his king with something more difficult to read.

"You come here now," Kole repeated, staring hard at the Ember, who lowered his glowing palm ever so slightly.

"I do."

The flames at his back curled menacingly, shadowed wisps leaking from his red armor.

"You come to kill, not to liberate," Kole said.

There was a pause.

"Is that not why you came?" the Ember responded.

Kole swallowed, but Linn spoke for him.

"You are the King of Ember?" she asked, her tone uncertain.

"I was," and the Sage chortled sickly.

"And now you serve our enemy? You serve the Eastern Dark?"

Tears shone in her eyes.

"The World is much wider than this Valley of yours," the Ember said. He looked down at the Sage, whose light was dimming even as the flames in the keep brightened. "Friends become enemies."

He glanced at Kole before settling those orange eyes back on Linn. The darkness that draped him did not touch his eyes. Those were his own.

"Nothing has happened as I wanted it to, but my people endure. You endure."

"What happened between you?" Kole asked, indicating the pitiful Sage at their feet, though the melted helm still came up nearly to his chest.

"We rode out against the Eastern Dark, fearing that he would open pathways to the World Apart too great to close. I was cast down and he fled back to his mountain hole. The Eastern Dark, too weak to follow, sent his Night Lords. The rest ..." he drifted off, staring down at the Sage.

"You can thank your protector here, for corrupting the lands outside of the Valley and bringing the army to your woods and fields."

"We've been fighting the Dark Kind for a generation," Linn said.

"Waves of them, yes. Enough to keep you strong in the case of his need. To keep you from the wars without. The Eastern Dark witnessed my power first-hand. He knows what potential the Embers possess."

"You have agents in the Valley," Kole said and the Ember did not answer.

Kole ignited his blade, drawing a small laugh from the broken Sage.

"Other Landkist," the King of Ember said. "They are searching. Searching for others that might join—

"None would join you," Kole said. "None would join him."

"It is only through him that we end their scourge," he said, staring balefully at the White Crest.

"Through you, you mean," Linn said and the Ember did not argue.

"You hate them all," the King of Ember took a step toward Kole, who took a step back. "You have much to learn—much more than the Embers here can teach you."

Kole spat.

"How did he break you?"

The King of Ember's expression was inscrutable, but the flames around him swirled and edged closer. Given what he had seen them do, even Kole feared their touch.

"We grew up on tales of you," Kole said, refusing to back down. "The great King of Ember, hero of the desert and descendant of the First Keeper, a man that fought against the Dark Kind."

"The World is large. The World is complicated."

"You made it small enough for your people," Kole said, venom rising. "You trapped us at the edge of the World and set one monster to guard us from the rest."

"The World is full of monsters." The Ember indicated the Sage at his feet. "It's time we got rid of the worst."

"All of the worst?" Linn asked.

"All."

Those orange eyes did not waver, and Kole swallowed.

"The Dark Kind tore my mother apart," Kole said. His voice was calm, steady. But the flames snaking from the hilt of his blade up to his elbow were anything but.

"There will always be a need for the Keepers," the King of Ember said. "So long as the Dark Kind find gates into this World, pockets through which they can sow their disease and discord. But you are not the only ones harried by the World Apart."

"You serve their master," Kole said, the flames twining around his shoulder now. The fires in the chamber shifted and morphed, choosing their alliance carefully.

The White Crest wheezed out another choking laugh.

"Master," he chortled. "The Dark Kind have no master. He merely found them at their source. He knows where to push at the seams, where to let them in. But he'll push too far and the rip will open too wide to close. He almost did when he sent the Night Lords against me."

"Kole slew a Night Lord not a moon past," Linn said disdainfully, earning another maniacal bout.

"A Night Lord?" the White Crest cackled. "That ape was not fit to be one of their standard-bearers. It was nothing more than a Corrupted beast from the hills of your own Valley. The Sentinels did their work well."

"The problem remains," Kole said, ignoring him. "You serve our enemy."

"I serve mankind, in whichever way I can."

"And what of the Landkist at your back?" Linn asked.

"They follow me."

"For now," Kole said.

"You're here for him," Linn said, nodding at the melted mess of armor and wings. "Then what?"

"On to the next."

"Why is the Eastern Dark trying to eliminate the other Sages?" Kole asked.

"They have been warring for centuries," the King of Ember said. "This one held himself apart for a time, but he was not always so innocent. Power breeds envy. Envy breeds contempt."

He straightened, raising that glowing palm.

"No matter. They will pass. Some sooner than others."

"I was afraid."

The White Crest spoke in half a whisper.

"Your cowardice has never been in question."

"I was afraid," he said again, the blue orb peering up, surprisingly, at Kole.

"Did you think he was the chosen one?" the King of Ember asked, voice rising and flames rising with it. He looked from the Sage to Kole. "Did you?"

Kole shrank back, put suddenly on the defensive.

"The Line of Mena'Tch," the King of Ember scoffed, looking down at the White Crest. The blue flared before dying back down. "Is that what you feared? The only power in blood is given by the World, not scratched into cavern walls in the desert."

He looked back at Kole.

"You are powerful," he said. "To fight a Sage head-on—even one as compromised as this one—it's not a feat many Landkist are capable of. Maybe none. But you merely wield the flames; you do not become them. I felt your power in the fields from leagues away, as we made our way through the foothills where the Corrupted massed. You can only use your body as a blade for so long without understanding the fire. It is why the Embers have used Everwood for so long as a natural extension, a ward against their true selves."

"All but you," Kole said, looking down at the Ember's glowing palms.

"All but me."

"I should have known it was you I sensed," the Sage sobbed. "I should have known."

"You see this?" the King of Ember kicked the armored chest and stepped on it, leaning his weight down, the flames along the floor inching close as hungry lions. Beneath the deformed helm and warped beak, the blue brightened with fear.

Kole felt ill.

Was this not why he had come? To do the very thing the King of Ember was now?

"They fear us, as they should," the King of Ember said, denting the chest plate in with his heel, teeth gritted. "The Sages will die at the hands of their own prophecies."

The King of Ember's palm exploded into a comet, lancing down to shatter the plate, the red tail tracing its path and mixing with the blinding flare of blue that erupted from the open chasm in the writhing Sage's chest.

When the light cleared, Kole peered into the fiery maelstrom at the center of the titan's breast. There was no body within, only a swirling mass of wind and crackling light—and now the flaming heart of an Ember's fist at its core. The White Crest struggled in vain, but the Ember kept him locked in place, leering down with hateful intensity, his eyes glowing a deep amber that Kole for a second mistook for the ruby red of a Sentinel.

Linn reached forward, but stopped as the Sage's shrieking spasms morphed sharply into the most maniacal laughter yet.

"You think you have free will?" he said, heedless of the burning at his core or driven on because of it. "You think you are your own, just because a Sentinel isn't driving you? I see the darkness in you. His darkness. You are a pawn on a board of his making. You will never be free of him, no matter your private designs."

The flames dipped down all around them, their hunger abating for the moment. The chamber glowed like twilight, and Kole was aware that the sun had dropped below the horizon; he could see starlight shining down from the blasted roof. The faint echoes of battle still rang outside, but they were lesser now, more full of the grunts and commands of the Rivermen than the shrieks of the hawks.

The King of Ember withdrew his molten hand. He looked down at the Sage, his face blank.

"His time will come," he said, softly, as if he were speaking to himself. "Darkness is the absence of light. And there are still bright lights remaining in this world."

He looked at Kole as he said it.

"Are you one of them?" Kole asked.

"How could he know?" Linn asked, and the amber eyes switched to her, orange lights passing over the surface of his glowing hand.

"I thought I was protecting you," he said, eyes glazing in the haze of memories too distant for Kole to imagine.

"Protecting them!"

The White Crest was making the most of its death throes.

"By stocking the Valley with these jewels of the desert? You sealed their fate. You cut them off from the source of their power. You kept them safe from the wars without. Safe in his keeping. Until he had need of them, as he had need of you."

"We would never join him," Linn said, though her voice wavered.

"Do you think the sorry souls before the gates of Hearth had a choice when I set the Dark Hearts to calling?"

The blue eye flicked up to the King of Ember.

"This one had a choice."

"As did you," the King of Ember said. "And you ran."

"You do his bidding."

"I do what I must."

"By killing the only beings capable of standing up to him?" Linn asked.

"They are all the same. Or they will be, eventually." He almost looked sad as he considered the broken form at his feet, one who Kole had no doubt projected majesty a century ago. "We could have stopped him that day, you and I. You don't know what's coming. I have to do this."

There was a short silence.

"Step back," the King of Ember told them, and they did.

Another laugh, but this one was false, a cover for the fear the White Crest felt.

"Always beware the chained hound," the Sage said.

The light was blinding white, and for a moment, Kole was sure that Linn would burn up. As it dissipated, he realized the blast had been so concentrated that it had immolated the armored form at their feet without so much as an errant mote.

Where the White Crest had been, there was nothing but a smoking ruin.

The King of Ember sighed, sweat standing out on his brow. The darkness seemed to deepen about him, or maybe it was just the absence of his flames. The only light remaining in the chamber came from the stars above and the soft yellow cadence of Kole's Everwood blade.

Footfalls behind them, and Linn and Kole turned to see the sturdy outline of Baas Taldis against the opening, his shield held out before him. The Rockbled stopped when he saw the light of Kole's blade and then approached cautiously.

"The others?" Linn asked as he neared. Baas was made of something strong as stone, for he was none the worse for wear, his skin unmarked and the blood already drying beneath his nose.

Baas nodded, his attention caught up by the strange presence of the King of Ember standing over his smoking pit.

A flood of relief washed through Kole knowing that none of the others had perished, a feeling that did nothing to ease the terror that gripped him when the King of Ember uttered a single word at his back.

CHAPTER THIRTY-EIGHT

DEAD AND BORN

"No."

The horror that leaked from the word and the veritable god that spoke it cast a dread spell over the company.

The King of Ember was staring up into the starry sky through the gaping hole in the vaulted ceiling. Linn followed his gaze.

There, hanging in the space between roof and sky was a swirling current of air that shimmered and sparked. What at first looked to be two stars in the canopy beyond came clear as the same blue orbs that marked the White Crest's eyes, the avian head half-formed.

Kole and Baas followed her line of sight, but they squinted against the twilight. Linn had ever been blessed, but this time, the noticing got her noticed.

With a pop and crack that sounded like the breaking of a mountain spur, the spirit morphed from wind to arcing light and streaked down faster than an arrow. Linn brought the silver shaft around as a sorry shield and the King of Ember sent a jet of red fire, but it was to no avail.

"Kole!" Linn screamed, and the Ember's blade flared brightly. Baas readied his shield and shouldered her out of the way. She fell to the floor with a jolt and recoiled as the spirit dodged Kole's slash and made for her, unerring.

It slammed into her chest with enough force to drive the air from her lungs and take the sight from her eyes, her vision going white. She felt the arrow snap, the bow digging into her back as she convulsed. The current animated her body like a sick marionette and the pain was beyond reckoning.

She heard shouting—Kole, she thought. And through her pain and thrashing, she felt heat flood the chamber as both Embers brought their power to bear. The great shadow of Baas Taldis passed in front of her, shielding her from their hellish collision.

And then the physical world passed away and the pain with it. There was brief darkness and then light whiter than any she had seen. She could not see the White Crest, but she felt his presence in her mind, his thoughts coming up unbidden as images played before her.

She saw a clash of Embers unlike anything she could have imagined. There was Kole, single blade struggling to hold back the torrent the King of Ember sent against him. The latter was trying to get to her, she saw—trying to pry the Sage from her shell. Baas joined the fray, his shield striking out and granting Kole a reprieve. The flames danced their wicked dance, delighting in the chaos of combat, and both Embers drank it in and poured it out in equal measure.

Linn had thought it impossible for an Ember to be hurt by the fire unless he willed it so, but Kole was burning. She could see the pain etched onto his face. More than that, she could see the desperation, the knowing that he could not win.

The battle of the present faded and images from the distant past were called up like memories through a faraway fog. She saw bronze-skinned men and women arrayed in staggered ranks, perched among the red rocks of a foreign land. Their wings—white and gray—flapped gently.

They were Landkist unlike any she had seen or heard of. At their head was a great leader whom she recognized, his crown bedecked in white feathers, body encased in brilliant armor that shone gold and silver in the light.

There was a great host embattled across the plains before them. The number of combatants was beyond counting, but there was power among them. She saw Landkist of all manner locked in mortal combat. Some rode great beasts with eyes shining like the emerald of the Faeykin, while others turned their skin to armor, shattering weapons on impact. There were stone-throwers that reminded her of the Rockbled and there were archers who guided their shafts with thought alone.

Wings beat and the ranks of birdmen took off, eager to join the fray. She did not see the clash, but she saw its aftermath, the White Crest's armor cracked and pitted, feathers red with blood. Behind him, the last of his Landkist perished in the swirling dust and she felt the heartbreak almost as keenly as the guilt that threatened to choke him like so much bile.

Next, Linn saw the Valley that had ever been her home, but she saw it in a different time. She saw the white rocks poking up from the green fields where Hearth would be. She rode on great wings over the shining silver lake, its shores bare but for the moss and stone that littered them, no Long Hall in sight. She saw the children of the Faey duck between the branches of trees at his passing, the Rivermen turn from him in the gap that broke the mountains where his titanic clash with the Night Lords would later cave them in.

Most of all, she felt the loneliness and regret, as well as seeds of anger too deep to contain. She felt fear in the knowledge of the growing threat posed by the Eastern Dark and the tense anticipation of their inevitable conflict.

Finally, she saw Ninyeva standing in the rain, bloody before the wreckage of her tower at Last Lake. She stood taller than she was, casting a shadow against his violent light that frightened him.

And Linn's heart broke when he struck her down.

She felt his shame, then, and that was what lingered longest as he passed beyond her reach.

But some of him remained.

"He has to die!"

The King of Ember seemed able to fly, jetting around the chamber on blazing trails. He dodged the sorry tongues of flame Kole sent for him from the edges of his blade and absorbed the geysers with his glowing palms.

Kole had been struck twice by the beams those palms produced and the heat of it shocked him, leaving him shaking with an energy that threatened to break him apart. Blood dripped from his nose and burned up in a red mist.

He fought on.

He ducked and dodged, going to work with his blade and infusing his muscles with the fire they needed rather than wasting it on attacks the other Ember rendered moot.

If it were not for Baas, who took the latest beam off the crown of his great shield, Kole would have fallen in the third exchange. As it were, with the combination of his resistance to the fire and Baas's masterful defense, they were able to keep their adversary away from Linn, whose thrashing had given way to a stillness Kole feared to contemplate.

"Stop this!" Kole screamed, but the King of Ember only brought more power to bear. He sent Baas crashing into the far wall, his leather doublet smoking. Though the Rockbled's skin was unmarked, the glazed look in his eyes suggested that the heat was taking its toll, leeching the strength from him.

"He must be excised," the King of Ember said, ducking Kole's swing and slamming him hard in the side. The percussive blast was accentuated by a crack that had Kole falling to one knee, sword held before him in shaking fingers.

The King of Ember stood over him, comet fists at his sides, eyes glowing molten amber. For a moment, his look softened. He hesitated before a shadow passed over him, darkening his features like smoke.

He raised his hand and Kole tried to rise and found that he could not.

And then the King of Ember vanished, disappearing under the hurtling side of a section of black marble. Kole looked to the right and saw Baas on his hands and knees, chest heaving, face pale. A huge chunk of the keep's base was missing—a missile of Baas's make. Framed against the doorway, Kole could see the running forms of the other Rockbled warriors, iron-forged weapons held aloft.

An explosion rocked the gallery and night turned to day. Fragments of stone shot in all directions, embedding themselves in the crumbling soapstone pillars and throwing sparks up as they struck the glowing tiles in the floor. And the King of Ember approached in all his majesty, stepping over the ruins of the throne. Blood caked his forehead and ran hissing down his neck, but he was alive. And he was angry.

"You cannot have her," Kole said, rising on shaking legs. Two of Baas's warriors flanked him, weapons ready. Their breath was ragged in the furnace the keep had become, but they stood strong and unmoving.

"They must all die," the King of Ember said, steady in his approach.

Stones flew at him from each side, two Rockbled calling pieces from the broken floor and whipping them in rapid succession. But the Ember called up his flames and they burned so hot around him that the stones were reduced to ash before they bounced lightly against his red armor.

"The good in them is not worth saving in the face of man's fall," he said. "The White Crest was good once. So was the Sage of the Waste. It was he who told me of the Valley. It was he who repelled the Eastern Dark for generations, keeping the Night Lords from the cave doors so the Keepers would only have their minions to face."

"And you would kill him too? Or have you done it already?" Kole cried.

"His time will come," he said. "You of all people know the ruin their magic can bring. How many wars must we fight on their behalf?"

"A war of which you're a part!"

"The final war. A war the Eastern Dark will finish, before I finish him."

"He'll never let you close again," Kole said, desperate. "He knows your mind."

"It won't save him. It won't save any of them."

The warriors on Kole's flanks charged. These Rivermen were not Landkist, and Kole screamed for them to stop, but it was too late. With a flare and the smallest of shrieks, they were gone, snuffed out. The Rockbled throwers were themselves thrown back, slamming against opposite walls before falling in dazed heaps.

The King of Ember stood over him, wreathed in flames. He was like a god to look upon. In that moment, looking up into a face turned golden, Kole knew this man could do anything he said.

He raised a glowing palm, and Kole braced for a heat unlike anything he had ever felt.

It was cold.

The King of Ember's face contorted, his expression morphing, and Kole felt the heat drain from his body, absorbed into the other Ember's outstretched palm. His skin turned blue and he felt like death, ice in his veins and heart slowing. He knew what it must be like to freeze and drown all at once.

Just before his vision faded, the sensation ceased, and he crumbled to the floor, his fire snuffed out but his life still clinging.

———◆—◆———

Linn squeezed her eyes shut tight against the pain as she was thrown back into her body, but all was calm. Her arms felt light as feathers. Her body thrummed with energy, as if the shifting currents in the embattled chamber passed through rather than around her. Her heart beat strong and steady, and with each pulse, there was a buzz like the building charge in a storm cloud.

Most of all, her sight—long the keenest in the Valley—was now truly akin to that of an eagle. Though the vaulted ceiling was too high even to be lit by the clashing Embers before the broken throne, Linn could see the details in the carved obsidian, the tiny motes of ash floating beneath the skylight. She saw far out into the blue-black night sky, and it nearly took her breath away, so clear did it appear, so in reach.

And then she heard Kole's anguished cry.

Linn went to stand and felt none of the agony she had expected. She brought the bow with her, which had stayed together where the silver shaft had split in two.

Kole cried out again and Linn cursed, snatching up the fletched end and setting it to the string. She settled down onto one knee. The arrow was halved, but the broken end still had enough length to scrape the bow when drawn; it would have to do.

As she aimed, Linn saw the ending of the Embers' duel in vivid detail. Though they battled thirty strides away or more, she saw the veins standing out in the King of Ember's hand as he turned Kole's blade aside and raised that glowing palm.

Kole tried to rise, but he was too weak. A look of pity crossed the King of Ember's features before his palm began to dull. Kole's skin turned ashen blue, and as she watched, Linn felt something stirring within her. Her palms tingled, hair waving with a breeze she had not felt moments before. There was an energy about her. It teased the tips of her fingers and played softly along the edges of her lips.

Linn smiled, feeling the storm as the clouds wheeled overhead. The orange and red in the chamber was swallowed by a brilliant blue as the rift in the roof opened further, the force of the passing lightning widening the breach.

It came for her, and this time, Linn did not recoil. She breathed in as the bolt struck, closing her eyes and feeling the electricity infuse her body and charge her heart. And then she harnessed it, passing the lightning through her veins and moving the wind with her will. She directed it all into the missing point of the shaft and let fly, reveling in the look of shock in those amber eyes as they turned her way.

The bolt struck true, blasting the Ember back even as he brought his palms around to block. He screamed out as the shaft went tumbling, teeth clenched as the storm wracked his body.

Linn was standing over him by the time he hit the ground, his red armor blackened and his eyes losing their glow.

"You will not take him from me," she said.

The King of Ember coughed, spots of blood standing out on his chin. "I would not kill him."

"You wouldn't. But then, you are not truly you."

He looked up at her with a mix of awe and denial.

"You don't understand," he said. "Their war will consume—

Linn knelt beside him.

"Maybe you're right. But it'll be us who decide. The Sages are in for a reckoning, but I'll be damned if I'm going to let one of them decide it. There is good to be found in all, even the Sages. I have felt it. Perhaps your master is the exception."

"The power," he said, reaching out for her hand, which was orbited by blue motes of light she hadn't noticed before—remnants of the blast that clung to her protectively. "It will consume you."

"We'll see."

A part of Linn knew she should end it then and there. But she could not. Rather, she chose not to.

"Mother Ninyeva believed in you," she said in a whisper, eyes watering.

The name seemed to strike something within him. His eyes widened as footfalls broke the silence.

Linn whirled and was relieved to see Misha Ve'Gah and the remainder of the Rockbled enter the moonlit gallery. The Ember had shed her armor and now sported nothing but her leggings and an immodest sash of cloth that she had tied from wounded hip to scraped shoulder. One of the warriors carried Jenk over one shoulder as if he were a child, and another set Nathen down to rest by the doorway before racing to check on Baas, who laid face-down by the blasted hole in the wall.

"What's this, then?" Misha asked, her voice echoing oddly in the recent stillness.

The King of Ember shot up faster than Linn could have anticipated. He put his back to the nearest pillar and Misha ignited Jenk's sword and sprinted forward, her wounds forgotten in the rush.

Linn stood surely, her hair fanning as the wind greeted her through the open roof. The Rockbled ringed the cornered Ember, weapons twisting silently in their hands.

"He is an enemy?" one of them asked, curious as to why Linn had not pressed her advantage.

"I don't know," Linn said, earning a confused and frustrated look from Misha. "And I don't think he does either."

The wild look in his eyes painted a stark contrast to the power he had displayed just minutes before. Something more than Linn's bolt had rattled him. Something much like doubt.

Misha seemed ready to decide things for them all when a piece of tile fell with a clatter from the skylight above. All eyes in the chamber shot up, and even Linn could not make out the figure clearly as it crouched over the lip of the yawning gap.

"Is it done?" the voice asked, lilting and certainly female.

The King of Ember stared at Linn a long while. And then he gave the slightest of nods.

"Good."

"Who—

Before Linn could finish, the form had melted into the shadows. There was a hint of movement, a rustling like the shifting of leaves, and a pale arm curled out of the closer dark to grasp the King of Ember on one armored shoulder.

"We must be going, then."

"What of the others?" he asked as he began to recede into the shadows with her.

"No luck," she purred. Linn caught a glimpse of a lavender iris glinting and the sheen of teeth that were impossibly white.

"Brega waits with the rest. We must be going."

"Like hell you are," Misha said, her blade flaring hungrily as she launched it like a spear toward the swirling patch of ink before the pillar. The Everwood blade passed through the air harmlessly, extinguishing with a hiss as the pale shadow danced out of the way.

The pale arms returned a moment later, pulling the King of Ember into the deeper dark, his eyes leaving golden trails that floated like burning ash.

"Well met, Ember King," Linn said. It was as much a warning as a farewell.

"My name is T'Alon Rane."

The voice came from above, and Linn looked up toward the blasted roof.

The King of Ember stood on the edge of the chasm, the shadow girl to his right, purple irises peering down at them.

"This Valley is no longer safe," he said and Linn scoffed.

"The Eastern Dark will not leave it lying free and open," he continued unabated. "He may come in a year. He may come in a generation. But he will not suffer the Embers to live once his work is done. I suggest you be gone by then."

"Gone where? You want us to leave the Valley you brought us to after killing the guardian you appointed?"

"You belong in the deserts," he said. "There is a Sage there called the Red Waste. He could—"

"Until you come for him as well," Linn challenged.

The King of Ember whose name was T'Alon Rane was silent, the lavender-eyed shadow staring up at him thoughtfully, considering.

"He is the least of," he paused. "The least of my master's worries right now."

"And who, pray tell, is the Eastern Dark worried about now?"

"So many questions," the shadow said, sparkling eyes staring at Linn as a cat examines a bird. "So many answers," she said, shifting them to the Ember King.

"There are quarrels the World over," he said. "One is growing very tense. The Emerald Road is not the safest place for traveling anymore."

The little shadow glared openly now, at him more than her, but the Ember ignored his companion. He watched one of the Rockbled lift

Kole like a sack. "The worse those quarrels between Sages get, the closer our master's hand gets to the door."

"Then I guess we'd better stop him," Linn said evenly, a spark lighting her own eyes that had the shadow shifting uneasily.

"For your sake and for his," he said, "I hope we find ourselves on the same side when next we meet. I wonder," he looked back to Kole, "if the two of you will be, given your hearts and their courses."

Linn was silent.

"So long, Linn Ve'Ran," he said, and the shadows grew thick about them, blocking the stars in the sky above.

"Right, then," Misha said, squatting down and pressing a hand to her bloody cloth. She looked up at Linn. "Who was that, and what was he on about?"

CHAPTER THIRTY-NINE

ASHES

"I was beginning to get used to waking up in unfamiliar surroundings," Kole said, rubbing his temples. He did not yet have the fortitude to open his eyes fully, but he had done enough squinting to recognize Captain Caru's sparse, cell-like quarters. "This one's old hat."

The Captain leaned against the mantle, watching Kole with a haggard look on his face.

"If you look that bad …"

"You are young," the Captain said. "Your worries dissolve with the rising of the sun. Mine linger."

"Tough to be young or old in this Valley of ours," Kole said, swinging his legs over the edge of the cot. The pine frame creaked in protest.

"If I hadn't seen first-hand how the Merchant Council treated you," he said, waving his hand at their surroundings, "this would do the trick."

"You're a simple man, Reyna, no matter what they say." Talmir donned a thick leather glove and handed Kole a steaming cup from the bed of glowing stones in the hearth.

The scalding liquid would have scarred a normal man from gullet to tailbone, but to Kole, it was a godsend. The memories of his battle with the King of Ember were flooding back. He supposed he should have tested his powers out before drinking boiling water, but there was no harm done.

"My father," Kole said, setting the stone cup down.

"Karin received a Runner from the Lake two days ago," Talmir said. His face worked through myriad emotions—none of them pleasant— before settling on sympathy. "The Faey Mother is dead."

It was like a glacier moving over Kole's heart. He swallowed.

"The White Crest came for her. He was driven off by Tu'Ren." Talmir paused. "Though, truth be told, there are plenty who say the old crone herself did the driving, including the First Keeper."

Kole nodded blankly.

"And Last Lake?" he asked, trying in vain to hope.

"No further casualties," Talmir said. "The sky broke before their walls had been breached."

The Captain spoke the last with a strange inflection, and Kole guessed he was trying to cover the bitterness seeping in.

He should have asked of Hearth. Still, all he could picture now was Iyana and her shining emerald eyes. She was safe.

"Your companions are in stable condition," Talmir said, his military staccato covering the momentary lapse. "Linn has been attending to them in the Bowl. She seems . . ."

Kole looked askance at him, but the Captain trailed off. There were fleeting images of Linn in the keep scattered in his mind's eye, but he couldn't sort them into the proper place.

"You'll see her soon enough."

The Captain of Hearth turned and leaned over the smoldering pit for a spell. Kole caught a glimpse of white bandages beneath his tunic, but the wounds he carried went far deeper than skin.

"The Rivermen?" Kole asked, breaking the silence.

"Baas and his people returned to the Steps to collect their own."

"They're coming into Hearth?"

"They could use us right now," Talmir said, frowning. "And, the Merchant Council reckons we could use them as well."

Kole did not want to imagine what damage the Dark Kind had visited upon Hearth. Had the Corrupted breached the walls? If they had, it was no wonder the Captain's voice held an edge where it concerned Last Lake, whose wooden stakes stood in the packed mud while his great white breakers of stone had been compromised.

"Jenk Ganmeer is up and moving already," the Captain said. "He's trying to get on the first caravan back. And your friend Nathen, the fisher's boy has been eating everything in sight. I daresay we would not have the stock to feed him if the siege still stood."

Kole laughed and Talmir turned a softer look on him. There was something like gratitude in it, spilling out through the pain. Kole did not feel much like a hero, having awoken on a sickbed for the third time in as many weeks. After all, it had not even been he who had toppled the White Crest in the end.

"We have you to thank for that," Talmir said. "You and yours. To think, our guardian had truly turned against us."

"He was a symptom of a larger problem," Kole said, voice hardening. "An older problem."

Talmir nodded.

"The Eastern Dark," he said. "He has found us, yes?"

"He never lost us. We were protected for a time, it's true, but the Breaking of the Valley marked a shift. The White Crest may have won the battle against the Night Lords, but the Eastern Dark won the war."

"Yes," Talmir said, looking through the misted window. "That was when the Dark Kind first entered the Valley."

"The Eastern Dark infected our protector with the hearts of the Night Lords sent against him," Kole said. "He was meant to test us." His voice took on an edge. "To cull us like a sown crop. But the White Crest awoke after the Dark Months. And when he did, he built an army of Corrupted and unleashed them on us so we could never be used against him."

Talmir blew out a long sigh.

"The Embers were the Eastern Dark's jewels," he said. "The Valley his chest."

Kole did not argue.

"But then," the Captain started, brows rising, "why has the Eastern Dark not come calling? Why has he not taken our Embers, taken you?"

"Because he already has the strongest one," Kole said. "And he's not one I'd fancy trying to control. I imagine we're a contingency plan."

The Captain's expression went from quizzical to confused.

"Linn didn't tell you? Misha?"

"I do not know Linn Ve'Ran," he said. "She's been more concerned with your condition than in keeping me informed. As for Misha, she hasn't been in a talkative mood. Dakken Pyr didn't make it through the siege. He was her man. A good man." He paused and swallowed. "There's been a lot to do, as you can imagine. Gathering the precise details of what occurred among those peaks hasn't been a priority, strange as that may seem. Who is this Ember?"

"An old one. One of several Landkist the Eastern Dark has ensnared."

"Our mortal enemy is amassing a secret force of Landkist," Talmir said with a cynical smile.

"Not a force," Kole said. "A handful of sycophants, I'd guess."

'Who is this Ember?" the Captain asked again.

"He is old," Kole said. "Before the Valley."

There was only one Ember that could be, but Talmir Caru, Kole knew, was a pragmatic man. The expression he wore now was one of disbelief.

"But we may not have lost him fully," Kole said, trying to cover the doubt in his voice.

Talmir shook his head slowly.

"What do you mean to do?"

"I mean to find him," Kole said.

"And then?"

"Find his strings, and follow them back to his dark master."

"'If' being the key," Talmir said. "The King of Ember." That look again. "If he was not strong enough to avoid falling to the Sage's spell, what makes you think you are?"

For a fleeting moment, Kole was back in the broken throne room. His skin was cold, his heart slow as death. The King of Ember stood over him, and just before the darkness closed in, a violent light shielded him from the Ember's wrath—a light with the face of Linn Ve'Ran.

"I won't be alone," Kole said, smirking.

"And what are we to do in the meantime?" Talmir asked. "Now that our enemy knows your strength? We've a city to mend, dead to bury, mourning ..."

He trailed off.

"He won't come for you," Kole said. "I'll make sure of that."

Talmir stared at him. It was a long time before he seemed satisfied, at least for the moment.

"I don't know how this Valley can ever feel like home again," the Captain said, sounding at once younger and older than his years.

"Maybe it's time our people went back to their true home, then."

Kole left Captain Talmir to stew in his thoughts. It suited him.

He made his way down the stairs, body aching like it never had before, and was relieved to see that the commons in the barracks below was not full of the wounded and dying this time. His relief lasted right up until he opened the door to the street outside.

Kole surveyed the grounds adjacent to the courtyard, which had been trampled into mush. To the west, they were still clearing the wreckage that had been the front gate. Beyond it, there was ruin far as the eye could see, the distant trees serving as silent sentinels of a different kind. What judgment they passed, Kole did not want to guess.

Around him, there was not a single soul not in motion. Soldiers still patrolled the battlements, watchful and weary, their armor shining once again under the returned sun. Tradesmen had put their carts to uses far less enterprising than usual, stocking them with debris, and what Kole at first took for a mound of Corrupted resolved itself into the form of a massive bear. The spears had yet to be removed from its flanks and workers and soldiers alike quickened their pace as they passed by it.

A cart laden with a bulging canvas trundled by, and Kole knew that if he had anything in his stomach to give, he'd have given it to the gutter.

What horrors had befallen the people of Hearth while he was away?

A flash of white stole over his vision as something crashed into his chest and laid him low.

"Hi, girl," Kole said, grabbing the hound by the scruff and rebuffing her kisses. An old woman laughed as she passed by dragging an empty stretcher stained brown with old blood.

Kole managed to gain his footing and cast about. Predictably, he saw the dark-haired boy standing under the eaves across the way. He wondered how many more had been orphaned this year. This week.

"Jakub," Kole called, waving.

Jakub looked startled that Kole had noticed him, but Kole smiled to put him at ease, scratching Shifa's flank as she twined around his legs, barking excitedly.

"Where there's smoke, there's fire," Kole said, affecting a laugh that seemed to draw Jakub out of the shadows even as it filled him with that familiar suspicion. "Care for a walk to the market?"

"No market anymore," the boy said. "Just a red bowl."

"That is what it's called, after all," Kole said, and the confused look he received in return clued him into the true devastation that had wracked his people.

Shifa did most of the talking on their walk, and for a change, Kole was happy for it. He felt a kinship with Jakub, a similarity of focus.

As Jakub had suggested, the Red Bowl earned its name that day. And if Talmir Caru was to be believed, things had improved substantially in the last few days. The tents still buzzed with activity, and most of the wounded he saw appeared in good spirits. But Kole could tell by the looks turned his way what had been lost.

He happened upon Rain Ku'Ral as she passed beneath an awning. They brushed shoulders before recognizing each other. Her attractive features were lined with the same exhaustion he had seen on the rest, but they drew up in an approximation of her former perkiness as she took him in.

They shared a hug that served as their exchange. There was no fire in it, only a knowing, and then she was off on whatever errand he had interrupted.

Kole thought Jakub had merely happened upon him, but he should have known the boy would not have come if not instructed by Talmir to do so. He tugged at Kole's britches and guided him toward the outskirts of the Red Bowl to the south, leaving him outside a small tent. Jakub sat down on a crate near the entrance and Shifa moved to join him.

"Guess I've got my work cut out for me winning you back, eh girl?"

Shifa merely tilted her head at him, tongue lolling as Jakub stroked her mane absently.

Taei was the first one he saw upon entering, and though he steeled himself for it, the guilt that welled in his gut was difficult to bear. He dreaded to see what lay on the other side of the flap the Ember guarded.

The two men nodded at one another, but the tension was palpable.

Kole made to move past him and Taei snatched his arm, pulling his sleeve roughly. They locked eyes, and, seeing whatever he saw in Kole's, Taei's own expression softened.

"She'll recover," he said, releasing Kole's arm and stepping out into the afternoon sun.

Her chin was wrapped in bandages, and for that Kole felt a sting, but most of her face was bare and absent scarring. Her arms were wrapped tightly and bowls of water littered the chamber, many of them soaking fresh wraps. Kole wondered how many times they had already been changed.

He sat by Fihn's side and took her hand. She winced as he did so, but did not wake.

Kole tried to say he was sorry, but all that emerged was the wracking of silent sobs.

He felt a flood of heat from Fihn's palm as a bandage came loose from his pressure, and she woke. Kole let her hand fall away with a start, and she looked him in the eyes, steady and alert.

Such a flood of emotions passed over her face, and each of them broke Kole's heart more than the last. She reached for him, and Kole thought she might strike him had she the strength for it, or else pull him close and whisper words of hatred and regret.

Instead, she unwrapped her hand and touched his own, her eyes hopeful. She tried to speak, but it came out muffled.

Kole felt the heat from her skin wash into him again and realization dawned. An image of the King of Ember came up unbidden, palms glowing molten gold as Kole's chest froze, heart slowing. He closed his eyes and focused on the heat, calling it to him like a mother cooing to her babe. He heard Fihn sigh and it was like the sweetest music. He made his body a conduit.

Soon Fihn's hand went limp and Kole released it, placing it back down by her side. Her eyes had closed and her chest rose and fell in a deep sleep, restful and painless.

Kole turned his hand over in the filtered light that spilled in through the canvas, marveling at his newfound abilities and wondering if he had possessed them all along—if all Embers did. His kind had long been able to draw the heat from flame, coal and stone, but from another person? That was something else entire.

He felt movement as the sheet was drawn back in a rush behind him. He turned to see Linn framed against the light of the opening, eyes shining. Taei was at her side, his expression concerned. He looked past Kole to Fihn and rushed to her, touching her bare hand and raising his brows in shock.

"What did you do?" he asked, not taking his eyes from his sister.

"What I could," Kole said, and Taei favored him with a curt nod that felt like a warm embrace.

———◆◆———

Linn did most of the talking as they rode.

There weren't many horses in the Valley; those there were belonged to Hearth, but the city gladly gave their strongest chargers to the small caravan that was bound for Last Lake. Hearth had been hit hard by the siege, and the burden now fell on the Emberfolk of the Lake to give what they could.

Of course, this caravan's only cargo was a grievously wounded Ember—Jenk had not so much as twitched in his sleep throughout the afternoon—and a fisherman's boy that was regaining his former strength and good humor with frightening speed.

Kole supposed they had to stop thinking of Nathen Swell as such after the role he had played in the destruction of the Dark Hearts. And the role he played in the rescue of the woman that rode beside him.

Linn described the state of Hearth when they had arrived before the still-smoking ruins of the front gate. The city had been in chaos. Although the sky had broken and the Corrupted had lost much of their vitality, the care of the wounded was too much for the healers in the Red Bowl to bear.

Luckily, the Faey had emerged from the forests to the east in some number, moving among the husks of the Corrupted like ghosts before lending their substantial gifts to those who needed it most. From the time their Faeykin arrived—more learned in the arts than those of Ember-birth—Hearth did not lose another soul. Kole wished he had the chance to thank them before they withdrew to their own villages, whose devastation was largely guessed at.

When all topics had been exhausted, including Linn's arduous trek through the Deep Lands and Kole's own trials, they exchanged feints and dodges, moving around the one subject both were uncertain how best to approach. Things felt strange between them, and Kole did not entirely know why, though he had a few guesses.

The closer they drew to the Lake, the thinner the roots grew, twining their way across the path that was not so far from that which Kole, Shifa and the Kane twins had traversed in a hellish sprint a week before. The longer roots reminded him of Misha Ve'Gah and her fallen spear, another ally he would not have made it far without.

And yet, how far had they made it, truly? They had played no small role in bringing down one tyrant only to learn he was merely the shadow cast by a larger one, one his people had called enemy for centuries. And though he truly felt the Valley was safe for the moment, he could not shake the knowledge that the wider World was suffering under the Sages even as the Emberfolk settled.

"What you did back there," Linn said, "in the sickbed with Fihn. "How did you do it?"

"For once," Kole said, "I didn't command the fire. I offered myself to it and it answered."

"That's new," she said. She meant it to come off light, Kole knew, and yet there was a heaviness as dusk filtered down through the hanging branches.

Kole was glad the Dark Months were far off. He wondered how much less the threat would be now that the Dark Hearts had been purged from their land. No rift had opened in the Valley before. He hoped it remained that way now.

"I'm not the only one with new tricks," Kole said and Linn looked away. She sighed, opened her mouth to speak and then closed it in a tight, worried line.

"Have you tried again?" Kole asked hesitantly.

"No. But I know I could. I can feel it."

"Will you?"

She looked at him, and for a moment her eyes flickered from striking to otherworldly.

"You mean to follow them," she said as much as asked, and Kole nodded slightly.

She sighed.

"Then I suppose I don't have much of a choice."

They both looked ahead.

"Is it," he started. "Is he still—

"No," she said after a time. Her brow worked, but she took her time choosing the next words.

"There was good in him, Kole," she said. "I saw it. I felt it. He was not so very different from the Landkist once."

"Power corrupts," Kole said softly, only realizing how many ways that went after he had said it.

They rode in silence for a time, and Kole was sorry to know that it was a tense one. Soon enough, familiar trails turned to those inseparable from the memories of the childhood they both shared. The Dark Kind could never take that away. No one could.

The modest timber walls of Last Lake came into view.

"T'Alon Rane believes he's protecting us all by going after the Sages," Kole said. "Drawing the Eastern Dark's need away from us."

"There is darkness in him," Linn said. "And much more in those that follow him. Killing even one Sage—the wrong one, at the wrong time—could upset the balance completely."

"There is no balance in the World," Kole said.

"How would we know? We've never been a part of it."

Kole was silent.

"We may need them, Kole. If the Eastern Dark plans to open the doors to the World Apart. Who will stop it if not them?"

"He has to die," Kole said. "At the very least, he has to die."

"Yes. But we can't do that on our own. And Rane needs to be stopped. His enemies could be our allies. The other four Sages are no doubt powerful. Powerful enough that the Eastern Dark fears them."

They reached the front gate and hailed the lads on the sap-slick battlements. Timbers cracked and creaked, and the soft mud moved out of fresh-dug grooves as the doors bowed inward.

"I'm sorry I was late," Kole said quietly as Nathen yawned and stretched under the flap behind them.

"I'm sorry I left without you," Linn said. "Left you."

Kole turned a light smile on her and she returned it.

"I guess we'd better make peace with ourselves and each other," he said. "Because your sister won't be having it with either one of us."

<hr />

They burned Ninyeva that night.

The notes of mourning carried to the furthest branches of the Valley that had been her home as the sun dipped below the salt lake and turned it to liquid fire. And Kole knew the Faey Mother's death marked both an ending and a beginning, just as he knew the tears amidst the smoke were as much for her as for Kaya Ferrahl and Larren Holspahr, two more Embers lost.

He stood with his father. They watched Doh'Rah take the flame from Tu'Ren and offer it to the pyre. Across the way, in the flickering shadows of the Long Hall, Linn and her sister swayed shoulder-to-shoulder. Iyana's eyes glowed like fireflies, embers brighter than any in the Valley.

Kole and Iyana embraced after the ceremony, but he let them have each other for the night. Tu'Ren took charge of Jenk Ganmeer, who offered Kole a solemn look that said all it needed to as the Emberfolk filled their homes with fires for cooking, warming and remembering rather than killing.

Karin told Kole the complete story of the battle for Hearth over dinner, sparing his own heroics, though Kole had already gleaned them from other sources.

"Talmir may need you," Karin said, coming back with two steaming bowls from the fireplace. "If what T'Alon Rane says is true—

"A big 'if,'" Kole said.

"If the Merchant Council won't support the expedition to resettle the deserts," Karin continued, undeterred, "then he may need you."

"He has other Reyna's to choose from."

"Not so many."

"No," Kole said, and Karin sighed and took a slurp from his bowl, eyes on the table. All told, he had taken the news that the last King of Ember was still alive and in league with the most dangerous foe their people had ever known quite well. His thoughts, however, were treading different paths. Kole knew because he knew his father's looks; this was a look that had never been far from Karin's face since a stormy night when three hearts became two.

Kole could still remember seeing his mother walking toward him through the burning throne room, her green eyes sparkling, her face stern. There was little closure in it all. Sarise had still died, and though the White Crest may not have done the killing, he had held himself from the saving.

"Linn thinks we can use them—the Sages," Kole said, bringing the conversation back around.

"And what do you think?"

"I don't know."

"Do you need so many enemies, Kole?"

"I know my enemy."

"Do you?"

Karin stared at him hard and Kole found himself looking away.

"We all do the best we can," Karin said after a while.

"Even T'Alon Rane?" Kole asked, and it was a long time before his father gave an answer.

———◆◆———

Iyana was different.

Linn could tell. They were all different, now.

They had burned the Faey Mother tonight, and already her thoughts turned to the future. Despite the light she felt teasing the edges of her fingertips and ticking the lashes on the ends of her lids, it seemed a dark one to her.

She sat alone on the roof and felt the soft breaths of her sister in sleep below the shingles and beams their father had built. She heard the wind whistling along the water, a sound more soothing to her now than the lapping of the waves along the docks.

The moon was out, and nothing stirred beneath it. It would be some time before the animals made their way back onto the forest paths.

"Am I good?" Linn asked the skies.

She wondered whether the White Crest had asked that of himself, even toward the end. She wondered if T'Alon Rane did, and she thought that he might.

Last, her thoughts turned to Kole Reyna.

With her new sight, Linn could see the northern peaks this time of night. She felt the Valley was a small place. She could see the light in Kole's window from here, too. It burned on into the night long after the wax had run, and the glass splintered and cracked with his dreaming.

About the Author

STEVEN is a fighter turned writer who resides in the Boston area. He wishes all disputes were still settled with a friendly game of hand-to-hand combat, is a fan of awesome things, and tries to write books he'd want to read. He hopes you like them.

You can find him and his musings at his official web site…

STEVENKELLIHER.COM

52510100R00267

Made in the USA
San Bernardino, CA
22 August 2017